Modern Ghost Stories

by

Noted Women Writers

Modern Ghost Stories

by

Noted Women Writers

WITH AN INTRODUCTION BY
SARA MAITLAND

EDITED BY RICHARD DALBY

BARNES
&NOBLE
BOOKS
NEW YORK

Originally published by Carroll & Graf Publishers, Inc. as
Modern Ghost Stories by Eminent Women Writers

Collection, Preface, and Notes copyright © 1991 by Richard Dalby
Introduction copyright © 1991 by Sara Maitland

This edition published by Barnes & Noble, Inc.,
by arrangement with Carroll & Graf Publishers, Inc.

1996 Barnes & Noble Books

ISBN 0-76070-351-5

Printed and bound in the United States of America

M 9 8 7 6 5 4 3 2 1

BVG

CONTENTS

ACKNOWLEDGEMENTS

PERMISSION to use the stories in this collection has kindly been granted by the following: 'The July Ghost', A.S. Byatt, from *Sugar and Other Stories*, Copyright © A.S. Byatt 1987, by Chatto & Windus and the Peters, Fraser & Dunlop Group Ltd; 'Don't Tell Cissie', Celia Fremlin, from *By Horror Haunted*, Copyright © Celia Fremlin 1974, by Gregory & Radice; 'The Book', Margaret Irwin, from *Madame Fears the Dark*, by the Peters, Fraser & Dunlop Group Ltd; 'The Grey Men', Rebecca West, by the Peters, Fraser & Dunlop Group Ltd; 'The Pool', Daphne du Maurier, from *The Breaking Point*, Copyright © Daphne du Maurier 1959, by Curtis Brown on behalf of the Chichester Partnership and by Doubleday, a division of Bantam Doubleday Dell Publishing Group Inc.; 'The Station Road', Ann Bridge, from *The Song in the House*, by the Peters, Fraser & Dunlop Group Ltd; 'Black Dog', Penelope Lively, from *Pack of Cards*, William Heinemann Ltd and Penguin Books Ltd, Copyright © Penelope Lively 1986, by Murray Pollinger and by Grove Press, Inc.; 'Prelude', Pamela Sewell, Copyright © Pamela Sewell 1991, by the author; 'The Pestering', D.K. Broster, from *Couching at the Door*, Copyright D.K. Broster 1942; 'I Used to Live Here Once', Jean Rhys, from *Sleep it Off Lady*, Copyright © Jean Rhys 1976, by Andre Deutsch Ltd; 'Whittington's Cat', Eleanor Smith, from *Satan's Circus*, Copyright Eleanor Smith 1934, by Aitken & Stone; 'The Haunting of Shawley Rectory', Ruth Rendell, by the Peters, Fraser & Dunlop Group Ltd; 'Mare Amore', Margery Lawrence, from *The Terraces of the Night*, Copyright Margery Lawrence 1932; 'Who's been Sitting in my Car?', © Antonia Fraser 1976, by Curtis Brown; 'The Ghosts of Calagou', Elizabeth Fancett, Copyright © Elizabeth Fancett 1991, by the author; 'The Thingummyjig', Mary Williams, from *The Haunted Valley and Other Stories*, Copyright © Mary Williams 1978, by Laurence Pollinger Ltd; 'The House of Shadows', Mary Elizabeth Counselman, Copyright © Mary Elizabeth Counselman 1933; 'Rosalind', Richmal Crompton, from *Mist and Other Stories*, Copyright Richmal Crompton 1928, by A.P. Watt Ltd on behalf of Richmal Ashbee; 'Redundant', Dorothy K. Haynes, Copyright © Dorothy K. Haynes 1991, by the author's Estate; 'The Dream of Fair

Women', A.L. Barker, from *Stories of Haunted Inns*, William Kimber, 1983, Copyright (©) A.L. Barker 1983, by Jennifer Kavanagh; 'The Chauffeur', Rosemary Pardoe, from *The Angry Dead*, Copyright (©) Rosemary Pardoe 1986, by the author; 'The Traitor', Joan Aiken, Copyright (©) Joan Aiken Enterprises Ltd 1991; 'The Landlady', Elinor Mordaunt, from *People, Houses & Ships*, Copyright 1924.

Every effort has been made to trace copyright holders in all copyright material in this book. The editor regrets if there has been any oversight and suggests the publisher is contacted in any such event.

The editor would also like to acknowledge the helpful assistance and encouragement given by Lynn Knight, Karen Millyard, Robert Adey and David Rowlands.

PREFACE

IN this second volume of twentieth-century ghost stories by women writers, I have selected twenty-seven more tales by some of the best practitioners in this timeless genre, the majority of whom did not appear in the previous anthology. Once again, I trust the reader will find that the shocks and delights of these stories will contain some unforeseen surprises, and an infinite variety ranging from the humorous and the horrific to the sad and poignant.

The contributors range from some of the most highly regarded Edwardian writers – Edith Wharton, Clotilde Graves and E. Nesbit – through the inter-war 'Golden Age' of the ghost story, to the active revival of the genre in the 1960s and up to the present day.

Some of these stories are already recognized worldwide as undoubted classics of the genre, like Edith Wharton's 'Afterward' and Margaret Irwin's 'The Book', whereas several others – including those by Richmal Crompton, Margery Lawrence, Eleanor Smith and D.K. Broster – have been unaccountably neglected, so I am very pleased to revive them for a new audience today.

The stories by Joan Aiken, Elizabeth Fancett, Pamela Sewell, and the late Dorothy K. Haynes, appear here for the first time.

Edith Wharton freely admitted that it is not easy to write a thoroughly convincing ghost story, adding: 'It is luckier for a ghost to be vividly imagined than dully "experienced"; and nobody knows better than a ghost how hard it is to put him or her into words shadowy, yet transparent enough . . . If a ghost story sends a cold shiver down one's spine, it has done its job and done it well.'

Richard Dalby

INTRODUCTION

THE previous collection, *Victorian Ghost Stories*, included a story by me: it was called 'Lady with Unicorn' and told the tale of a young woman haunted (or perhaps possessed) by the spirit (or perhaps the ghost) of the virgin from the two great series of medieval tapestries: The Hunt of the Unicorn (now in New York) and La Dame au Licorne (now in Cluny, France). I myself thought it was a classic ghost story, closely following the requirements of the genre—and in particular it ended as mysteriously as it began, with no clear internal commitment as to whether the protagonist was suffering from delusions or whether something external and objective (namely being raped by an 'imaginary' unicorn) had actually happened. I hope I am not introducing this story purely in a spirit of boastfulness; the point is that I have frequently been asked if I thought it was 'a real ghost story'. Of course I did. But there was still something in it which gave the reader pause.

What is a 'real' ghost story? One of the things that this collection suggests is that the ghost story is as nebulous as the ghosts themselves. It is an extraordinarily open genre: perhaps the only proper answer is that a real ghost story is one that doesn't make you protest when you find it in a collection of ghost stories. With other forms of so-called genre literature the options are considerably more tightly defined. A detective story *must* have something to detect, and that something must be detected; sci-fi *must* be based, however preposterously, on the logical extension of an acceptable material premise; romantic novels *must* untangle a complex couple-relationship to the point of simple resolution (happy or sad) and then stop. Even when the proposed story is funny or satirical, it operates within the accepted boundaries of the formal expectations.

But a ghost story? They don't seem to work like that. There are no such clear boundaries. The rules evaporate as fast as I attempt to pin them down. Taking the stories in this volume as a yardstick (and there are no stories in this collection which I would want to eliminate on formal grounds—they are all 'real ghost stories'), there do not seem to be any rules at all. Even such woolly restrictions as 'they must have some element of contact with the supernatural' prove too restrictive: some of the ghostlinesses you will find here take place solely within the psychological sphere. Some are not remotely frightening: they are tender, touching, funny, fantastic or intellectually challenging. Some are open-ended – it is left to the reader to decide what, if anything, happened. Some are closed – the author gives the reader the explanation (which can be entirely material) as a gift, packaged and sealed.

But, but . . . the stories *do* have a unity, a feeling of belonging together, a sense of being 'real ghost stories'. It is a unity not of form, I think, but of atmosphere; and I do mean atmosphere, not mood. The *mood* of ghost stories is infinitely varied – compare quickly Fremlin's 'Don't Tell Cissie', Irwin's 'The Book' and du Maurier's 'The Pool' from this collection and you will see what I mean. But despite their extreme differences of tone, these stories do have an atmosphere in common, a literary atmosphere: all of them, and indeed all the stories in this book, are trying to talk in two voices at once; trying to deal with two discourses, two languages, two ways of speaking, at the same time. The language of social realism and the language of the subterranean, the not-explained. This second language either is the mode of the supernatural, or draws directly on it; but it is the attempt to write from within *both worlds at once* that distinguishes the ghost story from other forms of fantasy, rather than the specific content of the second mode.

In order for the ghost story to work, the realist elements of it have to be firmly fixed: it is worth noting just how much of many of these stories is taken up with straightforward descriptive writing. 'There was once a house somewhere . . .' simply is not enough: each window of the house, each turn of the path, each petal of the flower and – perhaps most noticeably of all – each flicker of the weather has to be filled in. As the demands on the reader's credulity (or at very least on her 'willing suspension of disbelieve') are to be so high, each author gives as much solidity as possible to the bits that will be easiest to believe. For the story to work a lot is needed from the reader, who must therefore be given a lot in exchange. E. Nesbit, a mistress of fantasy writing, makes this explicit in her story 'No. 17', which is as near as this collection offers you to a satire of the genre, and is therefore among the most conscious and revealing about what, technically speaking, is going on: her narrator, in response to a ghost story already told, says:

> 'Very good story . . . but it's not what I call realism. You don't tell us half enough, sir. You don't say when it happened or where, or the time of year, or what colour your aunt's second cousin's hair was. Nor yet you don't tell us what it was she saw, nor what the room was like where she saw it, nor why she saw it, nor what happened afterwards.'

and what is true in the commercial bar of Nesbit's fiction is true for the fiction reader too. We need a solid realism, with the aunt's cousin's hair colour firmly fixed, which makes the first fictional world clear so that the second, less realist, language can be accessible.

Now in a sense all fiction writing is ghost-story writing: the author wants to make the reader believe that she believes in these mysterious, unreal, unliving, undead characters, places, situations, emotions or ideas. The reader, of course, does not really have to believe in them: most adult readers know perfectly well that the book *Anna Karenina* exists, is real, but that the woman 'Anna Karenina' does not (and did not). The 'trick' is to persuade that reader – for the duration of the read at least – that the reverse is in fact the case. You will not be 'haunted' by the black-spined paperback, or the leather-bound three-volume edition, or whatever; you will be haunted by the disturbing presence of the woman. When the author is successful the reader does enter genuinely into another world, because it is equally impossible to say that Anna Karenina does not exist or that Anna Karenina does exist; she does not exist because she is a fiction; she does exist because a reader believes in her and through her experiences the reader's own have been changed – the reader feels differently about nineteenth-century Russia, about adultery, about what it is to be a woman, and about herself; these changes affect the way she thinks and acts; such effects are the stuff of 'being real'. But if a second, different person has not read *Anna Karenina* (the book) or has read it and is unmoved, untouched, by Anna Karenina (the character) they will have no sense of this impossibility. She will hardly be a ghost at all; at best she will be a ghost of whom the second reader can very simply say, 'She isn't real. I don't believe in her.' The social and imaginative details – of plot, description, other characters, ambiance – are essential to belief. (I pick Anna Karenina here, of course, only because of the convenient fact that the character and the book have the same name.)

What I am suggesting is that what binds ghost stories together is not their themes, their moods, or their narrative techniques but the fact that they all push to an extreme this strange mode that we call fictional narrative, where belief and disbelief are necessarily interdependent.

I will go further and suggest that it is precisely because of this that so many of these (and other) ghost stories can be produced by writers who excel in other genres. Although it is not one hundred per cent true, a quick glance at the contents page of this volume will reveal to you a whole group of women whose writing you know for completely different reasons: Aiken, Barker, Byatt, Fraser, Irwin, Lively, Nesbit, Rendell, Rhys, Smith, West. This would not be the case, I suspect, with an anthology of either romantic fiction or detective stories, where the demands of the genre are so much more specific and technical.

There remains, moreover, a particular point in reference to this volume.

These stories are not just ghost stories, they are ghost stories by women. Richard Dalby has argued that it is impossible to tell, given any particular ghost story, whether it was written by a woman or a man: I don't dispute this; partly because I don't have the depth of knowledge that he does, but partly also because that is my experience of literature more widely. But it remains worth saying that this was a genre more or less invented and developed by women – from Ann Radcliffe, whose *Mysteries of Udolpho* laid down the ground rules in 1794, through to Mary Shelley's *Frankenstein* (although any historian of science fiction would dispute this claim) and Emily Brontë's *Wuthering Heights* (though any historian of the romance would likewise protest). And despite this record, the better-known line of descent remains male: Walpole, Poe, Hawthorne, Stevenson, and on through to King. This pattern within the little genre of the ghost story reflects the larger history of the novel: women have always been the majority of both producers and consumers of fictional narratives, yet they are banished to a silenced, shady sub-world. Or, to put it a different way, women come to the ghostly task of writing as ghosts (even, for much of literary culture, as dangerous spectres). Our tradition is a tradition in the shadows; our past is lost and misty; our identity, as writers and as objects of men's writings, is both owned and denied.

Classical ghosts spring from many sources: from unfinished business, from undealt-with guilts, angers and revenges, from enormous sadnesses and reluctance to abandon hope, from the Devil and from the womb – 'the Devil's gateway'. If like calls to like, it is not at all surprising that the ghost story has so many female practitioners. There is a dense complex here: if all fiction is a ghostly process, and all women writers are in some senses already ghosts, the appeal of the genre is obvious. Of course women write good ghost stories. Of course women want to read good ghost stories.

I had hoped that this would be enough. Now I discover that I do not want to end here. Because along with the literary genre called the ghost story, there is another tradition – partly oral, partly buried within folk tale, within mythology, and within religious practice. It is the tradition, the mixture of terror and curiosity, about ghosts themselves (beyond or outside their socially constructed literary representations); they occupy an ambivalent space within the imagination.

My youngest child is nine. He has long ago dealt with fairies, giants and hobgoblins ('load of rubbish'). He has now dealt with Father Christmas (fundamentalist conviction from 15 December to 26 December; sceptical tolerance the rest of the year) and with other differences between fiction and non-fiction. He has learnt to operate 'the willing suspension of disbelief' more and more appropriately so that the thrill, the real thrill, of fear or excitement to be gained from books and films is enhanced, not spoilt, by their containment within the realm of the not-that-sort-of-true.

But ghosts are different. Still they hover in the unsettled domain. Still the dark corner, still the lonely moment, still the unresolved guilt may or may not contain their violent or mournful presences. He cannot be sure.

'Mummy, do you believe in ghosts?' A question freighted with neither straightforward fear nor pure intellectual curiosity, but with an odd combination of yearning and horror. It is a question of an entirely different calibre from 'Do you believe in dinosaurs?' or 'Do you believe in mermaids?' The question is asked always with the desire to receive the opposite answer to the one that is uppermost in his own mind. He does not want to be certain.

Me too. You too, dear reader, for you have picked up this book, opened it.

There is, of course, a possibility that you have solely literary curiosity: the list of authors is indeed beguiling. What could conceivably bring together so odd a mixture of twentieth-century women writers – several of whom you will definitely have heard of, many of whom you may not? There is also a possibility that you have an equally pure sociological curiosity – the question of gender and imagination still perplexes us all: given the demands of the genre, the tightness of the focus, perhaps we can see if women's ghosts are other than men's ghosts, and from there suggest ways in which our conscious and subconscious yearnings are different. Both these possibilities are perfectly real and perfectly proper. They are, in fact, just the sorts of question that I have tried to discuss in the first half of this introduction. But I am not convinced that anyone will be able to get much further into this volume and still maintain their purity of intellectual intention.

Because it is precisely our own ambivalence, the very mistiness of ghosts, that makes the genre so attractive, to both reader and writer. Since we cannot finally decide whether we want to believe in them at all, we can certainly leave wide open questions about their origin and form. Here you will find ghost stories that are even more cynical than you are, like 'No. 17'. At the same time you will also find ghostly presences whose origins are demonic, are the direct responsibility of the victim, are objective, are humorous, are lethal, are helpful, are harmless. They spring from child-hood losses or joys, from love, from memory, from guilt, from the grave, from the imagination; from insanity and from excessive rationalism. Some of these ghosts invite your belief, some repudiate it. This volume even offers, in one of my own favourite stories, the ghost of someone living; there are also ghosts from the future who haunt the present; ghosts that are never identified, and ghosts with full biographies centuries long. There are individual ghosts and numinous 'forces'. This variety does not matter; indeed, it is precisely the point: if there may be some sort of ghosts somewhere, then potentially there are all sorts of ghosts anywhere.

Elsewhere, beyond the covers of this book, things are getting pretty risky. The planet itself may be dying. Even if it isn't, inside the atom we learn that time can indeed move into reverse. Einstein was wrong – the Old Man does indeed throw dice. The Mandelbrot Set illuminates chaos, and reveals there patterns of intricacy and infinite repetition in regression. Nothing at the largest or the smallest scales behaves according to good sense. If there is any truth in that at all, then we need not expect self and identity, particularly when pushed by the largest storms or the smallest tremors of emotion, to behave within the mechanistic framework either. The ghost story may have started out as a protection against too much rationalism: the folk story creeping in where organized religion was driven out. But now, it seems to me, all ghost stories gain their power from our buried uncertainty.

When I am writing pieces like this, of course I don't believe in ghosts: I believe in genre and discourse and literary tradition and social constructs. But when I read these ghost stories, then I enjoy not simply the nineteenth century's 'willing suspension of disbelief' in exchange for thrill or aesthetic experience, but something else as well, something more contemporary: a willing suspension of one set of beliefs in exchange for space to indulge another set, totally contradictory and yet totally valid.

At their best – and many of the stories in this book do achieve this for me – ghost stories bring together old fears, old desires, old hopes and new dreams, new ideas, new possibilities. They play with the patterns of our own ambivalence. This is of course the work of all fiction, but in the ghost story there is a special focus on hidden materials, the stuff of the subconscious, of the analytical couch. But stories give that material in ways that are much cheaper and much more fun.

Sara Maitland, London, 1991

A. S. Byatt

❦

THE JULY GHOST

'**I** THINK I must move out of where I'm living,' he said. 'I have this problem with my landlady.'

He picked a long, bright hair off the back of her dress, so deftly that the act seemed simply considerate. He had been skilful at balancing glass, plate and cutlery, too. He had a look of dignified misery, like a dejected hawk. She was interested.

'What sort of problem? Amatory, financial, or domestic?'

'None of those, really. Well, not financial.'

He turned the hair on his finger, examining it intently, not meeting her eye.

'Not financial. Can you tell me? I might know somewhere you could stay. I know a lot of people.'

'You would.' He smiled shyly. 'It's not an easy problem to describe. There's just the two of us. I occupy the attics. Mostly.'

He came to a stop. He was obviously reserved and secretive. But he was telling her something. This is usually attractive.

'Mostly?' Encouraging him.

'Oh, it's not like *that*. Well, not . . . Shall we sit down?'

They moved across the party, which was a big party, on a hot day. He stopped and found a bottle and filled her glass. He had not needed to ask what she was drinking. They sat side by side on a sofa: he admired the brilliant poppies bold on her emerald dress, and her pretty sandals. She had come to London for the summer to work in the British Museum. She could really have managed with microfilm in Tucson for what little manuscript research was needed, but there was a dragging love affair to end. There is an age at which, however desperately happy one is in stolen moments, days, or weekends with one's married professor, one either prises him loose or cuts and runs. She had had a stab at both, and now considered she had successfully cut and run. So it was nice to be immediately appreciated. Problems are capable of solution. She said as much to him, turning her soft face to his ravaged one, swinging the long bright hair. It had begun a year ago, he told her in a rush, at another party actually; he had met this woman, the landlady in question, and had made, not immediately, a kind of *faux pas*, he now saw, and she had been very decent, all things considered, and so. . . .

He had said, 'I think I must move out of where I'm living.' He had been quite wild, had nearly not come to the party, but could not go on drinking alone. The woman had considered him coolly and asked, 'Why?' One could not, he said, go on in a place where one had once been blissfully happy, and was now miserable, however convenient the place. Convenient, that was, for work, and friends, and things that seemed, as he mentioned them, ashy and insubstantial compared to the memory and the hope of opening the door and finding Anne outside it, laughing and breathless, waiting to be told what he had read, or thought, or eaten, or felt that day. Someone I loved left, he told the woman. Reticent on that occasion too, he bit back the flurry of sentences about the total unexpectedness of it, the arriving back and finding only an envelope on a clean table, and spaces in the bookshelves, the record stack, the kitchen cupboard. It must have been planned for weeks, she must have been thinking it out while he rolled on her, while she poured wine for him, while . . . No, no. Vituperation is undignified and in this case what he felt was lower and worse than rage: just pure, childlike loss. 'One ought not to mind places,' he said to the woman. 'But one does,' she had said. 'I know.'

She had suggested to him that he could come and be her lodger, then; she had, she said, a lot of spare space going to waste, and her husband wasn't there much. 'We've not had a lot to say to each other, lately.' He could be quite self-contained, there was a kitchen and bathroom in the attics; she wouldn't bother him. There was a large garden. It was possibly this that decided him: it was very hot, central London, the time of year when a man feels he would give anything to live in a room opening on to grass and trees, not a high flat in a dusty street. And if Anne came back, the door would be locked and mortice-locked. He could stop thinking about Anne coming back. That was a decisive move: Anne thought he wasn't decisive. He would live without Anne.

For some weeks after he moved in he had seen very little of the woman. They met on the stairs, and once she came up, on a hot Sunday, to tell him he must feel free to use the garden. He had offered to do some weeding and mowing, and she had accepted. That was the weekend her husband came back, driving furiously up to the front door, running in, and calling in the empty hall, 'Imogen, Imogen!' To which she had replied, uncharacteristically, by screaming hysterically. There was nothing in her husband,

Noel's, appearance to warrant this reaction; their lodger, peering over the banister at the sound, had seen their upturned faces in the stairwell and watched hers settle into its usual prim and placid expression as he did so. Seeing Noel, a balding, fluffy-templed, stooping thirty-five or so, shabby corduroy suit, cotton polo neck, he realized he was now able to guess her age, as he had not been. She was a very neat woman, faded blonde, her hair in a knot on the back of her head, her legs long and slender, her eyes downcast. Mild was not quite the right word for her, though. She explained then that she had screamed because Noel had come home unexpectedly and startled her: she was sorry. It seemed a reasonable explanation. The extraordinary vehemence of the screaming was probably an echo in the stairwell. Noel seemed wholly downcast by it, all the same.

He had kept out of the way, that weekend, taking the stairs two at a time and lightly, feeling a little aggrieved, looking out of his kitchen window into the lovely, overgrown garden, that they were lurking indoors, wasting all the summer sun. At Sunday lunch-time he had heard the husband, Noel, shouting on the stairs.

'I can't go on, if you go on like that. I've done my best, I've tried to get through. Nothing will shift you, will it, you won't *try*, will you, you just go on and on. Well, I have my life to live, you can't throw a life away . . . can you?'

He had crept out again on to the dark upper landing and seen her standing, halfway down the stairs, quite still, watching Noel wave his arms and roar, or almost roar, with a look of impassive patience, as though this nuisance must pass off. Noel swallowed and gasped; he turned his face up to her and said plaintively,

'You do see I can't stand it? I'll be in touch, shall I? You must want . . . you must need . . . you must . . .'

She didn't speak.

'If you need anything, you know where to get me.'

'Yes.'

'Oh, well . . .' said Noel, and went to the door. She watched him, from the stairs, until it was shut, and then came up again, step by step, as though it was an effort, a little, and went on coming past her bedroom, to his landing, to come in and ask him, entirely naturally, please to use the garden if he wanted to, and please not to mind marital rows. She was sure he understood . . . things were difficult . . . Noel wouldn't be back for some time. He was a journalist: his work took him away a lot. Just as well. She committed herself to the 'just as well'. She was a very economical speaker.

*　　　*　　　*

So he took to sitting in the garden. It was a lovely place: a huge, hidden, walled south London garden, with old fruit trees at the end, a wildly waving disorderly buddleia, curving beds full of old roses, and a lawn of overgrown, dense rye-grass. Over the wall at the foot was the Common, with a footpath running behind all the gardens. She came out to the shed and helped him to assemble and oil the lawnmower, standing on the little path under the apple branches while he cut an experimental serpentine across her hay. Over the wall came the high sound of children's voices, and the thunk and thud of a football. He asked her how to raise the blades: he was not mechanically minded.

'The children get quite noisy,' she said. 'And dogs. I hope they don't bother you. There aren't many safe places for children, round here.'

He replied truthfully that he never heard sounds that didn't concern him, when he was concentrating. When he'd got the lawn into shape, he was going to sit on it and do a lot of reading, try to get his mind in trim again, to write a paper on Hardy's poems, on their curiously archaic vocabulary.

'It isn't very far to the road on the other side, really,' she said. 'It just seems to be. The Common is an illusion of space, really. Just a spur of brambles and gorse-bushes and bits of football pitch between two fast four-laned main roads. I hate London commons.'

'There's a lovely smell, though, from the gorse and the wet grass. It's a pleasant illusion.'

'No illusions are pleasant,' she said, decisively, and went in. He wondered what she did with her time: apart from little shopping expeditions she seemed to be always in the house. He was sure that when he'd met her she'd been introduced as having some profession: vaguely literary, vaguely academic, like everyone else he knew. Perhaps she wrote poetry in her north-facing living-room. He had no idea what it would be like. Women generally wrote emotional poetry, much nicer than men, as Kingsley Amis has stated, but she seemed, despite her placid stillness, too spare and too fierce – grim? – for that. He remembered the screaming. Perhaps she wrote Plath-like chants of violence. He didn't think that quite fitted the bill, either. Perhaps she was a freelance radio journalist. He didn't bother to ask anyone who might be a common acquaintance. During the whole year, he explained to the American at the party, he hadn't actually *discussed* her with anyone. Of course he wouldn't, she agreed vaguely and warmly. She knew he wouldn't. He didn't see why he shouldn't, in fact, but went on, for the time, with his narrative.

They had got to know each other a little better over the next few weeks, at least on the level of borrowing tea, or even sharing pots of it. The weather had got hotter. He had found an old-fashioned deckchair, with faded striped canvas, in the shed, and had brushed it over and brought it out on to his mown lawn, where he sat writing a little, reading a little, getting up and pulling up a tuft of couch grass. He had been wrong about the children not bothering him: there was a succession of incursions by all sizes of children looking for all sizes of balls, which bounced to his feet, or crashed in the shrubs, or vanished in the herbaceous border, black and white footballs, beach-balls with concentric circles of primary colours, acid yellow tennis balls. The children came over the wall: black faces, brown faces, floppy long hair, shaven heads, respectable dotted sun-hats and camouflaged cotton army hats from Milletts. They came over easily, as though they were used to it, sandals, training shoes, a few bare toes, grubby sunburned legs, cotton skirts, jeans, football shorts. Sometimes, perched on the top, they saw him and gestured at the balls; one or two asked permission. Sometimes he threw a ball back, but was apt to knock down a few knobby little unripe apples or pears. There was a gate in the wall, under the fringing trees, which he once tried to open, spending time on rusty bolts only to discover that the lock was new and secure, and the key not in it.

The boy sitting in the tree did not seem to be looking for a ball. He was in a fork of the tree nearest the gate, swinging his legs, doing something to a knot in a frayed end of rope that was attached to the branch he sat on. He wore blue jeans and training shoes, and a brilliant tee shirt, striped in the colours of the spectrum, arranged in the right order, which the man on the grass found visually pleasing. He had rather long blond hair, falling over his eyes, so that his face was obscured.

'Hey, you. Do you think you ought to be up there? It might not be safe.'

The boy looked up, grinned, and vanished monkey-like over the wall. He had a nice, frank grin, friendly, not cheeky.

He was there again, the next day, leaning back in the crook of the tree, arms crossed. He had on the same shirt and jeans. The man watched him, expecting him to move again, but he sat, immobile, smiling down pleasantly, and then staring up at the sky. The man read a little, looked up, saw him still there and said:

'Have you lost anything?'

The child did not reply: after a moment he climbed down a little, swung along the branch hand over hand, dropped to the ground, raised an arm in salute, and was up over the usual route over the wall.

Two days later he was lying on his stomach on the edge of the lawn, out of the shade, this time in a white tee shirt with a pattern of blue ships and water-lines on it, his bare feet and legs stretched in the sun. He was chewing a grass stem, and studying the earth, as though watching for insects. The man said 'Hi, there,' and the boy looked up, met his look with intensely blue eyes under long lashes, smiled with the same complete warmth and openness, and returned his look to the earth.

He felt reluctant to inform on the boy, who seemed so harmless and considerate: but when he met him walking out of the kitchen door, spoke to him, and got no answer but the gentle smile before the boy ran off towards the wall, he wondered if he should speak to his landlady. So he asked her, did she mind the children coming in the garden. She said no, children must look for balls, that was part of being children. He persisted – they sat there, too, and he had met one coming out of the house. He hadn't seemed to be doing any harm, the boy, but you couldn't tell. He thought she should know.

He was probably a friend of her son's, she said. She looked at him kindly and explained. Her son had run off the Common with some other children, two years ago, in the summer, in July, and had been killed on the road. More or less instantly, she had added drily, as though calculating that just *enough* information would preclude the need for further questions. He said he was sorry, very sorry, feeling to blame, which was ridiculous, and a little injured, because he had not known about her son, and might inadvertently have made a fool of himself with some casual reference whose ignorance would be embarrassing.

What was the boy like, she said. The one in the house? 'I don't – talk to his friends. I find it painful. It could be Timmy, or Martin. They might have lost something, or want . . .'

He described the boy. Blond, about ten at a guess, he was not very good at children's ages, very blue eyes, slightly built, with a rainbow-striped tee shirt and jeans, mostly though not always – oh, and those football practice shoes, black and green. And the other tee shirt, with the ships and wavy lines. And an extraordinarily nice smile. A really *warm* smile. A nice-looking boy.

He was used to her being silent. But this silence went on and on and on. She was just staring into the garden. After a time, she said, in her precise conversational tone,

'The only thing I want, the only thing I want at all in this world, is to see that boy.'

She stared at the garden and he stared with her, until the grass began to dance with empty light, and the edges of the shrubbery wavered. For a brief moment he shared the strain of not seeing the boy. Then she gave a little sigh, sat down, neatly, as always, and passed out at his feet.

After this she became, for her, voluble. He didn't move after she fainted, but sat patiently by her, until she stirred and sat up; then he fetched her some water, and would have gone away, but she talked.

'I'm too rational to see ghosts, I'm not someone who would see anything there was to see, I don't believe in an after-life. I don't see how anyone can, I

· 6 ·

always found a kind of satisfaction for myself in the idea that one just came to an end, to a sliced-off stop. But that was myself; I didn't think *he* – not *he* – I thought ghosts were what people *wanted* to see, or were afraid to see . . . and after he died, and the best hope I had, it sounds silly, was that I would go mad enough so that instead of waiting every day for him to come home from school and rattle the letter-box I might actually have the illusion of seeing or hearing him come in. Because I can't stop my body and mind waiting, every day, every day, I can't let go. And his bedroom, sometimes at night I go in, I think I might just for a moment forget he *wasn't* in there sleeping, I think I would pay almost anything – anything at all – for a moment of seeing him like I used to. In his pyjamas, with his – his – his hair . . . ruffled, and, his . . . you said, his . . . that *smile*.

'When it happened, they got Noel, and Noel came in and shouted my name, like he did the other day, that's why I screamed, because it – seemed the same – and then they said, he is dead, and I thought coolly, *is* dead, that will go on and on and on till the end of time, it's a continuous present tense, one thinks the most ridiculous things, there I was thinking about grammar, the verb to be, when it ends to be dead. . . . And then I came out into the garden, and I half saw, in my mind's eye, a kind of ghost of his face, just the eyes and hair, coming towards me – like every day waiting for him to come home, the way you think of your son, with such pleasure, when he's – not there – and I – I thought – no, I won't *see* him, because he is dead, and I won't dream about him because he is dead, I'll be rational and practical and continue to live because one must, and there was Noel . . .

'I got it wrong, you see, I was so *sensible*, and then I was so shocked because I couldn't get to want anything – I couldn't *talk* to Noel – I – I – made Noel take away, destroy, all the photos, I – didn't dream, you can will not to dream, I didn't . . . visit a grave, flowers, there isn't any point. I was so sensible. Only my body wouldn't stop waiting and all it wants is to – see that boy. *That* boy. That boy you – saw.'

He did not say that he might have seen another boy, maybe even a boy who had been given the tee shirts and jeans afterwards. He did not say, though the idea crossed his mind, that maybe what he had seen was some kind of impression from her terrible desire to see a boy where nothing was. The boy had had nothing terrible, no aura of pain about him: he had been, his memory insisted, such a pleasant, courteous, self-contained boy, with his own purposes. And in fact the woman herself almost immediately raised the possibility that what he had seen was what she desired to see, a kind of mix-up of radio waves, like when you overheard police messages on the radio, or got BBC 1 on a switch that said ITV. She was thinking fast, and went on almost immediately to say that perhaps his sense of loss, his loss of Anne, which was what had led her to feel she could bear his presence in her house, was what had brought them – dare she say – near enough, for their wavelengths, to mingle, perhaps, had made him susceptible . . . You mean, he had said, we are a kind of emotional vacuum, between us, that must be filled. Something like that, she had said, and had added, 'But I don't believe in ghosts.'

Anne, he thought, could not be a ghost, because she was elsewhere, with someone else, doing for someone else those little things she had done so gaily for him, tasty little suppers, bits of research, a sudden vase of unusual flowers, a new bold shirt, unlike his own cautious taste, but suiting him, suiting him. In a sense, Anne was worse lost because voluntarily absent, an absence that could not be loved because love was at an end, for Anne.

'I don't suppose you will, now,' the woman was saying. 'I think talking would probably stop any – mixing of messages, if that's what it is, don't you? But – if – *if* he comes again' – and here for the first time her eyes were full of tears – 'if – you must promise, you will *tell* me, you must promise.'

He had promised, easily enough, because he was fairly sure she was right, the boy would not be seen again. But the next day he was on the lawn, nearer than ever, sitting on the grass beside the deckchair, his arms clasping his bent, warm brown knees, the thick, pale hair glittering in the sun. He was wearing a football shirt, this time, Chelsea's colours. Sitting down in the deckchair, the man could have put out a hand and touched him, but he did not: it was not, it seemed, a possible gesture to make. But the boy looked up and smiled, with a pleasant complicity, as though they now understood each other very well. The man tried speech: he said, 'It's nice to see you again,' and the boy nodded acknowledgement of this remark, without speaking himself. This was the beginning of communication between them, or what the man supposed to be communication. He did not think of fetching the woman. He became aware that he was in some strange way *enjoying the boy's company*. His pleasant stillness – and he sat there all morning, occasionally lying back on the grass, occasionally staring thoughtfully at the house – was calming and comfortable. The man did quite a lot of work – wrote about three reasonable pages on Hardy's original air-blue gown – and looked up now and then to make sure the boy was still there and happy.

He went to report to the woman – as he had after all promised to do – that evening. She had obviously been waiting and hoping – her unnatural calm had given way to agitated pacing, and her eyes were dark and deeper in. At this point in the story he found in himself a necessity to bowdlerize for the sympathetic American, as he had indeed already begun to do. He had mentioned only a child who had 'seemed like' the woman's lost son, and he now ceased to mention the child at all, as an actor in the story, with the result that what the American woman heard was a tale of how he, the man, had become increasingly involved in the woman's solitary grief, how their two losses had become a kind of *folie à deux* from which he could not extricate himself. What follows is not what he told the American girl, though it may be clear at which points the bowdlerized version coincided with what he really believed to have happened. There was a sense he could not at first analyse that it was improper to talk about the boy – not because he might not be believed; that did not come into it; but because something dreadful might happen.

'He sat on the lawn all morning. In a football shirt.'

'Chelsea?'

'Chelsea.'

'What did he do? Does he look happy? Did he speak?' Her desire to know was terrible.

'He doesn't speak. He didn't move much. He seemed – very calm. He stayed a long time.'

'This is terrible. This is ludicrous. There *is no boy*.'

'No. But I saw him.'

'Why you?'

'I don't know.' A pause. 'I do *like* him.'

'He is – was – a most likeable boy.'

Some days later he saw the boy running along the landing in the evening, wearing what might have been pyjamas, in peacock towelling, or might have been a track suit. Pyjamas, the woman stated confidently, when he told her: his new pyjamas. With white ribbed cuffs, weren't they? and a white polo neck? He corroborated this, watching her cry – she cried more easily now – finding her anxiety and disturbance very hard to bear. But it never occurred to him that it was possible to break his promise to tell her when he saw the boy. That was another curious imperative from some undefined authority.

They discussed clothes. If there were ghosts, how could they appear in clothes long burned, or rotted, or worn away by other people? You could imagine, they agreed, that something of a person might linger – as the Tibetans and others believe the soul lingers near the body before setting out on its long journey. But clothes? And in this case so many clothes? I must be seeing your memories, he told her, and she nodded fiercely, compressing her lips, agreeing that this was likely, adding, 'I am too rational to go mad, so I seem to be putting it on you.'

He tried a joke. 'That isn't very kind to me, to infer that madness comes more easily to me.'

'No, sensitivity. I am insensible. I was always a bit like that, and this made it worse. I am the *last* person to see any ghost that was trying to haunt me.'

'We agreed it was your memories I saw.'

'Yes. We agreed. That's rational. As rational as we can be, considering.'

All the same, the brilliance of the boy's blue regard, his gravely smiling salutation in the garden next morning, did not seem like anyone's tortured memories of earlier happiness. The man spoke to him directly then:

'Is there anything I can *do* for you? Anything you want? Can I help you?'

The boy seemed to puzzle about this for a while, inclining his head as though hearing was difficult. Then he nodded quickly and perhaps urgently, turned, and ran into the house, looking back to make sure he was followed. The man entered the living-room through the French windows, behind the running boy, who stopped for a moment in the centre of the room, with the man blinking behind him at the sudden transition from sunlight to comparative dark. The woman was sitting in an armchair, looking at nothing there. She often sat like that. She looked up, across the boy, at the man, and the boy, his face for the first time anxious, met the man's eyes again, asking, before he went out into the house.

'What is it? What is it? Have you seen him again? Why are you . . . ?'

'He came in here. He went – out through the door.'

'I didn't see him.'

'No.'

'Did he – oh, this is so *silly* – did he see me?'

He could not remember. He told the only truth he knew.

'He brought me in here.'

'Oh, what can I do, what am I going to *do*? If I killed myself – I have thought of that – but the idea that I should be with him is an illusion I . . . this silly situation is the nearest I shall ever get. To him. He was *in here with me*?'

'Yes.'

And she was crying again. Out in the garden he could see the boy, swinging agile on the apple branch.

* * *

He was not quite sure, looking back, when he had thought he had realized what the boy had wanted him to do. This was also at the party, his worst piece of what he called bowdlerization, though in some sense it was clearly the opposite of bowdlerization. He told the American girl that he had come to the conclusion that it was the woman herself who had wanted it, though there was in fact, throughout, no sign of her wanting anything except to see the boy, as she said. The boy, bolder and more frequent, had appeared several nights running on the landing, wandering in and out of bathrooms and bedrooms, restlessly, a little agitated, questing almost, until it had 'come to' the man that what he required was to be re-engendered, for him, the man, to give to his mother another child, into which he could peacefully vanish. The idea was so clear that it was like another imperative, though he did not have the courage to ask the child to confirm it. Possibly this was out of delicacy – the child was too young to be talked to about sex. Possibly there were other reasons. Possibly he was mistaken: the situation was making him hysterical, he felt action of some kind was required and must be possible. He could not spend the rest of the summer, the rest of his life, describing non-existent tee shirts and blond smiles.

He could think of no sensible way of embarking on his venture, so in the end simply walked into her bedroom one night. She was lying there, reading; when she saw him her instinctive gesture was to hide, not her bare arms and throat, but her book. She seemed, in fact, quite unsurprised to see his pyjamaed figure, and, after she had recovered her coolness, brought out the book definitely and laid it on the bedspread.

'My new taste in illegitimate literature. I keep them in a box under the bed.'

Ena Twigg, Medium. The Infinite Hive. The Spirit World. Is There Life After Death?

'Pathetic,' she proffered.

He sat down delicately on the bed.

'Please, don't grieve so. Please, let yourself be comforted. Please . . .'

He put an arm round her. She shuddered. He pulled her closer. He asked why she had had only the one son, and she seemed to understand the purport of his question, for she tried, angular and chilly, to lean on him a little, she became apparently compliant. 'No real reason,' she assured him, no material reason. Just her husband's profession and lack of inclination: that covered it.

'Perhaps,' he suggested, 'if she would be comforted a little, perhaps she could hope, perhaps . . .'

For comfort then, she said, dolefully, and lay back, pushing Ena Twigg off the bed with one fierce gesture, then lying placidly. He got in beside her, put his arms round her, kissed her cold cheek, thought of Anne, of what was never to be again. Come on, he said to the woman, you must live, you must try to live, let us hold each other for comfort.

She hissed at him 'Don't *talk*' between clenched teeth, so he stroked her lightly, over her nightdress, breasts and buttocks and long stiff legs, composed like an effigy on an Elizabethan tomb. She allowed this, trembling slightly, and then trembling violently: he took this to be a sign of some mixture of pleasure and pain, of the return of life to stone. He put a hand between her legs and she moved them heavily apart; he heaved himself over her and pushed, unsuccessfully. She was contorted and locked tight: frigid, he thought grimly, was not the word. *Rigor mortis*, his mind said to him, before she began to scream.

He was ridiculously cross about this. He jumped away and said quite rudely 'Shut up,' and then ungraciously 'I'm sorry.' She stopped screaming as suddenly as she had begun and made one of her painstaking economical explanations.

'Sex and death don't go. I can't afford to let go of my grip on myself. I hoped. What you hoped. It was a bad idea. I apologize.'

'Oh, never mind,' he said and rushed out again on to the landing, feeling foolish and almost in tears for warm, lovely Anne.

The child was on the landing, waiting. When the man saw him, he looked questioning, and then turned his face against the wall and leant there, rigid, his shoulders hunched, his hair hiding his expression. There was a similarity between woman and child. The man felt, for the first time, almost uncharitable towards the boy, and then felt something else.

'Look, I'm sorry. I tried. I did try. Please turn round.'

Uncompromising, rigid, clenched back view.

'Oh well,' said the man, and went into his bedroom.

So now, he said to the American woman at the party, I feel a fool, I feel embarrassed, I feel we are hurting, not helping each other, I feel it isn't a refuge. Of course you feel that, she said, of course you're right – it was temporarily necessary, it helped both of you, but you've got to live your life. Yes, he said, I've done my best, I've tried to get through, I have my life to live. Look, she said, I want to help, I really do, I have these wonderful friends I'm renting this flat from, why don't you come, just for a few days, just for a break, why don't you? They're real sympathetic people, you'd like them, I like them, you could get your emotions kind of straightened out. She'd probably be glad to see the back of you, she must feel as bad as you do, she's got to relate to her situation in her own way in the end. We all have.

He said he would think about it. He knew he had elected to tell the sympathetic American because he had sensed she would be – would offer – a way out. He had to get out. He took her home from the party and went back to his house and landlady without seeing her into her flat. They both knew that this reticence was promising – that he hadn't come in then, because he meant to come later. Her warmth and readiness were like sunshine, she was open. He did not know what to say to the woman.

In fact, she made it easy for him: she asked, briskly, if he now found it perhaps uncomfortable to stay, and he replied that he had felt he should move on, he was of so little use. . . . Very well, she had agreed, and had added crisply that it had to be better for everyone if 'all this' came to an end. He remembered the firmness with which she had told him that no illusions were pleasant. She was strong: too strong for her own good. It would take years to wear away that stony, closed, simply surviving insensibility. It was not his job. He would go. All the same, he felt bad.

He got out his suitcases and put some things in them. He went down to the garden, nervously and put away the deckchair. The garden was empty. There were no voices over the wall. The silence was thick and deadening. He wondered, knowing he would not see the boy again, if anyone else would do so, or if, now he was gone, no one would describe a tee shirt, a sandal, a smile, seen, remembered, or desired. He went slowly up to his room again.

The boy was sitting on his suitcase, arms crossed, face frowning and serious. He held the man's look for a long moment, and then the man went and sat on his bed. The boy continued to sit. The man found himself speaking.

'You do see I have to go? I've tried to get through. I can't get through. I'm no use to you, am I?'

The boy remained immobile, his head on one side, considering. The man stood up and walked towards him.

'Please. Let me go. What are we, in this house? A man and a woman and a child, and none of us can get through. You can't want that?'

He went as close as he dared. He had, he thought, the intention of putting his hand on or through the child. But could not bring himself to feel there was no boy. So he stood, and repeated,

'I can't get through. Do you want me to stay?'

Upon which, as he stood helplessly there, the boy turned on him again the brilliant, open, confiding, beautiful desired smile.

Mary Butts

WITH AND WITHOUT BUTTONS

I t is not only true, it is comforting, to say that incredulity is often no more than superstition turned inside out. But there can be a faith of disbelief as inaccurate as its excess, and in some ways more trying, for the right answers to it have not yet been thought up. It was only because Trenchard said at lunch that the mass was a dramatized wish-fulfilment that what came after ever happened. At least I wish we did not think so. It was trying to get out anyhow, but if he had not irritated us and made us want to show off, we would not have made ourselves serviceable to it. And it was we who came off lightly. To him it has been something that he has not been able to shake off. When it happened he behaved so well about it, but that didn't save him. Now he cannot think what he used to think, and he does not know what else there is that he might think.

I am seeing him now, more vividly than I like. He was our next-door neighbour in a remote village in Kent. A nest of wasps had divided their attention between us, and we had met after sunset to return their calls with cyanide and squibs.

He was a sanguine man, positive, hearty, actually emotional. He had known and done a great many things, but when he came to give his account of them, all he had to say was a set of pseudo-rationalizations, calling the bluff, in inaccurate language, of God, the arts, the imagination, the emotions. That is not even chic science for laymen today. He might have thought that way as much as he liked, but there was no reason, we said, to try and prove it to us all one hot, sweet, blue-drawn summer, in a Kentish orchard; to sweat for our conversion; to shame us into agreement. Until the evening I told him to stop boring us with his wish-fulfilments, for they weren't ours, and saw his healthy skin start to sweat and a stare come into his eyes. That ought to have warned me, as it did my sister, of whom I am sometimes afraid. It did warn us, but it wound us up also. We went home through the orchard in the starlight and sat downstairs in the midsummer night between lit candles, inviting in all that composed it, night hunting cries and scents of things that grow and ripen, cooled in the star-flow. A world visible, but not in terms of colour. With every door and every window open, the old house was no more than a frame, a set of screens to display night, midsummer, perfume, the threaded stillness, the stars strung together, their spears glancing, penetrating an earth breathing silently, a female power asleep.

'All he hears is nature snoring,' said my sister. 'Let's give him a nightmare.' It was a good idea.

'How?' I said.

'We'll find out tomorrow. I can feel one about.'

I got up to close the doors before we mounted with our candles. Through walls and glass, through open doors or shut, a tide poured in, not of air or any light or dark or scent or sound or heat or coolness. Tide. Without distinction from north or south or without or within; without flow or ebb, a Becoming; without stir or departure or stay: without radiance or pace. Star-tide. Has not Science had wind of rays poured in from interstellar space?

There is no kind of ill-doing more fascinating than one which has a moral object, a result in view which will justify the means without taking the fun out of them. All that is implied when one says that one will give someone something to cry about. It was that line which we took at breakfast.

'We'll try this simple faith,' we said. 'We'll scare him stiff and see how he stands the strain. We'll haunt him.' And asked each other if either of us knew of a practising vampire in the neighbourhood or a were-cow.

It was several days before we hit on a suitable technique, examining and rejecting every known variety of apparition, realizing that apparatus must be reduced to a minimum, and that when nothing will bear scrutiny, there must be very little given to scrutinize. In fact, what we meant to do was to suggest him into an experience – the worse the better – wholly incompatible with the incredulities of his faith. That it would be easy to do, we guessed; that it would be dangerous to him – that appeared at the moment as part of the fun. Not because we did not like him, because we wanted to have power over him, the power women sometimes want to have over men, the pure, not erotic power, whose point is that it shall have nothing to do with sex. We could have made him make love, to either or both of us, any day of the week.

This is what we planned, understanding that, like a work of art, once it had started, its development could be left to look after itself.

'Suppose,' said my sister, 'that we have heard a ridiculous superstition in the village that there is Something Wrong with the house. We will tell him that, and when he has gone through his reaction exercises – it may take a day or so and will depend on our hints, and if we make the right ones, the battle's won – he will ask us what the story is.'

'What is it to be?' I said, who can rarely attain to my sister's breadth of mind.

'That does not matter. Because before we begin we'll *do* something.

Anything. A last year's leaf for a start, so long as it can go into a series – on his blotter or his pillow. We're always in and out. We'll put them there and get asked round for the evening and start when we see one, and that's where our village story begins. All that he has to get out of us is that there *is* a story, and that wet leaves or whatever it is we choose are found about. Signatures, you know. If he doesn't rise the first night, he'll find that leaf when he goes to bed. It depends on how well we do it—'

I recognized a master's direction, but it all seemed to depend on our choice of stimulants. Last year's leaves, delicate damp articulations; coloured pebbles, dead flies, scraps of torn paper with half a word decipherable . . . A mixture of these or a selection?

'Keep it tangible,' my sister said – 'that's the way. Our only difficulty is the planting of them.'

'Which', I asked, 'are suitable to what?'

It seemed to be necessary in laying our train to determine the kind of unpleasantness for which they were ominous. But I could not get my sister to attend.

'It's not that way round,' she said at length – 'dead bees, feathers, drops of candle-grease? Old kid gloves? With and Without Buttons. That will do.'

I felt a trifle queer. 'Well,' I said, 'they're the sort of things a man never has in his house, so that's sound so far. But women do. Not the sort of things we wear, but he'd not know that. And how do we get hold of them?'

'There's a shoe-box in the loft full of them, by the door into his place when these houses were one.' (Our cottages were very old, side by side, with a common wall, our orchards divided by a hedge.) We had rented ours from a friend who had recently bought it as it stood from a local family which had died out, and of which very little seemed known. My sister said:

'Shiny black kid and brown, with little white glass buttons and cross stitching and braid. All one size, and I suppose for one pair of hands. Some have all the buttons and some have none and some have some—' I listened to this rune until I was not sure how many times my sister had said it.

'With and without buttons,' I repeated, and could not remember how often I had said that.

After that we said nothing more about it, and it was three days later that he asked us to supper, and we walked round through the gap in the hedge in the pure daylight, and sat in his little verandah, whose wooden pillars spread as they met the roof in fans of plaited green laths. Prim fantasy, with its French windows behind it, knocked out of walls of flint rubble three feet thick. Roses trailed up it. A tidy little home, with something behind it of monstrous old age one did as well to forget.

'By the way,' he said. (As I have said before, his name was Trenchard, and he had come back to his own part of England to rest, after a long time spent in looking after something in East Africa.) 'By the way, have either of you two lost a glove?'

'So she's got busy already and didn't tell me, the spoil sport,' I thought.

'No,' we said, 'but one always does. What sort of a glove?'

'A funny little thing of brown kid with no buttons. I didn't think it could be yours. I found it on the top of the loft stairs. Outside the door. Here it is.' He went inside and came out on to the verandah where we were having supper, a moment later, puzzled.

'Here it is,' he said. 'I put it in the bureau, and the odd thing is that when I went to look for it I found another. Not its pair either. This one's black.'

Two little ladylike shiny kid gloves, the kind worn by one's aunts when one was a child. I had not yet seen our collection. The black had three of its buttons missing. We told him that they were not the kind that women wore now.

'My landlady bought the place unfurnished,' he said. 'Must have come out of the things the old owners left behind when they died.' My sister gave a slight start, a slight frown and bit her lip. I shook my head at her.

'What's up?' he asked, simply.

'Nothing,' we said.

'I'm not going to be laughed at by you,' said my sister.

'I'm not laughing,' he said, his goodwill beaming at us, prepared even to be tolerant.

'Oh, but you'd have the right to—'

After that, he wanted to know at once.

'It's playing into your hands,' she said, 'but don't you know that your half of the house is the Village Haunt? And that it's all about gloves? With and without buttons?'

It was ridiculously easy. He was amiable rather than irritated at her story, while I was still hurt that she had not first rehearsed it with me. She began to tell him a story about old Miss Blacken, who had lived here with her brother, a musty old maid in horrible clothes, but nice about her hands; and how there was something – no, not a ghost – but something which happened that was always preceded by gloves being found about. This we told him and he behaved very prettily about it, sparing us a lecture.

'But it's not quite fair,' he said. 'I mustn't be selfish. She must leave some at your place. Remember, in her day, it was all one house.'

Then we talked about other things, but when we had gone home I found my sister a little pensive. I began on my grievance.

'Why didn't you tell me you had begun? Why didn't you coach me?' Then she said:

'To tell you the truth, I hadn't meant to begin. What I said I made up on the spot. All I'd done was that just before we left I ran up to the loft and snatched a glove from the box and left it on his bureau. That's the second one he found.'

'Then what about the one he found outside the loft door?'

'It's that that's odd. That's why he never thought it was us. I haven't had a chance to get to that part of his house. I didn't put it there.'

Well, now that the affair was launched, we felt it had better go on. Though I am not sure if we were quite so keen about it. It was as though – and we had known this to be possible before – it had already started itself. One sometimes feels this has happened. Anyhow, it was two days later before I thought it was my turn to lay a glove on his premises, and went up to our loft and took one out of the box. There was nothing in it but gloves. I took a white one, a little cracked, with only two buttons, and having made sure he was out, slipped through the hedge and dropped it at the foot of the stair. He startled me considerably by returning at that instant. I said I had come for a book. He saw the thing.

'Hallo,' he said, 'there's another. It's beginning. That makes four.'

'Four?' I said. 'There were only two the other night.'

'I found one in my bedroom. A grey. Are we never going to get a pair?'

Then it occurred to me that he'd seen through us all along, and was getting in ahead with gloves. I took my book and returned to my sister.

'That won't do,' she said, 'he's sharp, but we didn't begin it. He found his first.'

I said: 'I'm beginning to wonder if it mightn't be a good thing to find out in the village if anything is known about Miss Blacken and her brother.'

'You go,' said my sister, still pensive.

I went to the pub when it opened and drew blank. I heard about diseases of bees and chickens and the neighbours. The Post Office was no good. I was returning by a detour, along a remote lane, when a voice said:

'You *were* asking about Miss Blacken along at Stone Cottages?'

It was only a keeper who had been in the pub, come up suddenly through a gate, out of a dark fir planting. '—Seeing as you have the uses of her furniture,' said he. We passed into step. I learned that after fifty years' odd residence in the place there was nothing that you might have to tell about her and waited.

'—Now her brother, he was not what you might call ordinary.' Again that stopped at that.

'—Regular old maid she was. If maid she'd ever been. Not that you could be saying regular old man for him, for he wasn't either, if you take my meaning, Miss.'

I did. Finally I learned – and I am not quite sure how I learned – it was certainly not all by direct statement – that Miss Blacken had been a little grey creature, who had never seemed naturally to be living or dying; whose clothes were little bits and pieces, as you might say. Anyhow, she'd dropped something – an excuse me, Miss, petticoat, his wife had said – on the green, and run away without stopping to pick it up, opening and shutting her mouth. It was then it had begun. If you could call *that* beginning. I was asking to know what that was? In a manner of speaking he couldn't rightly say. It was the women took it to heart. What became of the petticoat? That was the meaning of it. 'Twasn't rightly speaking a petticoat at all. There weren't no wind, and when they came to pick it up, it upped and sailed as if there were a gale of wind behind it, right out of sight along the sky. And one day it had come back; hung down from the top of an elm and waved at them, and the women had it there were holes in it, like a face. And no wonder, seeing it had passed half a winter blowing about in the tops of the trees. Did it never come down to earth? Not it they said. Nor old Miss Blacken start to look for it, except that it was then that people remembered her about at nights.

A little pensive now myself, I asked about gloves and was told and no more than that 'they say that she's left her gloves about'.

I returned to my sister and we spent the evening doing a reconstruction of Miss Blacken out of Victorian oddments. It was most amusing and not in the least convincing.

'Tomorrow, shall we feed him a glove?' I said. It was then that it came across our minds, like a full statement to that effect, that it was no longer necessary. The gloves would feed themselves.

'I know what it is we've done,' said my sister, 'we've wound it up.'

'Wound up what?' I answered. 'Ghost of a village eccentric, who was careful about her hands?'

'Oh no,' said my sister. 'I don't know. Oh no.'

After another three days, I said:

'Nothing more has happened over there. I mean he's found no more gloves. Hadn't we better help things along a bit?'

'There was one yesterday in my room, unbuttoned,' she said. 'I didn't drop it.'

I was seriously annoyed. This seemed to be going too far. And in what direction? What does one do when this sort of thing happens? I was looking as one does when one has heard one's best friend talking about oneself, when the shadow of a heavy man fell across our floor. It was Trenchard. My sister looked up and said quickly:

'I've found one now.'

'Have you?' he said. 'So have I.' He hesitated. There was something very direct and somehow comforting in the way he was taking it, piece by piece as it happened, not as what he would think it ought to mean. It was then that we began to be ashamed of ourselves. He went on:

'You know my cat. She's her kittens hidden somewhere in the loft and I wanted to have a look at them. I went up softly not to scare her. You know it's dark on that top stair. I got there, and then I heard – well – a little thing falling off a step. Thought it was a kitten trying to explore. Peered and felt and picked up a glove.'

He pulled it out of his pocket and held it up by a finger with slight distaste. A brown one this time.

'One button,' he said. 'The kittens aren't big enough to have been playing with it and the cat wasn't about. There's no draught. Funny, isn't it? Reminded me of one of those humpty-dumpty toys we had, a little silk man with arms and legs and a painted face, and a loose marble inside him to make him turn over and fall about.'

My sister said:

'We've found a box of loose gloves in our attic close to your bricked-up door.'

His answer was that it was bricked up all right, and had we thought to count them in case either of our maids was up to some village trick. We hadn't, but I noticed that he mistrusted our maids as little as we did. Also that his behaviour was so reasonable because he had not yet thought that there was any cause for suspicion.

'Let's do it now,' he said. 'Put them all back, yours and mine. Count them and lock your door.'

He went back and fetched his five, and together we went upstairs. They sat on a basket trunk while I emptied the box.

'Twenty-seven. Eleven pairs in all and one missing.' I shovelled them back into the cardboard box, yellow with time and dust. I looked up at his broad straight nose and my sister's little one that turns up. Both were sniffing.

'There's a smell here,' they said. There was. Not the dust-camphor-mouse-and-apple smell proper to lofts.

'I know what it is,' Trenchard said, 'smelt it in Africa in a damp place. Bad skins.'

The loft went suddenly darker. We looked up. There was no window, but someone had cut the thatch and let in a skylight. Something was covering it, had suddenly blown across it, though outside there was no wind. I took the iron handle with holes in it to stick through the pin in the frame, and threw it up. The piece of stuff slid backwards into the thatch. I put my arm out, caught hold of it and pulled it in. A piece of calico with a stiff waxy surface, once used for linings, again some time ago. It seemed to have no shape, but there were holes in it. Holes not tears.

'Nasty slummy rag,' I said. 'I suppose it was lying about in the thatch.'

Our thatch was old and full of flowers. This thing went with dustbins and tin cans. One piece was clotted together. A large spider ran out of it. I dropped it on the floor beside the box and the gloves. I was surprised to see Trenchard look at it with disgust.

'Never could stand seeing things go bad,' he said. We left the attic, locking the door and went downstairs. We gave him the key. It seemed the decent thing to do.

Over a late and thoughtful tea, we talked of other things. We did not think it necessary to tell him what the keeper had said.

The evening was exquisite and the next day and the next night. Days refreshed with night-showers to draw out scent, and steady sun to ripen; a pattern on the world like the dry dew on a moth's wing, or the skin on a grape or a rose. And nothing more happened. The next evening Trenchard was to give a little party for his birthday, for some friends who would motor over; and my sister and I were to see that all was in order for it, flowers and fruit and wine and all the good cold things to eat. We had the delicate pleasant things to do; to slice the cucumbers and drench sprays of borage and balm-in-Gilead for the iced drinks. The almonds did not come, so we salted some ourselves, blanching them in the garden, getting hot in the kitchen over pans of burnt salt.

At about six o'clock we went back to dress. Trying, as was appropriate, to look like Paris, in compliment to Trenchard, but principally to the garden and to the weather and to the earth. There was a bump overhead from the attic.

'What's that?' said my sister, painting her face.

'I left the skylight open,' I said. 'It must have slipped. Let's leave it. Am I in a state of dress or undress to go up there?'

She was ready before I was, and said that she was going across to Trenchard's to have one more look to see if all was in order there. Half of our day's work had been to keep him out of the way. We had just sent him up to the village after more strawberries and hoped that he would be back in time – and there was still plenty of time – for him to dress. As she went, I heard his step at his front door, and a few moments later, my dressing finished, I went downstairs and out across the orchard to join them. He had gone upstairs to change, but just as I reached the verandah, I heard a short cry which must have come from him. I ran in with my sister, who was also outside, building a last pyramid of strawberries on a dish shaped like a green leaf. He came out of the dining room.

'Who's done this?' he said.

The supper table was set with food to be fetched and eaten when people pleased. There were little bowls of cut-glass set with sweets and almonds. One of these had been sprinkled with buttons, little white buttons that had been torn off, still ragged with red-brown threads.

'I filled it,' said my sister in a small weak voice, 'with those sugar rose leaves, and a real one on top.'

'Your servant—' I began, when he cried out again:

'What's that glove doing up the back of your dress?'

It was a little silver coat I had on to begin with. I pulled it off, and there fell off the collar, but with a tiny thud, another glove, a black one. It had no buttons on it and was open like a hand. Trenchard picked it up, and I thought I saw it collapse a little.

'No time to count them tonight,' he said, and looked round. It was too hot for a fire, but they were laid in all the rooms. He put the glove down and struck a match. The huge chimney used to roar with its draught, but the fire would not catch. He went out to the lavatory with the glove and the dish.

'Go up and dress,' we said when he came back; but instead he sniffed.

'It's what we smelt the other day,' he said. 'Up in the loft. Dead skin.'

Outside the air was hot and sweet and laced with coolness, but we noticed that here indoors it was cold, stale cold.

'Go and dress,' we said again, with the female instinct to keep the minutiae of things steady and in sequence.

'They won't be here till eight: there's plenty of time,' he said, feeling not fear or even much curiosity, but that it was not the proper thing to leave us alone with the inexplicable unpleasant.

'Your servant,' I began again.

'My servant's all right,' he said. 'Go out and wait in the verandah. I'll be down quickly.'

So he went up. We took a chair and sat each side of the open glass doors where we could see into the house. We remembered that his maid as well as ours had gone back to her cottage to get ready for company. So there was no one in either house.

'He's taking it well,' we said, and 'What is it?' And what we meant was:

'What have we stirred up?' And (for my sister and I cannot lie to one another) 'You did not do that with the buttons in the dish?' 'Dear God, I did not.'

'A dirty old woman,' said my sister, 'nice about her hands.'

I said: 'Dirty things done in a delicate way. There was that piece of stuff.'

The house and the little orchard were backed with tall trees. There was a hint of evening, and high branches black against strong gold. Was there something hanging high up, very high, that looked like a square of stuff that had holes in it?

Upstairs, Trenchard must have gone to the bathroom first. Then we heard him, moving about in his bedroom, just above the verandah roof. Then we heard him shout again, a cry he tried to stop. We ran out across the grass and called up at his window. He answered: 'No, don't come up.' Of course we ran up, in and through the sitting-room and up the stairs. The dining-room door was still open, and with a corner of my eye I saw a candle, guttering hideously in the windless room.

'Let us in,' we said at his door.

'Of all the filthy nonsense—' he was repeating: '—Look at my shirt.'

On the top of the chest of drawers out of which he had taken it, his shirt was lying; and on its stiff white linen was what looked like a patch of grey jelly. Only it had spread out from a clot into five ribbons, like a hand or the fingers of a glove.

'Fine sort of beastliness,' he said, 'that won't let you dress for dinner.' I heard myself saying:

'Are all your shirts like that?'

'No,' he said grimly, 'and if you don't mind waiting here till I've finished, we'll go downstairs and see what this is about.'

He took another shirt and finished his dressing, wincing as he touched things; while we felt as if there were slugs about, the things of which we are most afraid; and that we must keep our long dresses tight about us.

We went down together into the dining-room and there my sister screamed. On the top of the centre strawberry pyramid, hanging over the berries like a cluster of slugs, was a glove, yellow-orange kid-skin, still and fat. A colour we had not seen in the box. The wrist and the fingers open and swollen. No buttons.

'What witches' trick is this?' he cried, and stared at us, for we were women. And like a wave moving towards us, rearing its head, came the knowledge that we were responsible for this; that our greed and vanity in devising this had evoked this: that we would now have to show courage, courage and intelligence to put an end to this, to lay this. And we had no idea how.

'The fire must burn,' I said. 'A great fire.' He turned towards the outhouse.

'What's the lovely scent you wear?' he said to my sister. – 'I want to smell it. Get that.'

She ran away, and I stood still, aware of my shoulder-blades and the back of my neck, and all of my body that I couldn't *see*. Doors would not open easily. I heard him swearing and stumbling, the clang of a bucket tripped over and kicked away in the yard. My sister ran in, a scent-spray in her hand, crying:

'It's not scent any more. I tried it. It smells like the attic—'

She was squeezing the bulb and spraying us all violently; and I could not smell the dead smell of the loft, but the sweetness, like a ladylike animal, of old kid gloves.

Outside, the delicious evening was pouring in, to meet the original smell of the house; smell of flowers and tobacco, of polished furniture and wood-smoke and good things to eat. Trenchard had brought in a gallon jar of paraffin. He tipped and splashed it over the sitting-room fire.

'Get all the gloves,' he said, looking at our helpless skirts: 'I'll go across. I've got the loft key.'

We peered again into the dining-room, that the kitchen opened out of. The candle guttered in fat dripping folds; a spider ran across a plate. My sister said:

'It's got only five fingers. Like a glove.'

We waited. 'Let's have the fire ready,' we said, and I staggered with the can at arm's length to the sitting-room fire and drenched the piled wood. The ugly vulgar smell was sweet with reassurance. My sister threw in a match. A roar drowned the crackle of catching sticks.

'Now for it,' we said, and tore open the bureau drawer for the gloves. I ran up for Trenchard's shirt, and when I came back, my sister, her hands full of strawberries, threw them, yellow glove and all, on the leaping pillars of fire. I shook the guttering candle out of its stick; my sister unscrewed her spray and emptied the precious stuff, that waved blue and white fingers at us out of the fierce, shrill yellow flames.

'So much for that,' I said. 'Where is he?' said my sister. We looked at each other.

'This is our fault,' we said. – 'We must go over. If it starts here again when we're gone, God knows what we're to do.' Then she said:

'The loft's the place. It started there.'

Outside, the orchard was full of bird-conversation. Inside, in half an hour we were to give a birthday party. We ran through the gap in the hedge and into our side of the house, which had become again part of one house.

Inside it we expected to find one large, troubled man, upstairs collecting things. Instead there was quiet, a kind of dead quiet that came to meet us down the steep stair. The loft door was open. On the flight that led up to it he was lying, feet down, his head upon the sill; his head invisible, wrapped up in what looked like a piece of dark green cotton, dirty and torn. We dragged it off.

'Burn. Burn,' my sister said.

Some of it was in his mouth. We pulled it out. His tongue and mouth were stained. We slid him down to the foot of the flight and got water.

'Draw it fresh,' she said. And 'Keep it tight in your hand,' for I wanted to drop the cloth, to pull it away, as if it were trying to wrap itself round me, to stick to me.

We threw water on him. ('Two shirts already; what an evening!' thought a bit of me.) By this time I had hold of the cloth like grim death, for it felt as though it was straining away in a wind that wasn't there. 'Gloves,' he said. We went into the loft. The skylight was open, and the cardboard box lay open and full. She put on the lid, and put it under her arm, and we left him on the stairs and made off again, across the orchard to the fire. It was dying down. The room stifling, the wood sulky with oil-black. My sister flung in the box, drenched it with the oil, and stiff grey smoke poured out on us. She tossed a match on it, and there was the grunt of an explosion, and, as we jumped back, the fire poured up again. I felt a smart in my hand, as if the cloth was raw between my fingers.

'It mustn't fly up the chimney,' she said. 'If it does, it will come back all over again.'

There was a box of cigars on the table. We turned them out, and thrust it in between the thin cedar boards and shut it up. Flung it into the fire wall and held it down. The box rose once or twice, bucked under the poker and the shovel.

Then we went back to Trenchard. He had come round, and was sitting at the foot of the loft stair.

'Everything's burned,' we said. 'Tell us what happened to you.'

'God knows,' he said. And then: 'I was stooping to get the box, and something flapped against the skylight. Blew in, I suppose, and the next thing I knew it had wrapped itself round my head and I couldn't get it off. I tore at it and I tried to get out. Then I couldn't bear it any more. It was winding itself tight. Then I must have passed out. But, oh God, it was the smell of it . . .'

Celia Fremlin

DON'T TELL CISSIE

'FRIDAY, then. The six-ten from Liverpool Street,' said Rosemary, gathering up her gloves and bag. 'And don't tell Cissie!' she added, 'You *will* be careful about that, won't you, Lois?'

I nodded. People are always talking like this about Cissie, she's that kind of person. She was like that at school, and now, when we're all coming up towards retirement, she's like it still.

You know the kind of person I mean? Friendly, good-hearted, and desperately anxious to be in on everything, and yet with this mysterious knack of ruining things – of bringing every project grinding to a halt, simply by being there.

Because it wasn't ever her fault. Not really. 'Let me come! Oh, *please* let me come too!' she'd beg, when three or four of us from the Lower Fourth had schemed up an illicit trip to the shops on Saturday afternoon. And, because she was our friend (well, sort of – anyway, it was *our* set that she hovered on the fringe of all the time, not anyone else's) – because of this, we usually let her come; and always it ended in disaster. *She'd* be the one to slip on the edge of the kerb outside Woolworth's, and cut her knee so that the blood ran, and a little crowd collected, and a kind lady rang up the school to have us fetched home. *She'd* be the one to get lost . . . to miss the bus . . . to arrive back at school bedraggled and tear-stained and late for evening preparation, hopelessly giving the game away for all of us.

You'd think, wouldn't you, that after a few such episodes she'd have given up, or at least have learned caution. But no. Her persistence (perhaps one would have called it courage if only it hadn't been so annoying) – well, her persistence, then, was indomitable. Neither school punishments nor the reproaches of her companions ever kept her under for long. 'Oh, *please* let me come!' she'd be pleading again, barely a week after the last débâcle. 'Oh, plee-ee-ease! Oh, don't be so *mean*!'

And so there, once again, she'd inexorably be, back in action once more. Throwing-up in the middle of the dormitory feast. Crying with blisters as we trudged back from a ramble out of bounds. Soaked, and shivering, and starting pneumonia from having fallen through the ice of the pond we'd been forbidden to skate on.

So you can understand, can't you, why Rosemary and I didn't want Cissie with us when we went to investigate the ghost at Rosemary's new weekend cottage. Small as our chances might be of pinning down the ghost in any case, Cissie could have been counted on to reduce them to zero. Dropping a tray of tea-things just as the rapping began . . . Calling out, 'What? *I* can't hear anything!' as we held our breaths trying to locate the ghostly sobbing . . . Falling over a tombstone as we tiptoed through the moonlit churchyard . . . No, Cissie must at all costs be kept out of our little adventure; and by now, after nearly half a century, we knew that the only way of keeping Cissie out of anything was to make sure that she knew nothing about it, right from the beginning.

But let me get back to Rosemary's new cottage. I say 'new', because Rosemary has only recently bought it – not because the cottage itself is new. Far from it. It is early eighteenth-century, and damp, and dark, and built of the local stone, and Rosemary loves it (*did* love it, rather – but let me not get ahead of myself). Anyway, as I was saying, Rosemary loved the place, loved it on sight, and bought it almost on impulse with the best part of her life's savings. *Their* life's savings, I suppose I should say, because she and Norman are still married to each other, and it must have been his money just as much as hers. But Norman never seems to have much to do with these sort of decisions – indeed, he doesn't seem to have much to do with Rosemary's life at all, these days – certainly, he never comes down to the cottage. I think that was part of the idea, really – that they should be able to get away from each other at weekends. During the week, of course, it's all right, as they are both working full-time, and they both bring plenty of work home in the evenings. Rosemary sits in one room correcting history essays, while Norman sits in another working out Export Quotas, or something; and the mutual non-communication must be almost companionable, in an arid sort of a way. But the crunch will come, of course, when they both retire in a year or so's time. I think Rosemary was thinking of this when she bought the cottage; it would become a real port in a storm then – a bolt-hole from what she refers to as 'the last and worst lap of married life'.

At one time, we used to be sorry for Cissie, the only one of our set who never married. But now, when the slow revolving of the decades has left me a widow and Rosemary stranded among the flotsam of a dead marriage – now, lately I have begun wondering whether Cissie hasn't done just as well for herself as any of us, in the long run. Certainly, she has had plenty of fun on the fringes of other people's lives, over the years. She wangles invitations to silver-wedding parties; worms her way into other people's family holidays – and even if it ends up with the whole lot of them in quarantine at the airport because of Cissie coming out in spots – well, at least she's usually had a good run for her money first.

And, to be fair to her, it's not just the pleasures and luxuries of our lives that she tries to share; it's the problems and crises, too. I remember she managed to be present at the birth of my younger son, and if only she hadn't dropped the boiling kettle on her foot just as I went into the second stage of labour, her presence would have been a real help. As it was, the doctor and midwife were both busy treating her for shock in the kitchen, and binding up her scalded leg, while upstairs my son arrived unattended, and mercifully without fuss. Perhaps even the unborn are sensitive to atmosphere? Perhaps he sensed, even then, that, with Cissie around, it's just *no use* anyone else making a fuss about anything?

But let me get back to Rosemary's haunted cottage (or not haunted, as the case may be – let me not prejudge the issue before I have given you all the facts). Of course, to begin with, we were half playing a game, Rosemary and I. The tension tends to go out of life as you come up towards your sixties. Whatever problems once tore at you, and kept you fighting, and alive, and gasping for breath – they are solved now, or else have died, quietly, while you weren't noticing. Anyway, what with one thing and another, life can become a bit dull and flavourless when you get to our age; and, to be honest, a ghost was just what Rosemary and I were needing. A spice of danger; a spark of the unknown to reactivate these waterlogged minds of ours, weighed down as they are by such a lifetime's accumulation of the known.

I am telling you this because I want to be absolutely honest. In evaluating the events I am to describe, you must remember, and allow for, the fact that Rosemary and I *wanted* there to be a ghost. Well, no, perhaps that's putting it too strongly; we wanted there to *might* be a ghost – if you see what I so ungrammatically mean. We wanted our weekend to bring us at least a small tingling of the blood; a tiny prickling of the scalp. We wanted our journey to reach a little way into the delicious outskirts of fear, even if it *did* have to start from Liverpool Street.

We felt marvellously superior, Rosemary and I, as we stood jam-packed in the corridor, rocking through the rainy December night. We glanced with secret pity at all those blank, commuter faces, trundling towards the security of their homes. *We* were different. *We* were travelling into the Unknown.

* * *

Our first problems, of course, were nothing to do with ghosts. They were to do with milk, and bread, and damp firewood, and why Mrs Thorpe from the village hadn't come in to air the beds as she'd promised. She hadn't filled the lamps, either, or brought in the paraffin . . . how did she think Rosemary was going to get it from the shed in all this rain and dark? And where were all those tins she'd stocked up with in the summer? They couldn't *all* have been eaten . . . ?

I'm afraid I left it all to Rosemary. I know visitors are supposed to trot around at the heels of their hostesses, yapping helpfully, like terriers; but I just won't. After all, I know how little help it is to *me*, when I am a hostess, so why should I suppose that everyone else is different? Besides, by this time I was half-frozen, what with the black, sodden fields and marshlands without, and the damp stone within; and so I decided to concentrate my meagre store of obligingness on getting a fire going.

What a job it was, though! It was as if some demon was working against me, spitting and sighing down the cavernous chimney, whistling wickedly along the icy, stone-flagged floor, blowing out each feeble flicker of flame as fast as I coaxed it from the damp balls of newspaper piled under the damper wood.

Fortunately there were plenty of matches, and gradually, as each of my abortive efforts left the materials a tiny bit drier than before, hope of success came nearer. Or maybe it was that the mischievous demon grew tired of his dance of obstruction – the awful sameness of frustrating me time and time again – anyway, for whatever reason, I at last got a few splinters of wood feebly smouldering. Bending close, and cupping my hands around the precious whorls to protect them from the sudden damp gusts and sputters of rain down the chimney, I watched, enchanted, while first one tiny speck of gold and then another glimmered on the charred wood. Another . . . and yet another . . . until suddenly, like the very dawn of creation, a flame licked upwards.

It was the first time in years and years that I had had anything to do with an open fire. I have lived in centrally heated flats for almost all of my adult life, and I had forgotten this apocalyptic moment when fire comes into being under your hands. Like God on the morning of creation, I sat there, all-powerful, tending the spark I had created. A sliver more of wood here . . . a knob of coal there . . . soon my little fire was bright, and growing, and needing me no more.

But still I tended it – or pretended to – leaning over it, spreading my icy hands to the beginnings of warmth. Vaguely, in the background, I was aware of Rosemary blundering around the place, clutching in her left hand the only oil-lamp that worked, peering disconsolately into drawers and cupboards, and muttering under her breath at each new evidence of disorder and depletion.

Honestly, it was no use trying to help. We'd have to manage, somehow, for tonight, and then tomorrow, with the coming of the blessed daylight, we'd be able to get everything to rights. Fill the lamps. Fetch food from the village. Get the place properly warm . . .

Warm! I shivered, and huddled closer into the wide chimney-alcove. Although the fire was burning up nicely now, it had as yet made little impact on the icy chill of the room. It was cold as only these ancient, little-used cottages *can* be cold. The cold of centuries seems to be stored up in their old stones, and the idea that you can warm it away with a single brisk weekend of paraffin heaters and hastily lit fires has always seemed to me laughable.

Not to Rosemary, though. She is an impatient sort of person, and it always seems to her that heaters *must* produce heat. That's what the word *means*! So she was first angered, then puzzled, and finally half-scared by the fact that she just *couldn't* get the cottage warm. Even in late August, when the air outside was still soft, and the warmth of summer lingered over the fields and marshes – even then, the cottage was like an ice-box inside. I remember remarking on it during my first visit – 'Marvellously cool!' was how I put it at the time, for we had just returned, hot and exhausted, from a long tramp through the hazy, windless countryside; and that was the first time (I think) that Rosemary mentioned to me that the place was supposed to be haunted.

'One of those tragic, wailing ladies that the Past specializes in,' she explained, rather facetiously. 'She's supposed to have drowned herself away on the marsh somewhere – for love, I suppose; it always was, wasn't it? My God, though, what a thing to drown oneself for! – if only she'd *known* . . . !'

This set us off giggling, of course; and by the time we'd finished our wry reminiscences, and our speculations about the less-than-ecstatic love-lives of our various friends – by this time, of course, the end of the ghost story had rather got lost. Something about the woman's ghost moaning around the cottage on stormy nights (or was it moonlight ones?), and about the permanent, icy chill that had settled upon the cottage, and particularly upon the upstairs back bedroom, into which they'd carried her body, all dripping wet from the marsh.

'As good a tale as any, for when your tenants start demanding proper heating,' I remember remarking cheerfully (for Rosemary, at that time, had vague and grandiose plans for making a fortune by letting the place for part of the year) and we had both laughed, and that, it had seemed, was the end of it.

But when late summer became autumn, and autumn deepened into winter, and the north-east wind, straight from Siberia, howled in over the marshes, then Rosemary began to get both annoyed and perturbed.

'I just *can't* get the place warm,' she grumbled. 'I can't understand it! And as for that back room – the one that looks out over the marsh – it's uncanny how cold it is! Two oil-heaters, burning day and night, and it's *still* . . . !'

I couldn't pretend to be surprised: as I say, I *expect* my friends' weekend cottages to be like this. But I tried to be sympathetic; and when, late in November, Rosemary confessed, half-laughing, that she really *did* think the place was haunted, it was I who suggested that we should go down together and see if we could lay the ghost.

She welcomed the suggestion with both pleasure and relief.

'If it was just the cold, I wouldn't be bothering,' she explained. 'But there seems to be something eerie about the place – there really does, Lois! It's like being in the presence of the dead.' (Rosemary never has been in the presence of the dead, or she'd know it's not like that at all, but I let it pass.) 'I'm getting to hate being there on my own. Sometimes – I know it sounds crazy, but sometimes I really *do* seem to hear voices!' She laughed, uncomfortably. 'I must be in a bad way, mustn't I? *Hearing voices . . . ! Me . . . !*'

To this day, I don't know how much she was really scared, and how much she was just trying to work a bit of drama into her lonely – and probably unexpectedly boring – trips down to her dream cottage. I don't suppose she even knows herself. All I can say for certain is that her mood of slightly factitious trepidation touched exactly on some deep need of my own, and at once we knew that we would go. And that it would be fun. And that Cissie must at all costs be kept out of it. Once *her* deep needs get involved, you've had it.

A little cry from somewhere in the shadows, beyond the circle of firelight, jerked me from my reverie, and for a moment I felt my heart pounding. Then, a moment later, I was laughing, for the cry came again:

'Spaghetti! Spaghetti Bolognese! Four whole tins of it, all stacked up under the sink! Now, *who* could have. . . ?'

And who could care, anyway? Food, real food, was now within our grasp! Unless . . . Oh dear . . . !

'I bet you've lost the tin-opener!' I hazarded, with a sinking heart – for at the words 'Spaghetti Bolognese' I had realized just how hungry I was – and it was with corresponding relief that, in the flickering firelight, I saw a smug smile overspreading her face.

'See?' She held up the vital implement; it flickered through the shadows like a shining minnow as she gesticulated her triumph. '*See?* Though of course, if *Cissie* had been here . . . !'

We both began to giggle; and later, as we sat over the fire scooping spaghetti bolognese from pottery bowls, and drinking the red wine which Rosemary had managed to unearth – as we sat there, revelling in creature comforts, we amused ourselves by speculating on the disasters which would have befallen us by now had Cissie been one of the party. How she would have dropped the last of the matches into a puddle, looking for a lost glove . . . would have left the front door swinging open in the wind, blowing out our only oil-lamp. And the tin-opener, of course, would have been a write-off from the word go; if she hadn't lost it in some dark corner, it would certainly have collapsed into two useless pieces under her big, willing hands . . . By now, we would have been without light, heat or food . . .

This depressing picture seemed, somehow, to be the funniest thing imaginable as we sat there, with our stomachs comfortably full and with our third helping of red wine gleaming jewel-like in the firelight.

'To absent friends!' we giggled, raising our glasses. 'And let's hope they *remain* absent,' I added, wickedly, thinking of Cissie; and while we were both still laughing over this cynical toast, I saw Rosemary suddenly go rigid, her glass an inch from her lips, and I watched the laughter freeze on her face.

'Listen!' she hissed. 'Listen, Lois! Do you *hear*?'

For long seconds, we sat absolutely still, and the noises of the night impinged, for the first time, on my consciousness. The wind, rising now, was groaning and sighing around the cottage, moaning in the chimney and among the old beams. The rain spattered in little gusts against the windows, which creaked and rattled on their old hinges. Beyond them, in the dark, overgrown garden, you could hear the stir and rustle of bare twigs and sodden leaves . . . and beyond that again there was the faint, endless sighing of the marsh, mile upon mile of it, half-hidden under the dry, winter reeds.

'No . . .' I began, in a whisper; but Rosemary made a sharp little movement, commanding silence. '*Listen!*' she whispered once more; and this time – or was it my imagination? – I did begin to hear something.

'Ee . . . ee . . . ee . . . !' came the sound, faint and weird upon the wind. 'Ee . . . ee . . . ee . . . !' – and for a moment it sounded so human, and so imploring, that I, too, caught my breath. It must be a trick of the wind, of course; it *must* – and as we sat there, tensed almost beyond bearing by the intentness of our listening, another sound impinged upon our preternaturally sharpened senses – a sound just as faint, and just as far away, but this time very far from ghostly.

'Pr-rr-rr! Ch-ch-ch . . . !' – the sound grew nearer . . . unmistakable . . . The prosaic sound of a car, bouncing and crunching up the rough track to the cottage.

Rosemary and I looked at each other.

'Norman?' she hazarded, scrambling worriedly to her feet. 'But it *can't* be Norman, he *never* comes! And at this time of night, too! Oh dear, I wonder what can have happened . . . ?' By this time she had reached the window, and she parted the curtains just as the mysterious vehicle screeched to a halt outside the gate. All I could see, from where I sat, was the triangle of darkness between the parted curtains, and Rosemary's broad back, rigid with disbelief and dismay.

Then, she turned on me.

'Lois!' she hissed. 'How *could* you . . . !'

I didn't ask her what she meant. Not after all these years.

'I didn't! Of course I didn't! What do you take me for?' I retorted, and I don't doubt that by now my face was almost as white as hers.

For, of course, she did not need to tell me who it was who had arrived. Not after nearly half a century of this sort of thing. Besides, who else was there who slammed a car door as if slapping down an invasion from Mars? Who else would announce her arrival by yelling 'Yoo-hoo!' into the midnight air, and bashing open the garden gate with a hat-box, so that latch and socket hurtled together into the night?

'Oops – sorry!' said Cissie, for perhaps the fifty-thousandth time in our joint lives; and she blundered forward towards the light, like an untidy grey moth. For by now we had got the front door open, and lamplight was pouring down the garden path, lighting up her round, radiant face and her halo of wild grey curls, all a-glitter with drops of rain.

'You naughty things! Fancy not *telling* me!' she reproached us, as she surged through the lighted doorway, dumping her luggage to left and right. It was, as always, like a one-man army of occupation. Always, she manages to fill any situation so totally with herself, and her belongings, and her eagerness, that there simply isn't *room* for anyone else's point of view. It's not selfishness, exactly; it's more like being a walking takeover bid, with no control over one's operations.

'A real, live ghost! Isn't it thrilling!' she babbled, as we edged her into the firelit room. 'Oh, but you *should* have told me! You *know* how I love this sort of thing . . . !'

On and on she chattered, in her loud, eager, unstoppable voice . . . and this, too, we recognized as part of her technique of infiltration. By the time her victims have managed to get a word in edgeways, their first fine fury has already begun to wilt . . . the cutting-edge of their protests has been blunted . . . their sense of outrage has become blurred. And anyway, by that time she is *there*. Inescapably, irreversibly, *there*!

Well, what can you do? By the time Rosemary and I got a chance to put a word in, Cissie already had her coat off, her luggage spilling on to the floor, and a glass of red wine in her hand. There she was, reclining in the big easy chair (mine), the firelight playing on her face, exactly as if she had lived in the place for years.

'But, Cissie, how did you find *out?*' was the nearest, somehow, that we could get to a reproof; and she laughed her big, merry laugh, and the bright wine sloshed perilously in her raised glass.

'Simple, you poor Watsons!' she declared. 'You see, I happened to be phoning Josie, and Josie happened to mention that Mary had said that Phyllis had told her that she'd heard from Ruth, and . . .'

See what I mean? You can't win. You might as well try to dodge the Recording Angel himself.

'And when I heard about the ghost, then of course I just *had* to come!' she went on. 'It sounded just *too* fascinating! You see, it just happens that at the moment I know a good deal about ghosts, because . . .'

Well, of course she did. It was her knowing a good deal about Classical Greek architecture last spring that had kept her arguing with the guide on the Parthenon for so long that the coach went off without us. And it was precisely because she'd boned-up so assiduously on rare Alpine plants that she'd broken her leg trying to reach one of them a couple of years ago, and we had to call out the Mountain Rescue for her. The rest of us had thought it was just a daisy.

'Yes, well, we don't even know yet that there *is* a ghost,' said Rosemary, dampingly; but not dampingly enough, evidently, for we spent the rest of the evening – and indeed far into the small hours – trying to dissuade Cissie from putting into practice, then and there, various uncomfortable and hazardous methods of ghost-hunting of which she had recently informed herself – methods which ranged from fixing a tape-recorder on the thatched roof, to ourselves lying all night in the churchyard, keeping our minds a blank.

By two o'clock, our minds were blank anyway – well, Rosemary's and mine were – and we could think about nothing but bed. Here, though, there were new obstacles to be overcome, for not only was Cissie's arrival unexpected and unprepared-for, but she insisted on being put in the Haunted Room. If it *was* haunted – anyway, the room that was coldest, dampest, and most uncomfortable, and therefore entitled her (well, what can you do?) to the only functioning oil-heater, and more than her share of the blankets.

'Of course, I shan't *sleep!*' she promised (as if this was some sort of special treat for me and Rosemary). 'I shall be keeping vigil all night long! And tomorrow night, darlings, as soon as the moon rises, we must each take a white willow-twig, and pace in silent procession through the garden . . .'

We nodded, simply because we were too sleepy to argue; but beyond the circle of lamplight, Rosemary and I exchanged glances of undiluted negativism. I mean, apart from anything else, you'd have to be crazy to embark on any project which depended for its success on Cissie's not falling over something.

But we did agree, without too much reluctance, to her further suggestion that tomorrow morning we should call on the Vicar and ask him if we might look through the Parish archives. Even Cissie, we guardedly surmised, could hardly wreck a call on a vicar.

But the next morning, guess what? Cissie was laid up with lumbago, stiff as a board, and unable even to get out of bed, let alone go visiting.

'Oh dear – Oh, please don't bother!' she kept saying, as we ran around with hot-water bottles and extra pillows. 'Oh dear, I do so hate to be a nuisance!'

We hated her to be a nuisance, too, but we just managed not to say so; and after a bit our efforts, combined with her own determination not to miss the fun (yes, she was still counting it fun) – after a bit, all this succeeded in loosening her up sufficiently to let her get out of bed and on to her feet; and at once her spirits rocketed sky-high. She decided, gleefully, that her affliction was a supernatural one, consequent on sleeping in the haunted room.

'Damp sheets, more likely!' said Rosemary, witheringly. 'If people *will* turn up unexpectedly like this . . .'

But Cissie is unsquashable. *Damp sheets?* When the alternative was the ghost of a lady who'd died two hundred years ago? Cissie has never been one to rest content with a likely explanation if there is an *un*likely one to hand.

'I know what I'm talking about!' she retorted. 'I know more about this sort of thing than either of you. I'm a Sensitive, you see. I only discovered it just recently, but it seems I'm one of those people with a sort of sixth sense when it comes to the supernatural. It makes me more *vulnerable*, of course, to this sort of thing – look at my bad back – but it also makes me more *aware*. I can *sense* things. Do you know, the moment I walked into this room last night, I could tell that it was haunted! I could feel the . . . Ouch!'

Her back had caught her again; all that gesticulating while she talked had been a mistake. However, between us we got her straightened up once more, and even managed to help her down the stairs – though I must say it wasn't long before we were both wishing we'd left well alone – if I may put it so uncharitably. For Cissie, up, was far, far more nuisance than Cissie in bed. In bed, her good intentions could harm no one; but once up and about, there seemed no limit to the trouble she could cause in the name of 'helping'. Trying to lift pans from shelves above her head; trying to rake out cinders without bending, and setting the hearth-brush on fire in the process; trying to fetch paraffin in cans too heavy for her to lift, and slopping it all over the floor. Rosemary and I seemed to be forever clearing up after her, or trying to un-crick her from some position she'd got stuck in for some maddening, altruistic reason.

Disturbingly, she seemed to get worse as the day went on, not better. The stiffness increased, and by afternoon she looked blue with cold, and was scarcely able to move. But nothing would induce her to let us call a doctor, or put her to bed.

'What, and miss all the fun?' she protested, through numbed lips. 'Don't you realize that this freezing cold is *significant*? It's the chilling of the air that you always get before the coming of an apparition . . . !'

By now, it was quite hard to make out what she was saying, so hoarse had her voice become, and so stiff her lips; but you could still hear the excitement and triumph in her croaked exhortations:

'Isn't it thrilling! This is the Chill of Death, you know, darlings! It's the warning that the dead person is now about to appear! Oh, I'm so thrilled! Any moment now, and we're going to know the truth . . . !'

We did, too. A loud knocking sounded on the cottage door, and Rosemary ran to answer it. From where I stood, in the living-room doorway, I could see her framed against the winter twilight – already the short December afternoon was nearly at an end. Beyond her, I glimpsed the uniforms of policemen, heard their solemn voices.

'"Miss Cecily Curtis?" – Cissie? Yes, of course we know her!' I heard Rosemary saying, in a frightened voice; and then came the two deeper voices, grave and sympathetic.

I could hardly hear their words from where I was standing, yet somehow the story wasn't difficult to follow. It was almost as if, in some queer way, I'd known all along. How last night, at about 10.30 p.m., a Miss Cecily Curtis had skidded while driving – too fast – along the dyke road, and had plunged, car and all, into deep water. The body had only been recovered and identified this morning.

As I say, I did not really need to hear the men's actual words. Already the picture was in my mind, the picture which has never left it: the picture of Cissie, all lit up with curiosity and excitement, belting through the rain and dark to be in on the fun. Nothing would keep her away, not even death itself . . .

A little sound in the room behind me roused me from my state of shock, and I turned to see Cissie smiling that annoying smile of hers, for the very last time. It's maddened us for years, the plucky way she smiles in the face of whatever adversity she's got us all into.

'You see?' she said, a trifle smugly, 'I've been dead ever since last night – it's no wonder I've been feeling so awful!' – and with a triumphant little toss of her head she turned, fell over her dressing-gown cord, and was gone.

Yes, gone. We never saw her again. The object they carried in, wet and dripping from the marsh, seemed to be nothing to do with her at all.

We never discovered whether the cottage had been haunted all along; but it's haunted now, all right. I don't suppose Rosemary will go down there much any more – certainly, we will never go ghost-hunting there again. Apart from anything else, we are too scared. There is so much that might go wrong. It was different in the old days, when we could play just any wild escapade we liked, confident that whatever went wrong would merely be the fault of our idiotic, infuriating, impossible, irreplaceable friend.

Margaret Irwin

THE BOOK

O N a foggy night in November, Mr Corbett, having guessed the murderer by the third chapter of his detective story, arose in disappointment from his bed and went downstairs in search of something more satisfactory to send him to sleep.

The fog had crept through the closed and curtained windows of the dining-room and hung thick on the air in a silence that seemed as heavy and breathless as the fog. The atmosphere was more choking than in his room, and very chill, although the remains of a large fire still burned in the grate.

The dining-room bookcase was the only considerable one in the house and held a careless unselected collection to suit all the tastes of the household, together with a few dull and obscure old theological books that had been left over from the sale of a learned uncle's library. Cheap red novels, bought on railway stalls by Mrs Corbett, who thought a journey the only time to read, were thrust in like pert, undersized intruders among the respectable nineteenth-century works of culture, chastely bound in dark blue or green, which Mr Corbett had considered the right thing to buy during his Oxford days; beside these there swaggered the children's large gaily bound story-books and collections of Fairy Tales in every colour.

From among this neat new cloth-bound crowd there towered here and there a musty sepulchre of learning, brown with the colour of dust rather than leather, with no trace of gilded letters, however faded, on its crumbling back to tell what lay inside. A few of these moribund survivors from the Dean's library were inhospitably fastened with rusty clasps; all remained closed, and appeared impenetrable, their blank, forbidding backs uplifted above their frivolous surroundings with the air of scorn that belongs to a private and concealed knowledge. For only the worm of corruption now bored his way through their evil-smelling pages.

It was an unusual flight of fancy for Mr Corbett to imagine that the vaporous and fog-ridden air that seemed to hang more thickly about the bookcase was like a dank and poisonous breath exhaled by one or other of these slowly rotting volumes. Discomfort in this pervasive and impalpable presence came on him more acutely than at any time that day; in an attempt to clear his throat of it he choked most unpleasantly.

He hurriedly chose a Dickens from the second shelf as appropriate to a London fog, and had returned to the foot of the stairs when he decided that his reading tonight should by contrast be of blue Italian skies and white statues, in beautiful rhythmic sentences. He went back for a Walter Pater.

He found *Marius the Epicurean* tipped sideways across the gap left by his withdrawal of *The Old Curiosity Shop*. It was a very wide gap to have been left by a single volume, for the books on that shelf had been closely wedged together. He put the Dickens back into it and saw that there was still space for a large book. He said to himself in careful and precise words: 'This is nonsense. No one can possibly have gone into the dining-room and removed a book while I was crossing the hall. There must have been a gap before in the second shelf.' But another part of his mind kept saying in a hurried, tumbled torrent: 'There was no gap in the second shelf. There was no gap in the second shelf.'

He snatched at both the *Marius* and *The Old Curiosity Shop*, and went to his room in a haste that was unnecessary and absurd, since even if he believed in ghosts, which he did not, no one had the smallest reason for suspecting any in the modern Kensington house wherein he and his family had lived for the last fifteen years. Reading was the best thing to calm the nerves, and Dickens a pleasant, wholesome and robust author.

Tonight, however, Dickens struck him in a different light. Beneath the author's sentimental pity for the weak and helpless, he could discern a revolting pleasure in cruelty and suffering, while the grotesque figures of the people in Cruikshank's illustrations revealed too clearly the hideous distortions of their souls. What had seemed humorous now appeared diabolic, and in disgust at these two favourites he turned to Walter Pater for the repose and dignity of a classic spirit.

But presently he wondered if this spirit were not in itself of a marble quality, frigid and lifeless, contrary to the purpose of nature. 'I have often thought', he said to himself, 'that there is something evil in the austere worship of beauty for its own sake.' He had never thought so before, but he liked to think that this impulse of fancy was the result of mature consideration, and with this satisfaction he composed himself for sleep.

He woke two or three times in the night, an unusual occurrence, but he was glad of it, for each time he had been dreaming horribly of these blameless Victorian works. Sprightly devils in whiskers and peg-top trousers tortured a lovely maiden and leered in delight at her anguish; the gods and heroes of classic fable acted deeds whose naked crime and shame Mr Corbett had never appreciated in Latin and Greek Unseens. When he had woken in a cold sweat from the spectacle of the ravished Philomel's torn and bleeding tongue, he decided there was nothing for it but to go down and get another book that would turn his thoughts in some more pleasant direction. But his increasing reluctance to do this found a hundred excuses. The recollection of the gap in the shelf now occurred to him with a sense of unnatural importance; in the troubled dozes that followed, this gap between two books seemed the most hideous deformity, like a gap between the front teeth of some grinning monster.

But in the clear daylight of the morning Mr Corbett came down to the pleasant dining-room, its sunny windows and smell of coffee and toast, and ate an undiminished breakfast with a mind chiefly occupied in self-congratulation that the wind had blown the fog away in time for his Saturday game of golf. Whistling happily, he was pouring out his final cup of coffee when his hand remained arrested in the act as his glance, roving across the bookcase, noticed that there was now no gap at all in the second shelf. He asked who had been at the bookcase already, but neither of the girls had, nor Dicky, and Mrs Corbett was not yet down. The maid never touched the books. They wanted to know what book he missed in it, which made him look foolish, as he could not say. The things that disturb us at midnight are negligible at 9 a.m.

'I thought there was a gap in the second shelf,' he said, 'but it doesn't matter.'

'There never is a gap in the second shelf,' said little Jean brightly. 'You can take out lots of books from it and when you go back the gap's always filled up. Haven't you noticed that? I have.'

Nora, the middle one in age, said Jean was always being silly; she had been found crying over the funny pictures in *The Rose and the Ring* because she said all the people in them had such wicked faces, and the picture of a black cat had upset her because she thought it was a witch. Mr Corbett did not like to think of such fancies for his Jeannie. She retaliated briskly by saying Dicky was just as bad, and he was a big boy. He had kicked a book across the room and said, 'Filthy stuff,' just like that. Jean was a good mimic; her tone expressed a venom of disgust, and she made the gesture of dropping a book as though the very touch of it were loathsome. Dicky, who had been making violent signs at her, now told her she was a beastly little sneak and he would never again take her for rides on the step of his bicycle. Mr Corbett was disturbed. Unpleasant housemaids and bad schoolfriends passed through his head, as he gravely asked his son how he had got hold of this book.

'Took it out of that bookcase of course,' said Dicky furiously.

It turned out to be the *Boy's Gulliver's Travels* that Granny had given him, and Dicky had at last to explain his rage with the devil who wrote it to show

· 41 ·

that men were worse than beasts and the human race a washout. A boy who never had good school reports had no right to be so morbidly sensitive as to penetrate to the underlying cynicism of Swift's delightful fable, and that moreover in the bright and carefully expurgated edition they bring out nowadays. Mr Corbett could not say he had ever noticed the cynicism himself, though he knew from the critical books it must be there, and with some annoyance he advised his son to take out a nice bright modern boy's adventure story that could not depress anybody. It appeared, however, that Dicky was 'off reading just now', and the girls echoed this.

Mr Corbett soon found that he too was 'off reading'. Every new book seemed to him weak, tasteless and insipid; while his old and familiar books were depressing or even, in some obscure way, disgusting. Authors must all be filthy-minded; they probably wrote what they dared not express in their lives. Stevenson had said that literature was a morbid secretion; he read Stevenson again to discover his peculiar morbidity, and detected in his essays a self-pity masquerading as courage, and in *Treasure Island* an invalid's sickly attraction to brutality.

This gave him a zest to find out what he disliked so much, and his taste for reading revived as he explored with relish the hidden infirmities of minds that had been valued by fools as great and noble. He saw Jane Austen and Charlotte Brontë as two unpleasant examples of spinsterhood; the one as a prying, sub-acid busybody in everyone else's flirtations, the other as a raving, craving maenad seeking self-immolation on the altar of her frustrated passions. He compared Wordsworth's love of nature to the monstrous egoism of an ancient bellwether, isolated from the flock.

These powers of penetration astonished him. With a mind so acute and original he should have achieved greatness, yet he was a mere solicitor and not prosperous at that. If he had but the money, he might do something with those ivory shares, but it would be a pure gamble, and he had no luck. His natural envy of his wealthier acquaintances now mingled with a contempt for their stupidity that approached loathing. The digestion of his lunch in the City was ruined by meeting sentimental yet successful dotards whom he had once regarded as pleasant fellows. The very sight of them spoiled his game of golf, so that he came to prefer reading alone in the dining-room even on sunny afternoons.

He discovered also and with a slight shock that Mrs Corbett had always bored him. Dicky he began actively to dislike as an impudent blockhead, and the two girls were as insipidly alike as white mice; it was a relief when he abolished their tiresome habit of coming in to say good night.

In the now unbroken silence and seclusion of the dining-room, he read with feverish haste as though he were seeking for some clue to knowledge, some secret key to existence which would quicken and inflame it, transform it from its present dull torpor to a life worthy of him and his powers.

He even explored the few decaying remains of his uncle's theological library. Bored and baffled, he yet persisted, and had the occasional relief of an ugly woodcut of Adam and Eve with figures like bolsters and hair like dahlias, or a map of the Cosmos with Hell-mouth in the corner, belching forth demons. One of these books had diagrams and symbols in the margin which he took to be mathematical formulae of a kind he did not know. He presently discovered that they were drawn, not printed, and that the book was in manuscript, in a very neat, crabbed black writing that resembled black-letter printing. It was moreover in Latin, a fact that gave Mr Corbett a shock of unreasoning disappointment. For while examining the signs in the margin, he had been filled with an extraordinary exultation as though he knew himself to be on the edge of a discovery that should alter his whole life. But he had forgotten his Latin.

With a secret and guilty air which would have looked absurd to anyone who knew his harmless purpose, he stole to the schoolroom for Dicky's Latin dictionary and grammar and hurried back to the dining-room, where he tried to discover what the book was about with an anxious industry that surprised himself. There was no name to it, nor of the author. Several blank pages had been left at the end, and the writing ended at the bottom of a page, with no flourish or superscription, as though the book had been left unfinished. From what sentences he could translate, it seemed to be a work on theology rather than mathematics. There were constant references to the Master, to his wishes and injunctions, which appeared to be of a complicated kind. Mr Corbett began by skipping these as mere accounts of ceremonial, but a word caught his eye as one unlikely to occur in such an account. He read this passage attentively, looking up each word in the dictionary, and could hardly believe the result of his translation. 'Clearly,' he decided, 'this book must be by some early missionary, and the passage I have just read the account of some horrible rite practised by a savage tribe of devil-worshippers.' Though he called it 'horrible', he reflected on it, committing each detail to memory. He then amused himself by copying the signs in the margin near it and trying to discover their significance. But a sensation of sickly cold came over him, his head swam, and he could hardly see the figures before his eyes. He suspected a sudden attack of influenza, and went to ask his wife for medicine.

They were all in the drawing-room, Mrs Corbett helping Nora and Jean with a new game, Dicky playing the pianola, and Mike, the Irish terrier, who had lately deserted his accustomed place on the dining-room hearth-rug, stretched by the fire. Mr Corbett had an instant's impression of this peaceful and cheerful scene, before his family turned towards him and asked in scared tones what was the matter. He thought how like sheep they looked and sounded; nothing in his appearance in the mirror struck him as odd; it was their gaping faces that were unfamiliar. He then noticed the extraordinary behaviour of Mike, who had sprung from the hearth-rug and was crouched in the furthest corner, uttering no sound, but with his eyes distended and foam round his bared teeth. Under Mr Corbett's glance, he slunk towards the door, whimpering in a faint and abject manner, and then as his master called him, he snarled horribly, and the hair bristled on the scruff of his neck. Dicky let him out, and they heard him scuffling at a frantic rate down the stairs to the kitchen, and then, again and again, a long-drawn howl.

'What *can* be the matter with Mike?' asked Mrs Corbett.

Her question broke a silence that seemed to have lasted a long time. Jean began to cry. Mr Corbett said irritably that he did not know what was the matter with any of them.

Then Nora asked, 'What is that red mark on your face?'

He looked again in the glass and could see nothing.

'It's quite clear from here,' said Dicky; 'I can see the lines in the fingerprint.'

'Yes, that's what it is,' said Mrs Corbett in her brisk staccato voice; 'the print of a finger on your forehead. Have you been writing in red ink?'

Mr Corbett precipitately left the room for his own, where he sent down a message that he was suffering from headache and would have his dinner in bed. He wanted no one fussing round him. By next morning he was amazed at his fancies of influenza, for he had never felt so well in his life.

No one commented on his looks at breakfast, so he concluded that the mark had disappeared. The old Latin book he had been translating on the previous night had been moved from the writing-bureau, although Dicky's grammar and dictionary were still there. The second shelf was, as always in the daytime, closely packed; the book had, he remembered, been in the second shelf. But this time he did not ask who had put it back.

That day he had an unexpected stroke of luck in a new client of the name of Crab, who entrusted him with large sums of money: nor was he irritated by the sight of his more prosperous acquaintances, but with difficulty refrained from grinning in their faces, so confident was he that his remarkable ability must soon place him higher than any of them. At dinner he chaffed his family with what he felt to be the gaiety of a schoolboy. But on them it had a contrary effect, for they stared, either at him in stupid astonishment, or at their plates, depressed and nervous. Did they think him drunk? he wondered, and a fury came on him at their low and bestial suspicions and heavy dullness of mind. Why, he was younger than any of them!

But in spite of this new alertness he could not attend to the letters he should have written that evening and drifted to the bookcase for a little light distraction, but found that for the first time there was nothing he wished to read. He pulled out a book from above his head at random, and saw that it was the old Latin book in manuscript. As he turned over its stiff and yellow pages, he noticed with pleasure the smell of corruption that had first repelled him in these decaying volumes, a smell, he now thought, of ancient and secret knowledge.

This idea of secrecy seemed to affect him personally, for on hearing a step in the hall he hastily closed the book and put it back in its place. He went to the schoolroom where Dicky was doing his homework, and told him he required his Latin grammar and dictionary again for an old law report. To his annoyance he stammered and put his words awkwardly; he thought that the boy looked oddly at him and he cursed him in his heart for a suspicious young devil, though of what he should be suspicious he could not say. Nevertheless, when back in the dining-room, he listened at the door and then softly turned the lock before he opened the books on the writing-bureau.

The script and Latin seemed much clearer than on the previous evening, and he was able to read at random a passage relating to a trial of a German midwife in 1620 for the murder and dissection of 783 children. Even allowing for the opportunities afforded by her profession, the number appeared excessive, nor could he discover any motive for the slaughter. He decided to translate the book from the beginning.

It appeared to be an account of some secret society whose activities and ritual were of a nature so obscure, and when not, so vile and terrible, that Mr Corbett would not at first believe that this could be a record of any human mind, although his deep interest in it should have convinced him that from his humanity at least it was not altogether alien.

He read until far later than his usual hour for bed and when at last he rose, it was with the book in his hands. To defer his parting with it, he stood turning over the pages until he reached the end of the writing, and was struck by a new peculiarity.

The ink was much fresher and of a far poorer quality than the thick rusted ink in the bulk of the book; on close inspection he would have said that it was of modern manufacture and written quite recently were it not for the fact that it was in the same crabbed late-seventeenth-century handwriting.

This, however, did not explain the perplexity, even dismay and fear, he now felt as he stared at the last sentence. It ran: 'Contine te in perennibus studiis', and he had at once recognized it as a Ciceronian tag that had been dinned into him at school. He could not understand how he had failed to notice it yesterday.

Then he remembered that the book had ended at the bottom of a page. But now, the last two sentences were written at the very top of a page. However long he looked at them, he could come to no other conclusion than that they had been added since the previous evening.

He now read the sentence before the last: 'Re imperfecta mortuus sum,' and translated the whole as: 'I died with my purpose unachieved. Continue, thou, the never-ending studies.'

With his eyes still fixed upon it, Mr Corbett replaced the book on the writing-bureau and stepped back from it to the door, his hand outstretched behind him, groping and then tugging at the door handle. As the door failed to open, his breath came in a faint, hardly articulate scream. Then he remembered that he had himself locked it, and he fumbled with the key in frantic ineffectual movements until at last he opened it and banged it after him as he plunged backwards into the hall.

For a moment he stood there looking at the door handle; then with a stealthy, sneaking movement, his hand crept out towards it, touched it, began to turn it, when suddenly he pulled his hand away and went up to his bedroom, three steps at a time.

There he behaved in a manner only comparable with the way he had lost his head after losing his innocence when a schoolboy of sixteen. He hid his face in the pillow, he cried, he raved in meaningless words, repeating: 'Never, never, never. I will never do it again. Help me never to do it again.' With the words, 'Help me', he noticed what he was saying, they reminded him of other words, and he began to pray aloud. But the words sounded jumbled, they persisted in coming into his head in a reverse order so that he found he was saying his prayers backwards, and at this final absurdity he suddenly began to laugh very loud. He sat up on the bed, delighted at this return to sanity, common sense and humour, when the door leading into Mrs Corbett's room opened, and he saw his wife staring at him with a strange, grey, drawn face that made her seem like the terror-stricken ghost of her usually smug and placid self.

'It's not burglars,' he said irritably. 'I've come to bed late, that is all, and must have waked you.'

'Henry,' said Mrs Corbett, and he noticed that she had not heard him, 'Henry, didn't you hear it?'

'What?'

'That laugh.'

He was silent, an instinctive caution warning him to wait until she spoke again. And this she did, imploring him with her eyes to reassure her.

'It was not a human laugh. It was like the laugh of a devil.'

He checked his violent inclination to laugh again. It was wiser not to let her know that it was only his laughter she had heard. He told her to stop being fanciful, and Mrs Corbett, gradually recovering her docility, returned to obey an impossible command, since she could not stop being what she had never been.

The next morning, Mr Corbett rose before any of the servants and crept down to the dining-room. As before, the dictionary and grammar alone remained on the writing-bureau; the book was back in the second shelf. He opened it at the end. Two more lines had been added, carrying the writing down to the middle of the page. They ran:

> Ex auro canceris
> In dentem elephantis.

which he translated as:

> Out of the money of the crab
> Into the tooth of the elephant.

From this time on, his acquaintances in the City noticed a change in the mediocre, rather flabby and unenterprising 'old Corbett'. His recent sour depression dropped from him: he seemed to have grown twenty years younger, strong, brisk and cheerful, and with a self-confidence in business that struck them as lunacy. They waited with a not unpleasant excitement for the inevitable crash, but his every speculation, however wild and hare-brained, turned out successful. He no longer avoided them, but went out of his way to display his consciousness of luck, daring and vigour, and to chaff them in a manner that began to make him actively disliked. This he welcomed with delight as a sign of others' envy and his superiority.

He never stayed in town for dinners or theatres, for he was always now in a hurry to get home, where, as soon as he was sure of being undisturbed, he would take down the manuscript book from the second shelf of the dining-room and turn to the last pages.

Every morning he found that a few words had been added since the evening before, and always they formed, as he considered, injunctions to himself. These were at first only with regard to his money transactions, giving assurance to his boldest fancies, and since the brilliant and unforeseen success that had attended his gamble with Mr Crab's money in African ivory, he followed all such advice unhesitatingly.

But presently, interspersed with these commands, were others of a meaningless, childish, yet revolting character such as might be invented by a decadent imbecile, or, it must be admitted, by the idle fancies of any ordinary man who permits his imagination to wander unbridled. Mr Corbett was startled to recognize one or two such fancies of his own, which had occurred to him during his frequent boredom in church, and which he had not thought any other mind could conceive.

He at first paid no attention to these directions, but found that his new speculations declined so rapidly that he became terrified not merely for his fortune but for his reputation and even safety, since the money of various of his clients was involved. It was made clear to him that he must follow the commands in the book altogether or not at all, and he began to carry out their puerile and grotesque blasphemies with a contemptuous amusement, which, however, gradually changed to a sense of their monstrous significance. They became more capricious and difficult of execution, but he now never hesitated to obey blindly, urged by a fear that he could not understand, but knew only that it was not of mere financial failure.

By now he understood the effect of this book on the others near it, and the reason that had impelled its mysterious agent to move the books into the second shelf so that all in turn should come under the influence of that ancient and secret knowledge.

In respect to it, he encouraged his children, with jeers at their stupidity, to read more, but he could not observe that they ever now took a book from the dining-room bookcase. He himself no longer needed to read, but went to bed early and slept sound. The things that all his life he had longed to do when he should have enough money now seemed to him insipid. His most exciting pleasure was the smell and touch of these mouldering pages as he turned them to find the last message inscribed to him.

One evening it was in two words only: 'Canem occide.'

He laughed at this simple and pleasant request to kill the dog, for he bore Mike a grudge for his change from devotion to slinking aversion. Moreover, it could not have come more opportunely, since in turning out an old desk he had just discovered some packets of rat poison bought years ago and forgotten. No one therefore knew of its existence and it would be easy to poison Mike without any further suspicion than that of a neighbour's carelessness. He whistled light-heartedly as he ran upstairs to rummage for the packets, and returned to empty one in the dog's dish of water in the hall.

That night the household was awakened by terrified screams proceeding from the stairs. Mr Corbett was the first to hasten there, prompted by the instinctive caution that was always with him these days. He saw Jean, in her nightdress, scrambling up on to the landing on her hands and knees, clutching at anything that afforded support and screaming in a choking, tearless, unnatural manner. He carried her to the room she shared with Nora, where they were quickly followed by Mrs Corbett.

Nothing coherent could be got from Jean. Nora said that she must have been having her old dream again; when her father demanded what this was, she said that Jean sometimes woke in the night, crying, because she had dreamed of a hand passing backwards and forwards over the dining-room bookcase, until it found a certain book and took it out of the shelf. At this point she was always so frightened that she woke up.

On hearing this, Jean broke into fresh screams, and Mrs Corbett would have no more explanations. Mr Corbett went out on to the stairs to find what had brought the child there from her bed. On looking down into the lighted hall, he saw Mike's dish overturned. He went down to examine it and saw that the water he had poisoned must have been upset and absorbed by the rough doormat, which was quite wet.

He went back to the little girls' room, told his wife that she was tired and must go to bed, and he would take his turn at comforting Jean. She was now much quieter. He took her on his knee where at first she shrank from him. Mr Corbett remembered with an angry sense of injury that she never now sat on his knee, and would have liked to pay her out for it by mocking and frightening her. But he had to coax her into telling him what he wanted, and with this object he soothed her, calling her by pet names that he thought he had forgotten, telling her that nothing could hurt her now he was with her.

At first his cleverness amused him; he chuckled softly when Jean buried her head in his dressing-gown. But presently an uncomfortable sensation came over him, he gripped at Jean as though for her protection, while he was so smoothly assuring her of his. With difficulty, he listened to what he had at last induced her to tell him.

She and Nora had kept Mike with them all the evening and taken him to sleep in their room for a treat. He had lain at the foot of Jean's bed and they had all gone to sleep. Then Jean began her old dream of the hand moving over the books in the dining-room bookcase; but instead of taking out a book, it came across the dining-room and out on to the stairs. It came up over the banisters and to the door of their room, and turned their door handle very softly and opened it. At this point she jumped up wide awake and turned on the light, calling to Nora. The door, which had been shut when they went to sleep, was wide open, and Mike was gone.

She told Nora that she was sure something dreadful would happen to him if she did not go and bring him back, and ran down into the hall where she saw him just about to drink from his dish. She called to him and he looked up, but did not come, so she ran to him, and began to pull him along with her, when her nightdress was clutched from behind and then she felt a hand seize her arm.

She fell down, and then clambered upstairs as fast as she could, screaming all the way.

It was now clear to Mr Corbett that Mike's dish must have been upset in the scuffle. She was again crying, but this time he felt himself unable to comfort her. He retired to his room, where he walked up and down in an agitation he could not understand, for he found his thoughts perpetually arguing on a point that had never troubled him before.

'I am not a bad man,' he kept saying to himself. 'I have never done anything actually wrong. My clients are none the worse for my speculations, only the better. Nor have I spent my new wealth on gross and sensual pleasures; these now have even no attraction for me.'

Presently he added: 'It is not wrong to try and kill a dog, an ill-tempered brute. It turned against me. It might have bitten Jeannie.'

He noticed that he had thought of her as Jeannie, which he had not done for some time; it must have been because he had called her that tonight. He must forbid her ever to leave her room at night, he could not have her meddling. It would be safer for him if she were not there at all.

Again that sick and cold sensation of fear swept over him: he seized the bedpost as though he were falling, and held on to it for some minutes. 'I was thinking of a boarding-school,' he told himself, and then, 'I must go down and find out – find out—' He would not think what it was he must find out.

He opened his door and listened. The house was quiet. He crept on to the landing and along to Nora's and Jean's door where again he stood, listening. There was no sound, and at that he was again overcome with unreasonable terror. He imagined Jean lying very still in her bed, too still. He hastened away from the door, shuffling in his bedroom slippers along the passage and down the stairs.

A bright fire still burned in the dining-room grate. A glance at the clock told him it was not yet twelve. He stared at the bookcase. In the second shelf was a gap which had not been there when he had left. On the writing-bureau lay a large open book. He knew that he must cross the room and see what was written in it. Then, as before, words that he did not intend came sobbing and crying to his lips, muttering, 'No, no, not that. Never, never, never.' But he crossed the room and looked down at the book. As last time, the message was in only two words: 'Infantem occide.'

He slipped and fell forward against the bureau. His hands clutched at the book, lifted it as he recovered himself and with his finger he traced out the words that had been written. The smell of corruption crept into his nostrils. He told himself that he was not a snivelling dotard, but a man stronger and wiser than his fellows, superior to the common emotions of humanity, who held in his hands the sources of ancient and secret power.

He had known what the message would be. It was after all the only safe and logical thing to do. Jean had acquired dangerous knowledge. She was a spy, an antagonist. That she was so unconsciously, that she was eight years old, his youngest and favourite child, were sentimental appeals that could make no difference to a man of sane reasoning power such as his own. Jean had sided with Mike against him. 'All that are not with me are against me,' he repeated softly. He would kill both dog and child with the white powder that no one knew to be in his possession. It would be quite safe.

He laid down the book and went to the door. What he had to do, he would do quickly, for again that sensation of deadly cold was sweeping over him. He wished he had not to do it tonight; last night it would have been easier, but tonight she had sat on his knee and made him afraid. He imagined her lying very still in her bed, too still. But it would be she who would lie there, not he, so why should he be afraid? He was protected by ancient and secret powers. He held on to the door handle, but his fingers seemed to have grown numb, for he could not turn it. He clung to it, crouched and shivering, bending over it until he knelt on the ground, his head beneath the handle which he still clutched with upraised hands. Suddenly the hands were loosened and flung outwards with the frantic gesture of a man falling from a great height, and he stumbled to his feet. He seized the book and threw it on the fire. A violent sensation of choking overcame him, he felt he was being strangled, as in a nightmare he tried again and again to shriek aloud, but his breath would make no sound. His breath would not come at all. He fell backwards heavily, down on the floor, where he lay very still.

In the morning, the maid who came to open the dining-room windows found her master dead. The sensation caused by this was scarcely so great in the City as that given by the simultaneous collapse of all Mr Corbett's recent speculations. It was instantly assumed that he must have had previous knowledge of this and so committed suicide.

The stumbling-block to this theory was that the medical report defined the cause of Mr Corbett's death as strangulation of the windpipe by the pressure of a hand which had left the marks of its fingers on his throat.

Rebecca West

THE GREY MEN

(An Experience)

I MUST begin the account of my experience by setting down my misfortunes, not in order that I may enjoy the delights of querulousness, but because I would not have had this experience if I had not been in a peculiar physical state. At the end of August I went down for a holiday to a remote village in Cornwall, and after a few days was taken ill with blood-poisoning, and transported to a nursing-home in one of the largest mining towns. I was in a state to respond extravagantly to the infection, because I had been in bad health for some years, and for the last eighteen months I had been more or less continuously ill; and when I caught the germ I could not get well. My temperature sank to normal, but the rate of my pulse and respiration were greatly excessive, amounting sometimes to twice what it ought to have been. I suffered from persistent insomnia; very often I would not fall asleep till after the mine hooters had gone, and an hour and a half later I would be awakened for breakfast by the implacable routine of the nursing-home. So I fell into a curious state. I lost my power of suppressing irrelevant impressions and co-ordinating those that remained. I felt obliged to watch the trees outside my window and their behaviour in the sunshine and wind, to note the characteristics of every person who spoke to me, with a quite disagreeable intensity, and I was so fatigued by this constant effort of apprehension that there was no continuity in the working of my brain. Every moment of consciousness was distinct and unrelated to any other. Instead of being a stream my mental life was a string of disparate beads.

There came a Monday when I was told I could go back to London two days later; and in the afternoon I was sent out to take a little walk round the town. The walk I chose was one straight up the face of a high heathery hill, with an obelisk and a tower on the humps of its saddleback, which stands a mile or so outside the town. I knew it was unwise, but I had heard there was a fine view of the North Coast from the obelisk, and I was sick of being prevented from doing things by my health. But when I got to the top I realized that the ascent had, as they say, put the lid on it. I could not see the view. I could see it in bits, but not as a whole. It was like trying to take a photograph of a view with a non-panoramic camera. And what I saw seemed

like meaningless painting on glass. The patchwork of colours carried no
suggestion of textures and contours. I had to work hard to interpret it; to see,
for example, that that spattered rhomboidal patch was a cornfield, starred
with arrish mows, that rolled its fourth corner over the bend of the hill. But I
did not look at it for long, because two miners and their dogs came up on to
the plateau round the obelisk, and my exaggerated disordered perceptions
took too much notice of them. This hill was certainly large enough to
support these four inoffensive creatures as well as myself, but I felt as
irritated and uncomfortable as if I were being jostled by a dense crowd. I
went down the hill and walked home, realizing at every step that my
mechanism was hopelessly out of gear, and that I was in a thoroughly
abnormal condition.

This feeling of strangeness remained throughout the evening till I fell
asleep about midnight; and about three hours later I began to dream. I
thought that I awoke with a sense of imminent danger and that I got out of
bed and ran to the window. The nursing-home consisted of two three-
storeyed semi-detached villas knocked into one; the two porches had been
left as they were in the middle of the frontage, and the two broad gravel
walks that had run from the gate of each villa-garden to its porch had been
joined and now formed a semicircular drive. I was sleeping in the
ground-floor room to the right of the porches, and, as it was built on a
half-basement that rose out of its well to an exceptional height, I had a good
view over the garden from my large bay-window. To my surprise, for
vehicles were supposed to stop in the road outside the gate lest they should
disturb the patients, a large grey limousine was drawn up in front of the
porch. As I looked at it I began to shake with fear, for sitting in the front seat
were two men of terrifying appearance. They were dressed in a uniform
which was rather like that of the AA scouts, but cut very tightly of
midnight-blue cloth, and their heads were covered with aviators' helmets.
They sat there with an inhuman immobility. They were the most sinister
people I had ever seen. They were not diabolical, but they were inexorable.
And I realized they had come here with the intention of abducting somebody
from the home, and I began to run to the door so that I could rouse the
household.

But as I crossed the floor I saw, not with the physical eye, for there was a
wall and a door of frosted glass and wood in between, but with what the
saints and mystics have called 'the eye of the mind', that there was another
man like these, standing on the balcony that opened off my room on the side
that was at right angles to the frontage. I stood a moment wondering how he
had got there, for no steps led to it from the garden, and it stood on smooth
iron pillars rather above the height of a man, and I then went to the door. But

I could not open it because there was a similar watchman guarding the other side of the door. I was conscious, somehow, of a thin cold stream of breath coming from between his lips. At that I realized that I could do nothing. I could not help the poor creature who was even now being laid hands on by the confederates of these people.

There was something very sinister about the way these sentinels were standing with their backs to the entrances they guarded. It suggested that they did not need to keep their fists ready to prevent my escape, but could rely on some invisible emanation from their bodies.

Then, high up on the staircase of the other villa there sounded muffled, thudding noises, which became recognizable while they descended from third flight to second flight, from second flight to first, as the footsteps of men carrying an unwieldy burthen.

I became aware that they were carrying a man or woman wrapped in some kind of envelope from which he or she was partly protruding. I visualized it that two of these men were carrying downstairs a person who had been put into one of these large unbleached calico bags in which one keeps one's fur coat, and who had succeeded in getting their head above the drawstring at the top. I knew that this wasn't exactly what the men were carrying, that it was merely a metaphorical image for something I did not like my mind to perceive directly. Here for the first time I detected myself trying to interfere with the dream, to forge it, as it were. I went on to try to recognize the person in the bag as a friend of mine whom I knew to be in very dangerous circumstances, obviously with the intention of explaining away the dream by interpreting it symbolically. But I could not keep it up. And I gave up the attempt when they passed through the hall and the captured person cried out to them: 'Say something to me!' and then sobbed softly, 'Oh, if they would only tell me who they are and where they are taking me.'

They did not reply. In silence they carried the person down the steep stone steps of the porch and lifted him or her into the car, which immediately started. I followed it for a little way along the road, watching the poor thing as it turned to its immobile captors and, flapping its pinioned arms, pleaded to know what was going to happen to it.

I half awoke, and in that borderland state tossed about and tried to pretend that it was not really a terrifying dream.

'What a situation for the movies,' I muttered, and tried to work out a plot to lead up to it. Then I really woke up and realized the dream had been one of the most horrible things that had ever happened to me, and I then passed immediately into a vivid recollection of an incident of my childhood.

I was eight or nine. I was having tea, in a room with folding doors, with two women. Behind the folding doors an old lady lay dead. We heard the padding of a cat about the room, the sound of its spring on to the creaking bedstead.

'Naughty kitty's jumped on to the bed. Go in and fetch kitty, dear.'

I had never liked the old lady's obese body, and when I was told to go into the room where she lay dead it appeared to me possible that death might have given her new resources of ugliness. She was probably looking dreadful. I cried so much that they did not make me go, but my imagination had been set working . . .

I shuddered out of this memory, but found myself obsessed by thoughts of death as a harsh abduction to a place of decay. I remembered a thousand threats I had noticed that the other side of death might be torment and petrifaction. I felt that I was going to die soon, and I was possessed by fear and by resentments against the people who had wasted my life by their demands. Then I burst into the exhausted weeping that follows prolonged pain, and lay crying till it was broad daylight.

I woke with the worst headache I have ever had in my life. All the morning I was heavy with it, and in the afternoon it had grown so intolerable that they gave me a large dose of aspirin. In the evening I became very restless, and could not bring myself to undress and go to bed. At half-past ten I was sitting wondering when the night nurse would come and rebuke me for my late hours, when I heard the sound of one of the gates being opened and wheels coming along the drive.

'That is the car I dreamed of last night,' I said to myself.

The horror did not revisit me; I even felt what psychologists call the pleasure of recognition. I was on the point of going to the window when my natural scepticism reasserted itself and I sat down again.

'Nonsense, that was a dream. Besides . . . it was a car I saw. This is something drawn by a horse.'

I heard people coming up the stone steps and going through the hall. I tried to pretend that really all this was not of the slightest importance, and began to undress; but presently I was compelled to go to the window and look out. There was nothing but a little low cart drawn by a sturdy pony. I said to myself that the most probable explanation of its presence there was a late delivery of the washing. But all the time I knew with absolute certainty that I was watching the incident of which my dream had been the fantastic rehearsal, and I was not surprised when I heard those muffled footsteps coming down the staircase of the other villa and passing through the hall as I heard them the night before. I was not surprised when two men carried out a coffin and laid it in the cart.

I have the intensest desire to believe that the soul is mortal and perishes with the body. But it is really very difficult for me not to suspect that I became aware of the death of this woman who had died the previous evening in a room on the third storey, by supernatural means. I had not come in contact with anyone who had been present at her death or was aware of it, as I had seen none of the day nurses after tea-time. She had not been expected to die; therefore I could not have derived my sense of the corpse in the house from anything in the conversation or manner of the people about me. And as I believed that only nurses slept on the third storey, I had not the slightest reason for my accurate location of the deathbed. I am forced to go a little further than this. I cannot deny that all my emotions are convinced that I overheard the tribulation of a soul that was terrified at finding itself stripped of the flesh in a world not this earth.

I wish greatly that I had not had this experience. I am amazed at the temerity of those people, spiritualists and the like, who try to force these unnatural contacts with life after it has been subjected to the extreme change of death. For the human mind, exquisitely adapted as it is to the task of carrying its possessor through the material world, is, I think, unable to handle life in that altered state. My mechanism, having gone out of gear, intercepted the emotions of a person who had passed into that different world, emotions that, no doubt, if I could have understood them, were not more significant, not more incompatible with the scheme of a kindly universe than the weeping of a newborn child. But my earthly mind could not deal with it. The special weakness that had made me liable to this revelation made me link it up with childish fears and clothe it in symbolism inspired by an infantile conception of death that I knew to be untrue. I am quite sure that it is untrue; for though there is, as I have learned, much that is disagreeable in this universe, and an almost profligate abundance of pain, I have never found any scrap of evidence in support of the existence of bogeys. But the reality that was contained in my experience gives a sanction to the rubbish with which my imagination surrounded it, and has therefore made that infantile conception take fresh root in my mind. I am degraded; I am more subject to terror than I was. To me, for some little time to come till I find my footing again, it will seem as if death has its sting and the grave its victory. I can imagine no more rash challenge to fear than the voluntary seeking of such an experience.

Daphne du Maurier

THE POOL

I

THE children ran out on to the lawn. There was space all around them, and light, and air, with the trees indeterminate beyond. The gardener had cut the grass. The lawn was crisp and firm now, because of the hot sun through the day; but near the summer-house where the tall grass stood there were dew-drops like frost clinging to the narrow stems.

The children said nothing. The first moment always took them by surprise. The fact that it waited, thought Deborah, all the time they were away; that day after day while they were at school, or in the Easter holidays with the aunts at Hunstanton being blown to bits, or in the Christmas holidays with their father in London riding on buses and going to theatres – the fact that the garden waited for them was a miracle known only to herself. A year was so long. How did the garden endure the snows clamping down upon it, or the chilly rain that fell in November? Surely sometimes it must mock the slow steps of Grandpapa pacing up and down the terrace in front of the windows, or Grandmama calling to Patch? The garden had to endure month after month of silence, while the children were gone. Even the spring and the days of May and June were wasted, all those mornings of butterflies and darting birds, with no one to watch but Patch gasping for breath on a cool stone slab. So wasted was the garden, so lost.

'You must never think we forget,' said Deborah in the silent voice she used to her own possessions. 'I remember, even at school, in the middle of French' – but the ache then was unbearable, that it should be the hard grain of a desk under her hands, and not the grass she bent to touch now. The children had had an argument once about whether there was more grass in the world or more sand, and Roger said that of course there must be more sand, because of under the sea; in every ocean all over the world there would be sand, if you looked deep down. But there could be grass too, argued Deborah, a waving grass, a grass that nobody had ever seen, and the colour of that ocean grass would be darker than any grass on the surface of the world, in fields or prairies or people's gardens in America. It would be taller than trees and it would move like corn in a wind.

They had run in to ask somebody adult, 'What is there most of in the world, grass or sand?', both children hot and passionate from the argument. But Grandpapa stood there in his old panama hat looking for clippers to trim the hedge – he was rummaging in the drawer full of screws – and he said, 'What? What?' impatiently.

The boy turned red – perhaps it was a stupid question – but the girl thought, he doesn't know, they never know, and she made a face at her brother to show that she was on his side. Later they asked their grandmother, and she, being practical said briskly, 'I should think sand. Think of all the grains,' and Roger turned in triumph. 'I told you so!' The grains. Deborah had not considered the grains. The magic of millions and millions of grains clinging together in the world and under the oceans made her sick. Let Roger win, it did not matter. It was better to be in the minority of the waving grass.

Now, on this first evening of summer holiday, she knelt and then lay full-length on the lawn, and stretched her hands out on either side like Jesus on the Cross, only face downwards, and murmured over and over again the words she had memorized from Confirmation preparation. 'A full, perfect and sufficient sacrifice . . . a full, perfect and sufficient sacrifice . . . satisfaction, and oblation, for the sins of the whole world.' To offer herself to the earth, to the garden, the garden that had waited patiently all these months since last summer, surely this must be her first gesture.

'Come on,' said Roger, rousing himself from his appreciation of how Willis the gardener had mown the lawn to just the right closeness for cricket, and without waiting for his sister's answer he ran to the summer-house and made a dive at the long box in the corner where the stumps were kept. He smiled as he lifted the lid. The familiarity of the smell was satisfying. Old varnish and chipped paint, and surely that must be the same spider and the same cobweb? He drew out the stumps one by one, and the bails, and there was the ball – it had not been lost after all, as he had feared. It was worn, though, a greyish red – he smelt it and bit it, to taste the shabby leather. Then he gathered the things in his arms and went out to set up the stumps.

'Come and help me measure the pitch,' he called to his sister, and looking at her, squatting in the grass with her face hidden, his heart sank, because it meant that she was in one of her absent moods and would not concentrate on the cricket.

'Deb?' he called anxiously. 'You are going to play?'

Deborah heard his voice through the multitude of earth sounds, the heartbeat and the pulse. If she listened with her ear to the ground there was a humming much deeper than anything that bees did, or the sea at Hunstanton. The nearest to it was the wind, but the wind was reckless. The humming of the earth was patient. Deborah sat up, and her heart sank just as her brother's had done, for the same reason in reverse. The monotony of the game ahead would be like a great chunk torn out of privacy.

'How long shall we have to be?' she called.

The lack of enthusiasm damped the boy. It was not going to be any fun at all if she made a favour of it. He must be firm, though. Any concession on his part she snatched and turned to her advantage.

'Half-an-hour,' he said, and then, for encouragement's sake, 'You can bat first.'

Deborah smelt her knees. They had not yet got the country smell, but if she rubbed them in the grass, and in the earth too, the white London look would go.

'All right,' she said, 'but no longer than half-an-hour.'

He nodded quickly, and so as not to lose time measured out the pitch and then began ramming the stumps in the ground. Deborah went into the summer-house to get the bats. The familiarity of the little wooden hut pleased her as it had her brother. It was a long time now, many years, since they had played in the summer-house, making yet another house inside this one with the help of broken deckchairs; but, just as the garden waited for them a whole year, so did the summer-house, the windows on either side, cobweb-wrapped and stained, gazing out like eyes. Deborah did her ritual of bowing twice. If she should forget this, on her first entrance, it spelt ill-luck.

She picked out the two bats from the corner, where they were stacked with old croquet-hoops, and she knew at once that Roger would choose the one with the rubber handle, even though they could not bat at the same time, and for the whole of the holidays she must make do with the smaller one, that had half the whipping off. There was a croquet clip lying on the floor. She picked it up and put it on her nose and stood a moment, wondering how it would be if for evermore she had to live thus, nostrils pinched, making her voice like Punch. Would people pity her?

'Hurry,' shouted Roger, and she threw the clip into the corner, then quickly returned when she was halfway to the pitch, because she knew the clip was lying apart from its fellows, and she might wake in the night and remember it. The clip would turn malevolent, and haunt her. She replaced him on the floor with two others, and now she was absolved and the summer-house at peace.

'Don't get out too soon,' warned Roger as she stood in the crease he had marked for her, and with a tremendous effort of concentration Deborah forced her eyes to his retreating figure and watched him roll up his sleeves and pace the required length for his run-up. Down came the ball and she lunged out, smacking it in the air in an easy catch. The impact of ball on bat stung her hands. Roger missed the catch on purpose. Neither of them said anything.

'Who shall I be?' called Deborah.

The game could only be endured, and concentration kept, if Roger gave her a part to play. Not an individual, but a country.

'You're India,' he said, and Deborah felt herself grow dark and lean. Part of her was tiger, part of her was sacred cow, the long grass fringing the lawn was jungle, the roof of the summer-house a minaret.

Even so, the half-hour dragged, and, when her turn came to bowl, the ball she threw fell wider every time, so that Roger, flushed and self-conscious because their grandfather had come out on to the terrace and was watching them, called angrily, 'Do try.'

Once again the effort at concentration, the figure of their grandfather – a source of apprehension to the boy, for he might criticize them – acting as a spur to his sister. Grandpapa was an Indian god, and tribute must be paid to him, a golden apple. The apple must be flung to slay his enemies. Deborah muttered a prayer, and the ball she bowled came fast and true and hit Roger's off-stump. In the moment of delivery their grandfather had turned away and pottered back again through the French windows of the drawing-room.

Roger looked round swiftly. His disgrace had not been seen. 'Jolly good ball,' he said. 'It's your turn to bat again.'

But his time was up. The stable clock chimed six. Solemnly Roger drew stumps.

'What shall we do now?' he asked.

Deborah wanted to be alone, but if she said so, on this first evening of the holiday, he would be offended.

'Go to the orchard and see how the apples are coming on,' she suggested, 'and then round by the kitchen garden in case the raspberries haven't all been picked. But you have to do it all without meeting anyone. If you see Willis or anyone, even the cat, you lose a mark.'

It was these sudden inventions that saved her. She knew her brother would be stimulated at the thought of outwitting the gardener. The aimless wander round the orchard would turn into a stalking exercise.

'Will you come too?' he asked.

'No,' she said, 'you have to test your skill.'

He seemed satisfied with this and ran off towards the orchard, stopping on the way to cut himself a switch from the bamboo.

As soon as he had disappeared Deborah made for the trees fringing the lawn, and once in the shrouded wood felt herself safe. She walked softly along the alley-way to the pool. The late sun sent shafts of light between the trees and on to the alley-way, and a myriad insects webbed their way in the beams, ascending and descending like angels on Jacob's ladder. But were they insects, wondered Deborah, or particles of dust, or even split fragments of light itself, beaten out and scattered by the sun?

It was very quiet. The woods were made for secrecy. They did not
recognize her as the garden did. They did not care that for a whole year she
could be at school, or at Hunstanton, or in London. The woods would never
miss her: they had their own dark, passionate life.

Deborah came to the opening where the pool lay, with the five alley-ways
branching from it, and she stood a moment before advancing to the brink,
because this was holy ground and required atonement. She crossed her
hands on her breast and shut her eyes. Then she kicked off her shoes.
'Mother of all things wild, do with me what you will,' she said aloud. The
sound of her own voice gave her a slight shock. Then she went down on her
knees and touched the ground three times with her forehead.

The first part of her atonement was accomplished, but the pool demanded
sacrifice, and Deborah had come prepared. There was a stub of pencil she
had carried in her pocket throughout the school term which she called her
luck. It had teeth marks on it, and a chewed piece of rubber at one end. This
treasure must be given to the pool just as other treasures had been given in
the past, a miniature jug, a crested button, a china pig. Deborah felt for the
stub of pencil and kissed it. She had carried and caressed it for so many
lonely months, and now the moment of parting had come. The pool must not
be denied. She flung out her right hand, her eyes still shut, and heard the
faint plop as the stub of pencil struck the water. Then she opened her eyes,
and saw in mid-pool a ripple. The pencil had gone, but the ripple moved,
gently shaking the water-lilies. The movement symbolized acceptance.

Deborah, still on her knees and crossing her hands once more, edged her
way to the brink of the pool and then, crouching there beside it, looked down
into the water. Her reflection wavered up at her, and it was not the face she
knew, not even the looking-glass face which anyway was false, but a
disturbed image, dark-skinned and ghostly. The crossed hands were like the
petals of the water-lilies themselves, and the colour was not waxen white but
phantom green. The hair too was not the live clump she brushed every day
and tied back with ribbon, but a canopy, a shroud. When the image smiled it
became more distorted still. Uncrossing her hands, Deborah leant forward,
took a twig, and drew a circle three times on the smooth surface. The water
shook in ever-widening ripples, and her reflection, broken into fragments,
heaved and danced, a sort of monster, and the eyes were there no longer, nor
the mouth.

Presently the water became still. Insects, long-legged flies and beetles
with spread wings hummed upon it. A dragon-fly had all the magnificence of
a lily leaf to himself. He hovered there, rejoicing. But when Deborah took
her eyes off him for a moment he was gone. At the far end of the pool,
beyond the clustering lilies, green scum had formed, and beneath the scum

were rooted, tangled weeds. They were so thick, and had lain in the pool so long, that if a man walked into them from the bank he would be held and choked. A fly, though, or a beetle, could sit upon the surface, and to him the pale green scum would not be treacherous at all, but a resting-place, a haven. And if someone threw a stone, so that the ripples formed, eventually they came to the scum, and rocked it, and the whole of the mossy surface moved in rhythm, a dancing-floor for those who played upon it.

There was a dead tree standing by the far end of the pool. He could have been fir or pine, or even larch, for time had stripped him of identity. He had no distinguishing mark upon his person, but with grotesque limbs straddled the sky. A cap of ivy crowned his naked head. Last winter a dangling branch had broken loose, and this now lay in the pool half-submerged, the green scum dripping from the withered twigs. The soggy branch made a vantage-point for birds, and as Deborah watched a nestling suddenly flew from the undergrowth enveloping the dead tree, and perched for an instant on the mossy filigree. He was lost in terror. The parent bird cried warningly from some dark safety, and the nestling, pricking to the cry, took off from the branch that had offered him temporary salvation. He swerved across the pool, his flight mistimed, yet reached security. The chitter from the undergrowth told of his scolding. When he had gone silence returned to the pool.

It was, so Deborah thought, the time for prayer. The water-lilies were folding upon themselves. The ripples ceased. And that dark hollow in the centre of the pool, that black stillness where the water was deepest, was surely a funnel to the kingdom that lay below. Down that funnel had travelled the discarded treasures. The stub of pencil had lately plunged the depths. He had now been received as an equal among his fellows. This was the single law of the pool, for there were no other commandments. Once it was over, that first cold headlong flight, Deborah knew that the softness of the welcoming water took away all fear. It lapped the face and cleansed the eyes, and the plunge was not into darkness at all but into light. It did not become blacker as the pool was penetrated, but paler, more golden-green, and the mud that people told themselves was there was only a defence against strangers. Those who belonged, who knew, went to the source at once, and there were caverns and fountains and rainbow-coloured seas. There were shores of the whitest sand. There was soundless music.

Once again Deborah closed her eyes and bent lower to the pool. Her lips nearly touched the water. This was the great silence, when she had no thoughts, and was accepted by the pool. Waves of quiet ringed themselves about her, and slowly she lost all feeling, and had no knowledge of her legs, or of her kneeling body, or of her cold, clasped hands. There was nothing but the intensity of peace. It was a deeper acceptance than listening to the earth, because the earth was of the world, the earth was a throbbing pulse, but the acceptance of the pool meant another kind of hearing, a closing in of the waters, and just as the lilies folded so did the soul submerge.

'Deborah . . . ? Deborah . . . ?' Oh, no! Not now, don't let them call me back now! It was as though someone had hit her on the back, or jumped out at her from behind a corner, the sharp and sudden clamour of another life destroying the silence, the secrecy. And then came the tinkle of the cowbells. It was the signal from their grandmother that the time had come to go in. Not imperious and ugly with authority, like the clanging bell at school summoning those at play to lessons or chapel, but a reminder, nevertheless, that Time was all-important, that life was ruled to order, that even here, in the holiday home the children loved, the adult reigned supreme.

'All right, all right,' muttered Deborah, standing up and thrusting her numbed feet into her shoes. This time the rather raised tone of 'Deborah?', and the more hurried clanging of the cowbells, brought long ago from Switzerland, suggested a more imperious Grandmama than the tolerant one who seldom questioned. It must mean their supper was already laid, soup perhaps getting cold, and the farce of washing hands, of tidying, of combing hair, must first be gone through.

'Come on, Deb,' and now the shout was close, was right at hand, privacy lost for ever, for her brother came running down the alley-way swishing his bamboo stick in the air.

'What *have* you been doing?' The question was an intrusion and a threat. She would never have asked him what he had been doing, had he wandered away wanting to be alone, but Roger, alas, did not claim privacy. He liked companionship, and his question now, asked half in irritation, half in resentment, came really from the fear that he might lose her.

'Nothing,' said Deborah.

Roger eyed her suspiciously. She was in that mooning mood. And it meant, when they went to bed, that she would not talk. One of the best things, in the holidays, was having the two adjoining rooms and calling through to Deb, making her talk.

'Come on,' he said, 'they've rung,' and the making of their grandmother into 'they', turned a loved individual into something impersonal, showed Deborah that even if he did not understand he was on her side. He had been called from play, just as she had.

They ran from the woods to the lawn, and on to the terrace. Their grandmother had gone inside, but the cowbells hanging by the French window were still jangling.

The custom was for the children to have their supper first, at seven, and it was laid for them in the dining-room on a hot-plate. They served themselves. At a quarter-to-eight their grandparents had dinner. It was called dinner, but this was a concession to their status. They ate the same as the children, though Grandpapa had a savoury which was not served to the children. If the children were late for supper then it put out Time, as well as Agnes, who cooked for both generations, and it might mean five minutes' delay before Grandpapa had his soup. This shook routine.

The children ran up to the bathroom to wash, then downstairs to the dining-room. Their grandfather was standing in the hall. Deborah sometimes thought that he would have enjoyed sitting with them while they ate their supper, but he never suggested it. Grandmama had warned them, too, never to be a nuisance, or indeed to shout, if Grandpapa was near. This was not because he was nervous, but because he liked to shout himself.

'There's going to be a heat-wave,' he said. He had been listening to the news.

'That will mean lunch outside tomorrow,' said Roger swiftly. Lunch was the meal they took in common with the grandparents, and it was the moment of the day he disliked. He was nervous that his grandfather would ask him how he was getting on at school.

'Not for me, thank you,' said Grandpapa. 'Too many wasps.'

Roger was at once relieved. This meant that he and Deborah would have the little round garden-table to themselves. But Deborah felt sorry for her grandfather as he went back into the drawing-room. Lunch on the terrace could be gay, and would liven him up. When people grew old they had so few treats.

'What do you look forward to most in the day?' she once asked her grandmother.

'Going to bed,' was the reply, 'and filling my two hot-water bottles.' Why work through being young, thought Deborah, to this?

Back in the dining-room the children discussed what they should do during the heat-wave. It would be too hot, Deborah said, for cricket. But they might make a house, suggested Roger, in the trees by the paddock. If he got a few old boards from Willis, and nailed them together like a platform, and borrowed the orchard ladder, then they could take fruit and bottles of orange squash and keep them up there, and it would be a camp from which they could spy on Willis afterwards.

Deborah's first instinct was to say she did not want to play, but she checked herself in time. Finding the boards and fixing them would take Roger a whole morning. It would keep him employed. 'Yes, it's a good idea,' she said, and to foster his spirit of adventure she looked at his notebook, as they were drinking their soup, and approved of items necessary for the camp while he jotted them down. It was all part of the day-long deceit she practised to express understanding of his way of life.

When they had finished supper they took their trays to the kitchen and watched Agnes, for a moment, as she prepared the second meal for the grandparents. The soup was the same, but garnished. Little croûtons of toasted bread were added to it. And the butter was made into pats, not cut in a slab. The savoury tonight was to be cheese straws. The children finished the ones that Agnes had burnt. Then they went through to the drawing-room to say good night. The older people had both changed. Grandmama had a dress that she had worn several years ago in London. She had a cardigan round her shoulders like a cape.

'Go carefully with the bathwater,' she said. 'We'll be short if there's no rain.'

They kissed her smooth, soft skin. It smelt of rose leaves. Grandpapa's chin was sharp and bony. He did not kiss Roger.

'Be quiet overhead,' whispered their grandmother. The children nodded. The dining-room was underneath their rooms, and any jumping about or laughter would make a disturbance.

Deborah felt a wave of affection for the two old people. Their lives must be empty and sad. 'We *are* glad to be here,' she said. Grandmama smiled. This was how she lived, thought Deborah, on little crumbs of comfort.

Once out of the room their spirits soared, and to show relief Roger chased Deborah upstairs, both laughing for no reason. Undressing they forgot the instructions about the bath, and when they went into the bathroom – Deborah was to have first go – the water was gurgling into the overflow. They tore out the plug in a panic, and listened to the waste roaring down the pipe to the drain below. If Agnes did not have the wireless on she would hear it.

The children were too old now for boats or play, but the bathroom was a place for confidences, for a sharing of those few tastes they agreed upon, or, after quarrelling, for moody silence. The one who broke silence first would then lose face.

'Willis has a new bicycle,' said Roger. 'I saw it propped against the shed. I couldn't try it because he was there. But I shall tomorrow. It's a Raleigh.'

He liked all practical things, and the trying of the gardener's bicycle would give an added interest to the morning of next day. Willis had a bag of tools in a leather pouch behind the saddle. These could all be felt and the spanners, smelling of oil, tested for shape and usefulness.

'If Willis died,' said Deborah, 'I wonder what age he would be.'

It was the kind of remark that Roger resented always. What had death to do with bicycles? 'He's sixty-five,' he said, 'so he'd be sixty-five.'

'No,' said Deborah, 'what age when he got *there*.'

Roger did not want to discuss it. 'I bet I can ride it round the stables if I lower the seat,' he said. 'I bet I don't fall off.'

But if Roger would not rise to death, Deborah would not rise to the wager. 'Who cares?' she said.

The sudden streak of cruelty stung the brother. Who cared indeed . . . The horror of an empty world encompassed him, and to give himself confidence he seized the wet sponge and flung it out of the window. They heard it splosh on the terrace below.

'Grandpapa will step on it, and slip,' said Deborah, aghast.

The image seized them, and choking back laughter they covered their faces. Hysteria doubled them up. Roger rolled over and over on the bathroom floor. Deborah, the first to recover, wondered why laughter was so near to pain, why Roger's face, twisted now in merriment, was yet the same crumpled thing when his heart was breaking.

'Hurry up,' she said briefly, 'let's dry the floor,' and as they wiped the linoleum with their towels the action sobered them both.

Back in their bedrooms, the door open between them, they watched the light slowly fading. But the air was warm like day. Their grandfather and the people who said what the weather was going to be were right. The heat-wave was on its way. Deborah, leaning out of the open window, fancied she could see it in the sky, a dull haze where the sun had been before; and the trees beyond the lawn, day-coloured when they were having their supper in the dining-room, had turned into night-birds with outstretched wings. The garden knew about the promised heat-wave, and rejoiced: the lack of rain was of no consequence yet, for the warm air was a trap, lulling it into a drowsy contentment.

The dull murmur of their grandparents' voices came from the dining-room below. What did they discuss, wondered Deborah. Did they make those sounds to reassure the children, or were their voices part of their unreal world? Presently the voices ceased, and then there was a scraping of chairs, and voices from a different quarter, the drawing-room now, and a faint smell of their grandfather's cigarette.

Deborah called softly to her brother but he did not answer. She went through to his room, and he was asleep. He must have fallen asleep suddenly, in the midst of talking. She was relieved. Now she could be alone again, and not have to keep up the pretence of sharing conversation. Dusk was everywhere, the sky a deepening black. 'When they've gone up to bed,' thought Deborah, 'then I'll be truly alone.' She knew what she was going to do. She waited there, by the open window, and the deepening sky lost the veil that covered it, the haze disintegrated, and the stars broke through.

Where there had been nothing was life, dusty and bright, and the waiting earth gave off a scent of knowledge. Dew rose from the pores. The lawn was white.

Patch, the old dog, who slept at the end of Grandpapa's bed on a plaid rug, came out on to the terrace and barked hoarsely. Deborah leant out and threw a piece of creeper on to him. He shook his back. Then he waddled slowly to the flower-tub above the steps and cocked his leg. It was his nightly routine. He barked once more, staring blindly at the hostile trees, and went back into the drawing-room. Soon afterwards, someone came to close the windows – Grandmama, thought Deborah, for the touch was light. 'They are shutting out the best,' said the child to herself, 'all the meaning, and all the point.' Patch, being an animal, should know better. He ought to be in a kennel where he could watch, but instead, grown fat and soft, he preferred the bumpiness of her grandfather's bed. He had forgotten the secrets. So had they, the old people.

Deborah heard her grandparents come upstairs. First her grandmother, the quicker of the two, and then her grandfather, more laboured, saying a word or two to Patch as the little dog wheezed his way up. There was a general clicking of lights and shutting of doors. Then silence. How remote, the world of the grandparents, undressing with curtains closed. A pattern of life unchanged for so many years. What went on without would never be known. 'He that has ears to hear, let him hear,' said Deborah, and she thought of the callousness of Jesus which no priest could explain. Let the dead bury their dead. All the people in the world, undressing now, or sleeping, not just in the village but in cities and capitals, they were shutting out the truth, they were burying their dead. They wasted silence.

The stable clock struck eleven. Deborah pulled on her clothes. Not the cotton frock of the day, but her old jeans that Grandmama disliked, rolled up above her knees. And a jersey. Sandshoes with a hole that did not matter. She was cunning enough to go down by the back stairs. Patch would bark if she tried the front stairs, close to the grandparents' rooms. The back stairs led past Agnes's room, which smelt of apples though she never ate fruit. Deborah could hear her snoring. She would not even wake on Judgement Day. And this led her to wonder on the truth of that fable too, for there might be so many millions by then who liked their graves – Grandpapa, for instance, fond of his routine, and irritated at the sudden riot of trumpets.

Deborah crept past the pantry and the servants' hall – it was only a tiny sitting-room for Agnes, but long usage had given it the dignity of the name – and unlatched and unbolted the heavy back door. Then she stepped outside, on to the gravel, and took the long way round by the front of the house so as not to tread on the terrace, fronting the lawns and the garden.

The warm night claimed her. In a moment it was part of her. She walked on the grass, and her shoes were instantly soaked. She flung up her arms to the sky. Power ran to her fingertips. Excitement was communicated from the waiting tree, and the orchard, and the paddock; the intensity of their secret life caught at her and made her run. It was nothing like the excitement of ordinary looking forward, of birthday presents, of Christmas stockings, but the pull of a magnet – her grandfather had shown her once how it worked, little needles springing to the jaws – and now night and the sky above were a vast magnet, and the things that waited below were needles, caught up in the great demand.

Deborah went to the summer-house, and it was not sleeping like the house fronting the terrace but open to understanding, sharing complicity. Even the dusty windows caught the light, and the cobwebs shone. She rummaged for the old lilo and the motheaten car rug that Grandmama had thrown out two summers ago, and bearing them over her shoulder she made her way to the pool. The alley-way was ghostly, and Deborah knew, for all her mounting tension, that the test was hard. Part of her was still body-bound, and afraid of shadows. If anything stirred she would jump and know true terror. She must show defiance, though. The woods expected it. Like old wise lamas they expected courage.

She sensed approval as she ran the gauntlet, the tall trees watching. Any sign of turning back, of panic, and they would crowd upon her in a choking mass, smothering protest. Branches would become arms, gnarled and knotty, ready to strangle, and the leaves of the higher trees fold in and close like the sudden furling of giant umbrellas. The smaller undergrowth, obedient to the will, would become a briary of a million thorns where animals of no known world crouched snarling, their eyes on fire. To show fear was to show misunderstanding. The woods were merciless.

Deborah walked the alley-way to the pool, her left hand holding the lilo and the rug on her shoulder, her right hand raised in salutation. This was a gesture of respect. Then she paused before the pool and laid down her burden beside it. The lilo was to be her bed, the rug her cover. She took off her shoes, also in respect, and lay down upon the lilo. Then, drawing the rug to her chin, she lay flat, her eyes upon the sky. The gauntlet of the alley-way over, she had no more fear. The woods had accepted her, and the pool was the final resting-place, the doorway, the key.

'I shan't sleep,' thought Deborah. 'I shall just lie awake here all the night and wait for morning, but it will be a kind of introduction to life, like being confirmed.'

The stars were thicker now than they had been before. No space in the sky without a prick of light, each star a sun. Some, she thought, were newly born, white-hot, and others wise and colder, nearing completion. The law encompassed them, fixing the riotous path, but how they fell and tumbled depended upon themselves. Such peace, such stillness, such sudden quietude, excitement gone. The trees were no longer menacing but guardians, and the pool was primeval water, the first, the last.

Then Deborah stood at the wicket-gate, the boundary, and there was a woman with outstretched hand, demanding tickets. 'Pass through,' she said when Deborah reached her. 'We saw you coming.' The wicket-gate became a turnstile. Deborah pushed against it and there was no resistance, she was through.

'What is it?' she asked. 'Am I really here at last? Is this the bottom of the pool?'

'It could be,' smiled the woman. 'There are so many ways. You just happened to choose this one.'

Other people were pressing to come through. They had no faces, they were only shadows. Deborah stood aside to let them by, and in a moment they had all gone, all phantoms.

'Why only now, tonight?' asked Deborah. 'Why not in the afternoon, when I came to the pool?'

'It's a trick,' said the woman. 'You seize on the moment in time. We were here this afternoon. We're always here. Our life goes on around you, but nobody knows it. The trick's easier by night, that's all.'

'Am I dreaming, then?' asked Deborah.

'No,' said the woman, 'this isn't a dream. And it isn't death, either. It's the secret world.'

The secret world . . . It was something Deborah had always known, and now the pattern was complete. The memory of it, and the relief, were so tremendous that something seemed to burst inside her heart.

'Of course . . .' she said, 'of course . . .' and everything that had ever been fell into place. There was no disharmony. The joy was indescribable, and the surge of feeling, like wings about her in the air, lifted her away from the turnstile and the woman, and she had all knowledge. That was it – the invasion of knowledge.

'I'm not myself, then, after all,' she thought. 'I knew I wasn't. It was only the task given,' and, looking down, she saw a little child who was blind trying to find her way. Pity seized her. She bent down and put her hands on the child's eyes, and they opened, and the child was herself at two years old. The incident came back. It was when her mother died and Roger was born.

'It doesn't matter after all,' she told the child. 'You are not lost. You don't have to go on crying.' Then the child that had been herself melted, and became absorbed in the water and the sky, and the joy of the invading flood intensified so that there was no body at all but only being. No words, only movements. And the beating of wings. This above all, the beating of wings.

'Don't let me go!' It was a pulse in her ear, and a cry, and she saw the woman at the turnstile put up her hands to hold her. Then there was such darkness, such dragging, terrible darkness, and the beginning of pain all over again, the leaden heart, the tears, the misunderstanding. The voice saying 'No!' was her own harsh, worldly voice, and she was staring at the restless trees, black and ominous against the sky. One hand trailed in the water of the pool.

Deborah sat up, sobbing. The hand that had been in the pool was wet and cold. She dried it on the rug. And suddenly she was seized with such fear that her body took possession, and throwing aside the rug she began to run along the alley-way, the dark trees mocking and the welcome of the woman at the turnstile turned to treachery. Safety lay in the house behind the closed curtains, security was with the grandparents sleeping in their beds, and like a leaf driven before a whirlwind Deborah was out of the woods and across the silver soaking lawn, up the steps beyond the terrace and through the garden-gate to the back door.

The slumbering solid house received her. It was like an old staid person who, surviving many trials, had learnt experience. 'Don't take any notice of them,' it seemed to say, jerking its head – did a house have a head? – towards the woods beyond. 'They've made no contribution to civilization. I'm man-made, and different. This is where you belong, dear child. Now settle down.'

Deborah went back again upstairs and into her bedroom. Nothing had changed. It was still the same. Going to the open window she saw that the woods and the lawn seemed unaltered from the moment, how long back she did not know, when she had stood there, deciding upon the visit to the pool. The only difference now was in herself. The excitement had gone, the tension too. Even the terror of those last moments, when her flying feet had brought her to the house, seemed unreal.

She drew the curtains, just as her grandmother might have done, and climbed into bed. Her mind was now preoccupied with practical difficulties, like explaining the presence of the lilo and the rug beside the pool. Willis might find them, and tell her grandfather. The feel of her own pillow, and of her own blankets, reassured her. Both were familiar. And being tired was familiar too, it was a solid bodily ache, like the tiredness after too much jumping or cricket. The thing was, though – and the last remaining conscious thread of thought decided to postpone conclusion until the morning – which was real? This safety of the house, or the secret world?

When Deborah woke next morning she knew at once that her mood was bad. It would last her for the day. Her eyes ached, and her neck was stiff, and there was a taste in her mouth like magnesia. Immediately Roger came running into her room, his face refreshed and smiling from some dreamless sleep, and jumped on her bed.

'It's come,' he said, 'the heat-wave's come. It's going to be ninety in the shade.'

Deborah considered how best she could damp his day. 'It can go to a hundred for all I care,' she said. 'I'm going to read all morning.'

His face fell. A look of bewilderment came into his eyes. 'But the house?' he said. 'We'd decided to have a house in the trees, don't you remember? I was going to get some planks from Willis.'

Deborah turned over in bed and humped her knees. 'You can, if you like,' she said. 'I think it's a silly game.'

She shut her eyes, feigning sleep, and presently she heard his feet patter slowly back to his own room, and then the thud of a ball against the wall. If he goes on doing that, she thought maliciously, Grandpapa will ring his bell, and Agnes will come panting up the stairs. She hoped for destruction, for grumbling and snapping, and everyone falling out, not speaking. That was the way of the world.

The kitchen, where the children breakfasted, faced west, so it did not get the morning sun. Agnes had hung up fly-papers to catch wasps. The cereal, puffed wheat, was soggy. Deborah complained, mashing the mess with her spoon.

'It's a new packet,' said Agnes. 'You're mighty particular all of a sudden.'

'Deb's got out of bed the wrong side,' said Roger.

The two remarks fused to make a challenge. Deborah seized the nearest weapon, a knife, and threw it at her brother. It narrowly missed his eye, but cut his cheek. Surprised, he put his hand to his face and felt the blood. Hurt, not by the knife but by his sister's action, his face turned red and his lower lip quivered. Deborah ran out of the kitchen and slammed the door. Her own violence distressed her, but the power of the mood was too strong. Going on to the terrace, she saw that the worst had happened. Willis had found the lilo and the rug, and had put them to dry in the sun. He was talking to her grandmother. Deborah tried to slip back into the house, but it was too late.

'Deborah, how very thoughtless of you,' said Grandmama. 'I tell you children every summer that I don't mind your taking the things from the hut into the garden if only you'll put them back.'

Deborah knew she should apologize, but the mood forbade it. 'That old rug is full of moth,' she said contemptuously, 'and the lilo has a rainproof back. It doesn't hurt them.'

They both stared at her, and her grandmother flushed, just as Roger had done when she had thrown the knife at him. Then her grandmother turned her back and continued giving some instructions to the gardener.

Deborah stalked along the terrace, pretending that nothing had happened, and skirting the lawn she made her way towards the orchard and so to the fields beyond. She picked up a windfall, but as soon as her teeth bit into it the taste was green. She threw it away. She went and sat on a gate and stared in front of her, looking at nothing. Such deception everywhere. Such sour sadness. It was like Adam and Eve being locked out of paradise. The Garden of Eden was no more. Somewhere, very close, the woman at the turnstile waited to let her in, the secret world was all about her, but the key was gone. Why had she ever come back? What had brought her?

People were going about their business. The old man who came three days a week to help Willis was sharpening his scythe behind the toolshed. Beyond the field where the lane ran towards the main road she could see the top of the postman's head. He was pedalling his bicycle towards the village. She heard Roger calling, 'Deb? Deb . . . ?' which meant that he had forgiven her, but still the mood held sway and she did not answer. Her own dullness made her own punishment. Presently a knocking sound told her that he had got the planks from Willis and had embarked on the building of his house. He was like his grandfather; he kept to the routine set for himself.

Deborah was consumed with pity. Not for the sullen self humped upon the gate, but for all of them going about their business in the world who did not hold the key. The key was hers, and she had lost it. Perhaps if she worked her way through the long day the magic would return with evening and she would find it once again. Or even now. Even now, by the pool, there might be a clue, a vision.

Deborah slid off the gate and went the long way round. By skirting the fields, parched under the sun, she could reach the other side of the wood and meet no one. The husky wheat was stiff. She had to keep close to the hedge to avoid brushing it, and the hedge was tangled. Foxgloves had grown too tall and were bending with empty sockets, their flowers gone. There were nettles everywhere. There was no gate into the wood, and she had to climb the pricking hedge with the barbed wire tearing her knickers. Once in the wood some measure of peace returned, but the alley-ways this side had not been scythed, and the grass was long. She had to wade through it like a sea, brushing it aside with her hands.

She came upon the pool from behind the monster tree, the hybrid whose naked arms were like a dead man's stumps, projecting at all angles. This side, on the lip of the pool, the scum was carpet-thick, and all the lilies, coaxed by the risen sun, had opened wide. They basked as lizards bask on hot stone walls. But here, with stems in water, they swung in grace, cluster upon cluster, pink and waxen white. 'They're asleep,' thought Deborah. 'So is the wood. The morning is not their time,' and it seemed to her beyond possibility that the turnstile was at hand and the woman waiting, smiling. 'She said they were always there, even in the day, but the truth is that being a child I'm blinded in the day. I don't know how to see.'

She dipped her hands in the pool, and the water was tepid brown. She tasted her fingers, and the taste was rank. Brackish water, stagnant from long stillness. Yet beneath . . . beneath, she knew, by night the woman waited, and not only the woman but the whole secret world. Deborah began to pray. 'Let it happen again,' she whispered. 'Let it happen again. Tonight. I won't be afraid.'

The sluggish pool made no acknowledgement, but the very silence seemed a testimony of faith, of acceptance. Beside the pool, where the imprint of the lilo had marked the moss, Deborah found a kirby-grip, fallen from her hair during the night. It was proof of visitation. She threw it into the pool as part of the treasury. Then she walked back into the ordinary day and the heat-wave, and her black mood was softened. She went to find Roger in the orchard. He was busy with the platform. Three of the boards were fixed, and the noisy hammering was something that had to be borne. He saw her coming, and as always, after trouble, sensed that her mood had changed and mention must never be made of it. Had he called, 'Feeling better?', it would have revived the antagonism, and she might not play with him all the day. Instead, he took no notice. She must be the first to speak.

Deborah waited at the foot of the tree, then bent, and handed him up an apple. It was green, but the offering meant peace. He ate it manfully. 'Thanks,' he said. She climbed into the tree beside him and reached for the box of nails. Contact had been renewed. All was well between them.

3

The hot day spun itself out like a web. The heat haze stretched across the sky, dun-coloured and opaque. Crouching on the burning boards of the apple-tree, the children drank ginger beer and fanned themselves with dock-leaves. They grew hotter still. When the cowbells summoned them for lunch they found that their grandmother had drawn the curtains of all the rooms downstairs, and the drawing-room was a vault and strangely cool. They flung themselves into chairs. No one was hungry. Patch lay under the piano, his soft mouth dripping saliva. Grandmama had changed into a sleeveless linen dress never before seen, and Grandpapa, in a dented panama, carried a fly-whisk used years ago in Egypt.

'Ninety-one,' he said grimly, 'on the Air Ministry roof. It was on the one o'clock news.'

Deborah thought of the men who must measure heat, toiling up and down on this Ministry roof with rods and tapes and odd-shaped instruments. Did anyone care but Grandpapa?

'Can we take our lunch outside?' asked Roger.

His grandmother nodded. Speech was too much effort, and she sank languidly into her chair at the foot of the dining-room table. The roses she had picked last night had wilted.

The children carried chicken drumsticks to the summer-house. It was too hot to sit inside, but they sprawled in the shadow it cast, their heads on faded cushions shedding kapok. Somewhere, far above their heads, an aeroplane climbed like a small silver fish, and was lost in space.

'A Meteor,' said Roger. 'Grandpapa says they're obsolete.'

Deborah thought of Icarus, soaring towards the sun. Did he know when his wings began to melt? How did he feel? She stretched out her arms and thought of them as wings. The fingertips would be the first to curl, and then turn cloggy soft, and useless. What terror in the sudden loss of height, the drooping power . . .

Roger, watching her, hoped it was some game. He threw his picked drumstick into a flowerbed and jumped to his feet.

'Look,' he said, 'I'm a Javelin,' and he too stretched his arms and ran in circles, banking. Jet noises came from his clenched teeth. Deborah dropped her arms and looked at the drumstick. What had been clean and white from Roger's teeth was now earth-brown. Was it offended to be chucked away? Years later, when everyone was dead, it would be found, moulded like a fossil. Nobody would care.

'Come on,' said Roger.

'Where to?' she asked.

'To fetch the raspberries,' he said.

'You go,' she told him.

Roger did not like going into the dining-room alone. He was self-conscious. Deborah made a shield from the adult eyes. In the end he consented to fetch the raspberries without her on condition that she played cricket after tea. After tea was a long way off.

She watched him return, walking very slowly, bearing the plates of raspberries and clotted cream. She was seized with sudden pity, that same pity which, earlier she had felt for all people other than herself. How absorbed he was, how intent on the moment that held him. But tomorrow he would be some old man far away, the garden forgotten, and this day long past.

'Grandmama says it can't go on,' he announced. 'There'll have to be a storm.'

But why? Why not for ever? Why not breathe a spell so that all of them could stay locked and dreaming like the courtiers in the *Sleeping Beauty*, never knowing, never waking, cobwebs in their hair and on their hands, tendrils imprisoning the house itself?

'Race me,' said Roger, and to please him she plunged her spoon into the mush of raspberries but finished last, to his delight.

No one moved during the long afternoon. Grandmama went upstairs to her room. The children saw her at her window in her petticoat drawing the curtains close. Grandpapa put his feet up in the drawing-room, a handkerchief over his face. Patch did not stir from his place under the piano. Roger, undefeated, found employment still. He first helped Agnes to shell peas for supper, squatting on the back-door step while she relaxed on a lopsided basket chair dragged from the servants' hall. This task finished, he discovered a tin bath, put away in the cellar, in which Patch had been washed in younger days. He carried it to the lawn and filled it with water. Then he stripped to bathing-trunks and sat in it solemnly, an umbrella over his head to keep off the sun.

Deborah lay on her back behind the summer-house, wondering what would happen if Jesus and Buddha met. Would there be discussion, courtesy, an exchange of views like politicians at summit talks? Or were they after all the same person, born at separate times? The queer thing was that this topic, interesting now, meant nothing in the secret world. Last night, through the turnstile, all problems disappeared. They were non-existent. There was only the knowledge and the joy.

She must have slept, because when she opened her eyes she saw to her dismay that Roger was no longer in the bath but was hammering the cricket-stumps into the lawn. It was a quarter-to-five.

'Hurry up,' he called, when he saw her move. 'I've had tea.'

She got up and dragged herself into the house, sleepy still, and giddy. The grandparents were in the drawing-room, refreshed from the long repose of the afternoon. Grandpapa smelt of eau-de-Cologne. Even Patch had come to and was lapping his saucer of cold tea.

'You look tired,' said Grandmama critically. 'Are you feeling all right?'

Deborah was not sure. Her head was heavy. It must have been sleeping in the afternoon, a thing she never did.

'I think so,' she answered, 'but if anyone gave me roast pork I know I'd be sick.'

'No one suggested you should eat roast pork,' said her grandmother, surprised. 'Have a cucumber sandwich, they're cool enough.'

Grandpapa was lying in wait for a wasp. He watched it hover over his tea, grim, expectant. Suddenly he slammed at the air with his whisk. 'Got the brute,' he said in triumph. He ground it into the carpet with his heel. It made Deborah think of Jehovah.

'Don't rush around in the heat,' said Grandmama. 'It isn't wise. Can't you and Roger play some nice, quiet game?'

'What sort of game?' asked Deborah.

But her grandmother was without invention. The croquet mallets were all broken. 'We might pretend to be dwarfs and use the heads,' said Deborah, and she toyed for a moment with the idea of squatting to croquet. Their knees would stiffen, though, it would be too difficult.

'I'll read aloud to you, if you like,' said Grandmama.

Deborah seized upon the suggestion. It delayed cricket. She ran out on to the lawn and padded the idea to make it acceptable to Roger.

'I'll play afterwards,' she said, 'and that ice-cream that Agnes has in the fridge, you can eat all of it. I'll talk tonight in bed.'

Roger hesitated. Everything must be weighed. Three goods to balance evil.

'You know that stick of sealing-wax Daddy gave you?' he said.

'Yes.'

'Can I have it?'

The balance for Deborah too. The quiet of the moment in opposition to the loss of the long thick stick so brightly red.

'All right,' she grudged.

Roger left the cricket stumps and they went into the drawing-room. Grandpapa, at the first suggestion of reading aloud, had disappeared, taking Patch with him. Grandmama had cleared away the tea. She found her spectacles and the book. It was *Black Beauty*. Grandmama kept no modern children's books, and this made common ground for the three of them. She read the terrible chapter where the stable-lad lets Beauty get overheated and gives him a cold drink and does not put on his blanket. The story was suited to the day. Even Roger listened entranced. And Deborah, watching her grandmother's calm face and hearing her careful voice reading the sentences, thought how strange it was that Grandmama could turn herself into Beauty with such ease. She *was* a horse, suffering there with pneumonia in the stable, being saved by the wise coachman.

After the reading, cricket was an anticlimax, but Deborah must keep her bargain. She kept thinking of Black Beauty writing the book. It showed how good the story was, Grandmama said, because no child had ever yet questioned the practical side of it, or posed the picture of a horse with a pen in its hoof.

'A modern horse would have a typewriter,' thought Deborah, and she began to bowl to Roger, smiling to herself as she did so because of the twentieth-century Beauty clacking with both hoofs at a machine.

This evening, because of the heat-wave, the routine was changed. They had their baths first, before their supper, for they were hot and exhausted from the cricket. Then, putting on pyjamas and cardigans, they ate their supper on the terrace. For once Grandmama was indulgent. It was still so hot that they could not take chill, and the dew had not yet risen. It made a small excitement, being in pyjamas on the terrace. Like people abroad, said Roger. Or natives in the South Seas, said Deborah. Or beachcombers who had lost caste. Grandpapa, changed into a white tropical jacket, had not lost caste.

'He's a white trader,' whispered Deborah. 'He's made a fortune out of pearls.'

Roger choked. Any joke about his grandfather, whom he feared, had all the sweet agony of danger.

'What's the thermometer say?' asked Deborah.

Her grandfather, pleased at her interest, went to inspect it.

'Still above eighty,' he said with relish.

Deborah, when she cleaned her teeth later, thought how pale her face looked in the mirror above the wash-basin. It was not brown, like Roger's, from the day in the sun, but wan and yellow. She tied back her hair with a ribbon, and the nose and chin were peaky sharp. She yawned largely, as Agnes did in the kitchen on Sunday afternoons.

'Don't forget you promised to talk,' said Roger quickly.

Talk. . . . That was the burden. She was so tired she longed for the white smoothness of her pillow, all blankets thrown aside, bearing only a single sheet. But Roger, wakeful on his bed, the door between them wide, would not relent. Laughter was the one solution, and to make him hysterical, and so exhaust him sooner, she fabricated a day in the life of Willis, from his first morning kipper to his final glass of beer at the village inn. The adventures in between would have tried Gulliver. Roger's delight drew protests from the adult world below. There was the sound of a bell, and then Agnes came up the stairs and put her head round the corner of Deborah's door.

'Your Granny says you're not to make so much noise,' she said.

Deborah, spent with invention, lay back and closed her eyes. She could go no further. The children called good night to each other, both speaking at the same time, from age-long custom, beginning with their names and addresses and ending with the world, the universe, and space. Then the final main 'Good night', after which neither must ever speak, on pain of unknown calamity.

'I must try and keep awake,' thought Deborah, but the power was not in her. Sleep was too compelling, and it was hours later that she opened her eyes and saw her curtains blowing and the forked flash light the ceiling, and heard the trees tossing and sobbing against the sky. She was out of bed in an instant. Chaos had come. There were no stars, and the night was sulphurous. A great crack split the heavens and tore them in two. The garden groaned. If the rain would only fall there might be mercy, and the trees, imploring, bowed themselves this way and that, while the vivid lawn, bright in expectation, lay like a sheet of metal exposed to flame. Let the waters break. Bring down the rain.

Suddenly the lightning forked again, and standing there, alive yet immobile, was the woman by the turnstile. She stared up at the windows of the house, and Deborah recognized her. The turnstile was there, inviting entry, and already the phantom figures, passing through it, crowded towards the trees beyond the lawn. The secret world was waiting. Through the long day, while the storm was brewing, it had hovered there unseen beyond her reach, but now that night had come, and the thunder with it, the barriers were down. Another crack, mighty in its summons, the turnstile yawned, and the woman with her hand upon it smiled and beckoned.

Deborah ran out of the room and down the stairs. Somewhere somebody called – Roger, perhaps, it did not matter – and Patch was barking; but caring nothing for concealment she went through the dark drawing-room and opened the French window on to the terrace. The lightning searched the terrace and lit the paving, and Deborah ran down the steps on to the lawn where the turnstile gleamed.

Haste was imperative. If she did not run the turnstile might be closed, the woman vanish, and all the wonder of the sacred world be taken from her. She was in time. The woman was still waiting. She held out her hand for tickets, but Deborah shook her head. 'I have none.' The woman, laughing, brushed her through into the secret world where there were no laws, no rules, and all the faceless phantoms ran before her to the woods, blown by the rising wind. Then the rain came. The sky, deep brown as the lightning pierced it, opened, and the water hissed to the ground, rebounding from the earth in bubbles. There was no order now in the alley-way. The ferns had turned to trees, the trees to Titans. All moved in ecstasy, with sweeping limbs, but the rhythm was broken up, tumultuous, so that some of them were bent backwards, torn by the sky, and others dashed their heads to the undergrowth where they were caught and beaten.

In the world behind, laughed Deborah as she ran, this would be punishment, but here in the secret world it was a tribute. The phantoms who ran beside her were like waves. They were linked one with another, and they were, each one of them, and Deborah too, part of the night force that made the sobbing and the laughter. The lightning forked where they willed it, and the thunder cracked as they looked upwards to the sky.

The pool had come alive. The water-lilies had turned to hands, with palms upraised, and in the far corner, usually so still under the green scum, bubbles sucked at the surface, steaming and multiplying as the torrents fell. Everyone crowded to the pool. The phantoms bowed and crouched by the water's edge, and now the woman had set up her turnstile in the middle of the pool, beckoning them once more. Some remnant of a sense of social order rose in Deborah and protested.

'But we've already paid,' she shouted, and remembered a second later that she had passed through free. Must there be duplication? Was the secret world a rainbow, always repeating itself, alighting on another hill when you believed yourself beneath it? No time to think. The phantoms had gone through. The lightning, streaky white, lit the old dead monster tree with his crown of ivy, and because he had no spring now in his joints he could not sway in tribute with the trees and ferns, but had to remain there, rigid, like a crucifix.

'And now . . . and now . . . and now . . .' called Deborah.

The triumph was that she was not afraid, was filled with such wild acceptance . . . She ran into the pool. Her living feet felt the mud and the broken sticks and all the tangle of old weeds, and the water was up to her armpits and her chin. The lilies held her. The rain blinded her. The woman and the turnstile were no more.

'Take me too,' cried the child. 'Don't leave me behind!' In her heart was a savage disenchantment. They had broken their promise, they had left her in the world. The pool that claimed her now was not the pool of secrecy, but dank, dark brackish water choked with scum.

4

'Grandpapa says he's going to have it fenced round,' said Roger. 'It should have been done years ago. A proper fence, then nothing can ever happen. But barrow-loads of shingle tipped in it first. Then it won't be a pool, but just a dewpond. Dewponds aren't dangerous.'

He was looking at her over the edge of her bed. He had risen in status, being the only one of them downstairs, the bearer of tidings good or ill, the go-between. Deborah had been ordered two days in bed.

'I should think by Wednesday,' he went on, 'you'd be able to play cricket. It's not as if you're hurt. People who walk in their sleep are just a bit potty.'

'I did not walk in my sleep,' said Deborah.

'Grandpapa said you must have done,' said Roger. 'It was a good thing that Patch woke him up and he saw you going across the lawn . . .' Then, to show his release from tension, he stood on his hands.

Deborah could see the sky from her bed. It was flat and dull. The day was a summer day that had worked through storm. Agnes came into the room with junket on a tray. She looked important.

'Now run off,' she said to Roger. 'Deborah doesn't want to talk to you. She's supposed to rest.'

Surprisingly, Roger obeyed, and Agnes placed the junket on the table beside the bed. 'You don't feel hungry, I expect,' she said. 'Never mind, you can eat this later, when you fancy it. Have you got a pain? It's usual, the first time.'

'No,' said Deborah.

What had happened to her was personal. They had prepared her for it at school, but nevertheless it was a shock, not to be discussed with Agnes. The woman hovered a moment, in case the child asked questions; but, seeing that none came, she turned and left the room.

Deborah, her cheek on her hand, stared at the empty sky. The heaviness of knowledge lay upon her, a strange, deep sorrow.

'It won't come back,' she thought. 'I've lost the key.'

The hidden world, like ripples on the pool so soon to be filled in and fenced, was out of her reach for ever.

Ann Bridge

THE STATION ROAD

THERE was a little pause when the last speaker finished. We sat round the fire, each occupied with his own thoughts; the mind of each seeking its own solution of the problems raised by the uncanny story to which we had just listened. It was Tredgold who broke the silence.

'That was a good story – very,' he said, meditatively filling a fresh pipe. 'I always wish the psychologists could get us a little nearer to understanding these happenings, or appearances, or whatever you like to call them. Sometimes they look like communications, and sometimes they don't.' He lit a pipe carefully, and then turned round in his chair towards his immediate neighbour. 'I always think that business of your wife's, Doctor, was one of the oddest I ever heard in that line.'

'The train story, eh?' said Dr Freeland. 'Yes, that was a queer business.'

Of course we were urgent with the Doctor to let us have it.

'Very well,' he said, 'you shall.' He also made preparations for a fresh pipe, pushing his chair back a little from the fire.

'It happened when we were living in the country,' began the Doctor, stuffing his tobacco well down into the bowl. 'I had no practice then, but a mixed sort of job – doing hospital work in London two or three days a week, and relieving a man at that big private place at Westlea over the weekends. It was rather an up-and-down sort of life, but it suited him and it suited me.

'One day – it was early in the week, a Tuesday, I think – I got a letter in town from a man I used to know well, saying that he was returning to England by a certain boat, and wished to see me at once when he arrived. I had – well, looked after him to some extent in old days, and he had got into the habit of coming to me for advice and so on; but he had been in Canada for several years, and I had seen very little of him. I had not seen him since my marriage, and he had never seen my wife. He was urgent about the necessity for seeing me immediately, but he did not say what the trouble was.

'Well, I looked up the boat in the paper, and then rang up the London office of the line, and I found that she was due to arrive at Plymouth two days later. In those days the boat trains used to slip a coach at Westbury, and from there a fast train up the other line slipped a couple of coaches at Hedworth

Junction, about seven miles from us. There was an hour's wait at Westbury, but it was far quicker than going right up to town by the boat train and down again.

'So I sent off a wire to this man, to meet him at Plymouth, telling him to come to Hedworth in this way, and I wrote a letter too, bidding him welcome. Also I sent a line to my wife, and told her to meet the 7.11 at Hedworth to fetch off this man. I explained who he was, for I couldn't be sure of getting down myself that night; but my wife is quite accustomed to having casual strangers shot on to her, and I knew she would deal with him well enough till I got home.'

The Doctor paused, lit another match, and puffed at his pipe.

'I must say I thought it a little odd', he went on, 'that he should want so urgently to see me, right off the boat, as it were. But I supposed he was in some trouble, and he had got into the habit, as I said, of coming to me for help. Ah well, it is generally the wrong thing that one thinks odd.

'Well, my wife, like a good sensible creature as she is, thought nothing odd at all. She prepared a room, and a dinner, and then set off in the car to meet the stranger at the Junction. I always rode my old motorbike in and out, so that she did not have to worry about meeting me.

'It was early winter, November, and by the time she started it was black dark. Of course we both knew the station road painfully well – there wasn't a bump in the whole seven miles that we weren't perfectly familiar with. It's a very ordinary bit of south-country road; first a straight stretch between pastures – clay, with oaks in the hedgerows, for about three miles – then a patch of thick woodland; and after that the road climbs over the open downs before it drops to the valley, where the river, the main road, and the railway all run together. It was a cold, dry, cloudy night, with no moon; my wife told me how she noticed, perhaps for the hundredth time, as she drove along, how white the dry road looked, except where the fallen leaves had moistened and stained it; and how the light from her lamps picked out the trunks of the oak trees as she passed them one after another. She was keeping rather a sharp lookout on the foot-passengers, because she half expected that a young brother of hers might be turning up that evening – he used to come, very casually, by any train, and walk out from the Junction with a knapsack.

'So she was, as I say, keeping a particularly sharp lookout, and somewhere about the middle of the first flat straight stretch I spoke of, she saw a man on foot coming towards her, walking on the right-hand side of the road. She slowed down, she said, the least little bit, to have time to see him. It wasn't Jim, her brother; it was a medium-tall man, in a very pale raincoat, which looked almost white in the strong light. She observed him, even when she had seen that it wasn't Jim, with the sort of involuntary precision with which one sometimes takes in unimportant details, and she noticed that there was a dark stain or mark showing up very clearly on the left side of this white trench-coat of his, and that he had a very noticeable cast or twist of his right eye and eyebrow. Of course she paid no attention to this at the time, but just registered the impression automatically, as it were.

'Well, she drove on perhaps another couple of miles, and was well into the stretch of wood – young beeches, planted thick, so that the trunks look like rain in a dim light – when she saw ahead another man walking towards her, again on the right-hand side of the road. She had met one or two cars and cyclists in between – it wasn't a particularly lonely road by any means; but nothing had passed her. She began to look carefully at this man, as before, as soon as she saw him; and as she got nearer, and could see him in increasing detail, she noticed, first, that he too had a very pale raincoat, and then that it had a dark stain on the left side – and then, as she actually passed him, and could see his face clearly, she saw that he had the same cast of the right eye and eyebrow as the man she had passed a couple of miles further back. *It was the same man.*

'She said that the full strangeness of it didn't strike her instantly – she was puzzled, for a few seconds, as to where she had seen him before. Then, as she remembered, she had a pronouncedly disagreeable sensation. She wasted a few moments more trying to make some hypothesis to account for the disquieting facts – it is the way we all treat disquieting facts. But it wouldn't do. She knew she had seen him, she knew where she had seen him; she remembered distinctly that nothing had passed her, going the same way as herself. She could not cheat herself into the belief that it wasn't the same man; her involuntary and spontaneous attention, in both cases, had registered too clear and sharp an impression for that.

'She began to feel very uncomfortable indeed. It was then that she looked back. But in the woods the road was no longer straight – it curved a good deal, and quick as her thoughts had passed, she had covered a good stretch; the man would anyhow, as she realized, have been out of sight. The road behind her was, of course, empty, between the chalky banks and grey walls of trees – what she could see of it, for the road behind your lights is very black.

'She drove on. But she was now perceptibly glad to meet another car or two, and she had a strong desire not to see any more foot-passengers. Nor, after that first pause, had she any further wish to look back – somehow the blackness of the road behind her, in that one glance, had begun to let something like horror in on her.

'She pushed on at a good pace, shoving the car up the long hill on to the down. Right at the top there is a signpost at four crossroads. Her light picked up the white post at a good distance, and she was glad to see it, for it meant that her drive was nearly over – there remained only the drop down to the valley and the station. But the next moment she saw that there was a man under the signpost. She stood on the accelerator, determined, in a panic-stricken way, not to look at him. But she had to look – she couldn't help herself; and she saw, as she rushed past, in the pitiless light, again the white raincoat, the dark stain on the left side, the twisted eyebrow, and the cast eye.

'This time she was terrified. For a little while, she said, she quite lost control of herself, and raced along blindly, her one idea to get to lights and faces and human speech. She found herself descending the hill at a perfectly reckless pace, and the sense of actual physical danger pulled her together. There is a bad turn at the pitch of the hill; she managed to slow down for that, and drove on, more reasonably, to the station.

'She left the car outside, and fairly ran in. It was ten minutes past seven by the station clock. The lobby was warm and brightly lit, passengers and porters were moving about, and the whole place was so *normal* that it steadied her. The old station-master, who was a great ally of ours, came up and began to talk to her, and his fatherly chat added to her comfort. He asked whom she had come to meet, and she told him; the reflection that she would have a companion on the drive home made her almost at ease. They went out together on to the platform and stood waiting for the express. It was fairly late, but at 7.32 – the station-master took out his watch and checked the fact aloud – it came roaring through, and the slipped coaches, grinding and groaning on the metals, came to a stop well up the platform. "Now we'll find your gentleman for you, ma'am," said the old boy.

'Well, they didn't find him. The coaches emptied themselves, and people collected their luggage and began to leave the station in the waiting cars, or afoot; but no one appeared to be hanging about in the inquiring way, so easy to spot, of the total stranger who hopes to be met. They were puzzled. The station-master consulted the guard who took charge of the slip coaches from Westbury to Hedworth, and stopped with them at the latter place. "This lady's come to meet a gentleman off the boat train – should have taken this train at Westbury." What was the name, the guard wanted to know? "Macmurdo," says my wife. Oh, yes, he was there all right; the guard had his stuff in the van. They went to look, and there, sure enough, were three boxes with his name, and the steamer labels. But there was by this time no one on the platform but themselves and the porters. "Well, that's a puzzle," said the guard, lifting his hat and rubbing his head. "I saw him at Westbury, took 'is stuff and talked to him. An American gentleman, isn't he? Talked like one, anyway." Then the blow fell, as it were. My wife was up to now merely rather annoyed and bored by the man's not turning up; she was standing quite at ease, under the lamps, when the guard called out to the porter who had been collecting tickets as the passengers went out: "George, seen a gentleman go out in a white mackintosh, with a twitch in 'is right eye?"

"*What* do you say?" she said to the guard – so sharply that she saw his surprise. But she was too agitated to care. "*What* do you say he was like?" she repeated.

"'Why, he's a tallish gentleman, isn't 'e?" said the guard. "And he had on a whitish coat, and this twitch in 'is eye; sort of affliction – I noticed 'im particular. That's right, isn't it?"

'Of course it was – the horror lay just in the guard having seen so precisely what she had seen. She was on the point of asking if the white mackintosh had a dark stain on the left side, when she remembered that for the purposes of a sane world, a world of guards and porters, she hadn't seen the man at all. She couldn't have, you see. The guard had seen him at Westbury, and no earthly power could have got him on to the station road, where she had seen him, before seven o'clock. For the second time that night she pulled herself together, and asked the proper, rational questions. Was he sure he had seen him get into the train? How did he know his name, that it was the man? The guard was quite positive and clear. The express was late in leaving Westbury, and this gentleman come fidgeting up to him and asked when the train would start. "'E gave me 'is luggage for the van, so I saw the name; and 'e asked for the refreshment room, and I showed 'im. We had quite a chat – he was very free, like most American gentlemen, in his talk. I *should* remember him," said the guard, "for he gave me half a Bradbury for that. A great roll of notes he had on him."

'Well, there was no doubt about it – Macmurdo she had clearly seen; but you can guess that my wife took no very active part in the search of the empty carriages that followed. They found nothing, though one carriage was a litter of papers which the guard tossed over a little, carelessly. Of Macmurdo there was no trace, nor did my wife expect to find him. She guessed him to be in another world. Poor soul, he was, sure enough. Next morning when the slipped coaches were cleaned, blood-stains were found on the seat and floor of the carriage which had been full of scattered newspapers, and before twenty-four hours were out a gang of plate-layers, making their daily round of that section, came on the corpse of a man lying halfway down the embankment of the line, between Westbury and Armlea. He had fallen with violence, but the fall was not the cause of death; a great stain of blood on the left side of his pale raincoat marked where he had been cruelly stabbed – murdered, there could be little doubt, for the sake of the "great roll of notes" which the guard had noticed when he got his tip. His watch, ring, and so on had not been touched, nor anything but his money; and among the papers which easily identified him was my letter of welcome, telling him his train.'

The Doctor paused, and knocked out his pipe against the grate.

'That letter took me to the inquest,' he went on, 'so I heard all that the police could put together. He was stabbed and thrown out at some time between 6.40, when the train left Westbury – late, as you remember – and when it reached Armlea about 7.17. Armlea was the one stop between Westbury and Hedworth; and my wife had been at the Junction for some time when the train left that place.'

'That is where the murderer must have got out, of course,' someone put in.

'That was the supposition,' said the Doctor, 'but it was confirmed afterwards.'

'How?' asked five voices at once.

'That's the most curious part of all,' said the Doctor. 'Over a year later my wife was at the Junction again, in the evening, to meet me, this time. She's a courageous creature, and she did not let her distaste for the station road after dark keep her off it for long. "Poor soul," she said more than once, "he wanted help, and he was coming to you for it, as usual – that was all. I wish I *could* have helped him." Well, there she was at the station, and this time the down train was late. She was sitting in the waiting-room, looking at the paper, just under the lamp, when a man came in. She looked up, as one does, when she heard him, so that the light fell, I suppose, on her face. There was no one else in the room. Well, when this man saw her she said that his whole face changed – "went ghastly" was her expression – he almost staggered back a step or two, and then turned and went out like a man who had received a blow. She was rather upset, as you may suppose, at producing this effect on a total stranger, and actually went and tried to look at herself in one of those faded pictures of ocean liners which always hang in waiting-rooms. She could find nothing odd in her appearance, so she went on reading the paper. Presently something made her look up, and there was the man again, peering in through the window which gave on to the platform. He went on hanging about for a bit, and at last came in, looking shockingly disordered, and said that he must speak to her. She made him sit down, for he was shaking in every limb, and there and then he made a full confession of the murder of my poor friend. My wife thought at first that he was raving, but there could be no mistake: he gave the name, the date, and the time of the train. He had been desperate for money, had seen the notes when Macmurdo tipped the guard at Westbury, and on a sudden impulse had committed the murder. He got out at Armlea, as the police had surmised, and got clear away.'

'But why in the world—' someone began.

'Did he tell my wife?' said the Doctor.

'"Exactly. She asked him that, and you must make what you can of his answer. "You should tell this to the police," she said. "Why have you told me?"

'"Because *you were there!*" he said.

'"How do you mean, 'there'?" says my wife, startled.

'"You came and looked at me," said the poor wretch, trembling like a leaf. "Three times, while I was putting the papers about, before I got to Armlea, you stood at the door and looked in at me. You don't suppose I could forget your face?" he almost shrieked. "I knew that one day I should see you again, and then I should have to tell you."'

The Doctor paused again, but this time nobody said anything.

'There,' he said after a few moments, 'make what you like of that.'

We asked what became of the murderer.

'Oh, we handed him over to the police,' said the Doctor. 'One could do nothing else, and he wished it. But before he could be tried he went completely insane, and he's in the asylum now, I believe.'

'And what do you make of it yourself, Doctor?' Tredgold asked, after another pause.

The Doctor leaned forward and knocked out his pipe for the last time against the grate.

'God knows!' he said.

Penelope Lively

❧

BLACK DOG

JOHN Case came home one summer evening to find his wife huddled in the corner of the sofa with the sitting-room curtains drawn. She said there was a black dog in the garden, looking at her through the window. Her husband put his briefcase in the hall and went outside. There was no dog; a blackbird fled shrieking across the lawn and next door someone was using a mower. He did not see how any dog could get into the garden: the fences at either side were five feet high and there was a wall at the far end. He returned to the house and pointed this out to his wife, who shrugged and continued to sit hunched in the corner of the sofa. He found her there again the next evening and at the weekend she refused to go outside and sat for much of the time watching the window.

The daughters came, big girls with jobs in insurance companies, wardrobes full of bright clothes and twenty-thousand-pound mortgages. They stood over Brenda Case and said she should get out more. She should go to evening classes, they said, join a health club, do a language course, learn upholstery, go jogging, take driving lessons. And Brenda Case sat at the kitchen table and nodded. She quite agreed, it would be a good thing to find a new interest – jogging, upholstery, French; yes, she said, she must pull herself together, and it was indeed up to her in the last resort, they were quite right. When they had gone she drew the sitting-room curtains again and sat on the sofa staring at a magazine they had brought. The magazine was full of recipes the daughters had said she must try; there were huge bright glossy photographs of puddings crested with Alpine peaks of cream, of dark glistening casseroles and salads like an artist's palette. The magazine costed each recipe; a four-course dinner for six worked out at £3.89 a head. It also had articles advising her on life insurance, treatment for breast cancer and how to improve her love-making.

John Case became concerned about his wife. She had always been a good housekeeper; now, they began to run out of things. When one evening there was nothing but cold meat and cheese for supper he protested. She said she had not been able to shop because it had rained all day; on rainy days the dog was always outside, waiting for her.

· 88 ·

The daughters came again and spoke severely to their mother. They talked to their father separately, in different tones, proposing an autumn holiday in Portugal or the Canaries, a new three-piece for the sitting-room, a musquash coat.

John Case discussed the whole thing with his wife, reasonably. He did this one evening after he had driven the Toyota into the garage, walked over to the front door and found it locked from within. Brenda, opening it, apologized; the dog had been round at the front today, she said, sitting in the middle of the path.

He began by saying lightly that dogs have not been known to stand up on their hind legs and open doors. And in any case, he continued, there is no dog. No dog at all. The dog is something you are imagining. I have asked all the neighbours; nobody has seen a big black dog. Nobody round here owns a big black dog. There is no evidence of a dog. So you must stop going on about this dog because it does not exist. 'What is the matter?' he asked, gently. 'Something must be the matter. Would you like to go away for a holiday? Shall we have the house redecorated?'

Brenda Case listened to him. He was sitting on the sofa, with his back to the window. She sat listening carefully to him and from time to time her eyes strayed from his face to the lawn beyond, in the middle of which the dog sat, its tongue hanging out and its yellow eyes glinting. She said she would go away for a holiday if he wished, and she would be perfectly willing for the house to be redecorated. Her husband talked about travel agents and decorating firms and once he got up and walked over to the window to inspect the condition of the paintwork; the dog, Brenda saw, continued to sit there, its eyes always on her.

They went to Marrakesh for ten days. Men came and turned the kitchen from primrose to eau-de-nil and the hallway from magnolia to parchment. September became October and Brenda Case fetched from the attic a big gnarled walking stick that was a relic of a trip to the Tyrol many years ago; she took this with her every time she went out of the house, which nowadays was not often. Inside the house, it was always somewhere near her – its end protruding from under the sofa, or hooked over the arm of her chair.

The daughters shook their tousled heads at their mother, towering over her in their baggy fashionable trousers and their big gay jackets. It's not fair on Dad, they said, can't you see that? You've only got one life, they said sternly, and Brenda Case replied that she realized that, she did indeed. Well then... said the daughters, one on each side of her, bigger than her, brighter, louder, always saying what they meant, going straight to the point and no nonsense, competent with income-tax returns and contemptuous of muddle.

When she was alone, Brenda Case kept doors and windows closed at all times. Occasionally, when the dog was not there, she would open the upstairs windows to air the bedrooms and the bathroom; she would stand with the curtains blowing, taking in great gulps and draughts. Downstairs, of course, she could not risk this, because the dog was quite unpredictable; it would be absent all day, and then suddenly there it would be squatting by the fence, or leaning hard up against the patio doors, sprung from nowhere. She would draw the curtains, resigned, or move to another room and endure the knowledge of its presence on the other side of the wall, a few yards away. When it was there she would sit doing nothing, staring straight ahead of her; silent and patient. When it was gone she moved around the house, prepared meals, listened a little to the radio, and sometimes took the old photograph albums from the bottom drawer of the bureau in the sitting-room. In these albums the daughters slowly mutated from swaddled bundles topped with monkey faces and spiky hair to chunky toddlers and then to spindly-limbed little girls in matching pinafores. They played on Cornish beaches or posed on the lawn, holding her hand (that same lawn on which the dog now sat on its hunkers). In the photographs, she looked down at them, smiling, and they gazed up at her or held out objects for her inspection – a flower, a seashell. Her husband was also in the photographs; a smaller man than now, it seemed, with a curiously vulnerable look, as though surprised in a moment of privacy. Looking at herself, Brenda saw a pretty young woman who seemed vaguely familiar, like some relative not encountered for many years.

John Case realized that nothing had been changed by Marrakesh and redecorating. He tried putting the walking stick back up in the attic; his wife brought it down again. If he opened the patio doors she would simply close them as soon as he had left the room. Sometimes he saw her looking over his shoulder into the garden with an expression on her face that chilled him. He asked her, one day, what she thought the dog would do if it got into the house; she was silent for a moment and then said quietly she supposed it would eat her.

He said he could not understand, he simply did not understand, what could be wrong. It was not, he said, as though they had a thing to worry about. He gently pointed out that she wanted for nothing. It's not that we have to count the pennies any more, he said, not like in the old days.

'When we were young,' said Brenda Case. 'When the girls were babies.'

'Right. It's not like that now, is it?' He indicated the 24-inch colour TV set, the video, the stereo, the microwave oven, the English Rose fitted kitchen, the bathroom with separate shower. He reminded her of the BUPA membership, the index-linked pension, the shares and dividends. Brenda agreed that it was not, it most certainly was not.

The daughters came with their boyfriends, nicely spoken confident young men in very clean shirts, who talked to Brenda of their work in firms selling computers and Japanese cameras while the girls took John into the garden and discussed their mother.

'The thing is, she's becoming agoraphobic.'

'She thinks she sees this black dog,' said John Case.

'We know,' said the eldest daughter. 'But that, frankly, is neither here nor there. It's a mechanism, simply. A ploy. Like children do. One has to get to the root of it, that's the thing.'

'It's her age,' said the youngest.

'Of course it's her age,' snorted the eldest. 'But it's also her. She was always inclined to be negative, but this is ridiculous.'

'Negative?' said John Case. He tried to remember his wife – his wives – who – one of whom – he could see inside the house, beyond the glass of the patio window, looking out at him from between two young men he barely knew. The reflections of his daughters, his strapping prosperous daughters, were superimposed upon their mother, so that she looked at him through the cerise and orange and yellow of their clothes.

'Negative. A worrier. Look on the bright side, *I* say, but that's not Mum, is it?'

'I wouldn't have said . . .' he began.

'She's unmotivated,' said the youngest. 'That's the real trouble. No job, no nothing. It's a generation problem, too.'

'I'm trying . . .' their father began.

'We know, Dad, we know. But the thing is, she needs help. This isn't something you can handle all on your own. She'll have to see someone.'

'No way', said the youngest, 'will we get Mum into therapy.'

'Dad can take her to the surgery,' said the eldest. 'For starters.'

The doctor – the new doctor, there was always a new doctor – was about the same age as her daughters, Brenda Case saw. Once upon a time doctors had been older men, fatherly and reliable. This one was good-looking, in the manner of men in knitting-pattern photographs. He sat looking at her, quite kindly, and she told him how she was feeling. In so far as this was possible.

When she had finished he tapped a pencil on his desk. 'Yes,' he said. 'Yes, I see.' And then he went on, 'There doesn't seem to be any very specific trouble, does there, Mrs Case?'

She agreed.

'How do you think you would define it yourself?'

She thought. At last she said that she supposed there was nothing wrong with her that wasn't wrong with – well, everyone.

'Quite,' said the doctor busily, writing now on his pad. 'That's the sensible way to look at things. So I'm giving you this . . . Three a day . . . Come back and see me in two weeks.'

When she had come out John Case asked to see the doctor for a moment. He explained that he was worried about his wife. The doctor nodded sympathetically. John told the doctor about the black dog, apologetically, and the doctor looked reflective for a moment and then said, 'Your wife is fifty-four.'

John Case agreed. She was indeed fifty-four.

'Exactly,' said the doctor. 'So I think we can take it that with some care and understanding these difficulties will . . . disappear. I've given her something,' he said, confidently; John Case smiled back. That was that.

'It will go away,' said John Case to his wife, firmly. He was not entirely sure what he meant, but it did not do, he felt sure, to be irresolute. She looked at him without expression.

Brenda Case swallowed each day the pills that the doctor had given her. She believed in medicines and doctors, had always found that aspirin cured a headache and used to frequent the surgery with the girls when they were small. She was prepared for a miracle. For the first few days it did seem to her just possible that the dog was growing a little smaller but after a week she realized that it was not. She continued to take the pills and when at the end of a fortnight she told the doctor that there was no change he said that these things took time, one had to be patient. She looked at him, this young man in his swivel chair on the other side of a cluttered desk, and knew that whatever was to be done would not be done by him, or by cheerful yellow pills like children's sweets.

The daughters came, to inspect and admonish. She said that yes, she had seen the doctor again, and yes, she was feeling rather more . . . herself. She showed them the new sewing-machine with many extra attachments that she had not used and when they left she watched them go down the front path to their cars, swinging their bags and shouting at each other, and saw the dog step aside for them, wagging its tail. When they had gone she opened the door again and stood there for a few minutes, looking at it, and the dog, five yards away, looked back, not moving.

The next day she took the shopping trolley and set off for the shops. As she opened the front gate she saw the dog come out from the shadow of the fence but she did not turn back. She continued down the street, although she could feel it behind her, keeping its distance. She spoke in a friendly way to a couple of neighbours, did her shopping and returned to the house, and all the while the dog was there, twenty paces off. As she walked to the front door she could hear the click of its claws on the pavement and had to steel herself so hard not to turn round that when she got inside she was bathed in sweat and shaking all over. When her husband came home that evening he thought her in a funny mood; she asked for a glass of sherry and later she suggested they put a record on instead of watching TV – *West Side Story* or another of those shows they went to years ago.

He was surprised at the change in her. She began to go out daily, and although in the evenings she often appeared to be exhausted, as though she had been climbing mountains instead of walking suburban streets, she was curiously calm. Admittedly, she had not appeared agitated before, but her stillness had not been natural; now, he sensed a difference. When the daughters telephoned he reported their mother's condition and listened to their complacent comments; that stuff usually did the trick, they said, all the medics were using it nowadays, they'd always known Mum would be OK soon. But when he put the telephone down and returned to his wife in the sitting-room he found himself looking at her uncomfortably. There was an alertness about her that worried him; later, he thought he heard something outside and went to look. He could see nothing at either the front or the back and his wife continued to read a magazine. When he sat down again she looked across at him with a faint smile.

She had started by meeting its eyes, its yellow eyes. And thus she had learned that she could stop it, halt its patient shadowing of her, leave it sitting on the pavement or the garden path. She began to leave the front door ajar, to open the patio window. She could not say what would happen next, knew only that this was inevitable. She no longer sweated or shook; she did not glance behind her when she was outside, and within she hummed to herself as she moved from room to room.

John Case, returning home on an autumn evening, stepped out of the car and saw light streaming through the open front door. He thought he heard his wife speaking to someone in the house. When he came into the kitchen, though, she was alone. He said, 'The front door was open,' and she replied that she must have left it so by mistake. She was busy with a saucepan at the stove and in the corner of the room, her husband saw, was a large dog basket towards which her glance occasionally strayed.

He made no comment. He went back into the hall, hung up his coat and was startled suddenly by his own face, caught unawares in the mirror by the hatstand and seeming like someone else's – that of a man both older and more burdened than he knew himself to be. He stood staring at it for a few moments and then took a step back towards the kitchen. He could hear the gentle chunking sound of his wife's wooden spoon stirring something in the saucepan and then, he thought, the creak of wickerwork.

He turned sharply and went into the sitting-room. He crossed to the window and looked out. He saw the lawn, blackish in the dusk, disappearing into darkness. He switched on the outside lights and flooded it all with an artificial glow – the grass, the little flight of steps up to the patio and the flowerbed at the top of them, from which he had tidied away the spent summer annuals at the weekend. The bare earth was marked all over, he now saw, with what appeared to be animal footprints, and as he stood gazing it seemed to him that he heard the pad of paws on the carpet behind him. He stood for a long while before at last he turned round.

E. Nesbit

NO. 17

I YAWNED. I could not help it. But the flat, inexorable voice went on.
  'Speaking from the journalistic point of view – I may tell you,
gentlemen, that I once occupied the position of advertisement editor to the
Bradford Woollen Goods Journal – and speaking from that point of view, I hold
the opinion that all the best ghost stories have been written over and over
again; and if I were to leave the road and return to a literary career I should
never be led away by ghosts. Realism's what's wanted nowadays, if you want
to be up to date.'

The large commercial paused for breath.

'You never can tell with the public,' said the lean, elderly traveller; 'it's like
in the fancy business. You never know how it's going to be. Whether it's a
clockwork ostrich or samite silk or a particular shape of shaded glass novelty
or a tobacco-box got up to look like a raw chop, you never know your luck.'

'That depends on who you are,' said the dapper man in the corner by the
fire. 'If you've got the right push about you, you can make things go, whether
it's a clockwork kitten or imitation meat, and with stories, I take it, it's just
the same – realism or ghost stories. But the best ghost story would be the
realest one, *I* think.'

The large commercial had got his breath.

'I don't believe in ghost stories myself,' he was saying with earnest
dullness; 'but there was rather a queer thing happened to a second cousin of
an aunt of mine by marriage – a very sensible woman with no nonsense about
her. And the soul of truth and honour. I shouldn't have believed it if she had
been one of your flighty, fanciful sort.'

'Don't tell us the story,' said the melancholy man who travelled in
hardware; 'you'll make us afraid to go to bed.'

The well-meant effort failed. The large commercial went on, as I had
known he would; his words overflowed his mouth, as his person overflowed
his chair. I turned my mind to my own affairs, coming back to the
commercial room in time to hear the summing-up.

'The doors were all locked, and she was quite certain she saw a tall, white
figure glide past her and vanish. I wouldn't have believed it if . . .' And so on

da capo, from 'if she hadn't been the second cousin' to the 'soul of truth and honour'.

I yawned again.

'Very good story,' said the smart little man by the fire. He was a traveller, as the rest of us were; his presence in the room told us that much. He had been rather silent during dinner, and afterwards, while the red curtains were being drawn and the red-and-black cloth laid between the glasses and the decanters and the mahogany, he had quietly taken the best chair in the warmest corner. We had got our letters written and the large traveller had been boring us for some time before I even noticed that there was a best chair and that this silent, bright-eyed, dapper, fair man had secured it.

'Very good story,' he said; 'but it's not what I call realism. You don't tell us half enough, sir. You don't say when it happened or where, or the time of year, or what colour your aunt's second cousin's hair was. Nor yet you don't tell us what it was she saw, nor what the room was like where she saw it, nor why she saw it, nor what happened afterwards. And I shouldn't like to breathe a word against anybody's aunt by marriage's cousin, first or second, but I must say I like a story about what a man's seen *himself*.'

'So do I,' the large commercial snorted, 'when I hear it.'

He blew his nose like a trumpet of defiance.

'But', said the rabbit-faced man, 'we know nowadays, what with the advance of science and all that sort of thing, we know there aren't any such things as ghosts. They're hallucinations; that's what they are – hallucinations.'

'Don't seem to matter what you call them,' the dapper one urged. 'If you see a thing that looks as real as you do yourself, a thing that makes your blood run cold and turns you sick and silly with fear – well, call it ghost, or call it hallucination, or call it Tommy Dodd; it isn't the *name* that matters.'

The elderly commercial coughed and said, 'You might call it another name. You might call it—'

'No, you mightn't,' said the little man, briskly; 'not when the man it happened to had been a teetotal Bond of Joy for five years and is to this day.'

'Why don't you tell us the story?' I asked.

'I might be willing,' he said, 'if the rest of the company were agreeable. Only I warn you it's not that sort-of-a-kind-of-a-somebody-fancied-they-saw-a-sort-of-a-kind-of-a-something-sort of a story. No, sir. Everything I'm going to tell you is plain and straightforward and as clear as a timetable – clearer than some. But I don't much like telling it, especially to people who don't believe in ghosts.'

Several of us said we did believe in ghosts. The heavy man snorted and looked at his watch. And the man in the best chair began.

'Turn the gas down a bit, will you? Thanks. Did any of you know Herbert Hatteras? He was on this road a good many years. No? Well, never mind. He was a good chap, I believe, with good teeth and a black whisker. But I didn't know him myself. He was before my time. Well, this that I'm going to tell you about happened at a certain commercial hotel. I'm not going to give it a name, because that sort of thing gets about, and, in every other respect, it's a good house and reasonable, and we all have our living to get. It was just a good, ordinary, old-fashioned commercial hotel, as it might be this. And I've often used it since, though they've never put me in that room again. Perhaps they shut it up after what happened.

'Well, the beginning of it was, I came across an old schoolfellow; in Boulter's Lock one Sunday it was, I remember. Jones was his name, Ted Jones. We both had canoes. We had tea at Marlow, and we got talking about this and that and old times and old mates; and do you remember Jim, and what's become of Tom, and so on. Oh, you know. And I happened to ask after his brother, Fred by name. And Ted turned pale and almost dropped his cup, and he said, "You don't mean to say you haven't heard?" "No," says I, mopping up the tea he'd slopped over with my handkerchief. "No; what?" I said.

'"It was horrible," he said. "They wired for me, and I saw him afterwards. Whether he'd done it himself or not, nobody knows; but they'd found him lying on the floor with his throat cut." No cause could be assigned for the rash act, Ted told me. I asked him where it had happened, and he told me the name of this hotel – I'm not going to name it. And when I'd sympathized with him and drawn him out about old times and poor old Fred being such a good old sort and all that, I asked him what the room was like. I always like to know what the places look like where things happen.

'No, there wasn't anything specially rum about the room, only that it had a French bed with red curtains in a sort of alcove; and a large mahogany wardrobe as big as a hearse, with a glass door; and, instead of a swing-glass, a carved, black-framed glass screwed up against the wall between the windows, and a picture of "Belshazzar's Feast" over the mantelpiece. I beg your pardon?' He stopped, for the heavy commercial had opened his mouth and shut it again.

'I thought you were going to say something,' the dapper man went on. 'Well, we talked about other things and parted, and I thought no more about it till business brought me to – but I'd better not name the town either – and I found my firm had marked this very hotel – where poor Fred had met his death, you know – for me to put up at. And I had to put up there too, because of their addressing everything to me there. And, anyhow, I expect I should have gone there out of curiosity.

'No, I didn't believe in ghosts in those days. I was like you, sir.' He nodded amiably to the large commercial.

'The house was very full, and we were quite a large party in the room – very pleasant company, as it might be tonight; and we got talking of ghosts – just as it might be us. And there was a chap in glasses, sitting just over there, I remember – an old hand on the road, he was; and he said, just as it might be any of you, "I don't believe in ghosts, but I wouldn't care to sleep in Number Seventeen, for all that"; and, of course, we asked him why. "Because," said he, very short, "that's why."

'But when we'd persuaded him a bit, he told us.

'"Because that's the room where chaps cut their throats," he said. "There was a chap called Bert Hatteras began it. They found him weltering in his gore. And since that, every man that's slept there's been found with his throat cut."

'I asked him how many had slept there. "Well, only two beside the first," he said; "they shut it up then." "Oh, did they?" said I. "Well, they've opened it again. Number Seventeen's my room!"

'I tell you those chaps looked at me.

'"But you aren't going to *sleep* in it?" one of them said. And I explained that I didn't pay half a dollar for a bedroom to keep awake in.

'"I suppose it's press of business has made them open it up again," the chap in spectacles said. "It's a very mysterious affair. There's some secret horror about that room that we don't understand," he said, "and I'll tell you another queer thing. Every one of those poor chaps was a commercial gentleman. That's what I don't like about it. There was Bert Hatteras – he was the first, and a chap called Jones – Frederick Jones, and then Donald Overshaw – a Scotsman he was, and travelled in child's underclothing."

'Well, we sat there and talked a bit, and if I hadn't been a Bond of Joy, I don't know that I mightn't have exceeded, gentlemen – yes, positively exceeded; for the more I thought about it the less I liked the thought of Number Seventeen. I hadn't noticed the room particularly, except to see that the furniture had been changed since poor Fred's time. So I just slipped out, by and by, and I went out to the little glass case under the arch where the booking-clerk sits – just like here, that hotel was – and I said, "Look here, Miss; haven't you another room empty except Seventeen?"

'"No," she said; "I don't think so."

'"Then what's that?" I said, and pointed to a key hanging on the board, the only one left.

'"Oh," she said, "that's Sixteen."

'"Anyone in Sixteen?" I said. "Is it a comfortable room?"

'"No," said she. "Yes; quite comfortable. It's next door to yours – much the same class of room."

'"Then I'll have Sixteen, if you've no objection," I said, and went back to the others, feeling very clever.

'When I went up to bed I locked my door, and, though I didn't believe in ghosts, I wished Seventeen wasn't next door to me, and I wished there wasn't a door between the two rooms, though the door was locked right enough and the key on my side. I'd only got the one candle besides the two on the dressing-table, which I hadn't lighted; and I got my collar and tie off before I noticed that the furniture in my new room was the furniture out of Number Seventeen; French bed with red curtains, mahogany wardrobe as big as a hearse, and the carved mirror over the dressing-table between the two windows, and "Belshazzar's Feast" over the mantelpiece. So that, though I'd not got the *room* where the commercial gentlemen had cut their throats, I'd got the *furniture* out of it. And for a moment I thought that was worse than the other. When I thought of what that furniture could tell, if it could speak . . .

'It was a silly thing to do – but we're all friends here and I don't mind owning up – I looked under the bed and I looked inside the hearse-wardrobe and I looked in a sort of narrow cupboard there was, where a body could have stood upright—'

'A body?' I repeated.

'A man, I mean. You see, it seemed to me that either these poor chaps had been murdered by someone who hid himself in Number Seventeen to do it, or else there was something there that frightened them into cutting their throats; and upon my soul, I can't tell you which idea I liked least!'

He paused, and filled his pipe very deliberately. 'Go on,' someone said. And he went on.

'Now, you'll observe', he said, 'that all I've told you up to the time of my going to bed that night's just hearsay. So I don't ask you to believe it – though the three coroners' inquests would be enough to stagger most chaps, I should say. Still, what I'm going to tell you now's *my* part of the story – what happened to me myself in that room.'

He paused again, holding the pipe in his hand, unlighted.

There was a silence, which I broke.

'Well, what *did* happen?' I asked.

'I had a bit of a struggle with myself,' he said. 'I reminded myself it was not that room, but the next one that it had happened in. I smoked a pipe or two and read the morning paper, advertisements and all. And at last I went to bed. I left the candle burning, though; I own that.'

'Did you sleep?' I asked.

'Yes. I slept. Sound as a top. I was awakened by a soft tapping on my door. I sat up. I don't think I've ever been so frightened in my life. But I made myself say, "Who's there?" in a whisper. Heaven knows I never expected anyone to answer. The candle had gone out and it was pitch-dark. There was a quiet murmur and a shuffling sound outside. And no one answered. I tell you I hadn't expected anyone to. But I cleared my throat and cried out, "Who's there?" in a real out-loud voice. And "Me, sir," said a voice. "Shaving-water, sir; six o'clock, sir."

'It was the chambermaid.'

A movement of relief ran round our circle.

'I don't think much of your story,' said the large commercial.

'You haven't heard it yet,' said the story-teller, drily. 'It was six o'clock on a winter's morning, and pitch-dark. My train went at seven. I got up and began to dress. My one candle wasn't much use. I lighted the two on the dressing-table to see to shave by. There wasn't any shaving-water outside my door, after all. And the passage was as black as a coal-hole. So I started to shave with cold water; one has to sometimes, you know. I'd gone over my face and I was just going lightly round under my chin, when I saw something move in the looking-glass. I mean something that moved was reflected in the looking-glass. The big door of the wardrobe had swung open, and by a sort of double reflection I could see the French bed with the red curtains. On the edge of it sat a man in his shirt and trousers – a man with black hair and whiskers, with the most awful look of despair and fear on his face that I've ever seen or dreamt of. I stood paralysed, watching him in the mirror. I could not have turned round to save my life. Suddenly he laughed. It was a horrid, silent laugh, and showed all his teeth. They were very white and even. And the next moment he had cut his throat from ear to ear, there before my eyes. Did you ever see a man cut his throat? The bed was all white before.'

The story-teller had laid down his pipe, and he passed his hand over his face before he went on.

'When I could look round I did. There was no one in the room. The bed was as white as ever. Well, that's all,' he said, abruptly, 'except that now, of course, I understood how these poor chaps had come by their deaths. They'd all seen this horror – the ghost of the first poor chap, I suppose – Bert Hatteras, you know; and with the shock their hands must have slipped and their throats got cut before they could stop themselves. Oh! by the way, when I looked at my watch it was two o'clock; there hadn't been any chambermaid at all. I must have dreamed that. But I didn't dream the other. Oh! and one thing more. It was the same room. They hadn't changed the room, they'd only changed the number. *It was the same room!*'

'Look here,' said the heavy man, 'the room you've been talking about. *My* room's Sixteen. And it's got that same furniture in it as what you describe, and the same picture and all.'

'Oh, has it?' said the story-teller, a little uncomfortable, it seemed. 'I'm sorry. But the cat's out of the bag now, and it can't be helped. Yes, it *was* this house I was speaking of. I suppose they've opened the room again. But you don't believe in ghosts; *you'll* be all right.'

'Yes,' said the heavy man, and presently got up and left the room.

'He's gone to see if he can get his room changed. You see if he hasn't,' said the rabbit-faced man, 'and I don't wonder.'

The heavy man came back and settled into his chair.

'I could do with a drink,' he said, reaching to the bell.

'I'll stand some punch, gentlemen, if you'll allow me,' said our dapper story-teller. 'I rather pride myself on my punch. I'll step out to the bar and get what I need for it.'

'I thought he said he was a teetotaller,' said the heavy traveller when he had gone. And then our voices buzzed like a hive of bees. When our story-teller came in again we turned on him – half-a-dozen of us at once – and spoke.

'One at a time,' he said gently. 'I didn't quite catch what you said.'

'We want to know,' I said, 'how it was – if seeing that ghost made all those chaps cut their throats by startling them when they were shaving – how was it *you* didn't cut *your* throat when you saw it?'

'I should have,' he answered gravely, 'without the slightest doubt – I should have cut my throat, only,' he glanced at our heavy friend, 'I always shave with a safety razor. I travel in them,' he added slowly, and bisected a lemon.

'But – but,' said the large man, when he could speak through our uproar, 'I've gone and given up my room.'

'Yes,' said the dapper man, squeezing the lemon, 'I've just had my things moved into it. It's the best room in the house. I always think it worth while to take a little pains to secure it.'

Pamela Sewell

❧

PRELUDE

ELAINE smiled as she opened the front door. 'All right, then. It's in the dining-room.'

The familiar sight of her daughter's dark curls as she ran into the house, made her stomach tighten: Lori was all she had in the world, since her husband had died six years ago. Just before Lori's birth . . . She shook her head, willing the tears away. There had been another side to Yves, after all; and in the circumstances, it was best that it had happened.

A delighted squeal from the dining-room brought back the smile to her face: she had had a feeling that Lori would be pleased. Her daughter had shown signs of her father's musical talent from an early age, quickly able to remember and hum songs and tunes, even before she could speak. It had been only natural that her teachers would notice it; and so they had persuaded Elaine to let Lori have piano lessons. Part of Elaine had shrivelled at the idea, remembering Yves; but the sensible side of her knew that she shouldn't deprive the child for the father's faults.

So Elaine had agreed; when she heard how quickly Lori was taking to her lessons, she secretly decided to buy an upright for her child to practise upon. She had only been able to afford a second-hand piano – there had been very little left from Yves's estate, despite moving to a much smaller house, and her salary did not run to luxuries – but it had seemed in good condition. And it had been remarkably cheap.

She sauntered casually into the dining-room. 'Like it?'

The child's face gleamed. 'Can I play now?'

'Of course you can! It's for you, you know. And I expect to hear you practising!' Elaine hugged her daughter, and set her gently on the stool. As she lifted the lid, Lori's face took on an almost magical expression: tentatively, she put a finger on a key, and pressed.

The note was pure: the child beamed with delight, and tried another. And another, and another . . .

'I'll leave you to it!' Elaine laughed, and walked out of the room, leaving behind the cacophony from her daughter's fingers.

Some time later, she walked back into the hall, head on one side: surely that was not Lori playing? She had heard the child practise at school, from the early attempts at 'Three Blind Mice' and the usual scales, to '*Alouette*' and simple harmonies – but this . . . She shook her head. No, it couldn't be. Lori must have tired of practising, and started playing her favourite record. Funny, it had been her father's favourite, too: Chopin's 'Raindrop' prelude. It always reminded Elaine of Sundays – Sundays when the rain had trickled down the windowpanes, grey and sad. Yves had often played it on Sundays, in autumn . . .

On edge, she walked into the dining-room: the tune abruptly ceased. Lori was still sitting by the piano, picking out nursery rhymes, experimenting with chords; the records were still in the cabinet. Elaine frowned: stupid. It must have been a trick of her memory: when they had lived in the city, Yves had had a piano in his study. Having a piano in the house again had probably affected her more than she had thought.

She put the event out of her mind; but several days later she was tidying up quickly, before going to meet Lori, when she heard it again. Very, very softly, almost as if someone was trying to make no noise, but was desperate to practise. As Yves had been, in the early years, when she was asleep; she had sometimes been woken by very, very soft chords in the next room. A shiver ran down her spine: surely, surely, she was imagining things?

Cautiously, she moved towards the dining-room. The sound was definitely becoming louder, almost as if whoever was playing could no longer resist the music. The gentle raindrop theme flowed into the stormy movement, *forte*: Elaine felt herself freeze. She was alone in the house. So who – or what – was there?

The door was ajar; almost afraid to look, she peered through the crack. The piano stood there, lid down; the room was empty. Still frowning, she pushed the door fully open, and walked into the room. She really was alone: and there was no music. Nothing at all. Elaine shook her head. Stupid – memory playing tricks again. Of course no one had been playing the piano. She placed her hand upon the top, almost patting it; and recoiled as she felt a very slight vibration.

She shivered. Ridiculous. She was thinking too much about Yves, that was all. And he was long dead: it was about time she faced up to it.

Some weeks later, she met Lori from school; the happy-go-lucky six-year-old seemed quieter these days. Preoccupied with something – unless Elaine's mind was playing tricks again. Ever since the piano had been delivered she had been jumpy, far away; Lori was probably copying her example. She made an effort, and smiled at her daughter; yet the answering smile was fainter than usual.

Elaine swallowed. The child was growing more and more like her father every day: the dark curls, the piercing blue eyes, and that faraway smile. Plus the constant desire to play the piano: Elaine had been woken early in the morning, before now, by music from the dining-room. She had gone downstairs, to find her daughter sitting at the piano, intently playing, frowning as she hit the wrong note, then trying again. Just as Yves had been: impatient with himself, and forcing himself on, on, until it was right.

No wonder the child was growing quiet. Worn out from concentrating on her music, no doubt. Elaine made up her mind to have a word with the teacher. The work she was giving Lori was much too hard for a six-year-old, even with Lori's undoubted talent. Both of them needed a break. She thought that her own nervousness was due to overwork, and Lori . . . She hated to see her child with those dark rings under her eyes, the bright blue gaze becoming sharp, rather than the softness she was used to. Growing up was one thing: this was another.

Lori had changed in other ways, too: she no longer wanted a story at bedtime. Just music. Elaine had tried to compromise: a story first, then some music. But the stories had grown shorter and shorter, as her daughter's boredom became more and more obvious. Lori wanted only music. Elaine had had to give in; she sighed. Something was happening to her daughter, and there was nothing she could do.

As she washed up that evening, she heard Lori playing again. It was hard to believe that the child was only six; she played brilliantly. In the same style as her father, too. The glass Elaine was drying fell to the floor with a crash, as she heard the familiar way Lori was playing the *étude*. Just as Yves had played it, with that little trill in the middle. Perhaps Lori had heard it on a record somewhere, she thought; then went cold as she remembered that Yves had never recorded it. Ever.

She walked into the dining-room, forcing a smile on her face. Maybe if she joined Lori, together they could beat whatever it was . . . 'Very good, Lori! Tell you what – shall we play together?'

Lori looked up at her mother. 'If you like.'

Elaine shivered inside at the coldness on her daughter's face. Like Yves, when she had disturbed him at an inconvenient moment. Lori was no longer the child who loved to go for walks with her mother, read stories together, play ball . . . She shook herself mentally. Just tiredness, that was all. Of course nothing had changed. She was just overreacting. Smiling again at her daughter, she sat down at the piano. As she moved towards the keys, the lid came crashing down, catching the tops of the fingers on her left hand.

Once more, Elaine felt that shiver run down her spine: Lori, far from crying out, asking if she was all right, just sat there, staring, as if Elaine were just an inconvenience . . . Ignoring the pain in her left hand, she tried to lift the lid again; it refused to budge. Ridiculous. It wasn't heavy, and there was nothing wrong with her right hand. She tried again; but it was almost as if something was holding down the lid, from inside.

She turned to Lori. 'I think the lid must have jammed as it fell. I'll get it fixed tomorrow; let's read a story, instead.'

The child stared at her, mutinous. 'No. I'm tired. I'll go to bed.'

Elaine sat thinking for a long time after she had put Lori to bed. Perhaps she was going mad; but it seemed to her that the child was being influenced, in some way, by the piano. Becoming more and more like her father . . . Elaine had lost her faith years ago, and had never believed in ghosts; but she was convinced that Yves was somehow reaching out to their child. It would be just like him to demand one more sacrifice.

She shivered. It had to be Yves: how else would Lori have been able to move so rapidly from 'Three Blind Mice' to Chopin, Rachmaninov, Mozart?

But perhaps she was imagining things. Perhaps Lori was, after all, a peculiarly gifted child, and she had just never noticed it before. Perhaps she just needed a holiday . . .

It took Elaine a long, long time to drift into sleep that night; she slept fitfully, waking from nightmares about the piano, Yves, and Lori. The third time she woke, she sat up, meaning to get herself a hot milky drink – and sat, rigid, listening.

Someone was playing downstairs.

The darkness seemed to envelop her, curtaining the sound; she strained to hear. The wind had risen during the night: even so, she knew that it was the piano. Nothing that she recognized instantly, could name; yet somehow, it was familiar. She had heard it before, many years ago . . . Yves. He had been composing a set of preludes when they were first married. She had heard part of it, once, when she had crept through the back of the house, to surprise him: the only time he had ever played it, in her hearing. She was not sure if he had ever finished it – the darker side of his nature had shadowed his talent – but she had the feeling that he was trying to finish it now. Through Lori.

Determined, she got out of bed and pulled on her dressing-gown. Whatever it was, it had to stop. As she reached the door, she heard the sound of footsteps walking up the stairs: small, childlike footsteps. She opened her door a crack; Lori passed, almost as if she were sleepwalking. Elaine frowned. She had heard of people making drinks and meals in their sleep; maybe Lori had been playing the piano in her sleep. Though she was convinced that there was more to it than that . . .

Slowly, she walked towards Lori's room. Her daughter was sleeping soundly, duvet nested round her, almost as if she had never left her bed. At the sight, Elaine's heart throbbed: Lori seemed again the daughter Elaine knew, a sunny, loving, carefree child. Not like the pale, surly creature she had been since the piano arrived ... Elaine's mouth twisted. It was time.

Softly, she walked down the stairs. This had gone on long enough. She stepped quietly into the dining-room and stared at the piano, hatred burning in her eyes. The way it affected her child, even breaking her sleep to make her play – rage flooded through her. Whatever it was, it had to stop. And there was only one way she knew . . . She closed the dining-room door gently behind her, and walked deliberately towards the piano. It sat smugly in the corner; she had the feeling that it was awaiting her next move and was almost laughing at her, sure in the knowledge that it could beat her. After all, didn't it have Lori?

Still calm, she picked up the piano stool. It felt hot in her hands – almost burning her – but she ignored it. Mental sensation, nothing more. She would not give in, let it – him, she was sure it was Yves – have Lori, without a fight. She raised it above her head; as she did so, she thought she could hear music again, below the wind. Soft, and very gentle: the pieces Yves had played to her, when they were first married. Almost a peace offering: *we can share her.*

She shook her head, refusing: Yves had played that game before. Always promising to be fair. Then demanding his own way, pushing her feelings to one side, doing as he pleased. This time, it would be different: she would not give in. Almost immediately, as if sensing her mood, the music changed, growing fierce, angry – discordant and stormy, demanding. Shaking, she brought the stool downwards, hard: it was as if the music resisted her, pushing the stool backwards.

With an effort, she finally hurled it on to the piano; the stool broke and large splinters flew through the air, showering her face and arms. She took no heed of the stabbing pains, nor of the blood that was beginning to stream down her cheek: she had to win. For Lori's sake.

Quickly, she turned to the fire: a poker lay on the hearth, more decorative than useful. But it was good, strong metal. Wood against wood had proved useless. Perhaps this would be better. Driven by anger at the mocking notes issuing from the piano, and fear for her daughter, she struck at it, again and again. Her arm began to ache with the effort, and *still* the thing seemed unharmed.

Terror began to seep through her. It was virtually indestructible: and she had to win. If it beat her . . . it didn't bear thinking about. Lori, her beautiful six-year-old daughter, forced to play, night after night, until the child became no more than a shadow of her former self, almost as much of a ghost as her father. While she was powerless to intervene, say that the child had had enough, needed to rest.

She dropped her arm; at once, the harsh mocking notes stopped, and gentle persuasive music began again. Yves – generous in victory? Having known the man, she doubted it. Suddenly, she thrust the poker through the wood, into the middle of the piano, wrenching at the strings. Notes tinkled, brittle, under the blow, as if something had been broken; a cry behind her made her shiver. *Noooooooo*, fading away like a child's wail, but sounding for all the world like Yves . . .

She turned to face her daughter. The child was crying openly. 'He didn't mean any harm, Mummy, he didn't want to hurt you, he only wanted to teach me . . .'

Elaine shivered inwardly as she heard Lori's words. *He* – what had Lori seen, heard, as she played? Had she seen her father's shade hovering beside her, showing her the right notes, then banging the piano in impatience as she stumbled? Or had he been *inside* her, taking over her thoughts and feelings?

Shuddering at the thought, she ran over to her daughter, gathered her up. 'Hush, hush, don't cry. It's all right now.'

The child sobbed into her mother's shoulder; Elaine held her, comforting. Only a few hours before, the child would have shunned all contact. And now? She stroked back the mop of curls. 'Come on, darling – you're tired. I'll read you a good-night story.'

The weeping stopped; relief flooded through Elaine. She had her daughter back again.

Some time later, when Lori was sleeping soundly, Elaine wandered thoughtfully downstairs, drawn to the piano. The one thing she couldn't understand was that Lori had been affected only by that piano – not the ones at school. Yves had never seen that house – so why? Unless it was something to do with the piano.

Frowning, she walked over to the instrument and lifted the top of the lid. Something white glinted among the strings: part of the ivories, no doubt, Elaine thought guiltily, remembering how she had smashed at the keyboard. Though whatever it was, it seemed too big to be a key. Puzzled, she reached down and brought out a few sheets of paper.

She took the bundle over to the table, and switched on the overhead light. As she glanced at the top of the first sheet, she recognized the handwriting – and the date. A shiver ran down her spine: a variation on the 'Raindrop' – by Yves, the day before they married, ten years before.

D.K. Broster

THE PESTERING

WHEN Evadne Seton and her husband bought the old cottage at
Timpsfield known as Hallows, it was not only because they had fallen
in love with its charming half-timbered exterior, but also because it was
remarkably cheap for its size. For they had very little money to spend. The
war had ruined Captain Seton's health, and left him at one and forty a man
who had, most unwillingly, to take care of himself; and his wife possessed no
particular talent save a light hand with cakes. The lease of their small and
inconvenient flat in West Kensington having come to an end, a chance visit
to Worcestershire, joined to a growing conviction that country air would be
better for gassed lungs than the petrol-laden atmosphere of London, had
resulted in the transference to them of the ownership of a house which
Evadne described in all her letters as 'absolutely heavenly'.

And though the Setons always spoke of Hallows as a cottage, it was really
large enough to claim the more important title. Off its little square hall there
opened on one side Ralph Seton's 'den', which had a long French window –
a later feature, of course; on the other quite a large sitting-room with
engaging latticed casements; there was also a third small room to serve as
dining-room. Above were three bedrooms, and an attic running over all; but
the rooms were low, so that in total height Hallows did not exceed the
dimensions of an ordinary two-storey house. All this accommodation,
together with an attractive garden, rendered its very modest price a matter of
self-congratulation, more especially as it was in good condition and had
indeed been recently redecorated, even to the distempering of the attic.

All the Setons' friends who came to see it spoke enthusiastically of the
extraordinary bargain which Ralph and Eve had picked up. 'Poor dears, they
needed it!' More than one made the remark (which caused Evadne to
shudder) that the extreme picturesqueness of the place almost called for the
title of 'Ye Olde' – something or other; and it was left for Ralph Seton
occasionally to wonder at the fact, which the title-deeds revealed, that
Hallows had so often changed hands after comparatively short periods of
occupancy or ownership. The agents, however, were able to give quite

satisfactory reasons for this, and in any case the drains were all right, for he
had had them tested.

The cottage, however, had one slight disadvantage; it stood almost on the
high road, at the turn just outside Timpsfield village, and though in that
byway of a notably placid countryside there was less motor traffic than would
have shrieked or pounded past elsewhere, still, when summer came, cars
bearing the rheumatic visitants to the neighbouring spa developed a habit of
pulling up outside to admire the 'sweetly pretty' cottage, the roses clam-
bering on the black and white, and the tall fluted Tudor chimneys, of which
two survived in their pristine elegance. The Setons were a little annoyed;
and one day when a car-load of lusty holidaymakers from Birmingham rang
and asked if they 'did teas', Mrs Seton dismissed the inquiries with some
curtness, and entered her husband's sanctum with a heightened colour.

'What's the matter?' asked Captain Seton, looking up from the printed
foolscap document at which he had been frowning. Evadne told him.

'Rage becomes you, I declare!' he observed; and indeed Evadne, who was
thirty-six and whose thick unshingled brown hair was threaded with grey,
looked for the moment quite handsome. But her husband's smile was
transient. 'Come here a moment, will you, and look at this. It's from the
Silverdale Trust. Even the mortgage debenture-holders will not receive a
penny this half-year!'

The flattering colour left Evadne's cheeks. 'Oh, Ralph – another invest-
ment gone wrong! . . . No, no, my dear; of course I'm not blaming you; I
know it's only the bad times, but— And I did so want you to have some of
that new treatment this autumn!'

Captain Seton had his new treatment in the autumn, even though he
received no dividend from the Silverdale mortgage debentures. The demand
of the trippers that afternoon had given Evadne an idea; and the more her
husband fought, the more she upheld it. She *would* 'do teas', and he was
absurd and abysmally behind the times to think of objecting to it. 'Heaps of
people like us do it; and you know I *can* make scrumptious cakes, and
Hallows does attract motorists. We can use the garden if it's fine, the large
room if it's not; I could probably hire tables, for it will only be for a couple of
months or so.'

So very soon old Jacob Friend, the builder, spectacles on nose and tongue
following the movements of his hand, was creating, with an intensity no less
concentrated in its way than was behind that brush which once swept the
ceiling of the Sistine, that one word TEAS, in large letters on a small
signboard, which was to provide Timpsfield with a topic of conversation, to

please thirsty wayfarers, and in about a month's time to cause opulent sufferers at the spa to say to their chauffeurs: 'I think we might drive round by Timpsfield today, Smithson; I hear there are very good cakes to be had at that tea place there – "Ye Olde Tudor House", I think it is called.'

The Setons had not at first realized that this particular spa had practically a ten-months' season, a fact which, while it proved financially profitable to them, meant that Evadne was never surprised to be asked for tea from half-past three onwards even in October. So it was only with a mild surprise that she had heard the bell ring as she was seated by the hearth late one afternoon reading *The Silver Spoon* by firelight, and rather unwillingly got up; yet the surprise deepened when she realized that it was already dusk outside. However, it took no time to boil a kettle on a primus, and her cakes were always freshly made.

Ralph had gone to Birmingham for treatment that afternoon, and the village maiden who helped her had departed home some time ago; but as Evadne was always prepared to serve teas herself if need arose, she went to the door without more ado, only regretting leaving the fire and the society of Michael Mont. When she opened it she was surprised again at the depth of the dusk outside. The creeper leaves which fringed the porch were drained by it of their bright colour; the porch, small as it was, seemed quite shadowy; and shadowy, too, was the figure who stood in it – an old man (as far as she could see) in a hat as wide as those beloved of the Chelsea artist and a cloak to match. Only she was not even quite sure about that – the light was so bad.

'Good evening,' she said briskly. 'I suppose you want tea?'

There was complete silence for a moment. Then the visitor said in a low, slightly hurried tone: 'I am come about the chest, Mistress.'

'Chest?' repeated Evadne, puzzled. 'What chest?' Then she remembered that a chest of tea ordered the previous week from London had not yet arrived. 'Oh, are you the carrier? You have got it there, then? I was afraid it had gone astray.'

The man moved a little. 'Aye, it has indeed gone astray. And I want it. I wish to take it with me . . . if you'll kindly allow me, Mistress.'

'There's some mistake,' replied Evadne. 'I'm expecting it – from Twining's. There's no question of sending it back – particularly as it hasn't arrived yet!'

The old man had come quite close to the door now. Somehow Evadne did not like his nearness, and wished that Ralph were not out, and she alone in the house.

'Not arrived!' he exclaimed; and still his voice sounded just as far off as before. 'I was told that it was brought to this inn long ago, when—'

'But this is not an inn!' interrupted Mrs Seton. 'You have certainly made a mistake. Good evening.' Yet she still held the door open, for despite her half-dislike of her visitant, she was curious about him.

'Not an inn!' he repeated. 'When folk come here every day for refreshment! Mistress, pray, pray let me have the chest!'

'How can I?' asked Evadne, more and more puzzled, 'When I don't know anything about a chest?'

'I am so weary of asking,' sighed the faraway voice. 'Have pity on me, sweet lady, and let me come in and fetch it away!'

'No, you cannot come in,' said Evadne, with decision, suddenly, she knew not why, afflicted not with pity but with a strange trickle of fright. 'There is no chest here.' And she shut the door.

After a while slow, dragging footsteps went out of the porch. The old man, thought Evadne, listening on the other side of the door, was probably a little crazy. She would make inquiries about him in the village. He gave, somehow, the impression of considerable age, like Hawkins, the ancient beekeeper; only that old boy certainly had all his wits about him, as witness the price he had asked her for his honey! And the idea of thinking that Hallows was an inn! She only wished that she were not obliged to admit strangers and give them tea. But there, beggars could not be choosers, and financially her enterprise was well on the way to fill up the hole left by the missing dividends.

When her husband came back about an hour later she told him of the old carrier body or whatever he was, and his request, and how he had stood in the porch asking—

Ralph Seton interrupted her. 'Eve, you must have been having an orgy of cocktails in my absence! Porch! What do you mean? Hallows has no porch!'

The Silver Spoon fallen to the floor, she stared up at him. 'No more it has! What can I have been thinking of?' She passed a hand over her forehead. 'But, Ralph, I . . . I saw it . . . I saw the edge of it, the leaves . . .'

'You might make your fortune if you could remember what you put in that cocktail,' was all her husband would say. 'No good assuring me that you didn't have one! Don't look so worried, old thing!'

'But I am worried!' responded Evadne. 'Ralph, do you think I can be going mental?'

'No; I think you were dazed with reading, and fancied yourself back at your old home, where I seem to remember there was a porch, or somewhere . . . No, I won't get you certified yet!'

October passed into November, and Evadne still dispensed a few teas. Ivy, the 'help' from the village, now stayed later, and it was about six o'clock one evening that she came up to her mistress, who was drying her just-washed hair by an oil-stove in her bedroom, with the intelligence that there was a queer sort of man at the door asking summat about a chest what he was to take away.

'What!' ejaculated Evadne, flinging down her towel. 'A chest! What was the man like? Never mind, I'll get your master to go.' And with her half-dried hair streaming over her dressing-gown she ran downstairs quite perturbed. It was, nevertheless, a fact that she had hardly given her visitant of last month much thought; his queerness had been swamped at the time by the fact of her own, in imagining an architectural feature which did not exist.

She burst into her husband's room. 'Ralph, there's that man again at the door – at least there's *a* man – after that chest. Do go to him!'

'Can't Ivy see to it?' asked her husband, who was writing a letter. A glance had shown him that his wife could not, at least with decorum. 'Oh, all right.' He got up and left the room. 'I wonder if Ralph also will see something that isn't there,' thought Evadne.

In a moment Captain Seton was back. 'There's not a soul at the door,' he said rather crossly. 'What did that little fool mean?'

'I suppose he has gone away again,' said Evadne, with a sense of relief. 'So sorry, dear. And I apologize for coming in like this!'

In the hall she encountered Ivy and, mildly upbraiding her, was met with the reply: 'Oh, mum, but it was the back door. And he's there still; I can 'ear 'im.'

'You haven't left it open?'

'Oh, *no*, mum!'

'Well, go back and tell him that there is no chest for him here, and that it is no good his coming like this. There's a mistake somewhere, as I told him before.'

Ivy hesitated, getting very red. 'Please, mum, I don't like to.'

'Nonsense! I can't disturb your master again; and *I* can't go like this.'

For all answer Ivy burst abruptly into tears. Interspersed with this watery and far from silent protest were phrases which sounded like: 'It's begun again . . . everybody said as it would . . .' and more intelligible ones displaying an immediate desire to go home to her mother.

'If you can't answer the door you'd certainly better go home!' remarked Mrs Seton drily, only to be met with fresh sobs and the declaration that for nothing on earth would the sobber go outside the house this night, now that It had begun again.

With a gesture of vexation, Evadne left the weeping nymph, ran upstairs, caught up her discarded towel, twisted it round her head and came down again.

'Since you are so useless I must go to the back door myself!' she said severely, half hoping to shame Ivy into doing her duty. 'And in any case, the man will have got tired of waiting by now.'

The handmaid lifted a flushed, scared face. 'Oh no, he don't never get tired; he's bin at it too long!' And she burst into a fresh howl, demanding her mother and lamenting that she had ever come to Hallows.

Thoroughly annoyed, Evadne Seton in her turban-like headgear marched through the warm homeliness of the kitchen with its gleaming saucepans and stolid ranks of canisters comfortingly labelled: 'Rice', 'Flour', and 'Sugar'. The outer door was fast shut; she could see that Ivy had shot the bolt. But what was that clinking sound proceeding from it? Evadne stopped, her hands tightening on themselves. The thumbpiece of the latch was lifting in a continuous and regular jiggle, as though someone were shaking it from outside.

Evadne drew her breath hard. Must she open that door? Yes, if only because she had scolded Ivy for her cowardice. And besides, there was always Ralph within call. Bracing herself, she set one hand on the bolt and took hold of the latch with the other. Under her thumb it thrilled gently to that pressure outside. 'I can't do it!' she whispered, suddenly frightened to her inmost soul; though all the time something in her brain was saying reassuringly: 'Rubbish; it's only a crazy old man . . . or the wind.'

Setting her teeth, she plucked open the kitchen door. And she would have been glad after all to see that crazy old man, for there was no one there – no one whatever, only empty, windless darkness.

'I was an idiot, of course,' she said half an hour later in her husband's den. 'But I really was scared for a moment – infected by that silly Ivy, I suppose. By the way, did she apologize at all as you took her home?' For it had ended in Captain Seton's having to escort his timid domestic back to her mother's cottage.

'She? My dear girl, is it likely? I don't think we either of us spoke, as a matter of fact. I confess that I was too much bored by the whole business. Mrs Miller was a bit apologetic. Come to think of it, I should never have imagined a country girl would get the wind up so easily. They must be more or less used to tramps.'

'If it *was* a tramp,' said Evadne in a low voice, as she bent to poke the fire.

Apparently Ivy Miller, country-bred though she was, had no fancy for possible further dealings with old men at back doors, or else her nervous system was unusually highly strung, for she did not turn up next morning. In the middle of luncheon, however, arrived a remarkably ill-spelt note from Mrs Miller, intimating that 'my dorter dount feel as she giv' – a word which from the context must have been 'satisfaction' – 'up at halloses and will you kinly tak her weaks nottis an will not hask no wags yours trueley Mrs miller.'

'Look at that,' said Evadne angrily, passing the missive across the table. 'Tiresome woman! I must go and reason with her. And Ivy was just getting nicely into the way of the teas.'

'Why go and reason?' asked her husband, cutting himself a piece of cheese. 'Ivy's a brainless chit. You can easily get another, can't you, and one who won't go into hysterics if she is asked to go to the door in the dark?'

'And have all the bother of training her? I shall make an effort to get to the bottom of this business first. I'll go this afternoon, before any tea-ers can turn up.'

But a party of these individuals came very early that afternoon, and it was not until dusk had begun to set in that Evadne was able to invade Mrs Miller's dwelling. Her interview there was most unsatisfactory. No, Ivy hadn't nothing to complain of; she had always been treated most kind by you and the Capting, mum; but she didn't feel she give satisfaction, and she didn't like coming back in the dark, and it wasn't in reason that the Capting should bring her home every evening, poor gentleman, him with that cough and all; in fact, she'd rather not stay out her week; we can quite manage, thank you, mum, without the wages; sorry to put you about, but we all know there's difficulties about Hallows and no offence intended, I'm sure, and I hope none taken.

'Difficulties?' exclaimed Evadne. 'What do you mean by that, Mrs Miller? What sort of difficulties? The people who come for teas? But most of them give Ivy a tip, and I make all the cakes myself. If it's the extra washing-up . . .'

Mrs Miller looked down and smoothed her apron; she was a neat body, which was one reason why Ivy had been selected for her post. 'Oh no, mum; it's not the people who come for teas; oh dear no!'

The slight peculiarity of her tone spurred on Evadne to further investigation. 'Then what people do you—' she was beginning, when unfortunately Mrs Miller's labourer son clumped into the cottage, home from work, and the sentence and the investigation were cut short. Evadne thereupon took her leave, not having seen the recalcitrant Ivy at all.

As she went homewards in the dusk she thought that perhaps Hallows, from standing empty (though it had not so stood for long), had gained a bad reputation as the haunt of tramps or undesirables. Yet it was not a solitary place. Anyhow, the affair was most annoying, and not too reassuring for the prospects of replacing Ivy. It was getting too late now to go round to other cottages and endeavour to find some female to come the next day. But tomorrow was Saturday; together with Sunday the heaviest day for teas. Wrathfully musing, Evadne went past the churchyard with its spiky yews, came to the turn of the road, and saw the light from the living-room at Hallows slipping out cheerfully through the half-drawn curtains.

Then she saw, too – but could only just see – that someone was standing inside the gate, as if waiting for her. Foolish of Ralph to do that in the damp! 'Go in, you old silly!' she called out. 'How long have you been there?'

The person standing inside the gate did not answer, so it was not Ralph, and she wished she had not called out to him. It was not until she actually had her hand on the gate to push it open that she recognized something familiar about the outlines of the figure – about the headgear in particular. Feeling rather sick, she paused with her hand on the wood. It was he, the . . . the tramp, and he was on the inner side of her own gate. She would have to pass him, and she most distinctly did not want to do so.

But she could not allow herself to be a second Ivy. Besides, he was in her own garden, where he had no right to be. Horribly afraid, all the same, that he was going to try to keep her out ('and if he does, I shall hit him!' she thought, with a tremulous vindictiveness), she pushed open the gate and went through. 'What do you want?' she demanded, without stopping; for the faster she walked the sooner she would pass him.

But she did not seem to have to pass him; he was not where she expected; he was beside her, shuffling along through the fallen leaves at the edge of the path, and keeping up with her as she went. 'What do you want?' she asked again sharply, looking straight ahead as she spoke, and continuing up the path. 'I can't have you coming here like this!'

'You have just told me to go in, Mistress,' said that flat, faraway voice. 'It is true that I am old and silly, as you said; but you told me to go in. You are kind, after all!'

At that Evadne stopped. 'I never told *you* to go in! I thought it was my husband. Go away at once, or I will call him!' She was shivering with a sudden unnameable disgust. And she began to run.

The becloaked old thing kept up with her. 'Kind, kind!' the voice repeated, almost in her ear. 'You told me to go in . . . you asked me how long I had been waiting . . . Kind . . . kind!'

Evadne struck out with her left arm, but she must have miscalculated the distance. Her hand merely brushed the lavender bush by the door. So she knew she was quite near safety. 'You shall not come in! You shall not come in!' she cried. Then she turned the handle, huddled through, banged the door and fell on her knees inside, pushing against it with all her might and shrieking – for at last she could keep it in no longer: 'Ralph, Ralph, come and lock the door. Ralph, come quick – he's trying to get in – Ralph, for God's sake . . .'

'Well, you did give me the dickens of a fright!' said Captain Seton. He was standing over his wife with brandy, and Evadne, to her surprise, was uncomfortably disposed on the little sofa in the living-room. 'Here, for heaven's sake, get this down!' Ralph was pale himself, paler even than he usually was.

Through chattering teeth Evadne swallowed the brandy, and felt better. 'I'm . . . I'm like Ivy, aren't I?' she said, trying to smile. 'You'll have to go to the police, I'm afraid.'

'But, look here,' said he, 'weren't you imagining things? No one was trying to get in, I'm sure.' He began to rub her hands. 'You're as cold as ice, my dear girl! Did he try to stop you coming in – was that what you meant?'

'No. He wanted to come in, too. He said I told him to . . . as if I should!' She shuddered. 'I thought it was you at first; he was standing just inside the gate.'

'But I can't think why you should have got the wind up so, if he didn't really threaten you?'

'He said I was kind! Me kind . . . to that creature! And Ralph, he sort of shuffled along beside me . . . and his clothes smelt so musty . . .'

'I shall go and light the stove in our bedroom and you must go straight to bed. Yes, I've locked the front door, and the kitchen door is fastened, too. Now, my good girl, you cut off upstairs, and I'll bring you up some hot soup. You said you had made some, didn't you?'

'No, sir,' responded Sergeant Cook, whom Captain Seton had the luck to meet next morning in the village.'No, I never heard of any old tramp in a cloak such as your lady describes, about these parts; nor I never heard as tramps were partial to Hallows. Now if you'd seen him yourself, Captain Seton—'

'Unfortunately I haven't, Sergeant. My wife, however, is not a fanciful person, nor one easily frightened. I wish you'd keep an eye lifting for a few evenings?'

'I will sir, certainly . . . Might he perhaps be a loonatic, do you think?'

'I haven't any theories, Cook. For all I know he might be; but there's no asylum near here. The first time this fellow came my wife says he appeared to think that Hallows was an inn. Does that throw any light?'

'Ah!' said the Sergeant deeply. 'Well, it might or it might not!'

'*Was* Hallows ever an inn?'

'Couldn't say, sir. Best ask some of the old villagers about that. Friend, for instance, or old Hawkins, him that keeps the bees.'

'Oh, the rustic with the protectionist ideas about the price of honey! And Jacob Friend . . . Now that I come to think of it, my wife reported a curious thing which Friend said to her when she gave him the order to paint us a sign. He told her that she was a brave lady – braver than she knew. She thought he meant – well, undertaking that sort of thing, you know.'

'Quite so, sir. But it may be as he meant more. Them old villagers . . . I'm not a Timpsfield man myself. But this here undesirable hasn't ever come to ask for refreshment, has he, sir?'

'No. What he wants, apparently, is a chest which he seems to think we have.'

'Ah, a chest! That sounds old-fashioned, don't it! I'd go and see Friend or Hawkins if I was you, sir.' And on that advice they parted.

Captain Seton had little knowledge of what bees did in winter, but it was plain what a beekeeper did, if he was of the age of Mr Hawkins; he kept by the fire and was careful not to admit the slightest breath of air into his retreat – for months probably, said the visitor to himself as he entered it. Hibernation, if not suffocation . . .

However, Mr Hawkins was not even hibernating. His little eyes were quite alert, and the hat which he presumably kept as a permanency on his aged head, lest after all his precautions some faint breath of air might visit it, lent him the appearance of being ready to set off out of doors, the more so since, sitting by his fireside, he leant both hands upon a stout stick. He had to the life the air of a stage rustic, and a badly made-up one at that. Captain Seton could have sworn that spirit gum was the medium which kept in place the unconvincing collarette of white beard which surrounded his pallid moon face, singularly unwrinkled for his age, which was reputed to be close on ninety. A little woman who referred to him once as 'Granfer', but otherwise, with some coldness, merely as 'He', did the honours of the cottage.

'Good morning, Mr Hawkins,' said his visitor; and so strong was his sense of taking part in amateur theatricals that he nearly added: 'And how be bees?' or something in that strain. However, he restricted himself to: 'I hope you are well?'

'Good marnin', sir,' responded the ancient in a little cracked voice. 'I be doin' nicely, thank 'ee.'

'He's not so troubled with the rheumatics as some winters,' observed the hostess, dusting a chair. 'Please to take a seat, sir.'

'Sometimes,' remarked 'He', taking up the cue, 'I has the lumbago pitched in me baack something cruel, so that I be fair stuck like.'

'You are a good age, Mr Hawkins, aren't you? – though you carry it remarkably well,' Ralph hastened to add.

The moon face emitted a chuckle. 'Aye, I be a hundred and three come next month – or be it a hundred and four, Bessy?'

''Tain't neither,' replied Bessy sharply. 'Don't take no notice of him when he talks like that, sir,' she advised the somewhat startled Ralph. 'He ain't no good at figgers.'

'No,' complacently agreed the ancient – for at any rate he was that – 'I never could be bothered with 'rithmetic. Rheumatics is more in my line now – hee, hee! But 'tis bees as I knaws about. Will it be aught to do with them little critters as ee've come about, sir?'

'No, Mr Hawkins. But whatever your exact age, you are undoubtedly, I believe, the oldest inhabitant of Timpsfield.'

'Aye, that I be,' responded the *soi-disant* centenarian proudly, and, possibly with the idea of prolonging this distinction, he settled his hat more firmly on his head. 'Years and years older than the rest of 'em put together, I rackon. Now, Bessy, hold thy tongue! I kin remember old Passon as allus wore a wig, and the big floods eighty years ago, and the times when a loaf of bread costed—'

'And a good deal about the houses in the village, too, I dare say,' put in Captain Seton, to whom general reminiscences were of no value. 'For instance, there's my present cottage – Hallows, you know, at the turn of the road – I'm naturally interested in that. Do you remember any old stories about that?'

The face within the collarette changed in some indefinable way; to Captain Seton it looked as if Mr Hawkins had said to himself: 'Now you be careful!' 'Ah, so you be the gentleman as has bought 'Allows,' he remarked slowly. 'And how do 'Allows suit 'ee, sir?'

'Very well, thank you, Mr Hawkins. But I should like to know something of its past history.'

'A many would like to knaw that,' responded the beekeeper, propping his chin on the top of his stick. 'Now, Bessy, quit fiddlin' there; 'tis time sure, 'ee went for to do some shopping!' And, to Ralph's surprise, Bessy rather resentfully withdrew.

'I can't abide wimmen,' observed Mr Hawkins as the door closed. ''Tis a great pity a man has to put up wi' 'em, buzzin' about like so many bees on'y not near so sensible. And so 'ee likes 'Allows, sir; don't find it to have no inconveniences?'

Ralph looked at him steadily. 'That depends on what you mean by inconveniences.'

Mr Hawkins tried to scratch his head without removing his hat, a proceeding which a good deal disturbed the poise of the latter. 'Well, sir, being as I'm so old, I remember there was talk of folk being pestered like . . . But that's a long time ago.'

'Pestered by what?'

The old man leant forward over his stick, glanced round and dropped his voice. 'By *him*, sir.'

Ralph's heart gave a queer little jump which surprised him. There *was* something in it, then – or was supposed to be. But he merely asked, after a moment: 'What him?'

'Him as is always asking for it,' replied Mr Hawkins, his piping voice sunk almost to a whisper. And then, as Ralph gave no sign, he went on hurriedly and with an air of relief: 'Oh then, sir, if you ain't been worried, no need to say no more about it. There's some as is, and some as isn't.'

'It's true that I personally have not been worried,' said Ralph, after a moment's consideration. 'But I must admit that my wife has.'

'Ah!' Mr Hawkins sucked his lips. Then he leant yet further forward in his chair, and said, still in a tone as if he feared to be overheard, 'Best tell her never to let the young man in – see as she never does that!'

'But – but as far as I can gather it's not a young man, it's an old one; at least that was my wife's impression. Though, of course, the whole thing is probably an illusion,' he added, half to himself.

'I wouldn't call it no names, sir,' advised Mr Hawkins gravely. He drew back in his chair and appeared to reflect. 'So it seems old now, do it? Well, it have been askin' a mort of years, by what folks do say. My father now, he remembered it; and my mother allus swore she saw it one evening knocking on the door of 'Allows . . . But as long as no one don't never, never ask it in, sir, I reckon 'tis all right; fur it seems it can't come in wi'out 'tis invited, like. 'Tisn't as if 'Allows was an inn—'

'Was it ever an inn? My wife said the – the man at the door spoke of this inn the first time he came.'

'Did he now! . . . I don't remember of its being an inn, nor my father didn't, but some says it was, once.'

Ralph Seton, puzzled, uncomfortable, turned to another point. 'This chest, now, that he asked for – a chest which he said had been left there—'

'Aye, he would,' murmured Mr Hawkins, nodding his head. 'Allus the same thing – a chest, it be.' And by this time Ralph no longer saw him as a comic rustic. He really did seem to have some roots back in a curious past which had small affinity with a present of unceasing loudspeakers and weekly record-breaking aeroplane flights.

'There *is* a tale about a chest, then?'

'There's a tale about him allus askin' for a chest. But there wasn't no man livin', even in Granfeyther's day, as knew aught about a chest, and no chest ain't never bin found in 'Allows.'

'Then it's not much use his keeping on asking for it!'

'No, sir, it ain't. But I suppose that's just what he will do, keep on askin', seein' as he don't never get it!'

'A nice lookout, that, for the occupants of Hallows!' exclaimed Captain

Seton. 'We have lost a maid over this business already, and I very much fear that my wife may have difficulty in finding another in the village if this tale gets about!'

''Tain't no question of its "gettin about," sir,' corrected the sage. ''Cos 'tain't no new tale, if you unnerstans me. Only, him not havin' been seen for some time, it might have bin a bit forgot. I wonner now what could 'a started him off again?'

The words woke an echo of what Evadne had reported Ivy to have said on that score. Evidently even the young people of Timpsfield knew, at any rate in theory, of the 'pestering' of Hallows. A cheerful prospect if Evadne failed to get a maid – just now, too, when they were making a little money over the teas . . . much as he himself disliked that method of earning it!

'But what is the legend, the tale, behind this . . . this . . .' he really did not know what to call it, and finally came out with, 'this nuisance? Can you recall having heard anything as to its origin? Who brought the chest to Hallows, and when – and what was supposed to be inside it?'

The old beekeeper was probably not conversant with the vulgarism of 'Now you're asking!' but his expression conveyed that sentiment as he slowly shook his ancient, behatted head.

Captain Seton went out through the blackened Michaelmas daisies and dahlias of Mr Hawkins's crowded little garden, not knowing what to think. By the time he got home he was almost wondering whether Evadne's importunate old man could be accounted for on the theory of mass suggestion. If not, he was faced by an uncomfortable dilemma: either he must believe in this spectre and his 'chest', which he could not bring himself to do, or else Evadne, of all people, was developing nerves or hysteria – delusions, in fact. His mind revolted from both alternatives. The immediate question was, what was he going to tell her about his inquiries? Wouldn't the best thing be to say that neither Sergeant Cook nor the oldest inhabitant knew anything about the business? But then he had not the habit of lying to his wife – nor to anybody else, for that matter.

He was relieved to find that he need not come to an immediate decision on this point. A notice was pinned on the front door which said: 'No teas provided today', and on the hall table he found a note informing him that his wife had had no luck servant-hunting in the village, and had taken the little Austin and gone over to Worcester to a registry office. 'May not be back to tea, so don't wait,' it concluded. 'Cold lunch (sorry!) on the table.'

So she *had* failed to get a maid in the village! Of all the cursed nuisances!

He went for a walk after lunch, by the old canal, long out of use and undisturbed, as picturesque under its drooping trees as any river. It had no trace of movement in its unstirred waters – so little, indeed, that the drift of red beech leaves and of green ash leaves lay upon its surface as upon ice – the stillest water he had ever seen. The beech trees in their last glory made of it an enchanted waterway. Ralph turned off from it after a while and did a round. When he got back to Hallows it was practically dark.

Evadne had not returned, evidently, for the little garage door was still open and the house was unlit. Captain Seton let himself in and went towards his own den, extracting his pocket lighter. Just outside, however, it slipped from his fingers, and while he was groping for it on the floor he became aware, to his surprise, that there must be someone in his room, for he could distinctly hear a noise in there. He raised himself and listened. Yes – a series of dull thuds or thumps, apparently against the panelling of the wall. Evadne must be back, then; but what on earth was she doing? He gave up hunting for his lighter, for Evadne would presumably have lit the lamp in there, opened the door, and said, 'What in thunder are you up to, Eve – and in the dark, too?' For the room was not lit, save by the merest scrap of glow from the hearth.

But no one answered him. The thudding had stopped; there was not a sound, nor could he see anyone in the room. Yet that someone was there he was certain. By the draught which the opening of the door had caused he knew that the long French window must be partly open. Had he left it so when he went out?

'Who is it? If it's you Eve, don't play the silly ass!'

For the only answer he heard what sounded like rough-skinned hands rasping over the panelling. It wasn't Eve in here! 'Here, you!' he called out threateningly, 'Get out of this!' and made a dash for the corner whence the rasping appeared to come. He touched nothing, it is true, but he had the impression of something bundling rapidly to the other side of the room, something that diffused a mouldy smell as it moved; he even thought that he saw it, very indistinctly, cross the somewhat lighter oblong which was the uncurtained French window. Filled both with rage and with something of which he had known the like before . . . in Flanders – Ralph hurled himself in the dark towards his bureau, on top of which he kept an electric hand-lamp for emergencies, found it, switched it on and threw its strong but narrow beam into the corner on the other side of the window. Nothing there! He swept the room with it – nothing. A long breath of relief shook him. Now if *he* had been having cocktails . . .

Then, as he was starting, electric lamp in hand, to leave the room in search of his dropped lighter, he did see something . . . something that sat, huddled almost into a ball, in his own chair by the dying fire, something covered with what looked like a rotten and tattered dark-brown sack, something that had earth-coloured hands clasped over the shrouded head which was bowed to its very knees . . . if it had knees . . . something that was whimpering to itself in a dusty, faraway voice, 'Not here . . . not here . . . not here . . .'

Ralph Seton, in a worse place than the trenches, and almost beside himself with fear, hurled the electric lantern like a bomb at the thing which sat in his chair. The heavy lamp hit the stone jamb of the fireplace, shivering its glass and bulb at once. A second afterwards, Ralph heard the window flung wide in the darkness; then he bolted from the room and, with the sweat running down his spine, fell into a chair in the unlit hall, his heart beating almost to suffocation.

After a while he sat up, pulled out his handkerchief and began to mop his forehead, and it was then that he heard the horn of the Austin. A moving beam of light traversed the hall. Ralph got up. Evadne must not find him like this; besides, It might be lurking outside and frighten her. He opened the hall door, and was disgusted to find that his legs would not carry him down the path.

'All in the dark, old thing?' exclaimed his wife a moment later, appearing with her arms full of parcels. 'Whyever haven't you lit up?'

'Just going to . . . dropped my lighter,' mumbled Ralph. 'Haven't found it yet.' To himself his voice sounded extraordinary.

'But there are matches on the hall mantelpiece,' observed Evadne, dumping her parcels on to the table. 'Are you only just in, then . . . There!'

She was lighting the hanging Aladdin lamp. Thank goodness, one had to leave the flame low at first. Anyhow, perhaps he wasn't looking as queer as he felt, and she wouldn't notice.

'Yes. I've been for a walk . . . Where are you going?'

'I've bought a new waste-paper basket for your room,' replied his wife briskly, picking up one of her parcels, 'and it might as well be put in there at once . . . Goodness, Ralph, two people can't get through this door at a time!'

For her husband had pushed past her without ceremony. *It* might still be in there for all he knew. But directly he had the door well open he stopped, unable to go a step farther, though he could see that the room was empty. And the fact that he *could* see this was exactly what paralysed him. One of the two never-used candles which decked the old pewter candlesticks on his mantelpiece had been lit . . . or was he dreaming? Evadne slipped past.

'Well, you managed to get some kind of illumination,' she observed. 'Oh, you criminal, what a mess, though! You poked the candle into the fire, I suppose, by the look of it!'

Staring at the bowing flame, her husband shook his head. A . . . that

Thing light a candle! But no, either it was . . . not what he felt it was, or some human being had come in through the window and lighted that candle – God knew why! Yet on the other hand, was it likely that anyone . . . But had the Thing come back, then? . . .

'Hallo!' said Evadne, stooping down to the hearth. 'How did this come here? My goodness! It's all smashed to pieces!' She held up in one hand the damaged oak-cased hand-lamp, and in the other a piece of the stout glass of its shattered bull's eye.

Before he answered, Ralph went to the French window, shut it and pulled the curtains. Then he came back to the hearth and the solitary candle which he had not lit. 'I'm afraid I'm the culprit about the electric lamp. I don't know whether I'm taking leave of my senses, but – no, for God's sake, don't sit in that chair, Evadne!'

'But whyever not?' exclaimed his wife in utter astonishment, catching the arm which had grabbed at her.

Ralph told her why not.

It was of no avail to turn the matter over and over, as they did that evening; they could come to no stable conclusion. On the one hand it seemed as if 'It' had really won entry to Hallows, and was searching there on its own account; on the other, Captain Seton had the fervent desire to banish the picture of the sitter by his fireside as a trick of eyesight, the memory of the dry earthy hands rustling over the wall and the whimpering voice as a trick of hearing, and the affair of the candle as a jest played by someone who had subsequently slipped in through the open window. He slept ill that night, worse than Evadne.

It was not until next day that his wife told him of the likely woman she had heard of in Worcester the preceding afternoon, whose references she had taken up in person, and whom she proposed to engage at once by letter. This domestic would naturally have to live entirely at Hallows, since she was not of the neighbourhood.

'But what shall we say to this Mrs Minter when she comes?' asked Evadne as she was brushing out her hair at bedtime. 'If we tell her never to leave anything open after dark she'll get frightened about burglars or something, and won't stay.' Neither of them had been out since tea-time that afternoon, and every door and window had then been securely fastened.

Ralph finished winding up his watch and gloomily surmised that anyhow she would hear talk about Hallows in the village.

Two days later the new servant arrived, respectable, middle-aged, and (they hoped) unimaginative. Peace descended again, though that Evadne's nerves were jangled was abundantly proved on the occasion when Minter came in to announce that 'a man had come for the chest—' and got no farther. Mrs Seton had sprung up with a half-suppressed scream, so that the worthy woman stared at her astounded.

'Chest?' cried Evadne wildly. 'No, no, Minter – send him away at once! We have no—'

Luckily her husband came at that instant into the room. He broke in with a loud laugh which did not ring very genuine. 'It's all right, Minter. Your mistress has forgotten that the sofa has to go away to be mended. The man is here with the van from Petty's, Evadne, to fetch the chesterfield away.'

Evadne had recovered herself with a gulp. 'I'll go and see about it,' she mumbled, and fled from the room.

The approach of St Martin's Summer, fine as usual, was bringing visitors again to Hallows, and for a few bright days teas were again in demand; Evadne was glad of the distraction. On Armistice Day itself there were quite a number of 'tea-ers' in the living-room (for no longer, in mid-November, could they be accommodated in the kind of arbour which had sheltered them in the summer). They all arrived about the same time, but there were three parties of them, that is, two parties and one solitary young man who had a table to himself. Evadne, who was helping Minter with the waiting, thought that he looked like an artist; his hair was rather long, his tie large, his collar soft and loose, and his hands almost a woman's – so long and slim and with such tapering fingers that they might, thought Evadne, as she served him, have come out of a Van Dyck portrait. He asked for coffee, and would have nothing to eat; and while he stirred it, sat looking round the room with evident interest. And as Evadne passed again with a tray, he addressed her:

'You have a beautiful old house, madam. Is it . . . do you permit your guests to see over it?'

'No, I'm afraid not,' answered Evadne, somewhat taken aback. 'Not more than this room. You see, we live here.'

The young man looked disappointed, much more disappointed than he need, thought Evadne, seeing his handsome face darken until it was almost sullen. Perhaps he was a connoisseur of old houses; but, all the same, they could not undertake to make their home a spectacle to unknown trippers who came for tea – though, indeed, 'tripper' was not exactly the word to apply to this young man. 'I am sorry,' she added.

His face still dark, he made her a sort of bow. 'It is your house, madam,' and she passed on, feeling that she had been discourteous. Next time she came into the room he had finished and gone – and paid (which was the important thing) since the sixpence for his coffee lay on the cloth by the cup.

It must have been about two o'clock in the morning when Evadne woke with a jump and the impression that she had heard a noise somewhere near her bed. She lay a moment with her heart beating; but in another there came the long rumble of thunder. It had no doubt been a previous clap which had awakened her, and, though she disliked thunder by night, she felt relieved. The wind was rising, too; she heard a door bang downstairs. Yes, a night thunderstorm always affected her with a sense of something sinister. If it went on she would wake Ralph, who was sleeping through it. There seemed to be no lightning, which was odd; she never knew which she disliked the more – at night.

Ah! a flash at last, a slight one; and almost on its heels another, of tropical intensity, blue and searing, which lit up the whole room. But it was not the lightning which drew Evadne's scream and flung her upon her sleeping husband in the bed by her side. The flash had shown her, standing at the foot of her own bed, his hands on the oaken rail, with a half-mocking smile on his face, the young man of the afternoon. And his hands were—

'Ralph, Ralph, wake up! He's here in the room with us . . . but he's *dead* . . . his hands are all bones . . . I saw them . . . a skeleton's hands . . . Ralph, he had coffee here this afternoon . . .'

Babbling on in terror, she was clinging so hard to him that it was difficult for Captain Seton to free himself and reach out for the matches, but he succeeded, and managed to light the candle just as a tremendous peal of thunder reverberated over Hallows.

'My dear girl, you've had – a bad dream. There's nothing, Eve, you are – you really are – strangling me!' And he broke into one of his uncontrollable fits of coughing.

It was perhaps lucky; nothing else could so have recalled Evadne to herself.

In the morning the theory of a nightmare seemed the only plank to cling to, if sanity were to be retained by either of them; and as they counted over the week's takings, Ralph Seton elaborated it with a great show of common sense.

'You know, Eve, how you hate thunder in the night; and the fact that you imported into the dream which it gave you a harmless young tourist or whatnot from the day before proves . . . That lot is ten florins, yes; and six half-crowns – you have been doing well! . . . and sixpences – all right, I'll count them again. I make them eighteen, but one of them's a dud. You've been had, old lady! Look at that! Is it foreign, or what?'

Evadne took up the rejected coin and looked at it closely, on both sides; examined it again, got very red, then pale, and let it fall on the table with a little gesture, as though it were something that would sting. 'It's not foreign; but it says "Jacobus Rex" . . . it's *his*, Ralph, that he left for the coffee. Oh, what shall we do, what shall we do?' And laying her head upon her arms, she burst into tears.

Dr Mildmay came out of the bedroom and followed Captain Seton down to the latter's den.

'Yes, I will certainly send your wife a sedative. And what about yourself – you're looking none too grand?'

'We're both in the same boat, my wife and I,' said Ralph, smiling mirthlessly. 'And unless this horrible business can be stopped, I really don't know what is going to happen. We can't give up the house; we've only just bought it.'

Dr Mildmay was a newcomer to the district, a slight, hatchet-faced, forcible man in his forties with a little beard and a sallow, dried-up skin. He looked keenly at the haggard man standing before him. Of his physical disabilities he was aware, for Ralph had consulted him soon after settling in Timpsfield, and it was Dr Mildmay who had put him on to the new treatment in Birmingham.

'Then you must make the . . . visitant leave,' he said briskly. 'Have you ever heard of exorcism?'

'Yes. But don't tell me that you, a twentieth-century medical man, believe in it! Besides, isn't the object of exorcism to "lay" a ghost in a house? There's no ghost in this house – at least, not permanently. He's outside it – though he evidently intends not to remain there. And after last night it seems as though nothing will keep him out.'

'Then the only course is to take away his reason for coming. What was it he began by asking for – a chest?'

'Look here, Dr Mildmay,' said Ralph roughly, 'I don't want to be humoured! I'm not insane – yet. You know quite well that you put down all I have told you to some kind of hallucination or delusion. It isn't possible for you, with your training, to do anything else. I'm not a child—'

'How do you know what my training has been?' interrupted Dr Mildmay coolly. 'I spent ten years as a medical missionary in East Africa. No man who has done that, unless he is unbelievably stupid or invincibly prejudiced, can dogmatize about hallucination or delusions. He has seen far too many strange things himself out there.'

Ralph stared at him. 'You – you really think that I actually saw what I thought I saw, feeling round these walls, sitting in that chair, and that poor Evadne—'

'I would not rule out the possibility. And so, one must take steps to put an end to this invasion. It is serious – for you and Mrs Seton.'

'God knows it is!' muttered Ralph. 'Look here, Mildmay, can't you use some of your African spells or incantations – or exorcize the house yourself – no, as I said, exorcism probably wouldn't answer.'

'It certainly wouldn't in my hands; I'm a layman, Captain Seton. Also, you see, I'm a Christian, and can't go in for spells. No, I suggest we start by using common sense. Have you ever tried to find this "chest" yourself?'

'No. But there's nowhere it could be; the place was as bare as my hand when we came into it.'

'No bricked-up cellars, no old wells, no hiding-places in the chimneys, or in the thickness of the walls?'

'I don't think so.'

'Well, get a good builder and go round the house with him and make sure. Don't have a local man; get someone out from Worcester or Birmingham. I will look in again tomorrow morning; or you can send for me if you want me. Meanwhile, I'll write off to a historically minded friend of mine in Oxford who has a fairly extensive knowledge of the literature of haunting, and see if he can throw any light on this case. Good morning, and don't frighten yourselves with the far worse bugbear of incipient mental trouble.'

The builder whom Ralph had out next day from Worcester possessed a certain amount of intelligence, though he was extremely sceptical. 'Folks is always trying to find what they calls "priests' holes" in these here old houses,' he observed disparagingly. 'Can't see what they wants 'em for – nasty insanitary little places when found, what no one but them old cunning Jesuits would have wanted to live in!' Ralph, who had not revealed the ultimate object of the search, replied that such retreats were not inhabited from choice, but was evidently not believed.

It was not until the quest, fruitless so far, was almost over that Mr Wiggins had his great idea, and descending from the attic, went outside the house, stared upwards for some time from the garden, and returned with an expression of satisfaction on his face, to the dispirited Ralph, who had been watching him from one of the attic windows.

'Have it ever occurred to you to wonder, Captain Seton, why this 'ere right-'and casement,' he slapped its frame as he spoke, 'is set so much nearer to the wall than t'other is to t'other wall?'

'No, I can't say that it has,' returned Ralph. 'Hallows is an old house, and many things in it are not symmetrical.'

'That's right. But it might have give you an idea, sir, same as it 'as me' – 'if you had my experience and intelligence,' seemed to be understood. 'Now, listen to this!' Mr Wiggins struck a resounding blow on what appeared to be the end of the attic nearest to the right-hand window. ''Ark at that, sir! It's false, that wall is – lath and plaster. There's space beyond, as can be calkilated from the outside; not much space, *hun*doubtedly – but enough for one of them skinny Jesuits, I dare say. You've only to give the word, sir, and a haperture's easy made.'

But Ralph had no intention of interior researches being pursued by Mr Wiggins, and did not respond to the suggestion. He himself came and thumped the wall, however, puzzled. 'It's got a beam down it, though,' he remarked doubtfully, for a wavy black beam, just a slice of a tree, like many of the timbers in Hallows, divided the distempered surface into two. But this, according to Mr Wiggins, was but camouflage on the part of them Jesuits (to whom he seemed to attribute the power of continued existence even after what would have amounted to walling up alive).

When Mr Wiggins had departed, Ralph Seton returned to stare at the shut-off slice of the attic. This could surely only be very narrow, and the departed Wiggins had really been sharp to deduce the possibility of its existence. Dr Mildmay was coming tomorrow morning; possibly he might induce that somewhat unorthodox, or at least singularly unprejudiced medical man to help him break in upon whatever was concealed there – if there were anything.

He went to tell Evadne, still in bed, that there was now a faint hope of the lifting of the siege.

Unfortunately there was also evidence that the blockade was becoming straiter. When the worthy Minter brought Ralph his solitary tea that afternoon she asked him, in a somewhat indignant tone, whether it were by his wish that the builder's man, as she supposed he was, should be sitting on the attic stairs in the dark, moaning to himself – drunk he must certainly be, and she would never have let him into the house in that state, but as it happened, she did not let him in. Her tone seemed to imply that her less observant master must have done so.

Ralph put back the tea cosy which he had begun to lift off. 'On the attic stairs, in the dark!' he exclaimed, with a sinking of the heart. 'But I never ordered—' Then he checked himself. 'All right, Minter, I'll see to it. He can't stay there, of course. But don't you tell him – I will.'

'Thank you, sir,' replied Minter, with dignity, and retired, while Ralph lay back in his chair and groaned. 'Sitting on the attic stairs . . . moaning to himself!' There could be no doubt what was doing that. And now he must go and dislodge the creature.

There was one gleam of comfort – Its being where It was seemed to show that Wiggins had been correct, that the attic was the right venue. It also seemed to show that It knew of their doings this morning, and that It could reason . . .

His teacup, the hot toast, the easy chair and the fire cried strongly to him to remain where he was, and let the horror sit and moan on the attic stairs for as long as It liked. The danger was, not a fright to Evadne, who was, he believed, asleep, but to the precious Minter, lest she got an inkling of the real nature of the 'builder's man'. . . . No, it wouldn't do; though how he was going to expel the thing he knew not, and his flesh crept at the idea of even approaching the narrow stairway leading to the attic. However, he pulled himself out of his chair.

Hardly had he got into the hall when he heard a shrill scream from the direction of the kitchen. Great heavens! He hurried there and found Minter, with a face like a sheet, leaning panting against the dresser clutching a pastry-board shield-wise in front of her.

'What's the matter?' asked her master, with a miserable attempt at jocularity. 'Have you seen a rat or something?'

'Oh, sir, oh, Captain Seton – the most 'orrible, 'orrible thing! No, not a rat – much worse!' She shuddered and let slip the board, which fell with a bang between them. 'I'd just got out me rolling-pin and put it on the table there by the door, and 'ad me back turned to reach the pastry-board when I 'ear a kind of a swish and a scratching like, and out of the corner of me eye I see something come round the hedge of the door and make a grab at the rolling-pin . . . something like a 'and with a bit of sacking over it, and—'

'Nonsense, Minter,' interrupted Ralph stoutly. 'It was a stray cat, of course! Pull yourself together, woman!'

'Then p'raps you'll tell me, sir,' choked Minter, 'how a cat could carry off me rolling-pin – because it's gone!'

There was certainly no rolling-pin visible anywhere, even on the floor. An attempt at a suggestion on Ralph's part that she had never put it on the table at all was met by a firm rejoinder that she was, as the Captain knew, a member of the Church of England and a strict teetotaller. Then Ralph said, with a sudden air of enlightenment, that of course it was that drunken fellow upstairs playing her a trick; he would send him about his business in double-quick time.

Never did anyone feel less like carrying out such a threat than Ralph Seton as he went slowly upstairs with his repaired electric lamp. All was quiet above – cheering thought, perhaps the invader had not returned to his place of vigil! No moaning, nothing. But just as he got to the corner on the landing which he must turn before he could see the attic stairs, he stood rooted. What was that rapid series of bumps, one after the other? His hair rising on his head, Ralph set his teeth, slid round the corner and flashed the lamp on to the steep empty stairs . . . down which was trundling sedately a pale, cylindrical object – the kitchen rolling-pin.

It came to rest a few stairs from the bottom. Ralph had no wish to pick it up, but stood staring at it as if it had been a cobra. What in the name of heaven – was It descending to the level of a *poltergeist* . . . had It been here a moment ago and dropped the thing . . . why had It taken it?

Evadne's voice on the landing, sleepy and rather querulous. 'Ralph, I do think you needn't have chosen just the time when I had got off to sleep to do hammering up here!'

'But there's been no—' he was beginning, when it occurred to him that perhaps there had . . . on the attic door . . . with the rolling-pin. But he could offer neither that explanation nor the other possible one of the bumping descent of that object. He went and induced Evadne to return to bed, humbly apologizing for his thoughtlessness; he had not thought she could hear.

But he did not go to bed at all that night; he sat up till dawn in their bedroom with Jeans's *Mysterious Universe* (which he did not read) and, foolishly enough, his service revolver – loaded.

'It seems almost a pity, though,' said the doctor, surveying the new distemper. 'It will cost you something to have this mended up again, even if we only make a sort of doorway in it.'

'I don't care what it costs,' returned the owner of Hallows, hatchet in hand. 'I'm going to hoof that damned "chest" out of here before we both go mad, my wife and I. Come on!' And he struck the first blow.

It was a messy job, but not very difficult, to cut an entranceway through the lath and plaster; and when it was done the two men, candle in hand, stepped one after the other into a narrow, darkish place – wider none the less than Ralph had expected. It was neither cold nor damp, but felt very stuffy. 'Wonder the candles will burn!' muttered Ralph, but the air was not really foul. The rafters showed vaguely on high, but draped with cobwebs so filthy that they looked like dirty cloths hung out to dry, and the floor might have been covered with equally dirty flannel, for the foot sank soundlessly into its thick sediment of dust. In one or two places the candlelight gleamed on small white scraps of bone – relics of bird or mouse or bat. But of a chest, nothing – nothing at first, till Ralph pointed out, at the left-hand end of the slice of room, a small oblong mound on the floor, a shape not more than fifteen inches high and three feet or so long.

'I will fetch the broom I brought up,' he said, stepping back through the gap into the attic. He had foreseen dust, but not so much of it.

Dr Mildmay had vetoed Evadne's presence in her unstrung condition, and she was downstairs helping Minter in the kitchen. Nevertheless, Ralph had bolted the attic door – there was no key. It was wrong of her, therefore, to disobey orders, and, after trying the handle, to keep on tapping like that.

'Go away, Eve!' he shouted. 'You can come in afterwards. Yes, it's all right, we've found something.'

'You promise that I may come in afterwards?' came indistinctly through the door.

'Yes, yes; but go away now!' And to his relief he heard her going down the stairs again.

'I believe this may prove to be a child's coffin,' observed Dr Mildmay, as Ralph, back in the narrow candlelit space, started cautiously to use the broom on the dust-covered mound which, save that the sides were straight, had an outline that gave colour to the doctor's surmise.

At last Ralph got rid of most of this age-long deposit, and both men, coughing a little, stooped with their candles over a narrow box covered with hide or leather fastened with blackened nails to the wood beneath. In many places this leather was cracked and curled, and the little 'chest' was held together by a couple of thin iron bands going right round it.

'Let's get it out into daylight,' said the doctor. 'By Jove, it's heavy!'

'Treasure, perhaps,' commented Ralph; yet, though a memory of *Treasure Island* brought 'pieces of eight' for a moment into his mind, he did not really believe in such good fortune. And as he got his hands under the narrow leather-covered box he was conscious of such a spasm of aversion towards it that he had much ado to retain his hold. If it were not that the weight was much too great he would have said that it contained a skeleton – only, surely, the skeleton of a dwarf. Together, with difficulty owing to its weight, they got the receptacle through the aperture in the false wall. And when they set it down in full daylight on the clean bare boards Ralph was aware that Dr Mildmay, too, looked strange. Their eyes met.

'Whatever is in there is evil,' said the man from East Africa in a low voice, and Ralph nodded. Nevertheless, he selected from the tools he had brought up with him a stout chisel and a hammer.

'I wish I had asked Eve for a duster when she came to the door just now,' he thought, for the box was still pretty grimy. With some difficulty he got the chisel under the first of the iron bands, which, at any rate, was thin and almost rusted away; and indeed, it soon gave, starting up with a *cling*. The other band was more difficult and required the aid of pincers as well, but in the end he got it off. And then, as the lock was broken and the leathern hinges rotted away, there was no more to do than raise the lid.

'I suppose we had better?' suggested Ralph, hesitating after all.

'I think we must,' answered his companion firmly; and with that he lifted it off and laid it on the floor.

A strange smell, half of damp, half of some withered perfume, came out of the narrow box, out of the folds of rotting brocade, crimson and gold, which loosely covered what was within. And what was within showed enough of its shape to testify that it was a human body – but a body only three feet long. Summoning all his resolution, Ralph Seton pulled the tinder-thin stuff aside; and there met his eyes the greenish shape of a perfectly formed woman, clad only in a thin pleated kirtle from waist to knees, save where a fold climbed upwards over one breast and shoulder . . . a woman, yes, but one who had never lived. For after one wild second's thought of some impossible process of embalming, both men together gasped: 'Why, it's . . . it's a statue!'

It was; a bronze statue of rather more than half life-size of beautiful workmanship, a nymph, perhaps, for one hand held an arrow, and there were buskins on the feet. But it was not the work of the ancient world, that was clear; and, though the statue was perfect and unworn, it was not modern, either. There was a smile on the face, subtle and enigmatic, a little like the smile that Leonardo knew how to paint, and Luini and Boltraffio, too; but it was not an evil smile. Why, then, had they both been conscious of that feeling of repulsion and almost of fear?

'What is this?' asked Dr Mildmay suddenly, pointing. 'That, surely, is no part of the original design!'

For between the breasts of the figure, the one covered, the other exposed, protruded a blackened, cross-shaped object, like the hilt of a small dagger – a silver-hilted dagger, perhaps. Below it, indeed, when they looked closer, some half-inch of rusty blade was visible, fitting but ill into a jagged rent a little larger than itself. But there was more than the dagger blade in the bosom which had never felt the wound; there was a strip of paper wound about the rusty steel. The dagger itself would not come away; but Dr Mildmay with neat fingers picked and unwound the flimsy piece of paper. Even so, when he began to unfold it, it tore. Very silently he held out the tattered thing to Ralph. Captain Seton could not make sense of what was written on it – words which seemed no words, and signs that conveyed nothing. Shaking his head, he gave it back.

'This is rubbish, Doctor. Or, well, I suppose it may prove of interest. What are you after?'

He got no answer for a moment. Dr Mildmay, looking grim, went back into the recess and returned with one of the still lighted candles.

'Oh, wait a minute!' cried Ralph. 'Isn't that a pity? The paper may be—'

'If you want to be free from that unhappy creature I fancy this is the way,' answered the doctor. 'Don't you want to be free?'

'God knows I do!' answered Captain Seton, who, after all, was no antiquary. Evadne's health and peace of mind, not to speak of his own, were a great deal more to him than cabalistic writings. So he watched the candle-flame making short work of what Dr Mildmay had unwound, and saw, falling to the floor, a few blackened flakes flimsier than the cobwebs in the place which had hidden – for how many years, he wondered – this poniarded nymph lying there before them, with that changeless and secret smile, her head on a little green satin pillow spotted with mould.

It was night. Evadne's even breathing showed him that she was soundly asleep; but Ralph could not imitate her example. She had been told everything, had viewed with astonishment and admiration the secret of the 'chest', and, like her husband, had thankfully accepted Dr Mildmay's opinion that with the burning of the strip of paper wound about the dagger, they might reasonably expect Hallows to be free from its importunate visitor. Nevertheless, Ralph was restless; he almost felt fevered. That little statue; he lay picturing it set up on a pedestal. It would surely look even more beautiful so. They had not yet lifted it out of its bed, its coffin. What was to be done with it eventually? Had they a right to keep it? He supposed so. Then he would have that evasive smile to look at always, and the turn of the head, which must be more lovely, more significant, if the nymph were as she was created to be, upright against a forest tapestry of greens and browns . . .

For nearly an hour he lay thinking about her, and then rose very quietly from his bed, put on his dressing-gown and crept out of the room carrying a candlestick; he did not strike a match until he was outside. Why not be the first to see what she looked like, standing in her half-naked loveliness up there in the bare attic? Though she was heavy, she was not large; he was sure that he could lift her out of the coffer unaided.

Odd, he thought, as he went stealthily up the attic stairs, that that antiquated word should have come thus unbidden into his mind. He wished now that he had not allowed the strip of paper with the writing to be burnt. It might have told him something about his nymph – for she was his now. Dr Mildmay was . . . well, he had been a missionary, apparently; he was a man of very narrow ideas. Yes, he himself had been a damned fool to let him burn that writing!

This reflection reminded him of the dagger, that cruel dagger whose thrust had not destroyed her imperishable life, but which he hated to think of. He would have another try at getting it out – an excellent, an almost imperative reason for this nocturnal visit. All the same, he must be a trifle feverish, for he opened the attic door almost as though he were entering a shrine; he was aware of this, and knew the feeling to be absurd, more especially as the goddess which it contained was lying tied up in a box. For, the attic door having no key, Dr Mildmay and he had fastened up the chest again in two places with stout cord. However, he could soon undo it.

But even that was not necessary. He gazed down, astonished. The cords were no longer round the coffer . . . though they were still underneath it, lying spread upon the floor. And by the ends of them he saw – he could not help seeing – that they had neither been untied nor cut; they had been burst apart. Who on earth could have done such a thing – who could have had the strength?

Ralph set down the candle with a shaking hand and dropped to one knee. For a moment he dared not move the lid, which was still in place, though a little crooked. It was obvious what had happened; someone had got into Hallows and stolen her! She was no longer there; he should never see that smile again. There would only be the empty coffin.

Steeling himself, he took away the lid. His heart leapt up – she was there still, she was there! He took up the candle from the floor and held it over her, drinking in her beauty. And it was only after a moment or two that he noticed something different about her. The blackened dagger hilt was gone – the weapon was gone altogether . . . there was only the tiny rent between her shapely little breasts . . .

Ralph Seton felt an immense relief and gladness. Now there was nothing to mar her beauty . . . and nothing any longer to cause her pain! He could kneel on for ever, just looking at her . . .

Not, however, if he continued to have this strong conviction that he was being watched, and watched by someone or something hostile. He tore his gaze away and sent it searching round the dark and empty attic. No one, of course . . . nothing . . . unless that *was* a face peering at him through the breach in the false wall. No, mere fancy! He looked down again fondly at that perfect visage. Her hair rose high above her lovely brow – higher than in classical statues which he had seen; she was more human than they. The Gioconda smile seemed to flicker about her mouth as the candle-flame bent and wavered in the draught; it seemed to invite him. And had he not a right to it, he who had freed her from her long entombment, who was restoring her to the light of day and to her meed of admiration, to a background of woodland tapestry, with perhaps a crystal bowl of flowers at her feet?

'My beautiful one!' he whispered, and bent to kiss the smile.

How cold she was; how long and unsatisfying the kiss; how curious the sensation that a heavy weight upon the back of his neck, almost like a hand, was pressing his head down into the coffer, against the unyielding bronze and the rotting, faintly scented brocade! . . . But there *was* something gripping him there and pressing, pressing unmercifully! He tried to shout, but it was like a nightmare, for he was dumb; he struggled as desperately and as powerlessly as one struggles in a nightmare. . . . Then, thank God, the nightmare broke, and he was crouching on the floor by the box, sweating all over, his hands to his neck.

What had he been doing, he, Ralph Seton, stealing up at dead of night to kiss a statue – a *statue!* He must have gone mad, quite mad, shamefully mad! . . . But was it madness, or returning sanity, which brought to his ears a sound like a low laugh, which seemed to come from that dark place of discovery at the end of the attic? No, he was not mistaken – he *had* been watched at his indefensible worship!

Shame and sudden fury set him on his feet. Leaving the candle where it was on the floor, he made a rush at that dark cavity. 'Come out, whoever you are – come out and don't snigger in there!'

He caught his foot as he rushed in and half tripped, so that only the close proximity of the opposite wall saved him from falling; then, as he recovered and turned, beating about in the darkness to discover the invisible mocker, he thought instantly: 'Mustn't stop in here more than a moment . . . the air *is* foul . . . my poor old lungs won't stand it!' So he swung round to face the opening – and then stood motionless. Framed by the jagged aperture, bright and clear, though the only light there was the candle on the floor, a young man in a ruff and a short black velvet cloak was kneeling by the open coffer, his head bowed, his hands outstretched in a gesture that looked like entreaty. Every slash of purple in his green doublet, every stiffened fold of his ruff, every curl of the gold galon round the edge of his cloak was as distinct as the details in a pre-Raphaelite picture, even to the glint of a jewel in his left ear. His face Ralph could not see; and the whole vision, sharp-cut though it was, lasted but the space of a lightning flash . . . and when it was gone, left the dark of a night of thunderstorm behind it.

Captain Seton gasped, put a hand for a moment over his eyes, and then groped unsteadily for the aperture. Though the candlelight in the room beyond had been so unaccountably swallowed up he could find the gap by feeling, since, for one thing, it could not be more than a foot or two from his hand . . . God! what had become of it? He could feel nothing, not even the false wall . . . there was nothing round him anywhere, in any direction, but darkness, a thick, soft, choking darkness. And now his heart, his brain, were beating fit to burst; when he tried to draw a deep breath there was nothing to breathe but dust, dust. He fell on his knees in dust, dust was whirling down upon him in the warm gloom, dust was up his nostrils, in his mouth, in his very vitals. The way out of this place was lost, blocked, gone . . . with his damaged lungs he must stifle here . . . he *was* stifling. 'Dust thou art and to dust shalt thou return!' But *she* had not been dust . . . and that was why this had happened . . . Poor Eve . . . but his life was insured . . . 'Gas-masks, men – gas-masks, quick!' . . . He went down and down through spinning eternities of dust and suffocation.

If Evadne had not wakened and missed him, if she had not heard the sound of hasty feet in the attic above, if her husband had not left the attic door ajar, so that the light shone down – who knows? But these things told Evadne with voices of alarm, and with another candle she ran up the stairs, and saw the first one still burning on the floor by the side of the open coffer.

It did not take her long to find Ralph; but, strong though she was, she had to tug hard to pull him out, asking herself all the time what could have possessed him to enter that place at such a time. She flung the attic windows wide, she fetched remedies; gradually the blueness ebbed from his lips and he began to come round. She helped him to bed, asking for no explanation. As soon as it was daylight she went herself for Dr Mildmay.

What Ralph told the doctor she did not know; to her, later, he merely said that he had undoubtedly had a touch of fever – had had it before he went to bed, but had not bothered to tell her. But he avoided her eyes, and seemed altogether strange as well as ill.

However, he recovered, and recovered so completely as to be able to inform her a few days later that he was going to supper with Dr Mildmay and might be back rather late. She herself had helped the doctor to fasten up the nymph again and to wrap the whole chest in brown paper, so that it looked an entirely modern and ordinary parcel, though out of the ordinary heavy; and the doctor had had it fetched away to his own house. She understood that some art dealer was coming to look at it there.

But on the evening that Captain Seton supped with him, Dr Mildmay fetched out his car afterwards, and he and Ralph lifted the box into it, and they drove through the sleeping village without a single touch on the horn, until they came to the old canal where earlier the autumn leaves had lain unstirring, as on some road of glass. They took the wrapped coffer out and carried it along the verge to the old wooden high-arched bridge which – somewhat shakily now – spanned the canal; and from the middle of this they lowered what they carried with a rope – so much precaution to avoid the sound of a splash in the still autumn night. The heavy thing slid gently into the sluggish water, and the rope, weighted at the end, followed it down; thick bubbles came up as it reached the mud, bubbles of marsh gas. After that the water rocked a little and the widening circles spread out more and more faintly under the stars, and that was all.

Dr Mildmay wiped his forehead. 'May she rest in peace, and he, too!'

Ralph Seton was silent for a moment. After that night he had never wished to look upon the face of his nymph again, nor had he.

'Do you think he will sleep . . . or will he look for her here?'

'Who can tell? At least he can vex no human now. But I think that after he had withdrawn the dagger it was over for him, and that you witnessed his very last appearance. Come back with me now, and I will show you what my friend at Oxford has sent me, and you shall judge.'

The doctor's study was homely and comfortable after the sleeping canal and that midnight drowning.

'Come to the fire; you are shivering,' said its owner, and when he had settled his guest in a chair and mixed him a whisky and soda – against his principles, as he informed him – he drew out a letter.

'This is what my friend, Dawkins of Corpus, says. I must tell you first, though, that I only put the case to him as a ghost story which I had recently heard; I did not state that it was actually the present experience of a patient of mine.

'"I have identified your ghost for you, I think, though I have not come across its name. I remembered to have read the tale you passed on to me some years ago in a book called *Curiosities of the Supernatural*, a collection made by a rather credulous Victorian parson, the Rev. Thomas White, who died about 1860. I got out this volume at the Bodleian and found (what I had forgotten) that the reverend author of the *Curiosities* had not told the story in his own words, but had lifted it bodily from a seventeenth-century pamphlet containing, apparently, several such yarns. But the tiresome old cleric omits to mention either the title of the pamphlet or the name of its writer. Here, however, is the passage as he gives it.

'"And what shall be said of that young Gallant of the time of good King *James*, who, being violently enamoured of a young and fair *French* gentlewoman that would none of his suit and but mocked at him, caused make a copy in bronze of that beauteous *Diana* wherein that sculptor of so great parts, Monsieur *Jean Goujon*, did immortalize both the lady *Diane of Poictiers* and himself, the which statue was held to resemble as closely this young scornful Beauty as once it had resembled that famous bedfellow of a king; what shall be said of this disdained lover, that took with him to *England* this simulacrum of his lady in a coffer, and, being come there, did wickedly pierce the breast of the twice-likened *Artemis*, and in that bloodless wound set a silver dagger wound about with charms; which charms, whether by his knowledge and consent or against it, did cause the death of his proud mistress within the year. And he, being gone (it is thought) to the *Indies* or the *Spanish Main*, knew naught of it; and then, in captivity of the *Spaniards*, still less than naught; but, after many years, returning to England, and desiring to see again the image of his dearest love whom he had done to death, sought it over the length and breadth of the land and could not by any means find it: till, about the time the late bloody tyrant *Oliver* began to raise his horn, he was near finding it; but by ill fortune, before he came at it, was himself slain, being then about sixty-five years of age, bearing arms for our late sovereign Lord King *Charles the Second* at *Worcester* fight, and that by a mortal thrust in the very spot where he had so impiously transfixed the statue. Which statue continues lost until this day, and 'tis said that he still seeks after it, sometimes in the semblance of a young man, sometimes as an old one. Yet, since it appears that he may enter no place in search of it that he be not bidden to enter, 'twould seem that this poor Phantome must continue his quest for ever. Nevertheless, 'tis certain that the effigy lies somewhere hid in the county of Worcester.'"

'I was right about the paper, you see,' said Dr Mildmay, laying down the letter.

'Yes, you were right. And so the nymph was Diana herself. And now we have drowned her . . . Goujon was a famous Renaissance sculptor, wasn't he? But she was a copy, the . . . the one we found?'

'Yes, and a copy, apparently, of a work of his which is now lost. I don't know much about him myself, but Dawkins, who is a perfect mine of information, has a postscript on that point.' Dr Mildmay took up his friend's letter again and turned it sideways. 'He says that it has been supposed by some critics that there existed another masterpiece besides the famous Diana now in the Louvre, the one where the goddess is seated with her arm round the neck of a stag, because in the eighteenth century somebody called – can't quite make it out, but it looks like Piganiol – spoke enthusiastically of another nymph in the orangery of the château of Anet, where the Diana of the Louvre comes from.'

'Yes, I see,' said Ralph Seton, looking fixedly at his untouched glass. 'But why did you wait until after our expedition of this evening to read me this, Doctor?'

'To be perfectly frank with you, because I thought the nymph was better out of the way. But if you regret what we did, if you think that she is valuable and that you could sell her – why, she is not yet sunk so deep that she cannot be fished up again!'

Dr Mildmay spoke cheerfully, but he was looking at his visitor with a gaze not devoid of anxiety.

'No, no,' answered Ralph Seton with a slight shiver. 'I would not condemn even an art collector to the possibility of going through what we have been going through . . . I suppose, by the way, that *he* was encouraged to begin again by our opening a tea shop at Hallows, which gave him a kind of right of entry, as into an inn . . . And I myself must have invited him into the attic, for my wife denies that it was she at the door when I shouted, "You can come in afterwards" – No, let's have no more of that! I'm all for the Englishman's castle, now, the sanctity of the home and that sort of thing!' And with a rather strained laugh he drank off his whisky and soda.

Jean Rhys

I USED TO LIVE HERE ONCE

S HE was standing by the river looking at the stepping-stones and remembering each one. There was the round unsteady stone, the pointed one, the flat one in the middle – the safe stone where you could stand and look round. The next wasn't so safe, for when the river was full the water flowed over it and even when it showed dry it was slippery. But after that it was easy and soon she was standing on the other side.

The road was much wider than it used to be but the work had been done carelessly. The felled trees had not been cleared away and the bushes looked trampled. Yet it was the same road and she walked along feeling extraordinarily happy.

It was a fine day, a blue day. The only thing was that the sky had a glassy look that she didn't remember. That was the only word she could think of. Glassy. She turned the corner, saw that what had been the old pavé had been taken up, and there too the road was much wider, but it had the same unfinished look.

She came to the worn stone steps that led up to the house and her heart began to beat. The screw pine was gone, so was the mock summer-house called the ajoupa, but the clove tree was still there and at the top of the steps the rough lawn stretched away, just as she remembered it. She stopped and looked towards the house that had been added to and painted white. It was strange to see a car standing in front of it.

There were two children under the big mango tree, a boy and a little girl, and she waved to them and called 'Hallo' but they didn't answer her or turn their heads. Very fair children, as Europeans born in the West Indies so often are: as if the white blood is asserting itself against all odds.

The grass was yellow in the hot sunlight as she walked towards them. When she was quite close she called again, shyly: 'Hallo.' Then, 'I used to live here once,' she said.

Still they didn't answer. When she said for the third time 'Hallo' she was quite near them. Her arms went out instinctively with the longing to touch them.

It was the boy who turned. His grey eyes looked straight into hers. His expression didn't change. He said: 'Hasn't it gone cold all of a sudden. D'you notice? Let's go in.' 'Yes let's,' said the girl.

Her arms fell to her sides as she watched them running across the grass to the house. That was the first time she knew.

Clotilde Graves

🪶

A SPIRIT ELOPEMENT

WHEN I exchanged my maiden name for better or worse, and dearest Vavasour and I, at the conclusion of the speeches – I was married in a travelling-dress of Bluefern's – descended the steps of Mamma's house in Ebury Street – the Belgravian, *not* the Pimlican end – and, amid a hurricane of farewells and a hailstorm of pink and yellow and white confetti, stepped into the brougham that was to convey us to Waterloo Station, *en route* for Southampton – our honeymoon was to be spent in Guernsey – we were perfectly well satisfied with ourselves and each other. This state of mind is not uncommon at the outset of wedded life. You may have heard the horrid story of the newly-wedded cannibal chief, who remarked that he had never yet known a young bride to disagree with her husband in the early stages of the honeymoon. I believe if dearest Vavasour had seriously proposed to chop me into *côtelettes* and eat me, with or without sauce, I should have taken it for granted that the powers that be had destined me to the high end of supplying one of the noblest created beings with an *entrée* dish.

We were idiotically blissful for two or three days. It was flowery April, and Guernsey was looking her loveliest. No horrid hotel or boarding-house sheltered our lawful endearments. Some old friends of Papa's had lent us an ancient mansion standing in a wild garden, now one pink riot of almond blossom, screened behind lofty walls of lichened red brick and weather-worn wrought-iron gates, painted yellow-white like all the other iron- and woodwork about the house.

'Mon Désir' the place was called, and the fragrance of potpourri yet hung about the old panelled salons. Vavasour wrote a sonnet – I have omitted to speak before of my husband's poetic gifts – all about the breath of new Passion stirring the fragrant dust of dead old Love, and the kisses of lips long mouldered that mingled with ours. It was a lovely sonnet, but crawly, as the poetical compositions of the Modern School are apt to be. And Vavasour was an enthusiastic convert to, and follower of, the Modern School. He had often told me that, had not his father heartlessly thrown him into his brewery business at the outset of his career – Sim's Mild and Bitter Ales being the foundation upon which the family fortunes were originally reared – he,

Vavasour, would have been, ere the time of speaking, known to Fame, not only as a Minor Poet, but a Minor Decadent Poet – which trisyllabic addition, I believe, makes as advantageous a difference as the word 'native' when attached to an oyster, or the guarantee 'new laid' when employed with reference to an egg.

Dear Vavasour's temperament and tastes having a decided bias towards the gloomy and mystic, he had, before his great discovery of his latent poetical gifts, and in the intervals of freedom from the brain-carking and soul-stultifying cares of business, made several excursions into the regions of the Unknown. He had had some sort of intercourse with the Swedenborgians, and had mingled with the Muggletonians; he had coquetted with the Christian Scientists, and had been, until Theosophic Buddhism opened a wider field to his researches, an enthusiastic Spiritualist. But our engagement somewhat cooled his passion for psychic research, and when he was questioned by me with regard to table-rappings, manifestations, and materializations, I could not but be conscious of a reticence in his manner of responding to my innocent desire for information. The reflection that he probably, like Canning's knife-grinder, had no story to tell, soon induced me to abandon the subject. I myself am somewhat reserved at this day in my method of dealing with the subject of spooks. But my silence does not proceed from ignorance.

Knowledge came to me after this fashion. Though the April sun shone bright and warm upon Guernsey, the island nights were chill. Waking by dear Vavasour's side – the novelty of this experience has since been blunted by the usage of years – somewhere between one and two o'clock towards break of the fourth day following our marriage, it occurred to me that a faint cold draught, with a suggestion of dampness about it, was blowing against my right cheek. One of the windows upon that side – our room possessed a rather unbecoming cross-light – had probably been left open. Dear Vavasour, who occupied the right side of our couch, would wake with toothache in the morning, or, perhaps, with mumps! Shuddering, as much at the latter idea as with cold, I opened my eyes, and sat up in bed with a definite intention of getting out of it and shutting the offending casement. Then I saw Katie for the first time.

She was sitting on the right side of the bed, close to dear Vavasour's pillow; in fact, almost hanging over it. From the first moment I knew that which I looked upon to be no creature of flesh and blood, but the mere apparition of a woman. It was not only that her face, which struck me as both pert and plain; her hands; her hair, which she wore dressed in an old-fashioned ringlety mode – in fact, her whole personality was faintly luminous, and surrounded by a halo of bluish phosphorescent light. It was not only that she was transparent, so that I saw the pattern of the old-fashioned, striped, dimity bed-curtain, in the shelter of which she sat, quite plainly through her. The consciousness was further conveyed to me by a voice – or the toneless, flat, faded impression of a voice – speaking faintly and clearly, not at my outer, but at my inner ear.

'Lie down again, and don't fuss. It's only Katie!' she said.

'Only Katie!' I liked that!

'I daresay you don't,' she said tartly, replying as she had spoken, and I wondered that a ghost could exhibit such want of breeding. 'But you have got to put up with me!'

'How dare you intrude here – and at such an hour!' I exclaimed mentally, for there was no need to wake dear Vavasour by talking aloud when my thoughts were read at sight by the ghostly creature who sat so familiarly beside him.

'I knew your husband before you did,' responded Katie, with a faint phosphorescent sneer. 'We became acquainted at a *séance* in north-west London soon after his conversion to Spiritualism, and have seen a great deal of each other from time to time.' She tossed her shadowy curls with a possessive air that annoyed me horribly. 'He was constantly materializing me in order to ask questions about Shakespeare. It is a standing joke in our Spirit world that, from the best-educated spook in our society down to the most illiterate astral that ever knocked out "rapport" with one "p", we are all expected to know whether Shakespeare wrote his own plays, or whether they were done by another person of the same name.'

'And which way was it?' I asked, yielding to a momentary twinge of curiosity.

Katie laughed mockingly. 'There you go!' she said, with silent contempt.

'I wish *you* would!' I snapped back mentally. 'It seems to me that you manifest a great lack of refinement in coming here!'

'I cannot go until Vavasour has finished,' said Katie pertly. 'Don't you see that he has materialized me by dreaming about me? And as there exists *at present*' – she placed an annoying stress upon the last two words – 'a strong sympathy between you, so it comes about that I, as your husband's spiritual affinity, am visible to your waking perceptions. All the rest of the time I am hovering about you, though unseen.'

'I call it detestable!' I retorted indignantly. Then I gripped my sleeping husband by the shoulder. 'Wake up! Wake up!' I cried aloud, wrath lending power to my grasp and a penetrative quality to my voice. 'Wake up and leave off dreaming! I cannot and will not endure the presence of this creature another moment!'

'*Whaa*—' muttered my husband with the almost inebriate incoherency of slumber, '*whasamaramydarling?*'

'Stop dreaming about that creature,' I cried, 'or I shall go home to Mamma!'

'Creature?' my husband echoed, and as he sat up I had the satisfaction of seeing Katie's misty, luminous form fade slowly into nothingness.

'You know who I mean!' I sobbed. 'Katie – your spiritual affinity, as she calls herself!'

'You don't mean', shouted Vavasour, now thoroughly roused, 'that you have seen *her*?'

'I do mean it,' I mourned. 'Oh, if I had only known of your having an entanglement with any creature of the kind, I would never have married you – never!'

'Hang her!' burst out Vavasour. Then he controlled himself, and said soothingly: 'After all, dearest, there is nothing to be jealous of—'

'I jealous! And of that—' I was beginning, but Vavasour went on:

'After all, she is only a disembodied astral entity with whom I became acquainted – through my fifth principle, which is usually well developed – in the days when I moved in Spiritualistic society. She was, when living – for she died long before I was born – a young lady of very good family. I believe her father was a clergyman . . . and I will not deny that I encouraged her visits.'

'Discourage them from this day!' I said firmly. 'Neither think of her nor dream of her again, or I will have a separation.'

'I will keep her, as much as possible, out of my waking thoughts,' said poor Vavasour, trying to soothe me; 'but a man cannot control his dreams, and she pervades mine in a manner which, even before our engagement, my pet, I began to find annoying. However, if she really is, as she has told me, a lady by birth and breeding, she will understand' – he raised his voice as though she were there and he intended her to hear – 'that I am now a married man, and from this moment desire to have no further communication with her. Any suitable provision it is in my power to make—'

He ceased, probably feeling the difficulty he would have in explaining the matter to his lawyers; and it seemed to me that a faint mocking snigger, or rather the auricular impression of it, echoed his words. Then, after some more desultory conversation, we fell soundly asleep. An hour may have passed when the same chilly sensation as of a damp draught blowing across the bed roused me. I rubbed my cheek and opened my eyes. They met the pale, impertinent smile of the hateful Katie, who was installed in her old post beside Vavasour's end of the bolster.

'You see,' she said, in the same soundless way, and with a knowing little nod of triumph. 'It is no use. He is dreaming of me again!'

'Wake up!' I screamed, snatching the pillow from under my husband's head and madly hurling it at the shameless intruder. This time Vavasour was almost snappish at being disturbed. Daylight surprised us in the middle of our first connubial quarrel. The following night brought a repetition of the whole thing and so on, *da capo*, until it became plain to us, to our mutual disgust, that the more Vavasour strove to banish Katie from his dreams, the more persistently she cropped up in them. She was the most ill-bred and obstinate of astrals – Vavasour and I the most miserable of newly-married people. A dozen times in a night I would be roused by that cold draught upon my cheek, would open my eyes and see that pale, phosphorescent, outline perched by Vavasour's pillow – nine times out of the dozen would be driven to frenzy by the possessive air and cynical smile of the spook. And although Vavasour's former regard for her was now converted into hatred, he found the thought of her continually invading his waking mind at the most unwelcome seasons. She had begun to appear to both of us *by day as well as by night* when our poisoned honeymoon came to an end, and we returned to town to occupy the house which Vavasour had taken and furnished in Sloane Street. I need only mention that Katie accompanied us.

Insufficient sleep and mental worry had by this time thoroughly soured my temper no less than Vavasour's. When I charged him with secretly encouraging the presence I had learned to hate, he rudely told me to think as I liked! He implored my pardon for this brutality afterwards upon his knees, and with the passage of time I learned to endure the presence of his attendant shade with patience. When she nocturnally hovered by the side of my sleeping spouse, or in constituence no less filmy than a whiff of cigarette smoke, appeared at his elbow in the face of day, I saw her plainly, and at these moments she would favour me with a significant contraction of the eyelid, which was, to say the least of it, unbecoming in a spirit who had been a clergyman's daughter. After one of these experiences it was that the idea which I afterwards carried into execution occurred to me.

I began by taking in a few numbers of a psychological publication entitled *The Spirit-Lamp*. Then I formed the acquaintance of Madame Blavant, the renowned Professoress of Spiritualism and Theosophy. Everybody has heard of Madame, many people have read her works, some have heard her lecture. I had heard her lecture. She was a lady with a strong determined voice and strong determined features. She wore her plentiful grey hair piled in sibylline coils on the top of her head, and – when she lectured – appeared in a white oriental silk robe that fell around her tall gaunt figure in imposing folds. This robe was replaced by one of black satin when she held her *séances*. At other times, in the seclusion of her study, she was draped in an ample gown of Indian chintz innocent of cut, but yet imposing. She smiled upon my newborn desire for psychic instruction, and when I had subscribed for a course of ten private *séances* at so many guineas apiece she smiled more.

Madame lived in a furtive, retiring house, situated behind high walls in Endor's Grove, NW. A long glass tunnel led from the garden gate to the street door, for the convenience of Mahatmas and other persons who preferred privacy. I was one of those persons, for not for spirit worlds would I have had Vavasour know of my repeated visits to Endor's Grove. Before these were over I had grown quite indifferent to supernatural manifestations, banjos and accordions that were thrummed by invisible performers, blood-red writing on mediums' wrists, mysterious characters in slate-pencil, Planchette, and the Table Alphabet. And I had made and improved upon acquaintance with Simon.

Simon was a spirit who found me attractive. He tried in his way to make himself agreeable, and, with my secret motive in view – let me admit without a blush – I encouraged him. When I knew I had him thoroughly in hand, I attended no more *séances* at Endor's Grove. My purpose was accomplished upon a certain night, when, feeling my shoulder violently shaken, I opened the eyes which had been closed in simulated slumber to meet the indignant glare of my husband. I glanced over his shoulder. Katie did not occupy her usual place. I turned my glance towards the armchair which stood at my side of the bed. It was not vacant. As I guessed, it was occupied by Simon. There he sat, the luminously transparent appearance of a weak-chinned, mild-looking young clergyman, dressed in the obsolete costume of eighty years previously. He gave me a bow in which respect mingled with some degree of complacency, and glanced at Vavasour.

'I have been explaining matters to your husband,' he said, in that soundless spirit-voice with which Katie had first made me acquainted. 'He understands that I am a clergyman and a reputable spirit, drawn into your life-orbit by the irresistible attraction which your mediumistic organization exercises over my—'

'There, you hear what he says!' I interrupted, nodding confirmatively at Vavasour. 'Do let me go to sleep!'

'What, with that intrusive beast sitting beside you?' shouted Vavasour indignantly. 'Never!'

'Think how many months I have put up with the presence of Katie!' said I. 'After all, it's only tit for tat!' And the ghost of a twinkle in Simon's pale eye seemed to convey that he enjoyed the retort.

Vavasour grunted sulkily, and resumed his recumbent position. But several times that night he awakened me with renewed objurgations of Simon, who with unflinching resolution maintained his post. Later on I started from sleep to find Katie's usual seat occupied. She looked less pert and confident than usual, I thought, and rather humbled and fagged, as though she had had some trouble in squeezing her way into Vavasour's sleeping thoughts. By day, after that night, she seldom appeared. My husband's brain was too much occupied with Simon, who assiduously haunted us. And it was now my turn to twit Vavasour with unreasonable jealousy. Yet though I gloried in the success of my stratagem, the continual presence of that couple of spooks was an unremitting strain upon my nerves.

But at length an extraordinary conviction dawned on my mind, and became stronger with each successive night. Between Simon and Katie an acquaintance had sprung up. I would awaken, or Vavasour would arouse, to find them gazing across the barrier of the bolster which divided them with their pale negatives of eyes, and chatting in still, spirit-voices. Once I started from sleep to find myself enveloped in a kind of mosquito tent of chilly, filmy vapour, and the conviction rushed upon me that He and She had leaned across our couch and exchanged an intangible embrace. Katie was the leading spirit in this, I feel convinced – there was no effrontery about Simon. Upon the next night I, waking, overheard a fragment of conversation between them which plainly revealed how matters stood.

'We should never have met upon the same plane,' remarked Simon silently, 'but for the mediumistic intervention of these people. Of the man' – he glanced slightingly towards Vavasour – 'I cannot truthfully say I think much. The lady' – he bowed in my direction – 'is everything that a lady should be!'

'You are infatuated with her, it is plain!' snapped Katie, 'and the sooner you are removed from her sphere of influence the better.'

'Her power with me is weakening,' said Simon, 'as Vavasour's is with you. Our outlines are no longer so clear as they used to be, which proves that our astral individualities are less strongly impressed upon the brains of our earthly sponsors than they were. We are still materialized; but how long this will continue—' He sighed and shrugged his shoulders.

'Don't let us wait for a formal dismissal, then,' said Katie boldly. 'Let us throw up our respective situations.'

'I remember enough of the Marriage Service to make our union, if not regular, at least respectable,' said Simon.

'And I know quite a fashionable place on the Outside Edge of Things, where we could settle down,' said Katie, 'and live practically on nothing.'

I blinked at that moment. When I saw the room again clearly, the chairs beside our respective pillows were empty.

Years have passed, and neither Vavasour nor myself has ever had a glimpse of the spirits whom we were the means of introducing to one another. We are quite content to know ourselves deprived for ever of their company. Yet sometimes, when I look at our three babies, I wonder whether that establishment of Simon's and Katie's on the Outside Edge of Things includes a nursery.

Eleanor Smith

WHITTINGTON'S CAT

MARTIN was the name of the young man who went alone nearly every evening to the local pantomime. Usually, he sat in the dress circle, but sometimes he patronized the stalls, and he had even been seen on more than one occasion seated – still quite alone – in a stage box. The programme girls knew him by sight, and discussed him very frequently, for the regularity of his attendance made him appear something of an oddity in their eyes. Always, however, they decided that he must be in love either with the Principal Boy or with the Principal Girl. Very often, when they had nothing better to do, they had bets with one another as to which of the two had caught his eye. Unless, of course, this eye had fallen upon someone else – upon Columbine, for instance, or upon the Fairy Queen. . . .

Martin himself was quite unconscious of their interest. Nor was he in love with anyone, with the possible exception of Marlene Dietrich. His reasons for visiting the Burford Hippodrome so constantly were, in fact, purely aesthetic – he was engaged in compiling a book that was to be entitled *Pantomime throughout the Ages*.

Why such a subject ever in the first place appealed to him is impossible to understand; he knew nothing of pantomime, nor was he acquainted with anyone likely to be of assistance to him in this direction; all he knew was that he felt the urge to write, and to write, what is more, upon this particular subject. Hence these nightly visits to the Burford Hippodrome.

Early that autumn, visiting a local curiosity shop, he had stumbled by chance upon a series of spangled prints representing characters from popular pantomimes; fascinated by the glitter and gaiety of these little pictures, he had bought the lot, and hung them in his bedroom; he was determined to reproduce them as illustrations to the book, and it is conceivable that his fondness for the collection may have influenced his choice of subject.

There was no particular reason why Martin should have bothered to write a book at all. He was rich, and had no need to work. In Burford and its neighbourhood he was considered a *parti*, and the eyes of those mothers whose daughters were marriageable rested very fondly and very frequently upon him.

His own mother had died when he was very young, and his father, a retired mill-owner, had left him pleasantly endowed upon departing this life about a year before the pantomime mania became manifest.

Life, then, for Martin, was comfortable if dull. He continued to inhabit the ancestral home, a large pleasant villa in a fashionable suburb of Burford, and his every want was ministered to by Mr and Mrs Renshaw, who were respectively manservant and cook, and who had attended to his father many years before. His life was perhaps inclined to be lonely. He was only twenty-five. Provincial society sometimes seemed tedious to him, and then he would toy with the idea of living in London, or cruising round the world, or spending a winter in Monte Carlo. But in the end he was always too timid, too conservative, to embark upon adventures so tremendous. Burford had, after all, been good enough for his father before him and for his grandfather before that, and he had a curious idea that he might, in London, find himself more lonely than was already the case. In Burford he knew everyone, everyone of Burford consequence, that is, and he dined out regularly, and was respected by the tradesmen, and made an impressive appearance each Sunday in his parish church.

He supposed that one day he would have to marry, and beget children, and carry on his family name, but whenever this idea occurred to him he felt slightly uncomfortable, for he had never, with the sole exception of the doctor's niece met anyone who in the least attracted him, and his own natural shyness made it difficult for him to appear at his ease in the society of women. He invariably decided, after such reflections, to live a life of great austerity, a life devoted uniquely to the pursuit of literature. Then he discovered the pantomime prints, and from that moment his destiny seemed assured.

Unfortunately, the famous book was by no means swift in materializing. He had always supposed that it would keep him occupied for at least five years, but whenever he came to ponder upon the magnitude of his task and his own ignorance of his subject, he decided that ten years might be an optimistic time-limit to put upon his labours.

And now every night he sat at the Burford Hippodrome to watch *Dick Whittington*, and it was really discouraging to realize how very little nearer he was even to beginning his book. So many trivial matters seemed to occupy his mind whenever he tried to concentrate upon the technique of panto-mime. He could not help speculating, for instance, upon the adenoids of the Principal Girl, and wondering why she had never had them removed in childhood; it irritated him when the Principal Boy sang flat, which he very often did; and sometimes he suspected the Dame of being ever so slightly intoxicated.

That it would have been possible to scrape up an acquaintance with any of these people never once occurred to him; he would have been too timid, in any case, to take the first step, and actually he was interested in them not as people, nor as actors, but merely as the traditional characters of Christmas pantomime.

One frosty day, early in January, he informed Mrs Renshaw that he would once again be dining at six o'clock.

'Yes, sir,' she answered politely, but she seemed to hover in the doorway, and he was conscious that she had not yet finished with him. He was correct in this surmise; she coughed for a moment, and then asked, casually:

'The pantomime again, Mr Martin?'

He was conscious that the Renshaws must think his behaviour absurd, and he therefore answered curtly, 'Yes', hoping that that would be an end of the matter.

And it seemed to be, for Mrs Renshaw changed the subject. She said: 'I hope that cat didn't keep you awake last night, Mr Martin?'

'What cat? I didn't hear anything. . . .'

'There was one howling all night on the roof. Renshaw threw a shoe at it, and then it stopped for a bit.'

'No, I didn't hear anything,' Martin repeated.

He was bored with the subject, for he disliked cats at the best of times. He added, hoping to get rid of Mrs Renshaw: 'Six o'clock, then.'

And this time she went.

That night, Martin sat in the front row of the dress circle to watch the tribulations of Dick, Alice Fitzwarren and the Emperor of Baghdad. During the performance something happened that he had always known would happen if he continued to haunt the Burford Hippodrome. His natural shyness made him long to avoid such an embarrassing encounter, yet to many men, less courageous perhaps than himself, what he dreaded would not have seemed so very terrible.

During a certain scene, Dick Whittington's Cat left the stage to climb up to one of the stage boxes, thence to swing itself along the circle, where it was wont to engage one or other of the specators in badinage, much to the delight of the entire audience.

Now it was Martin's turn to be picked out, and the odd thing is that he had known this all night. He turned scarlet, gripping the rail with both hands, while the Cat scrambled straight towards him, and small boys nearly split their sides with laughter. Just opposite to him the Cat paused, balancing itself astride the circle; it thrust its mask close to him, and as he flinched away, the audience roared its delight at the embarrassment of this young ninny.

The Cat wore a suit of shaggy black hair. It seemed enormous, almost like a giant, as it peered towards him, and he could discover no human lineaments beneath the fiercely whiskered mask. Even as he recoiled he tried to force a ghastly smile, and then the Cat, approaching nearer still, whispered to him:

'Poor Tom's a-cold . . .'

Then it vanished, swinging away faster than it had come.

Martin felt self-conscious for the remainder of the evening. He decided that he would never again patronize the circle – he was too well known locally to endure such ridicule. He went home, made a few notes, and poured himself out a glass of beer. As he was finishing his drink, his eye fell upon the open notebook at his side. He read:

Origin of the Catskin

This hairy, faun-like garb, the introduction into pantomime of the feline grotesque, is believed to date from the days of Daemonology, or Devil-Worship. The Cat . . .

He read the paragraph once more, shaking his head. It was, after all, entirely surmise. He shut the book and went to bed.

That night his sleep was inclined to be fitful, and once when he woke just before dawn, he could hear distinctly the miowling of that stray cat which had already disturbed the Renshaws. Too sleepy, too comfortable to care very much one way or the other, he buried his head in his pillows and soon dozed off once more. Then he dreamed, a vague, perplexing dream, during the course of which he sat once more in the Hippodrome circle, and the Pantomime Cat, thrusting its mask close to his face, muttered in his ear: 'Poor Tom's a-cold.'

When he woke in the morning he found that he himself was cold, the bedclothes having tumbled upon the floor during the course of his restless night. It was a clear frosty day, and there were ice-flowers trailing across his windowpane. He ate his breakfast with enjoyment and remembered that he was lunching with his oldest friend, the doctor who had brought him into the world.

Dr Browning was a sharp-witted little man in appearance rather like a dried-up russet apple. He was something of a gourmet; he had a pretty niece named Gwen, and Martin always enjoyed lunching with him very much indeed.

Today they were alone; Gwen was spending Christmas with an aunt in London.

'Still haunting the pantomime, Martin?' the doctor asked quizzically.

'Yes. I go nearly every night.'

'Do tell me what it is that fascinates you so much about that very shoddy show? Is she blonde, brunette, or auburn-haired?'

'I've told you, sir, about fifty times, that—'

'Oh, I know all about that famous book. And a very excellent excuse, if I may say so. I only wish I'd practised authorship instead of surgery.'

While the doctor was engaged in his favourite pursuit of teasing Martin, something uncomfortable happened. The household cat, a large sluggish tabby, suddenly saw fit to spring from beneath the table where she was concealed, on to the guest's knee; with an exclamation of horror, Martin flung out his hand and threw poor Tabitha most violently from his lap, whereupon she gave a screech of anger and bolted from the room.

'I'm so sorry,' Martin cried. He had jumped to his feet all prepared to brandish his napkin, to which he clung as though it were a sword.

'There's no need to be so rough!' rebuked the doctor, who was exceedingly fond of Tabitha, and who much disliked seeing her upset. 'Nerves a bit jumpy, aren't they?'

'I'm so sorry,' Martin said again.

He sat down, feeling incredibly foolish.

The doctor repeated his question.

'No,' said Martin, in reply to this, 'my nerves aren't in the least jumpy, really they're not. It's only – you know cats always give me the creeps. I know it sounds idiotic, but honestly it's the truth.'

'Pantomimes – cats – what on earth next?' was the doctor's retort to these excuses. 'God bless my soul, Martin, you're growing into an old maid before my very eyes! Why don't you get away from Burford for a bit – travel – see the world – meet other young people? Cats, indeed!'

And he snorted most violently, with the result that his guest felt sulky and resentful, and the lunch immediately turned into something of a failure.

None the less Martin went off to the pantomime once more that same evening.

He was sitting all alone in a box, musing as to the probable origin of Pantaloon, when the Frightful Thing occurred. And it was really very frightful indeed. On the stage, a transformation scene was in progress. Tinsel roses were melting into a gilded bower, peopled with dancing elves, when suddenly he felt a touch upon his neck. This touch was indescribably horrible – it was so soft, so furtive, so obviously the contact, not of a hand, but of a padded, cushiony paw. He turned, to see the Cat bending over him. In the darkness of the box the Cat's eyes gleamed emerald. In one second Martin realized the appalling truth – the Cat was no longer an actor in a shaggy suit, but a real Cat, a giant Cat, a Cat nearly six feet tall.

Martin sprang to his feet. He felt faint, but had no desire to cry out. The Cat said again, suggestively: 'Poor Tom's a-cold.' It put its paw upon his shoulder, patting him, obviously conciliatory, and with that sickening and velvety caress his will-power suddenly failed him. He had no longer any will of his own; it was all in one moment surrendered.

Swiftly it had passed, this will of his, like a dark wave, right away from him into the personality of the Cat.

He watched his companion dumbly, waiting to see what was wanted of him.

And it pointed, with one paw, at his overcoat, that hung upon a peg in the box, together with his hat and muffler. Vaguely he grasped what this gesture signified; it was desirous of escape, and it could only succeed in this project were it disguised in the outward lineaments of a human being.

He picked up his overcoat and held it out towards his companion. Slowly, snake-like, the Cat slid itself into the coat. It twined the muffler dexterously about its chin, so that the black mask was at least partly concealed; the felt hat it jammed forward upon its ears so that still more was hidden; then having regarded itself critically in the mirror at the back of the box, it motioned to Martin.

'Home,' it commanded briefly.

And Martin, that was now no longer Martin so much as an animated puppet, a Robot taught only to obey, found himself opening the door of the box that his companion might precede him. The Cat strolled through this door with an air almost nonchalant; had it not been for a plume of black tail protruding beneath the overcoat, it might well have passed for some sober Burford citizen.

Outside it was snowing.

The air was thick with a cloud of drifting snowflakes, and the pavement was already powdered as though with icing sugar.

The Cat moved quietly by Martin's side.

Martin wondered whether this was some ghastly nightmare from which he would presently awake. Glancing behind him, fearful of curiosity, he observed with a curious detachment the footprints of the Cat, walking beside his own in the snow, round, padded, clear-cut, the prints not of a man but of the gigantic beast that it was. He shivered. They walked on in silence. Soon they had arrived at Martin's house, and he was obediently fumbling for his latchkey even while he prayed most desperately for escape.

How could he possibly introduce this fiend, this spectre, into the pleasant, humdrum security of his own home? For one second, then, his apathy changed into the fierce frightened rebellion of a wild thing, and then he turned to face the Cat, although his tongue clove to the roof of his mouth and his knees were shaking.

'You can't—'

But two eyes, like fixed and glaring emeralds, bore like searchlights into his own, and in one moment his defiance had withered away, so that he was once more the slave of this thing that his own imagination had created from an actor's motley. The Cat stepped over the threshold before him, and that he knew was a significant moment in the history of this strange adventure. From that instant he realized that the Cat was to be master of his home.

He shut the door behind him.

Very deliberately the Cat divested itself of overcoat, hat and muffler. It stretched itself, then, so that a ripple of movement slid through all its body, and he was reminded of the many dozing tabbies that he had seen stretch thus on the hearthrugs of his friends.

It said: 'Supper?'

He could not in any way define its voice. He would have been unable to describe it. Was it husky, miowling, high-pitched, or gruff? Was it perhaps not so much a voice as the sinister reflection, perfectly comprehended by him, of the Cat's own immediate desires? The interpretative shadow of its dark mind? He did not know; all he knew was he himself moved, spoke, and thought in some hideous trance; he was passive obedience to the will of the Cat; he felt sick, and would have cut his own throat had he been so commanded.

'What sort of supper?'

And his own voice for the matter of that, sounded totally unfamiliar to him. A rusty creak that seemed to come from a long way away. If he pinched himself, perhaps he would awake from all that this nightmare meant . . . he pinched, but nothing happened. The nightmare was still there.

The Cat appeared to ponder.

'Some fish, some milk,' it said, at length.

He tried to tell himself: 'That's all right. Fish and milk – why, of course. It's just an ordinary cat. Nothing at all to worry about.'

Aloud, he said: 'Will you come into the dining-room?'

The Cat at once followed him into the respectability of this apartment, where Martin's father had so often stayed alone to drink his port. It sat down – at the head of the table. Its bushy tail stuck out from behind the chair. It said, and again he sensed a menacing inflection:

'Don't be long. Tom's hungry.'

He found himself in the larder without knowing how he got there. He discovered some tinned sardines, half a lobster and a jug of milk. He hastened back into the dining-room.

The Cat ate – like other cats. Exactly like other cats. That, too, should have been reassuring, but it wasn't. When it had finished eating, it washed its face meticulously, licking its great paws first, again like other cats.

It looked at Martin.

'Where is poor Tom's room?'

He was not astonished by this question. He had known from the first moment his companion entered the front door that it was there to stay. He knew, too, that sleep for him would not be possible with such a presence in his home.

'I'll show you', he said, 'the three spare rooms.'

In silence they made a tour of the bedroom floor. On the threshold of each room the Cat hesitated, peered and shook its head. One room was too cold, another faced the wrong way, and the third looked damp.

'Show your room.'

So that was it! He longed, at that moment, for some last remaining feeble flicker of defiance, or courage, or self-respect; he longed in vain; his will was still the will of the Cat. When it ordered, he must obey, since he could not cast off this hateful thrall.

'This is my room.'

The Cat glanced at the great glowing fire, the soft comfortable bed, the warm curtains, all the luxury and security of this pleasant apartment.

It seemed to grin.

'This will do.'

And in one moment, the detestable black furry form had glided into Martin's own bed, had insinuated itself beneath his silk eiderdown, had cushioned its whiskered head upon his own pillows. He was dispossessed; the Cat was most certainly master now.

He returned to the farthest spare room, where he made himself up a bed. The night passed slowly; he was too terrified to sleep, and, even had he wished to do so, the persistent yowling of cats on the roof outside would probably have interfered with his slumbers.

Mrs Renshaw, the next morning, was disturbed by Martin at an unusually early hour. He looked ghastly, and demanded a cup of tea. He then said to her in hesitating accents:

'Mrs Renshaw, I don't want either you or Renshaw to go near my room today.'

Mrs Renshaw seemed astonished.

He continued:

'I – the fact of the matter is that I met an old friend of mine last night. He – he's ill; he's got a bad chill, and what's more, he's in quarantine for – for scarlet fever. I'm going to nurse him myself, and I don't want anyone else to go near him.'

Mrs Renshaw continued to look astonished. She said, at length:

'But I've had the scarlet fever, Mr Martin, and if there's any trouble—'

He interrupted her harshly.

'I shall look after my friend myself. I don't wish germs to be carried all over the house. And now, will you get some haddock for breakfast? Some haddock, and a glass of warm milk. . . .'

'Whatever's happened to Martin?' Gwen Browning asked her uncle, about a week later.

The doctor glanced vaguely up from his crossword.

'I didn't know anything had happened to him. I haven't seen him for about a fortnight.'

'That's just what I mean,' said the girl. 'He's never even been to see me since I got back from London. Shall I ring him up and ask him to supper?'

'Of course, my dear. Ask him by all means.'

The doctor thought, not for the first time, how pleased he would be if Martin married his niece, and then at once forgot them both in the mysteries of his crossword.

'I don't think Mr Martin can come to the telephone,' Renshaw told Gwen shortly afterwards, in a cautious tone of voice.

'Why not? He's in, isn't he? I'll hold on.'

'He's upstairs. He's engaged. Could you leave a message, miss?'

Gwen gave her message, not without a slight feeling of rebuff. That afternoon, Renshaw rang her up to say that Martin was sorry he would be unable to come to supper – he was confined to the house with a bad cold.

'We'll ask him again in a day or two,' commented the doctor. He added that Martin's cold did not surprise him – the weather was as treacherous as he ever remembered.

That same evening, just before dusk, as the doctor was returning home after his rounds, he heard from the kerb opposite to where he was walking the well-known wail of the cats'-meat man. He crossed the road immediately; he was always ready to give Tabitha a treat. He was, however, just too late. As he approached he heard the man say to another customer:

'That's the lot, sir. You've cleared me out for the day.'

The customer turned, saw the doctor, and looked thoroughly dismayed. It was Martin, his pockets stuffed full of cats' meat.

'Thought you had a cold?' the doctor said, with brisk humour.

Martin hesitated. At length, he stammered: 'I – I have.'

The doctor suddenly noticed that even by twilight the boy looked drawn and ill.

'You ought to be indoors, you know.'

'I'm just going home.'

'Whatever possessed you to come out, with an east wind like this? Surely not just to buy cats' meat?'

And the doctor roared with laughter at his own joke.

'I'm going now,' Martin muttered.

'Well, I'll walk with you to the corner.'

They set off in silence.

'Come in and have supper, when you're feeling better. Gwen hasn't seen you since she went away.'

'Is she well?' Martin asked listlessly.

'She's all right. But you've lost weight since I saw you last, Martin. Sure you wouldn't like me to look you up professionally?'

'Oh, no, indeed not,' Martin protested, with such violence that the doctor was almost inclined to take offence. He was, however, good-natured; he felt sorry for the boy, and at length he tried another topic of conversation.

'You probably caught a chill at your beloved pantomime.'

'I haven't been there for a week.'

'By the way, talking of the pantomime, did you read about that odd theft down at the theatre, the other day?'

'No. What was it?'

'You remember Dick Whittington's Cat? But of course you do, as you went every night. Well, someone apparently stole the Cat costume from a dressing-room just before the show, and so the poor fellow who acts the Cat had to go on and play the part in his ordinary clothes. They got another costume down from London the next day, but the funny part is, they've never found the other one. Fancy you not seeing that!'

Here, to his great astonishment, the doctor found that he was addressing the air. Martin had vanished round the corner with a quite extraordinary celerity and with no word of farewell whatsoever.

'That boy's mad,' the doctor told Gwen later, 'stark, staring mad. Mooning about, looking like death, buying enough cats' meat to stock a Cats' Home, and treating me, *me*, who brought him into the world, with the most infernal puppy-dog impudence! Running away from me, I tell you! He's as mad as a hatter!'

Gwen said: 'But Martin hates cats.'

'He's mad, I tell you,' the doctor repeated.

'But I tell you he hates them. He dreads them. He can't even be in the room with Tabitha.'

'I don't wish to discuss the young cub any further.'

But the doctor had by no means finished with Martin, although at the moment he really imagined that he had.

The next morning Renshaw arrived, while Gwen and her uncle were at breakfast, requesting the favour of an immediate interview.

'Show him in,' said the doctor, 'and give me another cup of tea, Gwen.'

Gwen obeyed.

'Do you want to see the doctor alone?' she asked Renshaw, who appeared perturbed.

'No, Miss, not particularly. That is, what I have to say is private, but I'd be glad all the same, and so I'm sure would Mrs Renshaw, if you'd listen to what I have to say, as well as Dr Browning.'

'Influenza, I suppose?' queried the doctor, eating toast and marmalade.

'Nobody's ill, sir, not at home. Not as far as we know, that is. But Mrs Renshaw will be soon, if it isn't stopped.'

The doctor began to show signs of interest.

'Suppose you sit down, Renshaw, and tell us quite slowly what's worrying you. Take your time – I'm in no particular hurry at the moment. It's Mr Martin, I suppose?'

'In a way,' Renshaw admitted cautiously.

He sat down as he was told, and began:

'More than a week ago Mr Martin told us he had this friend sick in his own bedroom, and that we weren't to go inside the room or disturb him in any way. He said the gentleman was an old friend of his, and eccentric – didn't like servants, and would only eat food brought to him by Mr Martin.'

'Did you see this mysterious friend when he arrived?'

'No, sir. He came back with Mr Martin late one night. We didn't know he was in the house until the next morning. We thought it queer, but we did just as Mr Martin said. Mrs Renshaw cooked for him, and Mr Martin always took it up, and meanwhile Mr Martin was sleeping in the spare room. At last I asked whether one of us mightn't go up to the gentleman, just to sweep, and make his bed.'

He paused.

'Well?'

'Well, sir, Mr Martin flew into the most dreadful passion. He turned pale, and shouted at me, and swore, and asked me if I didn't understand plain English. He said that if he ever found either of us messing about near that bedroom, he'd have to make different arrangements. I asked him, then, how long the gentleman was going to stay, and he flew up again. Said it was none of my business, and told me to get out of the room and not interfere.'

'And then?' the doctor wanted to know.

'For the last few days Mr Martin has looked as white as a sheet, and seems a regular bundle of nerves – quite unlike his usual self. He keeps on complaining, too, to Mrs Renshaw, about the gentleman's food – says it isn't fit to eat, and the gentleman *must* be humoured. He's never complained about Mrs Renshaw's cooking before, sir, nor has anyone else.'

'What sort of food, by the way, is being sent up to the gentleman?' Dr Browning asked.

'Fish, sir, mostly. Sometimes a little chicken, and any amount of milk. The odd thing is, sir, that – well, he must eat all the bones, for none ever come down on the tray. We can't quite make it out.'

There was a pause. For the first time a vague sensation of apprehension obtruded itself into the pleasant room.

Then the doctor asked: 'Anything else, Renshaw?'

The man glanced across at him, and then dropped his eyes. 'Yes, sir, since you mention it. Something a bit queer. I don't scarcely expect you to believe it, although Mrs Renshaw will bear me out.'

'I think we'd better hear it,' the doctor decided, in a kind tone of voice, 'if I am to be of any help to you. What was this queer thing, eh?'

Renshaw licked his lips, smiled nervously, and began:

'Well, it was like this. The cats have been very bad round the house, lately, screeching all night. It hasn't been easy to sleep, with so much row. Last night I'd just dropped off when Mrs Renshaw woke me up. She said she heard someone moving about downstairs. It was nearly two o'clock, so it worried us both. I listened and heard footsteps. I thought it was perhaps Mr Martin, in a restless fit, but all the same, we couldn't very well leave it at that. We got out of bed and went downstairs, as quiet as we could. I had my electric torch.'

He paused.

'Go on,' encouraged the doctor. 'What happened then?'

'There was nothing, sir, although we'd both heard footsteps. But all the same, there was something funny in the drawing-room – you know the great goldfish bowl that belonged to Mr Martin's mother? Well, there it was, standing in the middle of the floor, with a lot of water slopped out of it, and all the fish gone – every one.'

'An odd thing to steal, goldfish!'

'That's not all, sir. As we tiptoed upstairs we determined to go past Mr Martin's bedroom, to see if the strange gentleman was awake.'

'Yes!' Gwen's voice was eager now.

'We did so, Miss. There was a thread of light under the door. We stopped a minute to listen.'

He paused once more, averting his eyes.

'Well?'

'Dr Browning, there's something in that room that's not human. I swear there is: I'm not easily scared.'

'Go on, Renshaw.'

'We stopped to listen, as I told you. We both heard it moving about. It wasn't walking – it was *padding*, like a great beast. And we heard it snarling, as though it was growling away to itself, and I tell you that noise made your blood run cold.'

'Anything else?'

'No, sir. Only, while it was still growling, the cats outside started again, and then the Thing in the room became quiet. We went back to bed, and this morning, after we'd talked it over, we both decided I should come to you.'

'A queer story,' commented the doctor; 'tell me, Mr Martin has been nervous and irritable since the arrival of this mysterious guest, I think you said. Has he shown any other signs of being unlike himself?'

Renshaw said simply: 'He seems afraid, sir.' He added: 'And he looks very bad.'

The doctor jumped up.

'I'll come over with you now, Renshaw. Wait while I get my hat.'

'Can I come, too?' Gwen wanted to know.

Her uncle looked doubtful.

'Oh, do let me! Perhaps – if he's ill – perhaps Martin might want me.'

'All right, you can come. But hurry up.'

They were silent, all three of them, as they walked across the busy streets of Burford towards Martin's home.

When they arrived at the house they were admitted by Mrs Renshaw, who looked pale and anxious.

'Where's Mr Martin?' asked the doctor.

'I don't know, sir. I haven't seen him since he took the gentleman's breakfast upstairs.'

'How long ago was that?'

'It must be about an hour, sir.'

'We'll go and see for ourselves,' the doctor said to Renshaw. 'Don't worry – I'll take all responsibility. Gwen, you go into the drawing-room and wait.'

'But, Uncle—'

'Do as I tell you, there's a good girl. For all we know, there may be a lunatic at large upstairs. Come on, Renshaw, and bring a stout walking-stick from the umbrella stand there. I've got mine.'

The house seemed very still as they walked upstairs. Only the guttural ticking of a grandfather clock disturbed the silence of the hall. They paused outside the bedroom, but all was quiet there, as well.

'If it's locked,' whispered the doctor, 'we must break it open. Are you ready?'

But the door was not locked. When the doctor turned the handle, it opened immediately, and they walked in without any difficulty whatsoever.

The room was in a strange condition. Sheets and blankets had been stripped off the bed and flung haphazard about the floor, which was still further cluttered up with piles of feathers, as though someone had been plucking chickens, gnawed bones, dirty plates, dishes, and empty glasses that had at one time probably contained milk. The windows were closed, and the room smelled of stale food. There was another odour, too, one more difficult to define – the strong, harsh stink of an animal's body.

At first sight, the room was empty.

Then the two men caught sight of something dark lying on the floor, at the foot of the bed.

'That's it,' the doctor muttered.

Gingerly they approached the heap of black fur that lay coiled so still. A second afterwards the doctor burst out laughing. His laughter was rather forced.

'Fooled again,' he said.

For the black object upon the floor was nothing more nor less than a shaggy suit, with mask attached, of the kind worn by actors impersonating animals in Christmas plays. For a moment all horror was removed; the hairy skin, the papier-mâché mask, brought back immediately reassuring memories of *Peter Pan*, of other pleasant, childish, homely amusements. The doctor picked up the suit and held it, dangling limply from his hand, nothing more nor less than an empty, grotesque, tousled cat's skin.

Then Renshaw, moving across to the other side of the bed, gave a sudden cry of fear and horror. The doctor dropped the cat's suit more abruptly than he had picked it up.

'Look, sir!'

On the floor near the fireplace Martin's body lay sprawled. It was concealed by the bed; that was why they had not seen it before.

The doctor knelt down and gently lifted the boy's head. It was then, as he afterwards said, that he himself, with all his fund of grim experience, felt physically sick. Martin's throat was bleeding profusely. It was lacerated, torn – a mass of fiendish, slashing, brutal wounds. The mark of the Beast; for such fury of destruction by tooth and claw no human being could ever have been responsible.

'Good God!' whispered Renshaw. 'Is he dead?'

The doctor answered brusquely: 'Get me a basin of water. Quickly, do you hear? *Quickly!*'

*   *   *

It was many, many weeks afterwards that Martin, still looking ghastly pale and with his neck swathed in bandages, lay back on his sofa and asked Dr Browning if he might speak to him for a few minutes.

'It's about all this,' he said. 'I've never felt like mentioning it before, either to you or to Gwen, but I've got to face it one day, and I believe I'm feeling up to it at last. Won't you please sit down?'

The doctor obeyed. He looked worried; he had been dreading this moment.

'Well, Martin?'

'Well, doctor? Won't you tell me the truth? Did I go off my head for a time? Did I live like an animal and in the end try to commit suicide? Or did a real lunatic dress himself in that skin and take possession of my house?'

'What do you yourself really think?' the doctor asked him gravely.

'What do I think? My opinion has never changed – I think as I did then. I am still convinced, absolutely and completely convinced, that some frightening thing, materializing as a gigantic cat, took entire possession, not only of my house, but of my mind and of my soul. Hypnotism – it was more than that, far far more. I was the *will* of this creature, whatever it may have been. I existed only to do its bidding. Then, one day, I suppose it grew angry with me for some reason or other, or perhaps grew tired of being here, and it attacked me, before it disappeared. That sounds like a madman's explanation, doesn't it? But frankly, I have no other. Now tell me what you think.'

The doctor lighted his pipe.

'I think you're very lucky to be alive.'

'What else?'

'I'll tell you, Martin, since you want to know. What I've got to say is unethical and the world would probably laugh me out of the medical profession if it heard me talking to you, but I'll chance that.' He took a pull at his pipe. 'Look here, Martin, it's not good for any young man to live so much alone as you've been doing. This lonely house, these books – it's not a healthy existence. You're inclined to be imaginative, you're a bit neurotic into the bargain, and all that combined is tempting Providence.'

'Well?'

'Merely this: let us suppose for a moment that there do dwell, on the borders of this world and some other world, unclean spirits, evil elementals, forever in search, so to speak, of pliable human minds on which to impose their own will – suppose, I say, just suppose, such creatures exist, you yourself would undoubtedly have been an ideal victim for their experiments. Do you see?'

There was a pause.

'I see', Martin said, slowly, 'that at least you understand my story and don't think me mad.'

'I don't think you mad. . . . Go abroad for six months, and when you come back to Burford try to interest yourself in something less solitary than study. Buy a car, but learn to repair it yourself. Keep a horse, but groom it. And don't go mooning about by yourself at pantomimes any more. Take some children with you next time.'

'There won't be any next time,' said Martin.

It was only when he was alone once again that Martin noticed something curious.

He was looking – for the first time for many weeks – at the pantomime prints of which he was so fond. How pretty they were, how gay, how bright were their spangles – there were Pantaloon and Harlequin, and the Demon King, and there was Columbine, and there the Cat – but no, that was the funny thing – the form of the Cat had disappeared entirely from its frame, and although the spangled background of the print remained the same, the space once occupied by the little figure was now blank and empty.

The Cat had vanished; could it, he hoped, be for ever?

Ruth Rendell

THE HAUNTING OF
SHAWLEY RECTORY

I DON'T believe in the supernatural, but just the same I wouldn't live in Shawley Rectory.

That was what I had been thinking and what Gordon Scott said to me when we heard we were to have a new rector at St Mary's. Our wives gave us quizzical looks.

'Not very logical,' said Eleanor, my wife.

'What I mean is,' said Gordon, 'that however certain you might be that ghosts don't exist, if you lived in a place that was reputedly haunted you wouldn't be able to help wondering every time you heard a stair creak. All the normal sounds of an old house would take on a different significance.'

I agreed with him. It wouldn't be very pleasant feeling uneasy every time one was alone in one's own home at night.

'Personally,' said Patsy Scott, I've aways believed there are no ghosts in the Rectory that a good central-heating system wouldn't get rid of.'

We laughed at that, but Eleanor said, 'You can't just dismiss it like that. The Cobworths heard and felt things even if they didn't actually see anything. And so did the Bucklands before them. And you won't find anyone more level-headed than Kate Cobworth.'

Patsy shrugged. 'The Loys didn't even hear or feel anything. They'd heard the stories, they *expected* to hear the footsteps and the carriage wheels. Diana Loy told me. And Diana was quite a nervy highly strung sort of person. But absolutely nothing happened while they were there.'

'Well, maybe the Church of England or whoever's responsible will install central heating for the new person,' I said, 'and we'll see if your theory's right, Patsy.'

Eleanor and I went home after that. We went on foot because our house is only about a quarter of a mile up Shawley Lane. On the way we stopped in front of the Rectory, which is about a hundred yards along. We stood and looked over the gate.

I may as well describe the Rectory to you before I get on with this story. The date of it is around 1760 and it's built of pale dun-coloured brick with plain classical windows and a front door in the middle with a pediment over it. It's a big house with three reception rooms, six bedrooms, two kitchens and two staircases – and one poky little bathroom made by having converted a linen closet. The house is a bit stark to look at, a bit forbidding; it seems to stare straight back at you, but the trees round it are pretty enough and so are the stables on the left-hand side with a clock in their gable and a weathervane on top. Tom Cobworth, the last Rector, kept his old Morris in there. The garden is huge, a wilderness that no one could keep tidy these days – eight acres of it including the glebe.

It was years since I had been inside the Rectory. I remember wondering if the interior was as shabby and in need of paint as the outside. The windows had that black, blank, hazy look of windows at which no curtains hang and which no one has cleaned for months or even years.

'Who exactly does it *belong* to?' said Eleanor.

'Lazarus College, Oxford,' I said. 'Tom was a Fellow of Lazarus.'

'And what about this new man?'

'I don't know,' I said. 'I think all that system of livings has changed but I'm pretty vague about it.'

I'm not a churchgoer, not religious at all really. Perhaps that was why I hadn't got to know the Cobworths all that well. I used to feel a bit uneasy in Tom's company, I used to have the feeling he might suddenly round on me and demand to know why he never saw me in church. Eleanor had no such inhibitions with Kate. They were friends, close friends, and Eleanor had missed her after Tom died suddenly of a heart attack and she had had to leave the Rectory. She had gone back to her people up north, taking her fifteen-year-old daughter Louise with her.

Kate is a practical down-to-earth Yorkshirewoman. She had been a nurse – a ward sister, I believe – before her marriage. When Tom got the living of Shawley she several times met Mrs Buckland, the wife of the retiring incumbent, and from her learned to expect what Mrs Buckland called 'manifestations'.

'I couldn't believe she was actually saying it,' Kate had said to Eleanor. 'I thought I was dreaming and then I thought she was mad. I mean really psychotic, mentally ill. Ghosts! I ask you – people believing things like that in this day and age. And then we moved in and I heard them too.'

The crunch of carriage wheels on the gravel drive when there was no carriage or any kind of vehicle to be seen. Doors closing softly when no doors had been left open. Footsteps crossing the landing and going downstairs, crossing the hall, then the front door opening softly and closing softly.

'But how could you bear it?' Eleanor said. 'Weren't you afraid? Weren't you terrified?'

'We got used to it. We had to, you see. It wasn't as if we could sell the house and buy another. Besides, I love Shawley – I loved it from the first moment I set foot in the village. After the harshness of the north, Dorset is so gentle and mild and pretty. The doors closing and the footsteps and the wheels on the drive – they didn't do us any harm. And we had each other, we weren't alone. You can get used to anything – to ghosts as much as to damp and woodworm and dry rot. There's all that in the Rectory too and I found it much more trying!'

The Bucklands, apparently, had got used to it too. Thirty years he had been Rector of the parish, thirty years they had lived there with the wheels and the footsteps, and had brought up their son and daughter there. No harm had come to them; they slept soundly, and their grown-up children used to joke about their haunted house.

'Nobody ever seems to *see* anything,' I said to Eleanor as we walked home. 'And no one ever comes up with a story, a sort of background to all this walking about and banging and crunching. Is there supposed to have been a murder there or some other sort of violent death?'

She said she didn't know, Kate had never said. The sound of the wheels, the closing of the doors, always took place at about nine in the evening, followed by the footsteps and the opening and closing of the front door. After that there was silence, and it hadn't happened every evening by any means. The only other thing was that Kate had never cared to use the big drawing-room in the evenings. She and Tom and Louise had always stayed in the dining-room or the morning-room.

They did use the drawing-room in the daytime – it was just that in the evenings the room felt strange to her, chilly even in summer, and indefinably hostile. Once she had had to go in there at ten-thirty. She needed her reading glasses which she had left in the drawing-room during the afternoon. She ran into the room and ran out again. She hadn't looked about her, just rushed in, keeping her eyes fixed on the eyeglass case on the mantelpiece. The icy hostility in that room had really frightened her, and that had been the only time she had felt dislike and fear of Shawley Rectory.

Of course one doesn't have to find explanations for an icy hostility. It's much more easily understood as being the product of tension and fear than aural phenomena are. I didn't have much faith in Kate's feelings about the drawing-room. I thought with a kind of admiration of Jack and Diana Loy, that elderly couple who had rented the Rectory for a year after Kate's departure, had been primed with stories of hauntings by Kate, yet had neither heard nor felt a thing. As far as I know, they had used that drawing-room constantly. Often, when I had passed the gate in their time, I had seen lights in the drawing-room windows, at nine, at ten-thirty, and even at midnight.

The Loys had been gone three months. When Lazarus had first offered the Rectory for rent, the idea had been that Shawley should do without a clergyman of its own. I think this must have been the Church economizing – nothing to do certainly with ghosts. The services at St Mary's were to be undertaken by the Vicar of the next parish, Mr Hartley. Whether he found this too much for him in conjunction with the duties of his own parish or whether the powers-that-be in affairs Anglican had second thoughts, I can't say; but on the departure of the Loys it was decided there should be an incumbent to replace Tom.

The first hint of this we had from local gossip; next the facts appeared in our monthly news sheet, the *Shawley Post*. Couched in its customary parish magazine journalese it said: 'Shawley residents all extend a hearty welcome to their new Rector, the Reverend Stephen Galton, whose coming to the parish with his charming wife will fill a long-felt need.'

'He's very young,' said Eleanor a few days after our discussion of haunting with the Scotts. 'Under thirty.'

'That won't bother me,' I said. 'I don't intend to be preached at by him. Anyway, why not? Out of the mouths of babes and sucklings,' I said, 'hast Thou ordained strength.'

'Hark at the devil quoting scripture,' said Eleanor. 'They say his wife's only twenty-three.'

I thought she must have met them, she knew so much. But no.

'It's just what's being said. Patsy got it from Judy Lawrence. Judy said they're moving in next month and her mother's coming with them.'

'Who, Judy's?' I said.

'Don't be silly,' said my wife. 'Mrs Galton's mother, the Rector's mother-in-law. She's coming to live with them.'

Move in they did. And out again two days later.

The first we knew that something had gone very wrong for the Galtons was when I was out for my usual evening walk with our Irish setter Liam. We were coming back past the cottage that belongs to Charlie Lawrence (who is by way of being Shawley's squire) and which he keeps for the occupation of his gardener when he is lucky enough to have a gardener. At that time, last June, he hadn't had a gardener for at least six months, and the cottage should have been empty. As I approached, however, I saw a woman's face, young, fair, very pretty, at one of the upstairs windows.

I rounded the hedge and Liam began an insane barking, for just inside the cottage gate, on the drive, peering in under the hood of an aged Wolseley, was a tall young man wearing a tweed sports jacket over one of those black-top things the clergy wear, and a clerical collar.

'Good evening,' I said. 'Shut up, Liam, will you?'

'Good evening,' he said in a quiet, abstracted sort of way.

I told Eleanor. She couldn't account for the Galtons occupying Charlie Lawrence's gardener's cottage instead of Shawley Rectory, their proper abode. But Patsy Scott could. She came round on the following morning with a punnet of strawberries for us. The Scotts grow the best strawberries for miles around.

'They've been driven out by the ghosts,' she said. 'Can you credit it? A clergyman of the Church of England! An educated man! They were in that place not forty-eight hours before they were screaming to Charlie Lawrence to find them somewhere else to go.'

I asked her if she was sure it wasn't just the damp and the dry rot.

'Look, you know me. *I* don't believe the Rectory's haunted or anywhere *can* be haunted, come to that. I'm telling you what Mrs Galton told me. She came in to us on Thursday morning and said did I think there was anyone in Shawley had a house or a cottage to rent because they couldn't stick the Rectory another night. I asked her what was wrong. And she said she knew it sounded crazy – it did too, she was right there – she knew it sounded mad, but they'd been terrified out of their lives by what they'd heard and seen since they moved in.'

'*Seen?*' I said. 'She actually claims to have seen something?'

'She said her mother did. She said her mother saw something in the drawing-room the first evening they were there. They'd already heard the carriage wheels and the doors closing and the footsteps and all that. The second evening no one dared go in the drawing-room. They heard all the sounds again and Mrs Grainger – that's the mother – heard voices in the drawing-room, and it was then that they decided they couldn't stand it, they'd have to get out.'

'I don't believe it!' I said. 'I don't believe any of it. The woman's a psychopath, she's playing some sort of ghastly joke.'

'Just as Kate was and the Bucklands,' said Eleanor quietly.

Patsy ignored her and turned to me. 'I feel just like you. It's awful, but what can you do? These stories grow and they sort of infect people and the more suggestible the people are, the worse the infection. Charlie and Judy are furious, they don't want it getting in the papers that Shawley Rectory is haunted. Think of all the people we shall get coming in cars on Sundays and gawping over the gates. But they had to let them have the cottage in common humanity. Mrs Grainger was hysterical and poor little Mrs Galton wasn't much better. Who told them to expect all those horrors? That's what I'd like to know.'

'What does Gordon say?' I said.

'He's keeping an open mind, but he says he'd like to spend an evening there.'

In spite of the Lawrences' fury, the haunting of Shawley Rectory did get quite a lot of publicity. There was a sensational story about it in one of the popular Sundays and then Stephen Galton's mother-in-law went on television. Western TV interviewed her on a local news programme. I hadn't ever seen Mrs Grainger in the flesh and her youthful appearance rather surprised me. She looked no more than thirty-five, though she must be into her forties.

The interviewer asked her if she had ever heard any stories of ghosts at Shawley Rectory before she went there and she said she hadn't. Did she believe in ghosts? Now she did. What had happened, asked the interviewer, after they had moved in?

It had started at nine o'clock, she said, at nine on their first evening. She and her daughter were sitting in the bigger of the two kitchens, having a cup of coffee. They had been moving in all day, unpacking, putting things away. They heard two doors close upstairs, then footsteps coming down the main staircase. She had thought it was her son-in-law, except that it couldn't have been because as the footsteps died away he came in through the door from the back kitchen. They couldn't understand what it had been, but they weren't frightened. Not then.

'We were planning on going to bed early,' said Mrs Grainger. She was very articulate, very much at ease in front of the cameras. 'Just about half-past ten I had to go into the big room they call the drawing-room. The removal men had put some of our boxes in there and my radio was in one of them. I wanted to listen to my radio in bed. I opened the drawing-room door and put my hand to the light switch. I didn't put the light on. The moon was quite bright that night and it was shining into the room.

'There were two people, two figures, I don't know what to call them, between the windows. One of them, the girl, was lying huddled on the floor. The other figure, an older woman, was bending over her. She stood up when I opened the door and looked at me. I knew I wasn't seeing real people, I don't know how but I knew that. I remember I couldn't move my hand to switch the light on. I was frozen, just staring at that pale tragic face while it stared back at me. I did manage at last to back out and close the door, and I got back to my daughter and my son-in-law in the kitchen and I – well, I collapsed. It was the most terrifying experience of my life.'

Yet you stayed a night and a day and another night in the Rectory? said the interviewer. Yes, well, her daughter and her son-in-law had persuaded her it had been some sort of hallucination, the consequence of being overtired. Not that she had ever really believed that. The night had been quiet and so had the next day until nine in the evening when they were all this time in the morning-room and they heard a car drive up to the front door. They had all heard it, wheels crunching on the gravel, the sound of the engine, the brakes going on. Then had followed the closing of the doors upstairs and the footsteps, the opening and closing of the front door.

Yes, they had been very frightened, or she and her daughter had. Her son-in-law had made a thorough search of the whole house but found nothing, seen or heard no one. At ten-thirty they had all gone into the hall and listened outside the drawing-room door and she and her daughter had heard voices from inside the room, women's voices. Stephen had wanted to go in, but they had stopped him, they had been so frightened.

Now the interesting thing was that there had been something in the *Sunday Express* account about the Rectory being haunted by the ghosts of two women. The story quoted someone it described as a 'local antiquarian', a man named Joseph Lamb, whom I had heard of but never met. Lamb had told the *Express* there was an old tradition that the ghosts were of a mother and her daughter and that the mother had killed the daughter in the drawing-room.

'I never heard any of that before,' I said to Gordon Scott, 'and I'm sure Kate Cobworth hadn't. Who is this Joseph Lamb?'

'He's a nice chap,' said Gordon. 'And he's supposed to know more of local history than anyone else around. I'll ask him over and you can come and meet him if you like.'

Joseph Lamb lives in a rather fine Jacobean house in a hamlet – you could hardly call it a village – about a mile to the north of Shawley. I had often admired it without knowing who had lived there. The Scotts asked him and his wife to dinner shortly after Mrs Grainger's appearance on television, and after dinner we got him on to the subject of the hauntings. Lamb wasn't at all unwilling to enlighten us. He's a man of about sixty and he said he first heard the story of the two women from his nurse when he was a little boy. Not a very suitable subject with which to regale a seven-year-old, he said.

'These two are supposed to have lived in the Rectory at one time,' he said. 'The story is that the mother had a lover or a man friend or whatever, and the daughter took him away from her. When the daughter confessed it, the mother killed her in a jealous rage.'

It was Eleanor who objected to this. 'But surely if they lived in the Rectory they must have been the wife and daughter of a Rector. I don't really see how in those circumstances the mother could have had a lover or the daughter could steal him away.'

'No, it doesn't sound much like what we've come to think of as the domestic life of the English country parson, does it?' said Lamb. 'And the strange thing is, although my nanny used to swear by the story and I heard it later from someone who worked at the Rectory, I haven't been able to find any trace of these women in the Rectory's history. It's not hard to research, you see, because only the Rectors of Shawley had ever lived there until the Loys rented it, and the Rectors' names are all up on that plaque in the church from 1380 onwards. There was another house on the site before this present one, of course, and parts of the older building are incorporated in the newer.

'My nanny used to say that the elder lady hadn't got a husband, he had presumably died. She was supposed to be forty years old and the girl nineteen. Well, I tracked back through the families of the various Rectors and I found a good many cases where the Rectors had predeceased their wives. But none of them fitted my nanny's story. They were either too old – one was much too young – or their daughters were too old or they had no daughters.'

'It's a pity Mrs Grainger didn't tell us what kind of clothes her ghosts were wearing,' said Patsy with sarcasm. 'You could have pinpointed the date then, couldn't you?'

'You mean that if the lady had had a steeple hat on she'd be medieval or around 1850 if she was wearing a crinoline?'

'Something like that,' said Patsy.

At this point Gordon repeated his wish to spend an evening in the Rectory. 'I think I'll write to the Master of Lazarus and ask permission,' he said.

Very soon after we heard that the Rectory was to be sold. Notice boards appeared by the front gate and at the corner where the glebe abutted Shawley Lane, announcing that the house would go up for auction on October the 30th. Patsy, who always seems to know everything, told us that a reserve price of £60,000 had been put on it.

'Not as much as I'd have expected,' she said. 'It must be the ghosts keeping the price down.'

'Whoever buys it will have to spend another ten thousand on it,' said Eleanor.

'And central heating will be a priority.'

Whatever was keeping the price down – ghosts, cold, or dry rot – there were plenty of people anxious to view the house and land with, I supposed an idea of buying it. I could hardly be at work in my garden or out with Liam without a car stopping and the driver asking me the way to the Rectory. Gordon and Patsy got quite irritable about what they described as 'crowds milling about' in the lane and trippers everywhere, waving orders to view.

The estate agents handling the sale were a firm called Curlew, Pond and

66

Co. Gordon didn't bother with the Master of Lazarus but managed to get the key from Graham Curlew, whom he knew quite well, and permission to spend an evening in the Rectory. Curlew didn't like the idea of anyone staying the night, but Gordon didn't want to do that anyway; no one had ever heard or seen anything after ten-thirty. He asked me if I'd go with him. Patsy wouldn't – she thought it was all too adolescent and stupid.

'Of course I will,' I said. 'As long as you'll agree to our taking some sort of heating arrangement with us and brandy in case of need.'

By then it was the beginning of October and the evenings were turning cool. The day on which we decided to have our vigil happened also to be the one on which Stephen Galton and his wife moved out of Charlie Lawrence's cottage and left Shawley for good. According to the *Shawley Post*, he had got a living in Manchester. Mrs Grainger had gone back to her own home in London from where she had written an article about the Rectory for *Psychic News*.

Patsy shrieked with laughter to see the two of us setting forth with our oil-stove, a dozen candles, two torches, and half a bottle of Courvoisier. She did well to laugh, her amusement wasn't misplaced. We crossed the lane and opened the Rectory gate and went up the gravel drive on which those spirit wheels had so often been heard to crunch. It was seven o'clock in the evening and still light. The day had been fine and the sky was red with the aftermath of a spectacular sunset.

I unlocked the front door and in we went.

The first thing I did was put a match to one of the candles because it wasn't at all light inside. We walked down the passage to the kitchens, I carrying the candle and Gordon shining one of the torches across the walls. The place was a mess. I suppose it hadn't had anything done to it, not even a cleaning, since the Loys moved out. It smelled damp and there was even fungus growing in patches on the kitchen walls. And it was extremely cold. There was a kind of deathly chill in the air, far more of a chill than one would have expected on a warm day in October. That kitchen had the feel you get when you open the door of a refrigerator that hasn't been kept too clean and is in need of defrosting.

We put our stuff down on a kitchen table someone had left behind and made our way up the back stairs. All the bedroom doors were open and we closed them. The upstairs had a neglected, dreary feel but it was less cold. We went down the main staircase, a rather fine curving affair with elegant banisters and carved newel posts, and entered the drawing-room. It was empty, palely lit by the evening light from two windows. On the mantelpiece was a glass jar with greenish water in it, a half-burnt candle in a saucer, and a screwed-up paper table napkin. We had decided not to remain in this room but to open the door and look in at ten-thirty; so accordingly we returned to the kitchen, fetched out candles and torches and brandy, and settled down in the morning-room, which was at the front of the house, on the other side of the front door.

Curlew had told Gordon there were a couple of deckchairs in this room. We found them resting against the wall and we put them up. We lit our oil-stove and a second candle, and we set one candle on the window sill and one on the floor between us. It was still and silent and cold. The dark closed in fairly rapidly, the red fading from the sky, which became a deep hard blue, then indigo.

We sat and talked. It was about the haunting that we talked, collating the various pieces of evidence, assessing the times this or that was supposed to happen and making sure we both knew the sequence in which things happened. We were both wearing watches and I remember that we constantly checked the time. At half-past eight we again opened the drawing-room door and looked inside. The moon had come up and was shining through the windows as it had shone for Mrs Grainger.

Gordon went upstairs with a torch and checked that all the doors remained closed and then we both looked into the other large downstairs room, the dining-room, I suppose. Here a fanlight in one of the windows was open. That accounted for some of the feeling of cold and damp, Gordon said. The window must have been opened by some prospective buyer, viewing the place. We closed it and went back into the morning-room to wait.

The silence was absolute. We didn't talk any more. We waited, watching the candles and the glow of the stove, which had taken some of the chill from the air. Outside it was pitch-dark. The hands of our watches slowly approached nine.

At three minutes to nine we heard the noise.

Not wheels or doors closing or a tread on the stairs but a faint, dainty, pattering sound. It was very faint, it was distant, it was on the ground floor. It was as if made by something less than human, lighter than that, tiptoeing. I had never thought about this moment beyond telling myself that if anything did happen, if there was a manifestation, it would be enormously interesting. It had never occurred to me even once that I should be so dreadfully, so hideously, afraid.

I didn't look at Gordon, I couldn't. I couldn't move either. The pattering feet were less faint now, were coming closer. I felt myself go white, the blood all drawn in from the surface of my skin, as I was gripped by that awful primitive terror that has nothing to do with reason or with knowing what you believe in and what you don't.

Gordon got to his feet, and stood there looking at the door. And then I couldn't stand it any more. I jumped up and threw open the door, holding the candle aloft – and looked into a pair of brilliant golden-green eyes, staring steadily back at me about a foot from the ground.

'My God,' said Gordon. 'My God, it's Lawrences' cat. It must have got in through the window.'

He bent down and picked up the cat, a soft, stout, marmalade-coloured creature. I felt sick at the anticlimax. The time was exactly nine o'clock. With the cat draped over his arm, Gordon went back into the morning-room and I followed him. We didn't sit down. We stood waiting for the wheels and the closing of the doors.

Nothing happened.

I have no business to keep you in suspense any longer for the fact is that after the business with the cat nothing happened at all. At nine-fifteen we sat down in our deckchairs. The cat lay on the floor beside the oil-stove and went to sleep. Twice we heard a car pass along Shawley Lane, a remotely distant sound, but we heard nothing else.

'Feel like a spot of brandy?' said Gordon.

'Why not?' I said.

So we each had a nip of brandy and at ten we had another look in the drawing-room. By then we were both feeling bored and quite sure that since nothing had happened at nine nothing would happen at ten-thirty either. Of course we stayed till ten-thirty and for half an hour after that, and then we decamped. We put the cat over the wall into Lawrences' grounds and went back to Gordon's house where Patsy awaited us, smiling cynically.

I had had quite enough of the Rectory but that wasn't true of Gordon. He said it was well known that the phenomena didn't take place every night; we had simply struck an off-night, and he was going back on his own. He did too, half a dozen times between then and the 30th, even going so far as to have (rather unethically) a key cut from the one Curlew had lent him. Patsy would never go with him, though he tried hard to persuade her.

But in all those visits he never saw or heard anything. And the effect on him was to make him as great a sceptic as Patsy.

'I've a good mind to make an offer for the Rectory myself,' he said. 'It's a fine house and I've got quite attached to it.'

'You're not serious,' I said.

'I'm perfectly serious. I'll go to the auction with a view to buying it if I can get Patsy to agree.'

But Patsy preferred her own house and, very reluctantly, Gordon had to give up the idea. The Rectory was sold for £62,000 to an American woman, a friend of Judy Lawrence. About a month after the sale the builders moved in.

Eleanor used to get progress reports from Patsy, how they had rewired and treated the whole place for woodworm and painted and relaid floors. The central-heating engineers came too, much to Patsy's satisfaction.

We met Carol Marcus, the Rectory's new owner, when we were asked round to the Hall for drinks one Sunday morning. She was staying there with the Lawrences until such time as the improvements and decorations to the Rectory were complete. We were introduced by Judy to a very pretty, well-dressed woman in young middle age. I asked her when she expected to move in. April, she hoped, as soon as the builders had finished the two extra bathrooms. She had heard rumours that the Rectory was supposed to be haunted and these had amused her very much. A haunted house in the English countryside! It was too good to be true.

'It's all nonsense, you know,' said Gordon, who had joined us. 'It's all purely imaginary.' And he went on to tell her of his own experiences in the house during October – or his non-experiences, I should say.

'Well, for goodness' sake, I didn't *believe* it!' she said, and she laughed and went on to say how much she loved the house and wanted to make it a real home for her children to come to. She had three, she said, all in their teens, two boys away at school and a girl a bit older.

That was the only time I ever talked to her and I remember thinking she would be a welcome addition to the neighbourhood. A nice woman. Serene is the word that best described her. There was a man friend of hers there too. I didn't catch his surname but she called him Guy. He was staying at one of the local hotels, to be near her presumably.

'I should think those two would get married, wouldn't you?' said Eleanor on the way home. 'Judy told me she's waiting to get her divorce.'

Later that day I took Liam for a walk along Shawley Lane and when I came to the Rectory I found the gate open. So I walked up the gravel drive and looked through the drawing-room window at the new woodblock floor and ivory-painted walls and radiators. The place was swiftly being transformed. It was no longer sinister or grim. I walked round the back and peered in at the splendidly fitted kitchens, one a laundry now, and wondered what on earth had made sensible women like Mrs Buckland and Kate spread such vulgar tales and the Galtons panic. What had come over them? I could only imagine that they felt a need to attract attention to themselves which they perhaps could do in no other way.

I whistled for Liam and strolled down to the gate and looked back at the Rectory. It stared back at me. Is it hindsight that makes me say this or did I really feel it then? I think I did feel it, that the house stared at me with a kind of steady insolence.

Carol Marcus moved in three weeks ago, on a sunny day in the middle of

April. Two nights later, just before eleven, there came a sustained ringing at Gordon's front door as if someone were leaning on the bell. Gordon went to the door. Carol Marcus stood outside, absolutely calm but deathly white.

She said to him, 'May I use your phone, please? Mine isn't in yet and I have to call the police. I just shot my daughter.'

She took a step forward and crumpled in a heap on the threshold.

Gordon picked her up and carried her into the house and Patsy gave her brandy, and then he went across the road to the Rectory. There were lights on all over the house; the front door was open and light was streaming out on to the drive and the little Citroën Diane that was parked there.

He went into the house. The drawing-room door was open and he walked in there and saw a young girl lying on the carpet between the windows. She was dead. There was blood from a bullet wound on the front of her dress, and on a low round table lay the small automatic that Carol Marcus had used.

In the meantime Patsy had been the unwilling listener to a confession. Carol Marcus told her that the girl, who was nineteen, had unexpectedly driven down from London, arriving at the Rectory at nine o'clock. She had had a drink and something to eat and then said she had something to tell her mother, that was why she had come down. While in London she had been seeing a lot of the man called Guy and now they found that they were in love with each other. She knew it would hurt her mother, but she wanted to tell her at once, she wanted to be honest about it.

Carol Marcus told Patsy she felt nothing, no shock, no hatred or resentment, no jealousy. It was as if she were impelled by some external force to do what she did – take the gun she always kept with her from a drawer in the writing-desk and kill her daughter.

At this point Gordon came back and they phoned the police. Within a quarter of an hour the police were at the house. They arrested Carol Marcus and took her away and now she is on remand, awaiting trial on a charge of murder.

So what is the explanation of all this? Or does there, in fact, have to be an explanation? Eleanor and I were so shocked by what had happened, and awed too, that for a while we were somehow wary of talking about it even to each other. Then Eleanor said, 'It's as if all this time the coming event cast its shadow before it.'

I nodded, yet it didn't seem quite that to me. It was more that the Rectory was waiting for the right people to come along, the people who would *fit* its still unplayed scenario, the woman of forty, the daughter of nineteen, the lover. And only to those who approximated these characters could it show shadows and whispers of the drama; the closer the approximation, the clearer the sounds and signs.

The Loys were old and childless, so they saw nothing. Nor did Gordon and I – we were of the wrong sex. But the Bucklands, who had a daughter, heard and felt things, and so did Kate, though she was too old for the tragic leading role and her adolescent girl too young for victim. The Galtons had been nearly right – had Mrs Grainger once hoped the young Rector would marry her before he showed his preference for her daughter? – but the women had been a few years too senior for the parts. Even so, they had come closer to participation than those before them.

All this is very fanciful and I haven't mentioned a word of it to Gordon and Patsy. They wouldn't listen if I did. They persist in seeing the events of three weeks ago as no more than a sordid murder, a crime of jealousy committed by someone whose mind was disturbed.

But I haven't been able to keep from asking myself what would have happened if Gordon had bought the Rectory when he talked of doing so. Patsy will be forty this year. I don't think I've mentioned that she has a daughter by her first marriage who is away at the university and going on nineteen now, a girl that they say is extravagantly fond of Gordon.

He is talking once more of buying, since Carol Marcus, whatever may become of her, will hardly keep the place now. The play is played out, but need that mean there will never be a repeat performance . . . ?

Margery Lawrence

MARE AMORE

KITTY Bellasis, wife of Commander Norman Bellasis, retired, ex of the Royal Navy, stood at the long window of the drawing-room of her pretty country house and stared out at the garden, drumming on the panes with her fingers. Drumming a little impatiently, in truth, since her husband and the friend who had arrived to spend the day with them were already a little late for lunch, and there was an especially good lunch: fried fish, cutlets and new peas, and a cheese soufflé, all of which would spoil by waiting. . . . Little Mrs Bellasis sighed impatiently, and frowned as she glanced at her wrist-watch, then at the clock.

She might have known it would be like this. Was not the visitor old 'Pen' Rigby, boon companion of Bellasis in his seafaring days? And did not Norman Bellasis invariably lose all sense of time and duty when one of his old naval friends came down to Dorset to look him up, on their brief spells of time ashore? Devoutly little Mrs Bellasis wished they would not come at all! She would have given years of her life – and being already forty-one (although with her slim, alert figure, thick brown hair untouched by grey, and state of childlessness, she passed as a rule for a woman five to eight years younger) she did not utter the wish without due realization of what it meant – to have been able to divorce her husband from his old friends as completely as she had divorced him from his first love, the sea!

It had not been easy, that. Norman Bellasis was a born sailor, and his passion for the sea had been part of his very being – deep, abiding; indeed there were times when Kitty Bellasis uneasily wondered whether, after all, his love for herself did not come second, in his innermost heart, to another and older love? Ever since she had first fallen in love with him, when they were both young things in their early twenties, she had been jealous of the sea; jealous of the years of his early manhood spent upon it before she met him; jealous of the men who shared with him the great freemasonry of the ocean; jealous of the happy light that came into his eyes whenever he turned his steps towards his ship – even as he bade her farewell that light would flame high in them, and start a smouldering flame of bitterness within her heart. She was jealous of the knowledge he had, intimate and curious, of the great waters and their ways – jealous, above all, of the long periods he must perforce spend away from her, on the bosom of that ancient lover of men, the Sea!

Yet for many years, since they had nothing but his pay to live on, she endured it, albeit with a grim inner determination to terminate the endurance as soon as might be if the gods were kind. . . . And soon after her thirty-eighth birthday it seemed that they were minded to be kind at last. For a distant uncle died and left Kitty Bellasis heiress to all his money – sufficient to bring her in a regular income, small, yet larger than anything her husband could possibly make in the Navy; also (and more important still), a charming country house with farm-buildings already well stocked and staffed, in Dorsetshire.

Even thus, it had taken Kitty Bellasis many months of patient arguing, wrangling, pleading, to persuade her husband to 'chuck his job', as he put it. Bewildered, a little hurt, for the first time he realized how deeply and intensely his little wife hated the sea that meant so much to him; and was vaguely troubled by the realization.

He loved his profession; loved his ship, a lean, wicked-looking cruiser; loved his men, tanned, laughing fellows with bright eyes and the lilt of the sea in their walk – but he also loved his wife with the simplicity and sincerity peculiar to sailors, despite the rubbish that is talked about 'wives in every port', and for long the two warring forces rode his simple soul like a nightmare. He did not want to become a country gentleman in the very least; the idea of settling down 'on the land' for the rest of his life was entirely new and distasteful to him.

Vaguely he told his comrades that he was 'determined to stand his ground', but Kitty's determination was a hundred per cent more concentrated and intense than his own; and so, reluctant, bewildered, yet acquiescent, he found himself sending in his papers at the end of six months, buying unfamiliar tweeds and leggings, studying books on crops and cows, and getting out his seldom-used golf clubs, since Kitty said importantly that now he would have to take up golf, and there were some awfully nice people she knew down in Dorset who would put him up for the local golf club. So, with a strange aching blank at his heart, Norman Bellasis took his leave of the sea.

As she packed up the final batch of their possessions on the last day in the shabby little furnished flat in Plymouth that had seen so much of their married life, Mrs Bellasis felt a fierce surge of triumph seize her. It had come at last – they were leaving the sea and all that it meant! Now, at last, she would have her husband, her adored husband, with his blue, honest eyes; his merry laugh; his short, stocky, typically sailor's figure, all to herself, for all time. . . . She had beaten the sea!

She glanced out of the window – their apartment overlooked the bay – and laughed aloud in triumph! There it lay, wide and flat and grey, monotonous, that sinister waste that mysteriously held so much of her husband's heart . . . but tomorrow it would be left behind! So far behind that they would forget that it had ever existed. . . . Yet for many nights after they came down to 'Forest Farm' (so called for its proximity to a great rambling belt of woodland), even Kitty Bellasis found it difficult to sleep, missing for the first time in her life the purring murmur of the waves along the shore. The voice of the sea that lulls the world to sleep.

But it was many a long day now since she had even thought of those days; and today, all unexpectedly as she stood drumming her fingers against the pane, the remembrance popped up in her mind, like a jack-in-the-box, out of the void. . . . Then, smiling, she realized the reason, and laughed at herself for a fool. Of course. . . . It was the wind sweeping the forest! For two or three days now it had been blowing steadily now light, now strong, and as it swept the surface of the heaving plain of green, there were times when one might almost think one heard the sea; the hollow, distant roar of it, dying away and returning again, ceaselessly, eternally. . . . But even as she listened the wind dropped to a mere whisper, and the sound died away.

All the farm portion of the pretty little house lay at the back, surrounded by a substantial wall. The house itself fronted on to a large old-fashioned garden – it was a long, low structure, whitewashed, with a tiled roof weathered to a dozen shades of red and brown and green, and boasting several clusters of quaint and interesting chimney-stacks.

The garden was certainly a credit to its new owners. A pergola and summer shelter gave token of the Commander's handiness with carpenter's tools, while a wilderness of roses, Mrs Bellasis's particular care, ran all down one side of the charming little pleasance, and beds of gay 'annuals' vied with the window-boxes that bordered each window in lending the white house a lavish trimming of colour and scent. The whole group of buildings, garden and all, stood, as it were, at the far end, of a 'peninsula' of downland that ran up like an inquiring finger into the wide green sweep of the forest, so that it was both sheltered and open to the sunshine at one and the same time.

Forest Farm was certainly a charming little establishment, and one to please the heart of any woman. Stock and crops were doing well; the 'factor' was a reliable man, his wife a perfect cook; and the summer was for once being all an English summer should be and seldom is. There should have been no reason for Mrs Bellasis's somewhat hard little mouth to tighten as it did as she saw at last, against the dark wall of the woods just beyond the white gate, two figures approaching. Her husband and old Pen Rigby, square and bluff as ever, still wearing the naval blue he clung to even when on shore. . . . Her mouth tightened further, and she frowned on seeing it. The only fly in her ointment, the only cloud on her serene happiness, were these occasional 'reminders' of old days, after which her husband was already restless, irritable for hours and sometimes days.

Pen was in particular a visitor she dreaded. He *would* sport that uniform redolent of old times; would chat all the time of naval 'shop', chaff his old companion for having turned 'landlubber', and so on – and all that was inevitably disturbing. Acidly she wished he had not come, as she wished every time one of Bellasis's ex-colleagues visited him. . . . But there was no time for thought or speculation. With a hasty ring at the bell as an indication to Mrs Jenks to serve lunch, she shook her pretty spotted pink-and-white linen frock into place, and as the men entered the wide French windows, came forward holding out her hand with the usual conventional smile of welcome.

Captain Rigby greeted her with bluff courtesy, commented admiringly upon the garden, her looks, her husband's health, and assented eagerly to her suggestion of immediate lunch. Pecking at her share of the meal, a faint frown lurking between her alert hazel eyes, Kitty Bellasis listened as the two men talked; Rigby with his mouth full, eager, enthusiastic as his type invariably is; Bellasis more quiet, self-contained, less of a talker than a listener. . . .

'Charmin' little place you've got down here,' boomed the big man through a mouthful of cutlet. 'But I'm damned if I can place you as a country gent, my boy! Though I suppose by now you're used to it – don't miss the sea at all?'

Bellasis glanced quickly up. There was a faint gleam in his eyes, and he opened his mouth; then he glanced at his wife, and the words he meant to speak changed on his lips to something else.

'Oh, I don't know!' he said, with a faintly embarrassed laugh. 'After all, we've been here – how long, Kitty?'

'Three years!'

Her tone held a faint edge, and Bellasis glanced unhappily at her before he replied. His reply was obviously meant to conciliate – to attempt to square, as it were, the truth with what would be palatable to his wife's ears.

'Er – yes. Three years. Three years do make a difference to one's feelings, of course – and I've become quite the country squireen, as you can see!'

He laughed again, awkwardly, a flush mounting to his smooth brown cheek. At forty-four Norman Bellasis looked but little older, albeit a trifle squarer, more stolid, than he had looked at twenty-four; and Kitty Bellasis's heart yearned inarticulately over him as she watched him. Rigby bluffly interrupted, reaching for a fresh piece of toast.

'Squireen be hanged! You're a cut-and-dried tarryback, Bell, and always will be; nobody'll ever mistake you for anything else but a sailor!'

How often had people made that remark, thought the listening woman venomously. The fact that it was true made the stab all the sharper. . . . Rigby continued, all unconscious of the fury he was creating in the bosom of the quiet little woman at his side.

'You never ought to ha' left the sea, you know! Headquarters are always askin' after you. . . . I believe you could get another billet any time you wanted. Honestly, what you're doing, a damn' bluewater-man like you, settling down to grow roses and turnips and pinch pigs to see if they're fat enough for market, I'm blessed if I can think. . . .'

'My husband', said Kitty Bellasis acidly, 'left the Navy mainly because I asked him to!'

She was sitting very upright, a pink flush on either cheek and a dangerous glint in her eyes. The hint was not lost upon Rigby, imperceptive as he undoubtedly was. With a muttered apology he changed the subject, and nothing more was said about the sea. . . .

Unless, perhaps, during the men's subsequent wanderings about the farm, whither, disliking the effect of mud and dung upon her pretty slippers, Mrs Bellasis could not make up her mind to accompany them. Devoutly she hoped the latter had not been raised again. It would be too bad if after all her careful work, after these three years during which, apparently, Norman Bellasis had settled gradually down into the pleasant, monotonous life of a country gentleman, they were to be upset, all because of a casual remark made by a breezy insensitive fool in naval gold and blue!

It was late – between six and seven o'clock – when the two friends came in at last. There was only time for a brief cocktail and a biscuit before Norman Bellasis brought out the smart new Humber that last season's successful crops had brought them, and packing his stout friend into the little seat beside him, set out for the station to catch the London train. It was perhaps unfortunate that the very last remark Captain Rigby made, as he waved a hand in farewell to his hostess standing in the doorway in the slanting light of the dying sunshine, should have been flavoured with the one subject she disliked to hear.

'Listen to the way the wind's getting up in the forest out there! Sounds just like the sea, doesn't it?'

That evening Norman Bellasis was peculiarly silent. Always these visits – indeed, any reminder of his old life – disturbed and upset him for a time, but tonight there was a restless quality in his silence that faintly puzzled and distressed his wife. As they sat after dinner, each side of the flaming logs in the pretty old-world brick fireplace – despite the warmth of the June days, the evenings still demanded fires – the lamplight that they both preferred to electricity casting a mellow glow over old oak furniture, cosy velvet hangings, cushions, piano, all the rest of the little personal plenishings that they had chosen together, she eyed him furtively, wistfully, noting an added line or two in his pleasant suntanned face, an extra brushing of grey, like silver powder, each side of his crisp brown hair. He had aged during the last three years. Rebelliously she told herself that he would have aged anyway; that they were neither of them growing any younger. . . . But she could not gainsay the fact that he *had* aged more markedly and speedily since he had left the Navy!

While he had been at sea he had remained a boy despite the mounting years. Now he was definitely a middle-aged man, charming, affectionate, attentive, but lacking the gay, youthful element that, like the flame inside a lamp, makes all the difference between a thing really youthfully alive, and that same thing merely tamely existing. He was now – and she realized it for the first time tonight with grim and unmistakable force – he was a lamp with the flame turned down. . . .

Rising on a sudden irresistible impulse of panic she plumped herself down on her knees beside him, where he sat quietly reading, a large album open before him and, disregarding his exclamation of half-shy surprise – for he was an undemonstrative man, and she was not given to outward displays of affection as a rule – put her arms round his neck and held him close. Embarrassed, he laughed, and patted her on the back as he kissed her – she lay halfway across the book in his lap, hence he could not close it, but it did not escape her quick perception that he had made a clumsy, involuntary movement to do so. She glanced down at it – and her heart stood still; then moved onward with a faintly increased pulsation. It was an old book of sea-pictures. Postcards, large professional photographs, mere personal 'snaps' taken by himself or others . . . she could not speak for a moment, and he spoke, hastily, half-apologetically.

'Seeing old Rigby made me want to look up these rubbishy things, Kit. Just – just to remind me, you know.'

Crouched back on her heels, her small oval face in red shadow as she sat with her back to the blazing logs, she looked at him sideways. Her voice was bitter as gall.

'Must you always want – reminding, then?'

The sailor flushed, miserably enough.

'I don't know. Oh, Kit,' he paused and spread his hands vaguely, helplessly. 'It's *so* damn difficult to explain! We've had this out so often. . . .'

She rose to her feet and went over to the window. Pulling the heavy velvet curtain aside, she stood looking out towards the forest, trying to regain her temper. Angry, frightened in some dim undefined way, she yet knew that she must keep her temper, or she was lost . . . for a dramatic moment she stood still, striving for balance, for self-control, staring out at the outline of the forest-clad hills, like the line of a shadowy ocean heaving in dark irregular billows against the dusky star-patterned blueness of the sky. The restless wind had sprung up again, and through the window, now the heavy curtains were pulled aside, its voice sang, hollow, thunderous, among the distant tree-tops . . . an arm stole tentatively about her still slender waist.

'There's going to be a storm, if I'm any judge of wind!' said Bellasis's voice behind her.

She glanced up and managed a smile at his wistful anxious face at her shoulder. Like the small boy he so much resembled, he had come stealing up, longing to kiss and make friends, ready to do anything to bring the light to her eyes again – on impulse she laid her head against his shoulder, sighing, for the moment tranquillized. But his next words drove repose from her mind once more – set it afresh on its old course, angry, restless, frightened of she knew not what. . . .

'Sounds just like the sound of the sea, doesn't it?'

Releasing his clasp of her waist, Bellasis threw the windows widely apart, and stepped out upon the narrow paved verandah that ran across the front of the house. On the opening of the windows, the voice of the wind suddenly arose and rushed at them, shouting, triumphant – it had risen considerably since the afternoon, and indeed, in its singing roar, hollow, resounding, did undeniably resemble, and that with uncanny strength, the voice of the eternal sea, breaking on distant shores. Alone, triumphant, immortal. . . .

There was a tang of coming rain in the air, that brought with it a faint unpleasant chill – a chill, again, resembling the dank chilliness that precedes a storm at sea. With a curious dim fear stirring her heart, Kitty Bellasis stood watching her husband standing motionless upon the darkened lawn, his face turned towards the forest, his greying hair ruffled by the fingers of the wind, his eyes wide, remotely happy, as she had seen them so often in the old days, when, his shore leave over, he kissed her, turned on his heel and went away – back to the sea!

A gust of anger rose suddenly in the woman's breast, and took possession of her. Anger against herself, as much as anything else, in truth. It was, of course, mere chance, coupled with the presence of old Pen Rigby and his eternal talk of the sea and sea-faring things – that the ordinary wind that so often harried the forest and the downs should, this night of all nights, remind them both so strongly of the sea, that bogey she had dreamt laid, forgotten for good and all! The wind that went roaring tumultuously through the tree-tops, banging and thundering in the hollows with a sound like Gatling guns, ruffling the leaves sideways in sudden flurries till their silver under-sides looked like breaking foam on a lee-shore . . . muttering darkly in the distance, then coming nearer to break in crashing thunders about their ears as a storm breaks about a ship at sea . . . there she was again, comparing everything with the sea! A perfectly ordinary storm was rising, such as she had heard rise an indefinite number of times before, that was all. . . . She shivered suddenly and set her teeth, resolute.

This was mere nerviness! The result of worrying, the effect of suggestion, of one sort and another, upon both herself and her husband she adored – above all she must not add to it herself, or that would drive the rivets in still further. She must drive away again, and this time for good, the green ghost that seemed still to haunt them! Throwing back her head, she braced herself, and, stepping out upon the verandah, slipped a possessive hand through her husband's arm.

'Sounds just like the sea, as you say, dear!' No use in funking all mention of the subject – that was no way to fight a thing. 'Almost like old times, hearing it at our door!'

He turned a face curiously blank towards her. For a moment it seemed as if he neither saw nor heard her; as though he were withdrawn, as it were, into some distant world of the spirit where his soul wandered, remote, detached, ecstatic . . . then suddenly he was himself again, bluff, pleasant Commander Bellasis, RN, standing outside his charming country house on a stormy night, with his adored wife beside him, her hair blown abroad, like her filmy black chiffon skirts. Instantly he was all solicitude for her, lest she catch cold, spoil her frock, have her hair disturbed, and she smiled a triumphant smile as he guided her indoors, shut the windows once more, and drew the shutters close – and the voice of the wind, that was so like the voice of the sea she hated, faded almost into nothingness.

But not for long. Almost as soon as they had settled down to the nightly game of cards with which they invariably finished an evening, Jenks, the 'factor' who with his wife ran the small household, came in with a long face portending trouble.

It appeared that there was a bad storm rising and a gust of wind had just caught the back door, and banged it off its hinges very near, so that they couldn't fasten it – not to feel safe-like about it. . . . Even as he spoke, as if to confirm his words there came a fresh gust. A tinkling crash on the verandah betokened the fall of a loose tile from the ancient roof, the windows rattled furiously, and a puff of purple wood-smoke flared out into the warm room like a fairy balloon. Frowning – he hated to have his game of cards disturbed – the Commander rose and trod heavily out of the room after his henchman, while Kitty, chin on hand, stared sombrely after him. This wind – it was getting on her nerves . . . as he left the room her husband had left the door open, and through the open back door she could hear the wind again.

The house was a wide oblong, not a square, and the back door only just at the end of a short passage beyond the small entrance-hall – she could hear her husband's voice raised, discussing, arguing, hear the rougher voice of Jenks, as they wrangled over the broken hinge, but stronger than all she heard now the wind, risen, it seemed, even in the short half-hour since they had come in, to thrice its original force! Like a ranging animal it roamed about the house, thrusting its fingers into cranny and hole, puffing down the chimneys, rattling the windows, sniffing under lintels, and all the time singing hoarsely aloud with that strangely borrowed voice – that voice that in all her happy three years in Dorset, Mrs Bellasis had never heard before. The voice of the sea. . . .

She listened with strained ears, as through the now open back door the strange voice sang to her, but now it seemed, it sang in a curiously different tone. It sang to her alone. It pleaded . . . gone was the joyous defiance that had hurled itself against her as she stood, her hand through her husband's arm in the garden but a short half-hour ago! Now it was soft: pleading, beseeching, tender as the voice of a woman. Now it crooned, and wept and implored, begging for sympathy, for understanding. . . . Her eyes wide and frightened, but defiant still, Kitty Bellasis rose to her feet, staring before her at the open door, the *portière* of which still waved faintly in the draught. A little eddy of wind crept about her, lifted the curls of her hair and laid them down again; stole sighing to the flamelit fireplace, ruffled the flounces of her frock. . . . Something – something appallingly huge and powerful, laid siege to her pity – something ancient, colossal, before whose majesty she blenched and quivered in terror. Something that had laid aside, for love's sake, all arrogance, all ruthlessness, even all power, for the moment, was pleading with her . . . a vast inchoate Force, a Power before whom her very flesh dwindled and shrank, spoke to her, using the voice of the Wind and the Forest! Clutching the edge of the table she swayed, terrified, amazed, on the verge of fainting; listening, hearing, yet knowing all the time that it was with some inner ear that she listened, not with the ears of her body at all. . . . Through the veil of the shouting wind it sang to her, wordless, pleading its cause in a threnody vast and terrifying yet small and sweet as a woman's voice. Like a giant heartbeat it came to her, through the throbbing of the wind.

'Let go! He is not yours, you know it! You keep him trapped by reason of your love, your body, your woman's spell . . . but he was not yours in the beginning. He was mine, and he is still mine at heart! Let him go . . . and I will be kind. But defy me. . . .'

The unspoken threat throbbed and pulsated silently about her, but still the swaying woman held her ground, though the sweat poured down her brow, and she ground her teeth together to anchor her quivering self-control. She spoke at last, hoarsely, a little above a whisper and as she spoke, it seemed to her that something listened. . . .

'I will not! He is mine, and I will never let him go. Never, never, never! I will die first. . . .'

It seemed she had scarcely reached the last word when lo, the atmosphere of the room changed, totally and completely! It was suddenly – empty, and most horribly empty – then with a screech that rang most horribly like a howl of wild appalling laughter, the storm was upon them! The clap of banging doors accompanied it, the crash of a breaking window, and the shrieks of the frightened maids as they came running into the hall . . . dazed and shaken, Kitty Bellasis found herself in the hall too, her husband, his hair blown wildly awry, his coat wet with rain and spattered with stray leaves, at her side, panting a little but laughing like a boy.

'My God, what a storm we're in for!' He dusted both strong hands together – she noticed they were scratched and dirty. 'It's going to be a corker – hark at the wind! Come here. . . .'

He dragged her unresisting down the passage towards the back door. The back of the house faced directly upon the forest, and the sound of the wind was even stronger here, it seemed. Overhead the storm-clouds scudded helter-skelter, and the wet moon shone in blinks as the purple rags flapped hurrying across its face. Only just beyond the frail walls of the little farm rose the dark sweep of the forest, stretching away to the skyline, an endless vista of tree-tops undulating in waves and humps and hollows like a stretch of dark and restless waters. With the surface now uneasy, rising, falling, it looked uncannily like the sea itself – but like no real sea; it was a black and sinister ghost-sea, a nightmare ocean without glimmer of light or foam or ripple upon its bosom! A wide and terrible plain of heaving darkness, that yet spoke with the voice of the sea itself . . . far out it boomed and thundered, hollow, distant, menacing, but near at hand the rattle of a thousand leaves ruffled by the furious little winds that eddied, like guerrilla soldiers, about the flanks of the main armies, made a sound like the harsh crash and rattle of the pebbles on a lonely shore, dragged at by the fingers of the maddened waves. Now more than ever it sounded as though Ocean itself, unseen, but dreadfully actual, surged threatening, savage, about their very doors, and shivering, the woman turned away. She was very cold.

'Come,' she said, speaking very low – for of a sudden all Kitty Bellasis's fierce defiance had left her and only a simple frightened woman caught in a vast web of which she knew neither beginning nor ending, and did not dare to guess, remained. Barring the door with a shiver, she led the way towards the rickety stairs that led upwards to their bedroom.

'Come darling . . . it's late. Come – to sleep.'

Obediently he followed her, and she did not dare to glance behind, fearing to see the glow and radiance in his face as he listened to the shouting of the boisterous wind that now rocked the little house as a ship is rocked in the arms of a storm. She did not dare to look . . . but she knew too well that it was there. . . .

Only Mr and Mrs Jenks slept in the house, the other maids went down at nights to their homes in the village. The sound of their laughing voices as they struggled through the wind and rain down the garden path rose faintly to Kitty Bellasis's ears as she lay awake beside her sleeping husband, and on impulse she wished she had suggested that Bess and Ella had stayed for the night in the house. She felt curiously forlorn and alone; as though she longed to draw about her the protective mantle of human companionship, to hide beneath it from some vague alien force, or at least to use it to bolster up her flagging courage . . . for, alone in the darkness, hearing the windows creak and rattle, her husband's even breathing in the dark beside her, she realized that her courage was slowly slipping from her. She was afraid! She who had never known what fear was, afraid at last. Afraid of that huge elemental Force that dimly she felt was arrayed against her, to filch from her the thing she held dearest in life . . . was he yet to be drawn away from her, despite her fierce passion for him, her determination to hold him?

This stealthy sapping of her courage unnerved her – was this to be the way she was to be defeated? Was this to go on until she grew listless, apathetic, cowed, let him go from sheer lack of energy to keep him back? Clenching her hands under the bedclothes, she told herself fiercely not to be a fool. She had allowed an unlucky concatenation of circumstances to affect her nerves, to influence her strangely . . . her inner obsession about the Sea – a thing perhaps, rather exaggerated in itself – had caused her to exaggerate everything connected with it!

The appearance of old Rigby, with his ceaseless talk of old days and old ways, had helped things on, and the strange voice of the wind – which, of course, *could* not be anything but quite ordinary wind, only somehow today she could not help hearing in it something she did not seem to have heard before. Absurd, of course, but there it was. Through these simple things, all capable of the most ordinary explanation, she had allowed herself to actually imagine, for those fantastic moments in the drawing-room, to think that the Sea itself was speaking to her – speaking through and with the voice of the wind in the Forest – imploring her to release her lover, to let him return. . . . Now she saw that it was all quite absurd and childish, and she would compose herself to sleep, as Norman had done, bless him. Yet despite her brave words her skin crept and her hands grew clammy and in her ears still rang the sound of the wind roaring in the forest far out – roaring with the voice of the Sea. . . .

A gust caught the window – lightly latched as it was of necessity, since for artistic reasons the Bellasis had left the old house as much as possible in its original state – and it flew open with a crash that made her jump and quiver like a cornered hare . . . yet it did not wake her husband. The sky was still full of flying clouds, but for the moment the moon sailed clear of them, and in the silver gleam she saw her husband lying, his hands lightly crossed on his breast, his face turned sideways towards the window so that one brown cheek pressed the pillow. His lips were slightly parted as he slept, and in a moment's lull in the raging storm she heard a faint sound issuing from them. She bent close and listened, and her cheek blanched . . . for he was singing! Faintly, below his breath, but clearly and regularly, as he used to sing in his midshipman's days, an old sea-chanty.

> 'As I was a-walking down Paddington Street
> *(With a heave ho blow the man down!)*
> A pretty young maiden I chanced to meet.
> *(Give me some time to blow the man down!)*'

She sank back on her pillow, quivering. . . . It was no use. She would never eradicate this love of the sea – but with all her strength she would resist it! She would never let him go – she would twine her arms about his neck and weep and plead, did he suggest returning, as she had sometimes dreaded he might – but she did not think he would. He had long ago relinquished any effort to make her sympathize or understand his love of the sea. In anything else she was tolerant, sympathetic, charming, but in this she was fixed; immutable as Time itself. She would never let him go. Sooner death! Sooner death. . . .

Vaguely she stared out into the darkness of the room. The light had fled, as a veiling of black and angry clouds flung themselves across the moon's face, and only a glimmer here and there, reflected on small shining surfaces, the mirror, the clock-face, the brass andirons in the ancient fireplace, the glass in the framed photograph of her husband on the mantelpiece, lit the sombre darkness . . . yet as she stared, it seemed that the glimmerings *moved*! That they were not stable, as usual . . . and that there were more of them than there should be, all slipping and changing, melting into each other like ripples of light moving on the surface of a stealthily rising flood . . . she smiled faintly at herself and sighed.

How horribly nervy she had allowed herself to get tonight, to be sure. The worrying about the Sea seemed to have seeped into her very brain, so that she thought she saw it or heard it or sensed it at every turn. . . . Then suddenly she held still, stiff, paralysed, for she knew the truth. *The Sea was there* – in the room with her! Silently it pressed in, through every nook and cranny, pouring in through the window, rising through the floor, stealing, forcing its way under the cracks of the door . . . as she stared with bulging eyes, lying spellbound beside her sleeping husband, she watched it rise, and knew the exquisite perfection of terror! First a mere film upon the floor, dimly shining as it crawled and slithered, she saw the loose rug rise with the stealthy pressure of the water beneath it, until it lapped the legs of dressing-table, chairs and bed. . . . With distended eyes, utterly unable to move, she watched it rise and rise, stealthy, silent, inexorable, and as it rose it brought with it all the soul of the Sea!

No mere flood of water, real or imaginary, filled the tiny chamber in the farmhouse on the Dorset downs, but the great illimitable Sea itself, sea-green, luminous, eternal! Tall weeds, purple and olive and bronze, stretched their hungry fingers towards the bed, and tossed their streaming hair, beaded with gleaming crystal bubbles. Anemones, like starry living flowers, massed themselves in the corners, crimson and orange-coloured, yellow and mauve, while tiny blue crabs ran busily among them, and rainbow-coloured fish, their fins like trailing lengths of transparent gauze, swam in and out, their solemn unwinking eyes fixed like the glass eyes of automatons!

It did not seem strange to little Mrs Bellasis, now sunk in some strange sort of trance, to see the moonlight, as the moon sailed out at last, glint on a smooth sheet of water, now level with the bedclothes; it did not seem strange to her to see huge clams open and shut their scalloped mouths where her husband's shoe-box stood, or even to see, from a forest of giant sponges, a great black conger-eel glide by . . . and now the flood was level with the bed! It was lapping the fingers of her hand, hanging over the edge, but so gently, so softly that she never moved – so gently that at last she even smiled, happily, vaguely, the terror wiped completely from her face, so that it was the vacant, dreaming face of a little child. And the flood rose higher, and the soul of Kitty Bellasis, who had defied the Sea, floated out upon it, tranquilly, peacefully, so that she died without knowing that she died. So that it seemed that the Sea was kind in triumph, after all. . . .

The doctor from Titherton – the hamlet nearest to Forest Farm – hastily fetched by a white-faced Jenks on the morning following the terrible June storm – that storm that is still talked of in Dorset with bated breath – gave a certificate of death by heart-failure, of course; there was nothing else that he could say, in public at least, about Mrs Bellasis's strange and sudden death.

For many months Norman Bellasis mourned his dominant little wife deeply and sincerely. Yet since a sailor born is a sailor always, in the end he packed his grip, sold his farm to the nearest bidder, and took his way again towards the blue waters that had always held his heart – and only those who know the power the Sea has over her lovers can realize the light that was in his eyes as he turned his back, finally and for ever, upon the land!

Only one curiously interesting thing remains (and that unknown to the general public) about poor little Mrs Bellasis's death. A secret that, fortunately, will remain locked for ever in the breast of dour, self-contained Dr McPhail. There are times when he will discuss it – if you are a friend – but only in private even then, and under seal of the strictest confidence. . . .

'Whisht, mon!' (he will say, being a Scot). 'Wha would ha believed me, if I had tellt the truth? Which wis that the puir little body – the de'il knows how – was deid, not o' hearrt-failure, but o' droonin'?'

Antonia Fraser

WHO'S BEEN SITTING IN MY CAR?

'WHO'S been sitting in my car?' said Jacobine. She said it in a stern gruff voice, like a bear. In fact Jacobine looked more like Goldilocks with her pale fair hair pulled back from her round forehead. The style betokened haste and worry, the worry of a girl late for school. But it was Jacobine's children who were late, and she was supposed to be driving them.

'Someone's been smoking in my car,' Jacobine added, pointing to the ashtray crammed with butts.

'Someone's been driving your car, you mean.' It was Gavin, contradictory as usual. 'People don't just sit in cars. They drive them.' He elaborated. 'Someone's been driving my car, said the little bear—'

'People do sit in cars. We're sitting in a car now.' Tessa, because she was twelve months older, could never let that sort of remark from Gavin pass.

'Be quiet, darlings,' said Jacobine automatically. She continued to sit looking at the ashtray in front of her. It certainly looked quite horrible with all its mess of ash and brown stubs. And there was a sort of violence about the way it had been stuffed: you wondered that the smoker had not bothered to throw at least a few of them out of the window. Instead he had remorselessly gone on pressing them into the little chromium tray, hard, harder, into the stale pyre.

Jacobine did not smoke. Rory, her ex-husband, had been a heavy smoker. And for one moment she supposed that Rory might have used an old key to get into the Mini, and then sat endlessly smoking outside the house. . . . It was a mad thought and almost instantly Jacobine recognized it as such. For one thing she had bought the Mini second-hand after the divorce. Since ferrying the children had become her main activity these days, she had spent a little money on making it as convenient as possible. More to the point, Jacobine and Rory were on perfectly good terms.

'Married too young' was the general verdict. Jacobine agreed. She still felt rather too young for marriage, as a matter of fact: in an upside-down sort of way, two children seemed to be all she could cope with. She really quite liked Rory's new wife, Fiona, for her evident competence in dealing with the problem of living with him.

It was only that the mucky filled ashtray had reminded Jacobine of the household details of life with Rory. But if not Rory, who? And why did she feel, on top of disgust, a very strong sensation of physical fear? Jacobine, habitually timid, did not remember feeling fear before in quite such an alarmingly physical manner. Her terrors were generally projections into the future, possible worries concerned with the children. She was suddenly convinced that the smoker had an ugly streak of cruelty in his nature – as well as being of course a potential thief. She had a nasty new image of him sitting there in her car outside her house. Waiting for her. Watching the house. She dismissed it.

'Tessa, Gavin, stay where you are.' Jacobine jumped out of the driver's seat and examined the locks of the car.

'Mummy, we are going to be late,' whined Tessa. That decided Jacobine. Back to the car, key in lock and away. They had reached the corner of Melville Street when the next odd thing happened. The engine died and the little Mini gradually and rather feebly came to a halt.

'No petrol!' shouted Gavin from the back.

'Oh darling, do be quiet,' began Jacobine. Then her eye fell on the gauge. He was right. The Mini was out of petrol. Jacobine felt completely jolted as if she had been hit in the face. It was as uncharacteristic of her carefully ordered existence to run out of petrol as, for example, to run out of milk for the children's breakfast – a thing which had happened once and still gave Jacobine shivers of self-reproach. In any case, another unpleasantly dawning realization, she had only filled up two days ago. . . .

'Someone's definitely been driving this car,' she exclaimed before she could stop herself.

'That's what I said!' crowed Gavin. 'Someone's been driving my car, said the little bear.'

'Oh Mummy, we are going to be awfully late,' pleaded Tessa. 'Miss Hamilton doesn't like us to be late. She says Mummies should be more thoughtful.'

The best thing to do was to take them both to school in a taxi and sort out the car's problems later. One way and another, it was lunch-time before Jacobine was able to consider the intruding driver again. And then, sturdily, she dismissed the thought. So that, curiously enough, finding the Mini once more empty of petrol and the ashtray packed with stubs the following morning was even more of a shock. Nor was it possible to escape the sharp eyes of the children, or gloss over the significance of the rapid visit to the petrol station. In any case, Tessa had been agonizing on the subject of lateness due to petrol failure since breakfast.

'I shall go to the police,' said Jacobine firmly. She said it as much to reassure herself as to shut up the children. In fact the visit was more irritating than reassuring. Although Jacobine began her complaint with the statement that she had locked her car, and the lock had not been tampered with, she was left with the strong impression that the police did not believe any part of her story. They did not seem to accept either that the doors had been locked or that the petrol was missing, let alone appreciate the significance of the used ashtray. All the same, they viewed her tale quite indulgently, and were positively gallant when Jacobine revealed that she lived, as they put it, 'with no man to look after you'.

'Of course you worry about the car, madam, it's natural. I expect your husband did all that when you were married,' said the man behind the broad desk. 'Tell you what, I know where you live, I'll tell the policeman on the beat to keep a special watch on it, shall I? Set your mind at rest. That's what we're here for. Prevention is better than cure.'

Jacobine trailed doubtfully out of the station. Prevention is better than cure. It was this parting homily which gave her the inspiration to park the Mini for the night directly under the street light, which again lay under the children's window. If the police did not altogether believe her, she did not altogether believe them in their kindly promises. Anyway, the light would make their task easier, if they did choose to patrol the tree-shaded square.

That evening Jacobine paid an unusually large number of visits to the children's room after they went to sleep. Each time she looked cautiously out of the window. The Mini, small and green, looked like a prize car at the motor show, in its new spotlight. You could hardly believe it had an engine inside it. It might have been a newly painted dummy. The shock of seeing the Mini gone on her fifth visit of inspection was therefore enormous. At the same time, Jacobine did feel a tiny pang of satisfaction. Now let the police treat her as a hysterical female she thought, as she dialled 999 with slightly shaking fingers. Her lips trembled too as she dictated the number of the car: 'AST 5690. A bright green Mini. Stolen not more than ten minutes ago. I warned you it might happen.'

'Don't worry, madam, we'll put out a general call for it.' Why did everyone tell her not to worry?

'No, it's my car, not my husband's. I haven't got a husband.'

Jacobine tried to sleep after that, but her mind raced, half in rage at the impudence of the intruder, half in imagined triumph that he would be hauled before her, cigarette hanging from his lips, those tell-tale polluting cigarettes. . . . It was the door bell weaving in and out of these hazy dreams which finally ended them. At first she assumed they were bringing round the thief, even at this time of night.

It was a policeman, a new one from the morning's encounter. But he was alone.

'Mrs Esk? Sorry to call so late. About your stolen Mini—'

'Have you found it? Who took it?'

'Well that's the point, madam. A green Mini, number AST 5690, reported stolen twenty minutes ago at Ferry Road police station, is now outside your door.'

Jacobine stared. It was true. The Mini was back.

'He must have known you were looking for him.' She blurted out the remark and then regretted it. Silently, Jacobine in her quilted dressing-gown and slippers, and the policeman in his thick night-black uniform, examined the Mini from every angle. The locks were pristine, and the car itself was locked. They examined the dashboard. It was untouched.

'Perhaps there was some mistake?' suggested the policeman in the gentle tone Jacobine had come to associate with his colleagues. 'You only looked out of the window, you said. In the lamplight, you know. . . . Well, I'd better be getting back to the station and report that all is well. You don't want to be arrested for driving your own Mini tomorrow, do you?' He sounded quite paternal.

'Look, he only had time for two cigarettes,' said Jacobine suddenly. At least she had curtailed the nocturnal pleasures of her adversary. On the other hand there was a new and rather horrible development. The car positively *smelt*. It did. She did not like to point that out to the policeman, since he had not mentioned it. Perhaps he was embarrassed. It was a strong, pungent, human smell which had nothing to do with Jacobine or the children or even cigarettes. As Jacobine had envisaged someone cruel and even violent when she first saw the ashtray, she now conjured up involuntarily someone coarse and even brutal.

Jacobine had not thought much about sex since the end of her marriage. Now she found herself thinking of it, in spite of herself. It was the unmistakable animal smell of sex which overpoweringly filled her nostrils.

The next night she put the children to bed early. Still fully dressed, with a new large torch beside her, she took up her vigil in the lobby next to the front door. A little after eleven o'clock, with apprehension but also with excitement, she heard the noise of an engine running. It was close to the house. It was the peculiar coughing start of her own car.

Without considering what she was doing, Jacobine flung open the front door, ran towards the kerb and shouted: 'Stop it, stop it, stop, thief!' The engine stopped running instantly. It was as though it had been cut short in mid-sentence. She wrenched upon the handle of the passenger seat, her fingers trembling so much that she fumbled with the familiar door. It did not open. Even locked against her: her own car! In her passion, Jacobine rapped hard on the window.

Nothing happened. Very slowly, she realized that the driver's seat, and indeed the whole of the tiny car, was empty. In the ashtray, illuminated by the street lamp like a detail in a moonlight picture, lay one cigarette, still alight. Jacobine was now suddenly aware of her thumping heart as the anger which had driven her on drained away. For the first time she had no idea what to do. After a pause, during which she stood gazing at the locked Mini and the gradually disintegrating cigarette, she walked back into the house. She picked up the car keys. Even more slowly, she returned to the car and unlocked it. Deliberately, but very gingerly she climbed into the front seat and touched the cigarette. Yes, warm. The car smelt fearfully.

'Sweetheart,' said a voice very close to her ear. 'You shouldn't have told the police, you know. You shouldn't have done that. You have to be punished for that, don't you?'

Jacobine felt herself grasped roughly and horribly. What happened next was so unexpected in its outrageous nature that she tried to scream out her revulsion. But at the same time a pair of lips, thick hard rubbery lips, were pressed on to her own. The car was still, to her staring frantic eyes above her muted mouth, palpably empty.

'Oh God, I've been taken,' she thought, as she choked and struggled.

'But you like it, don't you, Sweetheart?' as though she had managed to speak aloud. It was not true.

'I'm going to be sick, I think,' said Jacobine. This time she did manage to say it out loud.

'But you'll come back for more tomorrow night, won't you, Sweetheart,' said the voice. 'And we'll go for a drive together.' She was released. Jacobine fumbled with the door once more and, half-retching, fled towards the house.

She did not dare leave it again that night but lay in her bed, trembling and shaking. Even a bath did not help to wash away her body's memories of the assault. The next morning, as soon as the children were at school, Jacobine went to the police station. From the start, the man behind the desk was altogether more wary of her, she thought. He listened to her new story with rather a different expression, no less kind, but somewhat more speculative. At the end, without commenting on Jacobine's nocturnal experience, he asked her abruptly if she had ever seen a doctor since the break-up of her marriage.

'I need the police, not a doctor, for something like this,' said Jacobine desperately. 'I need protection.'

'I'm not quite so sure, Mrs Esk,' said the policeman. 'Now look here, why don't you have a word first of all with your GP? It's not very pleasant being a woman on your own, is it, and maybe a few pills, a few tranquillizers. . . .'

When Jacobine left the station, it was with a sinking feeling that he had not believed her at all. The rest of the day she agonized over what to do. Ring Rory? That was ridiculous. But Jacobine had no other figure of authority in her life. A lawyer might help, she thought vaguely, remembering the sweet young man who had helped her over the divorce. Yet even a lawyer would ask for more proof, if the police had proved so sceptical. With dread, Jacobine realized that it was up to her to provide it.

About eleven o'clock that night, therefore, she took up her position in the driver's seat. She was not quite sure what to expect, except that there would be a moment's wait while she settled herself.

'I'm glad you're early, Sweetheart,' said the voice conversationally. Because we'll be able to go for a really long drive. We've got so much to talk about, haven't we? The children, for example. I don't really like your children. You'll have to get rid of them, you know.'

'Don't you dare touch my children,' gasped Jacobine.

'Oh, rather you than me,' said the voice. 'My methods aren't as pretty as yours. A car crash on the way to school, for example, which would leave you uninjured. . . .'

Jacobine gave a little sick cry. She envisaged those precious tender bodies . . . the recurring nightmare of motherhood.

'I know all about crashes and children, their precious bodies,' went on the voice. He seemed to read her thoughts, her ghastly images. 'Poor little mangled things.'

Jacobine could no longer bear it. The smell combined with terror overwhelmed her. And the police station was so near. Jumping out of the car, abandoning her persecutor, she ran along the road in the general direction of the station. A few minutes later she heard the engine start up. The car was following her. Her heart banged in her chest. She had time to think that it was more frightening being pursued by a car, an empty car, than by anything in the world human and alive, when she gained the safety of the steps. The car stopped, neatly, and remained still.

'He's threatening the children now. He says he's going to kill them,' Jacobine began her story. It seemed that she had hardly gulped it out before a policewoman was taking her back – on foot – to her house. The policewoman concentrated on the fact that Jacobine had left her children alone in the house while she went out to the car. Indeed, although it had not occurred to Jacobine at the time, it was very much outside her usual character. The car was driven back by a policeman. It looked very chic and small and harmless when it came to rest once more outside her front door.

It was two days later that Rory rang up. In between Jacobine had not dared to leave the intruder alone in the car at night in case he carried out his threat against the children during the day. On Saturday he performed the same act of possession which had initiated their relationship. On Sunday he brought up the subject of the children again. First he made Jacobine drive as far as Arthur's Seat, then round through silent Edinburgh. Jacobine was tired when she got back, and the Mini was allowed to park beside her house once more. A policeman noted her sitting there, a smouldering cigarette propped above the dashboard, and he heard her cry out. In answer to his questions, she would only point to the cigarette. She was wearing, he saw, a nightdress under her coat. At the time, the policeman was not quite sure whether Jacobine was crying out in terror or delight.

Actually what had forced that strange hoarse sound out of Jacobine was neither fear nor pleasure. It was, in its weird way, a sort of cry of discovery, a confirmation of a dread, but also bringing relief from the unknown.

She had got to know, perforce, the voice a little better during their long night drive. It was some chance remark of his about the car, some piece of mechanical knowledge, which gave her the clue. Proceeding warily – because the voice could often, but not always, read her thoughts – Jacobine followed up her suspicions. In any case, she preferred talking about the car to listening to the voice on the subject of her children. She tried to shut her mind to his gibes and sometimes quite surprisingly petty digs against Tessa and Gavin. He seemed to be out to belittle the children as well as eliminate them from Jacobine's life.

'Fancy Gavin not being able to read – at seven,' he would say. 'I heard him stumbling over the smallest words the other day. What a baby!' And again: 'Tessa makes an awful fuss about being punctual for one so young, doesn't she? I can just see her when she grows up. A proper little spinster. If she grows up, that is. . . .'

Jacobine interrupted this by wondering aloud how she had got such a bargain in the shape of a second-hand Mini which had hardly done a thousand miles.

'Oh yes, Sweetheart,' exclaimed the voice, 'you certainly did get a bargain when you bought this car. All things considered. It had always been very well looked after, I can tell you—'

'Then it was your car,' Jacobine tried to stop her own voice shaking as she burst out with her discovery. 'This was your car once, wasn't it?'

'There was an accident,' replied the voice. He spoke in quite a different tone, she noticed, dully, flatly, nothing like his usual accents which varied from a horrid predatory kind of lustfulness to the near frenzy of his dislike for the children.

'Tell me.'

'It was her children. On the way to school. There was an accident.' It was still quite a different tone, so much so that Jacobine almost thought – it was a ridiculous word to use under the circumstances – that he sounded quite human. The smell in the car lessened and even the grip which he habitually kept on her knee, that odious grip, seemed to become softer, more beseeching than possessing.

'She worked so hard. She always had so many things to do for them. I was just trying to help her, taking them to school for her. It was an accident. A mistake. Otherwise why didn't I save myself? An accident, I tell you. And she won't forgive me. Oh, why won't she forgive me? I can't rest till she forgives me.' It was piteous now and Jacobine heard a harsh, racking sobbing, a man's sobbing which hurts the listener. She yielded to some strange new impulse and tentatively put out her hand towards the passenger seat. The next moment she was grasped again, more firmly than before; the assault began again, the smell intensified.

'I've got you now, Sweetheart, haven't I?' said the voice. 'It doesn't matter about her any more. Let her curse me all she likes. We've got each other. Once we get rid of your children, that is. And I'm awfully good at getting rid of children.'

When Rory rang on Monday he was uneasy and embarrassed.

'It's all so unlike Jacobine,' he complained later to Fiona. 'She's really not the type. And you should have heard some of the things she told the policeman this fellow in the car had done to her.'

'Oh those quiet types,' exclaimed Fiona. Without knowing Jacobine intimately, she had always thought it odd that she should have surrendered such an attractive man as Rory, virtually without a struggle. 'Still waters,' Fiona added brightly.

Rory suggested a visit to the doctor. He also wondered whether the strain of running a car. . . . Jacobine felt the tears coming into her eyes. Why hadn't she thought of that? Get rid of him. Get rid of the car. Free herself.

'Oh, Rory,' she begged. 'Would you take Tessa and Gavin for a few days? I know it's not your time, and I appreciate that Fiona's job—'

'I'll have them at the weekend,' suggested Rory, always as placating as possible, out of guilt that Jacobine, unlike him, had not married again. 'Fiona's got a marketing conference this week and I'll be in Aberdeen.'

'No, please, Rory, today, I implore you. I tell you what, I'll send them round in a taxi. I won't come too. I'll just put them in a taxi this afternoon.'

But Rory was adamant. It would have to be the weekend.

That afternoon, picking up Tessa and Gavin from school, Jacobine very nearly hit an old woman on a zebra crossing. She had simply not seen her. She could not understand it. She always slowed down before zebra crossings and yet she had been almost speeding across this one. Both children bumped themselves badly and Gavin in the front seat who was not wearing his safety belt (another odd factor, since Jacobine could have sworn she fastened it herself), cut himself on the driving mirror.

'That's your warning,' he said that night. 'The children must go. You spend too much time thinking about them and bothering about them. Tiresome little creatures. I'm glad they hurt themselves this afternoon. Cry babies, both of them. Besides, I don't want you having any other calls on your time.'

And Jacobine was wrenched very violently to and fro, shaken like a bag of shopping. The next moment was worse. A cigarette was stubbed, hard, on her wrist, just where the veins ran.

Even at the instant of torture, Jacobine thought:

'Now they'll have to believe me.'

But it seemed that they didn't. In spite of the mark and in spite of the fact that surely everyone knew Jacobine did not smoke. A doctor came. And Rory came. Jacobine got her wish in the sense that Tessa and Gavin were taken away by Rory. Fiona had to break off halfway through her marketing conference, although you would never have guessed it from the cheery way she saluted the children.

'Just because their mother's gone nuts,' Fiona said sensibly to Rory afterwards, 'it doesn't mean that I can't give them a jolly good tea. And supper too. I have no idea what happened about meals with all that jazzing about at night, and running around in her nightie, and screaming.'

Then Rory took Jacobine down to a really pleasant countrified place not far from Edinburgh, recommended by the doctor. It had to be Rory: there was no one else to do it. Jacobine was very quiet all the way. Rory wondered whether it was because he was driving her car – the car. But Fiona needed the Cortina to fetch the children from school. Once or twice he almost thought Jacobine was listening to something in her own head. It gave him a creepy feeling. Rory put on the radio.

'Don't do that,' said Jacobine, quite sharply for her. 'He doesn't like it.' Rory thought it prudent to say nothing. But he made a mental note to report back to Fiona when he got home. For it was Fiona who felt some concern about despatching Jacobine in this way.

'It's really rather awful, darling,' she argued, 'taking her children away from her. They're all she had in her life. Poor dotty girl.'

'They are my children too,' said Rory humbly. But he knew just what Fiona meant. He admired her more than ever for being so resolutely kind-hearted: it was wonderful how well she got on with both Tessa and Gavin as a result. Fiona also took her turn visiting Jacobine when Rory was too busy. There were really no limits to her practical good nature. And so it was Fiona who brought back the news.

'She wants the car.'

'The car!' cried Rory. 'I should have thought that was the very last thing she should have under the circumstances.'

'Not to drive. She doesn't even want the keys. Just the car. She says she likes the idea of sitting in it. It makes her feel safe to know the car's there and not free to go about wherever it likes. I promise you, those were her very words.'

'What did Dr Mackie say? It seems very rum to me.'

'Oh, he seemed quite airy about it. Talked about womb transference – can that be right? – anyway that sort of thing. He said it could stay in the grounds. Like a sort of Wendy house, I suppose. She hasn't been making very good progress. She cries so much, you see. It's pathetic. Poor thing, let her have the car. She has so little,' ended Fiona generously.

So Jacobine got her car back. Dr Mackie had it parked as promised in a secluded corner of the gardens. He was encouraged to find that Jacobine cried much less now. She spent a great deal of time sitting alone in the driver's seat, talking to herself. She was clearly happier.

'It's much better like this,' said the voice. 'I'm glad we got rid of your children the *nice* way. You won't ever see them again, you know.' Jacobine did not answer. She was getting quite practised at pleasing him. He was generally waiting for her when she arrived at the Mini in its shady corner.

'Who's been sitting in my car?' she would say in a mock gruff voice, pointing to the heap of butts in the ashtray. But in spite of everything Jacobine still looked more like Goldilocks than a bear. Indeed, her face had come to look even younger since she lost the responsibility of the children – or so Fiona told Rory.

Jacobine had to be specially charming on the days when Fiona came down to see her, in case He got into her car and went back to find the children after all. She thought about them all the time. But she no longer cried in front of Him. Because that made Him angry and then He would leave her. She had to keep Him sitting beside her. That way the children would be safe. From Him.

Elizabeth Fancett

THE GHOSTS OF CALAGOU

REGUS stood in the grey of dawn beneath the great tree on the edge of the empty corral.

Empty now, but not for long. Soon his horses would come and his ranch would begin.

He could not see his shadow, but he did not worry. He knew that it would reveal itself later when the sun came up. He was glad the day was ahead of him, a sunny day, when he would have the surety of his shadow.

He looked about him at his lands and blessed the wealth that had made it possible. *His* gold, though they had sought it together, he and his erstwhile partners. They had worked as hard for it, suffered for it, died for it. And by their greed they had nearly killed him too.

But he had survived, and they had hated him for it. Beyond the grave they hated him. They tried to make him think he too was dead. Had they believed such tricks could drive him to madness, to take his own life maybe – when he really would have been one of them?

He cursed the day when he had taken them on.

He had come into the little town of Calagou, the last stop on his way to the legendary mountains that towered above the intervening valleys and prairies. He knew he would need more help, more hands, strong backs, but held little hope of getting them. For as legends told – indeed, as living men still said – there was more than gold in the high and haunted hills of Calagou.

Many had gone there in the past, few had stayed more than a night there, and many more had not returned. And those who had returned – without gold, though the hills were rich with it – had told their eerie tales in the comfort of lighted cabins or the cosy warmth of saloons, and had shuddered in the telling and in the remembering of the sounds they had heard there and the things they said they had seen there. And they had recalled, with the respect that terror brings, the legendary warning that no man takes gold from Calagou and lives!

Then Regus came, himself something of a legend in this part of the West. Regus could divine gold as some could find oil or water. And Regus was bound for the hills of Calagou.

He made his choice – three young strong men, Talley, deSeegar and Carney. They were willing, they said, but had Regus heard the legends?

Yes, he had heard the tales and scorned them. Tales of disappointed men, he had told them. Excuses for their failures and their stupidity. The voices they claimed to have heard were nothing but coyotes calling from the surrounding hills, the ghosts no more than fevered imaginings of gold-greedy men – not legendary dead men jealously guarding their treasure.

Dead men there were, no doubt. Buried in the mountains, trapped by their own stupidity, their own greed, when they refused to leave before the fierce, unmerciful summer came to the hills of Calagou, when the sun scorched their backs to cinder and fried their heads to madness.

But he, Regus, would be going in the springtime and would quit before the summer came.

They had agreed to go, were eager to go, for they were strong and courageous men. But above all, they were greedy men, possessing the one essential quality to override all fear, to scorn all tales, to laugh at all legends. They had the perfect combination – guts, and the greed for gold – and this pleased and suited Regus.

Calagou was to be his final venture, and his ultimate challenge. For the mountains were enormous, cragged and sheer, the canyons deep. One false move and hell could be waiting. But the rewards were greater than the dangers for any man brave enough – or fool enough – to try.

He'd been a fool! reflected Regus grimly. A fool to trust, a fool to take them. He should have gone alone. But how was he to have known?

And they had worked so hard. They had worked cheerfully, powerfully, pouring out their young strength into the great mountains, mining the areas where he had told them to dig and find.

And they had found – time and again, and again, and again. . . .

The weeks had been gruelling, packed tight with work, but they had also packed their storehouse tight with gold, harrowed out of the hills from dawn till dusk and after, and in all that time no ghostly voices called them from the heights, no spectres rose to haunt their work-filled days and they found no signs of the legendary long-since dead guarding their gold from all who dared to come to the hills of Calagou.

They had even stood on the mountain tops, Talley, deSeegar and Carney, and called in strong and mirthful voices if ghosts there be to show themselves. They had laughed about the legends in the cool nights when they rested from their labours or counted their growing sacks of gold.

But they had laughed too long! thought Regus. And they had worked too long. They should have quit when he'd said, gone when he'd decided they should leave. They had a magnificent store of gold, beyond even his wildest hopes. They should have quit when they were ahead, packed up and ridden out.

The long hot days were coming, he had warned them. The heat would be unbearable, the days unendurable, the nights unsleepable. They had not believed him. Not with the golden fire in their veins, not with the dust of gold grimed in the sweat of their calloused hands, clinging to their tattered clothing, not with the bright knowledge of the gold as yet uncovered, the riches untouched. They knew it was there, as he knew it was there. More and more and more. . . .

They had enough, he had urged them. Far, far more than enough, more than any man would need in his lifetime. But for them, enough was not sufficient. They wanted more. They had stayed for more. They had stayed one day too long, one week too many, one month too late.

The sun rose higher and fiercer in the long, hot days with no shade anywhere to receive them in rest from their labours. And at night even the shelter of their cabin was an oven for their baked and sweating bodies, a furnace of heat instead of a refuge.

At night, not even the coyotes called from the high hills about them and no birds flew in the fierce, bright scorch of days above the hills of Calagou.

Regus had begged them to pull out, but they would not. Then he himself would go, he had told them. He would take his share of gold and leave the mountains. But they needed him, they had said, to find more gold, and they would kill him if he tried to go. And he knew that they would have, without qualm or hesitation, for by this time they were all not a little mad.

At night, exhausted yet unrelenting, they took it in turns to guard him, lest in the dark he should take his share of gold and pull out on them.

But the day came when they could work no more, when their scorched and blistered bodies bowed beneath the increasing burn of the day. Their young strength broke and madness came upon them. Regus had done his best for them, though his own strength too was failing, but he buried them all eventually in the gold-flecked dirt of the mountains, in the last rich vein he had just uncovered before their strength gave out and the sun had robbed them of their reason.

And in the voiceless, windless, soundless silence, when the last echo of the last clod of earth upon their graves had died away, they came and stood before him, hating him, taunting him, reviling him, cursing him because they were dead.

Assuming that madness had come upon him too, he had crawled into the cabin and lain there. And all the while they cried to him and cursed him and tried to make him think that he was one of them, willing him to die – no, not to die – telling him, *telling* him, that he was already dead, that he, like them, would never leave the golden, ghostly hills of Calagou.

But he knew that he was not dead. Sick he was, delirious without doubt, but he was alive – and he had his shadow to prove it! And when his fever abated a little he had crawled out into the hot dust, that he might see his shadow and draw comfort from it, and by it know that he still lived.

But when the hot night brought its darkness again his shadow was no longer with him. And they came with their grey, gaunt faces, their dead voices, hating him, crying out for vengeance to which he knew they had no right. He had warned them, hadn't he, he'd told them. Had he not pleaded with them to leave? It had been their own fault they had died, their fault that he was stranded here, all food and water gone, the horses and pack mules dead.

His fever left him, but they did not. They walked with him or stood about him – gaunt, grey, haggard, dead. They stood on the high peaks at sunrise and looked down upon him. They stood on the edge of the canyons at sundown and cried to him and cursed him. They walked the beds of the dried-up creeks and mocked him.

But gradually his strength had returned, enough for him to make a rough sledge from the wood of the storehouse, to load it painfully and slowly with as much of the gold as it could bear – the gold garnered by four pairs of once willing hands throughout the cool sweet springtime of the hills of Calagou.

He had spent a night loading the sledge, dragging the gold bag by bag, inch by inch, until all was stacked and ready. He used his saddle rope to pull it by and he came down from the mountains, carefully, slowly, taking a full day, lest his precious load be spilled into the clefts and chasms of the hills of Calagou. And at night he had set out on his long, slow journey across the parched prairie, dragging his burden through the hot darkness, without his shadow . . . but not alone.

For *they* came with him. Shapes in the darkness, moving mists that called to him and taunted him and screamed at him that he was dead – dead with the gold, dead though he walked, dead though he hoped, dead though he thought that he lived.

'One of us, Regus! One of us! One of the walking dead!'

He had flung their taunts back at them, giving them shout for shout, curse for curse.

'Don't waste your eternity trying to drive me mad! I know that I live! For as long as I can cast my shadow I cannot be dead! As long as my shadow lives – *I* live!'

But they had not left him, they had not ceased to cry.

'One of us, Regus! One of us! Can you see your shadow, Regus? Tell us, Regus, where is your shadow?'

But he had lived. He had won through.

When the town was in sight he had hidden the gold. They had watched him as he buried it, silently grouped around him, ghosts in the sunlight, phantoms in the bright, bright day. But his shadow was with him now, and he drew strength from it.

He wondered if they would enter the town with him, if others would see them too. He knew that if he stayed, if they talked, if they cursed him, he must be careful not to show his awareness of their presence lest the townsfolk think that he was mad.

But at the prairie's end they faded as if the cooling air of the little valley town had blown away their images.

The inhabitants had believed him readily when he told of the greed of the others, their determination to stay on, their eventual deaths, his own sickness and the loss of their animals. Yes, they had believed him. Too many in the past had died defying the sun, too many had not come back. The fact that he had walked the long, dry prairie back, they had no trouble in believing either. Big Regus, strong, indomitable Regus, could outwork and outlive many a younger man.

But most of all they believed him because he had no gold. If he had come into town, dragging his laden sledge, he knew they would not have taken his word about the others' deaths. And because he was Regus they loaned to him fresh horses and mules, the necessities of his trade, accepting his promise to repay them as soon as he hit gold.

And at night he had returned to the desert, loaded the gold and ridden away – without his shadow, alone. His ghosts had left him. And there had been no sign nor sound of them, no sight nor breath nor cry of them . . . until yesterday.

He had thought he was safe here – a two-months' ride and more from Calagou. They belonged in the hills there for they were dead there, Talley, deSeegar and Carney, buried there among the gold. *That's* where their ghosts belonged. But they had come the previous sundown, when his shadow had left him, they had come in the night, calling his name. And there was more than malice in their voices, more than cursing in their callings. There was triumph . . . exultation. . . .

The sun was high now, warm, bright, comforting. Regus turned his eyes to his shadow and was reassured. No man could be dead and yet not know it. That was madness, against all reason – if reason still held, if he was still *able* to reason, if madness had not yet come upon him! For how does one know if one is mad? Maybe he was, and saw ghosts where there were none, heard voices calling when none called. Maybe it had started, his madness, back there in the mountains of Calagou, when he had buried them?

Maybe.

One thing he knew – he was not dead.

Regus paced the ground and his shadow walked beside him. And they came and stood about him, waiting. . . .

He looked at his shadow, his precious sentinel of hope. As long as he could see it he was safe. But his soul was weighted down with an unaccustomed dread.

Then there was the sound of hoofs pounding, of distant riders coming. Regus looked beyond the ranch gates for a glimpse of the horsemen. They rode, hard, rode fast.

And still they stood there, Carney, deSeegar and Talley transparent in the sunlight, silent and waiting, watching and waiting, and through them he could see the riders beyond the gates.

As they approached, Regus looked hard at the three men in the saddles. Their faces were grey with the stubble of many nights and days, their clothes white with prairie dust. They dismounted and strode towards him.

'You Regus?' asked one.

The eyes of his questioner were hard, cold, familiar, reminding Regus of someone. He glanced at the second man, at the also familiar features, and he looked at the third man and he knew that all three must be the fathers of the three men he had buried, of the three ghosts in the sunlight, silent, watching, waiting. . . .

And he knew why one of the men had a coil of stout rope in his hands as they stood before him in the sunlight, blotting out his shadow, their eyes accusing him.

He tried to deny that he was Regus, but the words would not come. And he could only shake his head.

'He's Regus sure enough!' said the second man. 'The description tallies.'

'We trailed you, Regus!' said the third man, who held the rope. 'For two months and nigh on eighteen days we trailed you, Regus!'

'Then state your business,' said Regus defiantly.

The rope twitched in the man's hand.

'If it's about the animals I borrowed,' went on Regus, 'I long since paid my debts to Calagou.'

'Not *all* your debts, Regus!' snarled the man. 'Regus the great gold hunter, Regus the robber, Regus the killer!'

Regus glanced swiftly at the three ghosts standing silent, watching. He looked at Talley, gaunt and haggard, at deSeegar, his wild eyes fever-bright, at Carney, staring evilly, and on the faces of all three – triumph, a devil's leer of victory, of a battle about to be won. And he knew that *they* had guided their fathers here, in ways known only to the ghostly heart.

'Only *you* came back, Regus! Our sons were with you – but only you came back!'

'We don't know how you worked it, Regus, how you managed to get out of those mountains on foot and with all the gold, but we're sure you found a way, Regus! You found a way!'

'We don't care about the gold, Regus. But our sons were with you – and only you came back!'

He began to protest, to tell them how it was, but the rope was uncoiled now, swung high over a branch of the great tree, and the noose was about his neck and he was up on a horse and the sunlight exploded into darkness from which the morning would never break.

The three men turned from their deed, mounted their horses and rode out past their watching phantom sons. Before the sounds of the horses' hoofs had died away, the three ghosts moved towards the tree.

'One of us, Regus! One of us!' they chorused, and with that final triumphant cry they faded in sunlight and troubled Regus no more.

In the warm, bright sunny day, on the edge of the empty corral, Regus swung beneath the great tree.

And in the last companionship of death, his shadow swung beside him.

But Regus could no longer see it.

Edith Wharton

AFTERWARD

I

'OH, there *is* one of course, but you'll never know it.'

The assertion, laughingly flung out six months earlier in a bright June garden, came back to Mary Boyne with a new perception of its significance as she stood, in the December dusk, waiting for the lamps to be brought into the library.

The words had been spoken by their friend Alida Stair, as they sat at tea on her lawn at Pangbourne in reference to the very house of which the library in question was the central, the pivotal 'feature'. Mary Boyne and her husband, in quest of a country place in one of the southern or southwestern counties, had, on their arrival in England, carried their problem straight to Alida Stair, who had successfully solved it in her own case; but it was not until they had rejected, almost capriciously, several practical and judicious suggestions that she threw out: 'Well, there's Lyng, in Dorsetshire. It belongs to Hugo's cousins, and you can get it for a song.'

The reason she gave for its being obtainable on these terms – its remoteness from a station, its lack of electric light, hot-water pipes, and other vulgar necessities – were exactly those pleading in its favour with two romantic Americans perversely in search of the economic drawbacks which were associated, in their tradition, with unusual architectural felicities.

'I should never believe I was living in an old house unless I was thoroughly uncomfortable,' Ned Boyne, the more extravagant of the two had jocosely insisted; 'the least hint of "convenience" would make me think it had been bought out of an exhibition, with the pieces numbered, and set up again.' And they had proceeded to enumerate, with humorous precision, their various doubts and demands, refusing to believe that the house their cousin recommended was *really* Tudor till they learned it had no heating system, or that the village church was literally in the grounds till she assured them of the deplorable uncertainty of the water-supply.

'It's too uncomfortable to be true!' Edward Boyne had continued to exult as the avowal of each disadvantage was successively wrung from her; but he had cut short his rhapsody to ask, with a relapse to distrust: 'And the ghost? You've been concealing from us the fact that there is no ghost!'

Mary, at the moment, had laughed with him, yet almost with her laugh, being possessed of several sets of independent perceptions, had been struck by a note of flatness in Alida's answering hilarity.

'Oh, Dorsetshire's full of ghosts, you know.'

'Yes, yes; but that won't do. I don't want to have to drive ten miles to see somebody else's ghost. I want one of my own on the premises. *Is* there a ghost at Lyng?'

His rejoinder had made Alida laugh again, and it was then that she had flung back tantalizingly: 'Oh, there *is* one, of course, but you'll never know it.'

'Never know it?' Boyne pulled her up. 'But what in the world constitutes a ghost except the fact of its being known for one?'

'I can't say. But that's the story.'

'That there's a ghost, but that nobody knows it's a ghost?'

'Well – not till afterward, at any rate.'

'Till afterward?'

'Not till long, long afterward.'

'But if it's once been identified as an unearthly visitant, why hasn't its *signalement* been handed down in the family? How has it managed to preserve its incognito?'

Alida could only shake her head. 'Don't ask me. But it has.'

'And then suddenly – ' Mary spoke up as if from cavernous depths of divination – 'suddenly, long afterward, one says to one's self: "*That was it?*"'

She was startled at the sepulchral sound with which her question fell on the banter of the other two, and she saw the shadow of the same surprise flit across Alida's pupils. 'I suppose so. One just has to wait.'

'Oh, hang waiting!' Ned broke in. 'Life's too short for a ghost who can only be enjoyed in retrospect. Can't we do better than that, Mary?'

But it turned out that in the event they were not destined to, for within three months of their conversation with Mrs Stair they were settled at Lyng, and the life they had yearned for, to the point of planning it in advance in all its daily details, had actually begun for them.

It was to sit, in the thick December dusk, by just such a wide-hooded fireplace, under just such black oak rafters, with the sense that beyond the mullioned panes the downs were darkened to a deeper solitude: it was for the ultimate indulgence of such sensations that Mary Boyne, abruptly exiled from New York by her husband's business, had endured for nearly fourteen years the soul-deadening ugliness of a Middle Western town, and that Boyne had ground on doggedly at his engineering till, with a suddenness that still made her blink, the prodigious windfall of the Blue Star Mine had put them at a stroke in possession of life and the leisure to taste it. They had never for a moment meant their new state to be one of idleness; but they meant to give themselves only to harmonious activities. She had her vision of painting and gardening (against a background of grey walls), he dreamed of the production of his long-planned book on the 'Economic Basis of Culture'; and with such absorbing work ahead no existence could be too sequestered: they could not get far enough from the world; or plunge deep enough into the past.

Dorsetshire had attracted them from the first by an air of remoteness out of all proportion to its geographical position. But to the Boynes it was one of the ever-recurring wonders of the whole incredibly compressed island – a nest of counties, as they put it – that for the production of its effects so little of a given quality went so far: that so few miles made a distance, and so short a distance a difference.

'It's that', Ned had once enthusiastically explained, 'that gives such depth to their effects, such relief to their contrasts. They've been able to lay the butter so thick on every delicious mouthful.'

The butter had certainly been laid on thick at Lyng: the old house hidden under a shoulder of the downs had almost all the finer marks of commerce with a protracted past. The mere fact that it was neither large nor exceptional made it, to the Boynes, abound the more completely in its special charm – the charm of having been for centuries a deep dim reservoir of life. The life had probably not been of the most vivid order: for long periods, no doubt, it had fallen as noiselessly into the past as the quiet drizzle of autumn fell, hour after hour, into the fishpond between the yews; but these backwaters of existence sometimes breed, in their sluggish depths, strange acuities of emotion, and Mary Boyne had felt from the first the mysterious stir of intenser memories.

The feeling had never been stronger than on this particular afternoon when, waiting in the library for the lamps to come, she rose from her seat and stood among the shadows of the hearth. Her husband had gone off, after luncheon, for one of his long tramps on the downs. She had noticed of late that he preferred to go alone; and, in the tried security of their personal relations, had been driven to conclude that his book was bothering him, and that he needed the afternoons to turn over in solitude the problems left from the morning's work. Certainly the book was not going as smoothly as she had thought it would, and there were lines of perplexity between his eyes such as had never been there in his engineering days. He had often, then, looked fagged to the verge of illness, but the native demon of 'worry' had never. branded his brow. Yet the few pages he had so far read to her – the introduction, and a summary of the opening chapter – showed a firm hold on his subject, and an increasing confidence in his powers.

The fact threw her into deeper perplexity, since, now that he had done with 'business' and its disturbing contingencies, the one other possible source of anxiety was eliminated. Unless it were his health, then? But physically he had gained since they had come to Dorsetshire, grown robuster, ruddier and fresher-eyed. It was only within the last week that she had felt in him the undefinable change which made her restless in his absence, and as tongue-tied in his presence as though it were *she* who had a secret to keep from him!

The thought that there *was* a secret somewhere between them struck her with a sudden rap of wonder, and she looked about her down the long room.

'Can it be the house?' she mused.

The room itself might have been full of secrets. They seemed to be piling themselves up, as evening fell, like the layers and layers of velvet shadow dropping from the low ceiling, the rows of books, the smoke-blurred sculpture of the hearth.

'Why, of course – the house is haunted!' she reflected.

The ghost – Alida's imperceptible ghost – after figuring largely in the banter of their first month or two at Lyng, had been gradually left aside as too ineffectual for imaginative use. Mary had, indeed, as became the tenant of a haunted house, made the customary inquiries among her rural neighbours, but, beyond a vague 'They dü say so, ma'am', the villagers had nothing to impart. The elusive spectre had apparently never had sufficient identity for a legend to crystallize about it, and after a time the Boynes had set the matter down to their profit-and-loss account, agreeing that Lyng was one of the few houses good enough in itself to dispense with supernatural enhancements.

'And I suppose, poor ineffectual demon, that's why it beats its beautiful· wings in vain in the void,' Mary had laughingly concluded.

'Or, rather,' Ned answered in the same strain, 'why, amid so much that's ghostly, it can never affirm its separate existence as *the* ghost.' And thereupon their invisible housemate had finally dropped out of their references, which were numerous enough to make them soon unaware of the loss.

Now, as she stood on the hearth, the subject of their earlier curiosity revived in her with a new sense of its meaning – a sense gradually acquired through daily contact with the scene of the lurking mystery. It was the house itself, of course, that possessed the ghost-seeing faculty, that communed visually but secretly with its own past; if one could only get into close enough communion with the house, one might surprise its secret, and acquire the ghost-sight on one's own account. Perhaps, in his long hours in this very room, where she never trespassed till the afternoon, her husband *had* acquired it already, and was silently carrying about the weight of whatever it had revealed to him. Mary was too well versed in the code of the spectral world not to know that one could not talk about the ghosts one saw: to do so was almost as great a breach of taste as to name a lady in a club. But this explanation did not really satisfy her. 'What, after all, except for the fun of the shudder,' she reflected, 'would he really care for any of their old ghosts?' And thence she was thrown back once more on the fundamental dilemma: the fact that one's greater or less susceptibilty to spectral influences had no particular bearing on the case, since, when one *did* see a ghost at Lyng, one did not know it.

'Not till long afterward,' Alida Stair had said. Well, supposing Ned *had* seen one when they first came, and had known only within the last week what had happened to him? More and more under the spell of the hour, she threw back her thoughts to the early days of their tenancy, but at first only to recall a lively confusion of unpacking, settling, arranging of books, and calling to each other from remote corners of the house as, treasure after treasure, it revealed itself to them. It was in this particular connection that she presently recalled a certain soft afternoon of the previous October, when, passing from the first rapturous flurry of exploration to a detailed inspection of the old house, she had pressed (like a novel heroine) a panel that opened on a flight of corkscrew stairs leading to a flat ledge of the roof – the roof which, from below, seemed to slope away on all sides too abruptly for any practised feet to scale.

The view from this hidden coign was enchanting, and she had flown down to snatch Ned from his papers and give him the freedom of her discovery. She remembered still how, standing at her side, he had passed his arm about her while their gaze flew to the long tossed horizon-line of the downs, and then dropped contentedly back to trace the arabesque of yew hedges about the fishpond, and the shadow of the cedar on the lawn.

'And now the other way,' he had said, turning her about within his arm; and closely pressed to him, she had absorbed, like some long satisfying draught, the picture of the grey-walled court, the squat lions on the gates, and the lime-avenue reaching up to the highroad under the downs.

It was just then, while they gazed and held each other, that she had felt his arm relax, and heard a sharp 'Hallo!' that made her turn to glance at him.

Distinctly, yes, she now recalled that she had seen, as she glanced, a shadow of anxiety, of perplexity, rather, fall across his face; and, following his eyes, had beheld the figure of a man – a man in loose greyish clothes, as it appeared to her – who was sauntering down the lime-avenue to the court with the doubtful gait of a stranger who seeks his way. Her short-sighted eyes had given her but a blurred impression of slightness and greyishness, with something foreign, or at least unlocal, in the cut of the figure or its dress; but her husband had apparently seen more – seen enough to make him push past her with a hasty 'Wait!' and dash down the stairs without pausing to give her a hand.

A slight tendency to dizziness obliged her, after a provisional clutch at the chimney against which they had been leaning, to follow him first more cautiously; and when she had reached the landing she paused again, for a less definite reason, leaning over the banister to strain her eyes through the silence of the brown sun-flecked depths. She lingered there till, somewhere in those depths, she heard the closing of a door; then, mechanically impelled, she went down the shallow flights of steps till she reached the lower hall.

The front door stood open on the sunlight of the court, and hall and court were empty. The library door was open, too, and after listening in vain for any sound of voices within, she crossed the threshold, and found her husband alone, vaguely fingering the papers on his desk.

He looked up, as if surprised at her entrance, but the shadow of anxiety had passed from his face, leaving it even, as she fancied, a little brighter and clearer than usual.

'What was it? Who was it?' she asked.

'Who?' he repeated, with the surprise still all on his side.

'The man we saw coming towards the house.'

He seemed to reflect. 'The man? Why, I thought I saw Peters; I dashed after him to say a word about the stable drains, but he had disappeared before I could get down.'

'Disappeared? But he seemed to be walking so slowly when we saw him.'

Boyne shrugged his shoulders. 'So I thought; but he must have got up steam in the interval. What do you say to our trying to scramble up Meldon Steep before sunset?'

That was all. At the time the occurrence had been less than nothing, had, indeed, been immediately obliterated by the magic of their first vision from Meldon Steep, a height which they had dreamed of climbing ever since they had first seen its bare spine rising above the roof of Lyng. Doubtless it was the mere fact of the other incident having occurred on the very day of their ascent to Meldon that had kept it stored away in the fold of memory from which it now emerged; for in itself it had no mark of the portentous. At the moment there could have been nothing more natural than that Ned should dash himself from the roof in the pursuit of dilatory tradesmen. It was the period when they were always on the watch for one or the other of the specialists employed about the place; always lying in wait for them, and rushing out at them with questions, reproaches or reminders. And certainly in the distance the grey figure had looked like Peters.

Yet now, as she reviewed the scene, she felt her husband's explanation of it to have been invalidated by the look of anxiety on his face. Why had the familiar appearance of Peters made him anxious? Why, above all, if it was of such prime necessity to confer with him on the subject of the stable drains, had the failure to find him produced such a look of relief? Mary could not say that any one of these questions had occurred to her at the time, yet, from the promptness with which they now marshalled themselves at her summons, she had a sense that they must all along have been there, waiting their hour.

2

Weary with her thoughts, she moved to the window. The library was now quite dark, and she was surprised to see how much faint light the outer world still held.

As she peered out into it across the court, a figure shaped itself far down the perspective of bare limes: it looked a mere blot of deeper grey in the greyness, and for an instant, as it moved towards her, her heart thumped to the thought 'It's the ghost!'

She had time, in that long instant, to feel suddenly that the man of whom, two months earlier, she had had a distant vision from the roof, was now, at his predestined hour, about to reveal himself as *not* having been Peters; and her spirit sank under the impending fear of the disclosure. But almost with the next tick of the clock the figure, gaining substance and character, showed itself even to her weak sight as her husband's; and she turned to meet him, as he entered, with the confession of her folly.

'It's really too absurd,' she laughed out, 'but I never *can* remember!'

'Remember what?' Boyne questioned as they drew together.

'That when one sees the Lyng ghost one never knows it.'

Her hand was on his sleeve, and he kept it there, but with no response in his gesture or in the lines of his preoccupied face.

'Did you think you'd seen it?' he asked, after an appreciable interval.

'Why, I actually took *you* for it, my dear, in my mad determination to spot it!'

'Me – just now?' His arm dropped away, and he turned from her with a faint echo of her laugh. 'Really, dearest, you'd better give it up, if that's the best you can do.'

'Oh, yes, I give it up. Have *you*?' she asked, turning round on him abruptly.

The parlour-maid had entered with letters and a lamp, and the light struck up into Boyne's face as he bent above the tray she presented.

'Have *you*?' Mary perversely insisted, when the servant had disappeared on her errand of illumination.

'Have I what?' he rejoined absently, the light bringing out the sharp stamp of worry between his brows as he turned over the letters.

'Given up trying to see the ghost.' Her heart beat a little at the experiment she was making.

Her husband, laying his letters aside, moved away into the shadow of the hearth.

'I never tried,' he said, tearing open the wrapper of a newspaper.

'Well, of course,' Mary persisted, 'the exasperating thing is that there's no use trying, since one can't be sure till so long afterward.'

He was unfolding the paper as if he had hardly heard her; but after a pause, during which the sheets rustled spasmodically between his hands, he looked up to ask, 'Have you any idea *how long?*'

Mary had sunk into a low chair beside the fireplace. From her seat she glanced over, startled at her husband's profile, which was projected against the circle of lamplight.

'No; none. Have *you?*' she retorted, repeating her former phrase with an added stress of intention.

Boyne crumpled the paper into a bunch, and then, inconsequently, turned back with it towards the lamp.

'Lord no! I only meant,' he explained, with a faint tinge of impatience, 'is there any legend, any tradition, as to that?'

'Not that I know of,' she answered; but the impulse to add 'What makes you ask?' was checked by the reappearance of the parlour-maid, with tea and a second lamp.

With the dispersal of shadows, and the repetition of the daily domestic office, Mary Boyne felt herself less oppressed by that sense of something mutely imminent which had darkened her afternoon. For a few moments she gave herself to the details of her task and when she looked up from it she was struck to the point of bewilderment by the change in her husband's face. He had seated himself near the farther lamp, and was absorbed in the perusal of his letters; but was it something he had found in them, or merely the shifting of her own point of view, that had restored his features to their normal aspect? The longer she looked the more definitely the change affirmed itself. The lines of tension had vanished, and such traces of fatigue as lingered were of the kind easily attributable to steady mental effort. He glanced up, as if drawn by her gaze, and met her eyes with a smile.

'I'm dying for my tea, you know; and here's a letter for you,' he said.

She took the letter he held out in exchange for the cup she proffered him, and, returning to her seat, broke the seal with the languid gesture of the reader whose interests are all enclosed in the circle of one cherished presence.

Her next conscious motion was that of starting to her feet, the letter falling to them as she rose, while she held out to her husband a newspaper clipping.

'Ned? What's this? What does it mean?'

He had risen at the same instant, almost as if hearing her cry before she uttered it, and for a perceptible space of time he and she studied each other, like adversaries watching for an advantage, across the space between her chair and his desk.

'What's what? You fairly made me jump!' Boyne said at length, moving towards her with a sudden half-exasperated laugh. The shadow of apprehension was on his face again, not now a look of fixed foreboding, but a shifting vigilance of lips and eyes that gave her the sense of his feeling himself invisibly surrounded.

Her hand shook so that she could hardly give him the clipping.

'This article – from the *Waukesha Sentinel* – that a man named Elwell has brought suit against you – that there was something wrong about the Blue Star Mine. I can't understand more than half.'

They continued to face each other as she spoke, and to her astonishment she saw that her words had the almost immediate effect of dissipating the strained watchfulness of his look.

'Oh, *that*!' He glanced down the printed slip, and then folded it with the gesture of one who handles something harmless and familiar. 'What's the matter with you this afternoon, Mary? I thought you'd got bad news.'

She stood before him with her undefinable terror subsiding slowly under the reassurance of his tone.

'You knew about this, then – it's all right?'

'Certainly I knew about it; and it's all right.'

'But what *is* it? I don't understand. What does this man accuse you of?'

'Pretty nearly every crime in the calendar.' Boyne had tossed the clipping down, and thrown himself into an armchair near the fire. 'Do you want to hear the story? It's not particularly interesting – just a squabble over interests in the Blue Star.'

'But who is this Elwell? I don't know the name.'

'Oh, he's a fellow I put into it – gave him a hand up. I told you all about him at the time.'

'I dare say. I must have forgotten.' Vainly she strained back among her memories. 'But if you helped him, why does he make this return?'

'Probably some shyster lawyer got hold of him and talked him over. It's all rather technical and complicated. I thought that kind of thing bored you.'

His wife felt a sting of compunction. Theoretically, she deprecated the American wife's detachment from her husband's professional interests, but in practice she had always found it difficult to fix her attention on Boyne's report of the transactions in which his varied interests involved him. Besides, she had felt during their years of exile that, in a community where the amenities of living could be obtained only at the cost of efforts as arduous as her husband's professional labours, such brief leisure as he and she could command should be used as an escape from immediate preoccupations, a flight to the life they always dreamed of living. Once or twice, now that this new life had actually drawn its magic circle about them, she had asked herself if she had done right; the retrospective excursions of an active fancy. Now, for the first time, it startled her a little to find how little she knew of the material foundation on which her happiness was built.

She glanced at her husband, and was again reassured by the composure of his face; yet she felt the need of more definite grounds for her reassurance.

'But doesn't this suit worry you? Why have you never spoken to me about it?'

He answered both questions at once. 'I didn't speak of it at first because it *did* worry me – annoyed me, rather. But it's all ancient history now. Your correspondent must have got hold of a back number of the *Sentinel*.'

She felt a quick thrill of relief. 'You mean it's over? He's lost his case?'

There was a just perceptible delay in Boyne's reply. 'The suit's been withdrawn – that's all.'

But she persisted, as if to exonerate herself from the inward charge of being too easily put off. 'Withdrawn it because he saw he had no chance?'

'Oh, he had no chance,' Boyne answered.

She was still struggling with a dimly felt perplexity at the back of her thoughts.

'How long ago was it withdrawn?'

He paused, as if with a slight return of his former uncertainty. 'I've just had the news now; but I've been expecting it.'

'Just now – in one of your letters?'

'Yes; in one of my letters.'

She made no answer, and was aware only, after a short interval of waiting, that he had risen, and, strolling across the room, had placed himself on the sofa at her side. She felt him, as he did so, pass an arm about her, she felt his hand seek hers and clasp it and turning slowly, drawn by the warmth of his cheek, she met his smiling eyes.

'It's all right – it's all right?' she questioned, through the flood of her dissolving doubts; and 'I give you my word it was never righter!' he laughed back at her, holding her close.

One of the strangest things she was afterward to recall out of all the next day's strangeness was the sudden and complete recovery of her sense of security.

It was in the air when she woke in her low-ceilinged, dusky room; it went with her downstairs to the breakfast table, flashed out at her from the fire, and reduplicated itself from the flanks of the urn, and the sturdy flutings of the Georgian teapot. It was as if, in some roundabout way, all her diffused fears of the previous day, with their moment of sharp concentration about the newspaper article – as if this dim questioning of the future, and startled return upon the past, had between them liquidated the arrears of some haunting moral obligation. If she had indeed been careless of her husband's affairs, it was, her new state seemed to prove, because her faith in him instinctively justified such carelessness; and his right to her faith had now affirmed itself in the very face of menace and suspicion. She had never seen him more untroubled, more naturally and unconsciously himself, than after the cross-examination to which she had subjected him: it was almost as if he had been aware of her doubts and had wanted the air cleared as much as she did.

It was as clear, thank Heaven! as the bright outer light that surprised her almost with a touch of summer when she issued from the house for her daily round of the gardens. She had left Boyne at his desk, indulging herself, as she passed the library door, by a last peep at his quiet face, where he bent, pipe in mouth, above his papers; and now she had her own morning's task to perform. The task involved, on such charmed winter days, almost as much happy loitering about the different quarters of her demesne as if spring were already at work there. There were such endless possibilities still before her, such opportunities to bring out the latent graces of the old place, without a single irreverent touch of alteration, that the winter was all too short to plan what spring and autumn executed. And her recovered sense of safety gave, on this particular morning, a peculiar zest to her progress through the sweet still place. She went first to the kitchen garden, where the espaliered pear trees drew complicated patterns on the walls, and pigeons were fluttering and preening about the silvery-slated roof of their cot. There was something wrong about the piping of the hothouse, and she was expecting an authority from Dorchester, who was to drive out between trains and make a diagnosis of the boiler. But when she dipped into the damp heat of the greenhouses, among the spiced scents and waxy pinks and reds of old-fashioned exotics – even the flora of Lyng was in the note! – she learned that the great man had not arrived, and, the day being too rare to waste in an artificial atmosphere, she came out again and paced along the springy turf of the bowling-green to the gardens behind the house. At their farther end rose a grass terrace, looking across the fishpond and yew hedges to the long house-front with its twisted chimney-stacks and blue roof angles all drenched in the pale gold moisture of the air.

Seen thus, across the level tracery of the gardens, it sent her, from open windows and hospitably smoking chimneys, the look of some warm human presence, of a mind slowly ripened on a sunny wall of experience. She had never before had such a sense of her intimacy with it, such a conviction that its secrets were all beneficent, kept, as they said to children, 'for one's good', such a trust in its power to gather up her life and Ned's into the harmonious pattern of the long long story it sat there weaving in the sun.

She heard steps behind her, and turned, expecting to see the gardener accompanied by the engineer from Dorchester. But only one figure was in sight, that of a youngish slightly built man who, for reasons she could not on the spot have given, did not remotely resemble her notion of an authority on hothouse boilers. The newcomer, on seeing her, lifted his hat, and paused with the air of a gentleman – perhaps a traveller – who wishes to make it known that his intrusion is involuntary. Lyng occasionally attracted the more cultivated traveller, and Mary half expected to see the stranger dissemble a camera, or justify his presence by producing it. But he made no gesture of any sort, and after a moment she asked, in a tone responding to the courteous hesitation of his attitude: 'Is there anyone you wish to see?'

'I came to see Mr Boyne,' he answered. His intonation, rather than his accent, was faintly American, and Mary, at the note, looked at him more closely. The brim of his soft felt hat cast a shade on his face, which, thus obscured, wore to her short-sighted gaze a look of seriousness, as of a person arriving 'on business', and civilly but firmly aware of his rights.

Past experience had made her equally sensible to such claims; but she was jealous of her husband's morning hours, and doubtful of his having given anyone the right to intrude on them.

'Have you an appointment with my husband?' she asked.

The visitor hesitated, as if unprepared for the question.

'I think he expects me,' he replied.

It was Mary's turn to hesitate. 'You see this is his time for work: he never sees anyone in the morning.'

He looked at her a moment without answering; then, as if accepting her decision, he began to move away. As he turned, Mary saw him pause and glance up at the peaceful house-front. Something in his air suggested weariness and disappointment, the dejection of the traveller who has come from far off and whose hours are limited by the timetable. It occurred to her that if this were the case her refusal might have made his errand vain, and a sense of compunction caused her to hasten after him.

'May I ask if you have come a long way?'

He gave her the same grave look. 'Yes – I have come a long way.'

'Then, if you'll go to the house, no doubt my husband will see you now. You'll find him in the library.'

She did not know why she had added the last phrase, except from a vague impulse to atone for her previous inhospitality. The visitor seemed about to express his thanks, but her attention was distracted by the approach of the gardener with a companion who bore all the marks of being the expert from Dorchester.

'This way,' she said, waving the stranger to the house; and an instant later she had forgotten him in the absorption of her meeting with the boiler-maker.

The encounter led to such far-reaching results that the engineer ended by finding it expedient to ignore his train, and Mary was beguiled into spending the remainder of the morning in absorbed confabulation among the flower-pots. When the colloquy ended, she was surprised to find that it was nearly luncheon-time, and she half expected, as she hurried back to the house, to see her husband coming out to meet her. But she found no one in the court but an under-gardener raking the gravel, and the hall, when she entered it, was so silent that she guessed Boyne to be still at work.

Not wishing to disturb him, she turned into the drawing-room, and there, at her writing-table, lost herself in renewed calculations of the outlay to which the morning's conference had pledged her. The fact that she could permit herself such follies had not yet lost its novelty; and somehow, in contrast to the vague fears of the previous days, it now seemed an element of her recovered security, of the sense that, as Ned had said, things in general had never been 'righter'.

She was still luxuriating in a lavish play of figures when the parlour-maid, from the threshold, roused her with an inquiry as to the expediency of serving luncheon. It was one of their jokes that Trimmle announced luncheon as if she were divulging a state secret, and Mary, intent upon her papers, merely murmured an absentminded assent.

She felt Trimmle wavering doubtfully on the threshold, as if in rebuke of such unconsidered assent; then her retreating steps sounded down the passage, and Mary, pushing away her papers, crossed the hall and went to the library door. It was still closed, and she wavered in her turn, disliking to disturb her husband, yet anxious that he should not exceed his usual measure of work. As she stood there, balancing her impulses, Trimmle returned with the announcement of luncheon, and Mary, thus impelled, opened the library door.

Boyne was not at his desk, and she peered about her, expecting to discover him before the bookshelves, somewhere down the length of the room; but her call brought no response, and gradually it became clear to her that he was not there.

She turned back to the parlour-maid.

'Mr Boyne must be upstairs. Please tell him that luncheon is ready.'

Trimmle appeared to hesitate between the obvious duty of obedience and an equally obvious conviction of the foolishness of the injunction laid on her. The struggle resulted in her saying: 'If you please, madam, Mr Boyne's not upstairs.'

'Not in his room? Are you sure?'

'I'm sure, madam.'

Mary consulted the clock. 'Where is he, then?'

'He's gone out,' Trimmle announced, with the superior air of one who has respectfully waited for the question that a well-ordered mind would have put first.

Mary's conjecture had been right, then. Boyne must have gone to the gardens to meet her and since she had missed him, it was clear that he had taken the shorter way by the south door, instead of going round to the court. She crossed the hall to the French window opening directly on the yew garden, but the parlour-maid, after another moment of inner conflict decided to bring out: 'Please, madam, Mr Boyne didn't go that way.'

Mary turned back. 'Where *did* he go? And when?'

'He went out of the front door, up the drive, madam.' It was a matter of principle with Trimmle never to answer more than one question at a time.

'Up the drive? At this hour?' Mary went to the door herself, and glanced across the court through the tunnel of bare limes. But its perspective was as empty as when she had scanned it on entering.

'Did Mr Boyne leave no message?'

Trimmle seemed to surrender herself to a last struggle with the forces of chaos.

'No, madam. He just went out with the gentleman.'

'The gentleman? What gentleman?' Mary wheeled about, as if to front this new factor.

'The gentleman who called, madam,' said Trimmle resignedly.

'When did a gentleman call? Do explain yourself, Trimmle!'

Only the fact that Mary was very hungry, and that she wanted to consult her husband about the greenhouses, would have caused her to lay so unusual an injunction on her attendant; and even now she was detached enough to note in Trimmle's eye the dawning defiance of the respectful subordinate who has been pressed too hard.

'I couldn't exactly say the hour, madam, because I didn't let the gentleman in,' she replied, with an air of discreetly ignoring the irregularity of her mistress's course.

'You didn't let him in?'

'No, madam. When the bell rang I was dressing, and Agnes—'

'Go and ask Agnes, then,' said Mary.

Trimmle still wore her look of patient magnanimity. 'Agnes would not know, madam, for she had unfortunately burnt her hand in trimming the wick of the new lamp from town' – Trimmle, as Mary was aware, had always been opposed to the new lamp – 'and so Mrs Dockett sent the kitchen-maid instead.'

Mary looked again at the clock. 'It's after two! Go and ask the kitchen-maid if Mr Boyne left any word.'

She went in to luncheon without waiting, and Trimmle presently brought her there the kitchen-maid's statement that the gentleman had called about eleven o'clock, and that Mr Boyne had gone out with him without leaving any message. The kitchen-maid did not even know the caller's name, for he had written it on a slip of paper, which he had folded and handed to her, with the injunction to deliver it at once to Mr Boyne.

Mary finished her luncheon, still wondering, and when it was over, and Trimmle had brought the coffee to the drawing-room, her wonder had deepened to a first faint tinge of disquietude. It was unlike Boyne to absent himself without explanation at so unwonted an hour, and the difficulty of identifying the visitor whose summons he had apparently obeyed made his disappearance the more unaccountable. Mary Boyne's experience as the wife of a busy engineer, subject to sudden calls and compelled to keep irregular hours, had trained her to the philosophic acceptance of surprises; but since Boyne's withdrawal from business he had adopted a Benedictine regularity of life. As if to make up for the dispersed and agitated years, with their 'stand-up' lunches and dinners rattled down to the joltings of the dining-cars, he cultivated the last refinements of punctuality and monotony, discouraging his wife's fancy for the unexpected, and declaring that to a delicate taste there were infinite gradations of pleasure in the recurrences of habit.

Still, since no life can completely defend itself from the unforeseen, it was evident that all Boyne's precautions would sooner or later prove unavailing, and Mary concluded that he had cut short a tiresome visit by walking with his caller to the station, or at least accompanying him part of the way.

This conclusion relieved her from further preoccupations, and she went out herself to take up her conference with the gardener. Thence she walked to the village post office a mile or so away; and when she turned towards home the early twilight was setting in.

She had taken a footpath across the downs, and as Boyne, meanwhile, had probably returned from the station by the highroad, there was little likelihood of their meeting. She felt sure, however, of his having reached the house before her; so sure that, when she entered it herself, without even pausing to inquire of Trimmle, she made directly for the library. But the library was still empty, and with an unwonted exactness of visual memory she observed that the papers on her husband's desk lay precisely as they had lain when she had gone in to call him to luncheon.

Then of a sudden she was seized by a vague dread of the unknown. She had closed the door behind her on entering, and as she stood alone in the long silent room, her dread seemed to take shape and sound, to be there breathing and lurking among the shadows. Her short-sighted eyes strained through them, half-discerning an actual presence, something aloof, that watched and knew; and in the recoil from that intangible presence she threw herself on the bell-rope and gave it a sharp pull.

The sharp summons brought Trimmle in precipitately with a lamp, and Mary breathed again at this sobering reappearance of the usual.

'You may bring tea if Mr Boyne is in,' she said, to justify her ring.

'Very well, madam. But Mr Boyne is not in,' said Trimmle, putting down the lamp.

'Not in? You mean he's come back and gone out again?'

'No, madam. He's never been back.'

The dread stirred again, and Mary knew that now it had her fast.

'Not since he went out with – the gentleman?'

'Not since he went out with the gentleman.'

'But who *was* the gentleman?' Mary insisted, with the shrill note of someone trying to be heard through a confusion of noises.

'That I couldn't say, madam.' Trimmle, standing there by the lamp, seemed suddenly to grow less round and rosy, as though eclipsed by the same creeping shade of apprehension.

'But the kitchen-maid knows – wasn't it the kitchen-maid who let him in?'

'She doesn't know either, madam, for he wrote his name on a folded paper.'

Mary, through her agitation, was aware that they were both designating the unknown visitor by a vague pronoun, instead of the conventional formula which, till then, had kept their allusions within the bounds of conformity. And at the same moment her mind caught at the suggestion of the folded paper.

'But he must have a name! Where's the paper?'

She moved to the desk, and began to turn over the documents that littered it. The first that caught her eye was an unfinished letter in her husband's hand with his pen lying across it, as though dropped there at a sudden summons.

'My dear Parvis' – who was Parvis? – 'I have just received your letter announcing Elwell's death, and while I suppose there is now no further risk of trouble, it might be safer—'

She tossed the sheet aside, and continued her search; but no folded paper was discoverable among the letters and pages of manuscript which had been swept together in a heap, as if by a hurried or a startled gesture.

'But the kitchen-maid *saw* him. Send her here,' she commanded, wondering at her dullness in not thinking sooner of so simple a solution.

Trimmle vanished in a flash, as if thankful to be out of the room, and when she reappeared, conducting the agitated underling, Mary had regained her self-possession, and had her questions ready.

The gentleman was a stranger, yes – that she understood. But what had he said? And, above all, what had he looked like? The first question was easily enough answered, for the disconcerting reason that he had said so little – had merely asked for Mr Boyne, and, scribbling something on a bit of paper, had requested that it should at once be carried in to him.

'Then you don't know what he wrote? You're not sure it *was* his name?'

The kitchen-maid was not sure, but supposed it was, since he had written it in answer to her inquiry as to whom she should announce.

'And when you carried the paper in to Mr Boyne, what did he say?'

The kitchen-maid did not think that Mr Boyne had said anything, but she could not be sure, for just as she had handed him the paper and he was opening it, she had become aware that the visitor had followed her into the library, and she had slipped out, leaving the two gentlemen together.

'But then, if you left them in the library, how do you know that they went out of the house?'

This question plunged the witness into a momentary inarticulateness, from which she was rescued by Trimmle, who, by means of ingenious circumlocutions, elicited the statement that before she could cross the hall to the back passage she had heard the two gentlemen behind her, and had seen them go out of the front door together.

'Then, if you saw the strange gentleman twice, you must be able to tell me what he looked like.'

But with this final challenge to her powers of expression it became clear that the limit of the kitchen-maid's endurance had been reached. The obligation of going to the front door to 'show in' a visitor was in itself so subversive of the fundamental order of things that it had thrown her faculties into hopeless disarray, and she could only stammer out, after various panting efforts: 'His hat, mum, was different-like, as you might say—'

'Different? How different?' Mary flashed out, her own mind, in the same instant, leaping back to an image left on it that morning, and then lost under layers of subsequent impressions.

'His hat had a wide brim, you mean? and his face was pale – a youngish face?' Mary pressed her with a white-lipped intensity of interrogation. But if the kitchen-maid found any adequate answer to this challenge, it was swept away for her listener down the rushing current of her own convictions. The stranger – the stranger in the garden! Why had Mary not thought of him before? She needed no one now to tell her that it was he who had called for her husband and gone away with him. But who was he, and why had Boyne obeyed him?

4

It leapt out at her suddenly, like a grin out of the dark that they had often called England so little – 'such a confoundedly hard place to get lost in.'

A confoundedly hard place to get lost in! That had been her husband's phrase. And now, with the whole machinery of official investigation sweeping its flashlights from shore to shore and across the dividing straits; now, with Boyne's name blazing from the walls of every town and village, his portrait (how that wrung her!) hawked up and down the country like the image of a hunted criminal; now the little compact populous island, so policed, surveyed and administered, revealed itself as a Sphinx-like guardian of abysmal mysteries, staring back into his wife's anguished eyes as if with the wicked joy of knowing something they would never know!

In the fortnight since Boyne's disappearance there had been no word of him, no trace of his movements. Even the usual misleading reports that raise expectancy in tortured bosoms had been few and fleeting. No one but the kitchen-maid had seen Boyne leave the house, and no one else had seen 'the gentleman' who accompanied him. All inquiries in the neighbourhood failed to elicit the memory of a stranger's presence that day in the neighbourhood of Lyng. And no one had met Edward Boyne, either alone or in company, in any of the neighbouring villages, or on the road across the downs, or at either of the local railway stations. The sunny English noon had swallowed him as completely as if he had gone out into Cimmerian night.

Mary, while every official means of investigation was working at its highest pressure, had ransacked her husband's papers for any trace of antecedent complications, of entanglements or obligations unknown to her, that might throw a ray into the darkness. But if any such had existed in the background of Boyne's life, they had vanished like the slip of paper on which the visitor had written his name. There remained no possible thread of guidance except

– if it were indeed an exception – the letter which Boyne had apparently been in the act of writing when he received his mysterious summons. That letter, read and reread by his wife, and submitted by her to the police, yielded little enough to feed conjecture.

'I have just heard of Elwell's death, and while I suppose there is now no further risk of trouble, it might be safer—' That was all. The 'risk of trouble' was easily explained by the newspaper clipping which had apprised Mary of the suit brought against her husband by one of his associates in the Blue Star enterprise. The only new information conveyed by the letter was the fact of its showing Boyne, when he wrote it, to be still apprehensive of the results of the suit, though he had told his wife that it had been withdrawn, and though the letter itself proved that the plaintiff was dead. It took several days of cabling to fix the identity of the 'Parvis' to whom the fragment was addressed, but even after these inquiries had shown him to be a Waukesha lawyer, no new facts concerning the Elwell suit were elicited. He appeared to have had no direct concern in it, but to have been conversant with the facts merely as an acquaintance, and possible intermediary; and he declared himself unable to guess with what object Boyne intended to seek his assistance.

This negative information, sole fruit of the first fortnight's search, was not increased by a jot during the slow weeks that followed. Mary knew that the investigations were still being carried on, but she had a vague sense of their gradually slackening, as the actual march of time seemed to slacken. It was as though the days, flying horror-struck from the shrouded image of the one inscrutable day, gained assurance as the distance lengthened, till at last they fell back into their normal gait. And so with the human imaginations at work on the dark event. No doubt it occupied them still, but week by week and hour by hour it grew less absorbing, took up less space, was slowly but inevitably crowded out of the foreground of consciousness by the new problems perpetually bubbling up from the cloudy cauldron of human experience.

Even Mary Boyne's consciousness gradually felt the same lowering of velocity. It still swayed with the incessant oscillations of conjecture; but they were slower, more rhythmical in their beat. There were even moments of weariness when, like the victim of some poison which leaves the brain clear, but holds the body motionless, she saw herself domesticated with the Horror, accepting its perpetual presence as one of the fixed conditions of life.

These moments lengthened into hours and days, till she passed into a phase of stolid acquiescence. She watched the routine of daily life with the incurious eye of a savage on whom the meaningless processes of civilization make but the faintest impression. She had come to regard herself as part of the routine, a spoke of the wheel, revolving with its motion; she felt almost like the furniture of the room in which she sat, an insensate object to be dusted and pushed about with the chairs and tables. And this deepening apathy held her fast at Lyng, in spite of the entreaties of friends and the usual medical recommendation of 'change'. Her friends supposed that her refusal to move was inspired by the belief that her husband would one day return to the spot from which he had vanished, and a beautiful legend grew up about this imaginary state of waiting. But in reality she had no such belief: the depths of anguish enclosing her were no longer lighted by flashes of hope. She was sure that Boyne would never come back, that he had gone out of her sight as completely as if Death itself had waited that day on the threshold. She had even renounced, one by one, the various theories as to his disappearance which had been advanced by the press, the police, and her own agonized imagination. In sheer lassitude her mind turned from these alternatives of horror, and sank back into the blank fact that he was gone.

No, she would never know what had become of him – no one would ever know. But the house *knew*; the library in which she spent her long lonely evenings knew. For it was here that the last scene had been enacted, here that the stranger had come, and spoken the word which had caused Boyne to rise and follow him. The floor she trod had felt his tread; the books on the shelves had seen his face; and there were moments when the intense consciousness of the old dusky walls seemed about to break out into some audible revelation of their secret. But the revelation never came, and she knew it would never come. Lyng was not one of the garrulous old houses that betray the secrets entrusted to them. Its very legend proved that it had always been the mute accomplice, the incorruptible custodian, of the mysteries it had surprised. And Mary Boyne, sitting face to face with its silence, felt the futility of seeking to break it by any human means.

5

'I don't say it *wasn't* straight, and yet I don't say it *was* straight. It was business.'

Mary, at the words, lifted her head with a start, and looked intently at the speaker.

When, half an hour before, a card with 'Mr Parvis' on it had been brought up to her, she had been immediately aware that the name had been a part of her consciousness ever since she had read it at the head of Boyne's unfinished letter. In the library she had found awaiting her a small sallow man with a bald head and gold eyeglasses, and it sent a tremor through her to know that this was the person to whom her husband's last known thought had been directed.

Parvis, civilly, but without vain preamble – in the manner of a man who has his watch in his hand – had set forth the object of his visit. He had 'run over' to England on business, and finding himself in the neighbourhood of Dorchester, had not wished to leave it without paying his respects to Mrs Boyne; and without asking her, if the occasion offered, what she meant to do about Bob Elwell's family.

The words touched the spring of some obscure dread in Mary's bosom. Did her visitor after all, know what Boyne had meant by his unfinished phrase? She asked for an elucidation of his question, and noticed at once that he seemed surprised at her continued ignorance of the subject. Was it possible that she really knew as little as she said?

'I know nothing – you must tell me,' she faltered out; and her visitor thereupon proceeded to unfold his story. It threw, even to her confused perceptions, and imperfectly initiated vision, a lurid glare on the whole hazy episode of the Blue Star Mine. Her husband had made his money in that brilliant speculation at the cost of 'getting ahead' of someone less alert to seize the chance; and the victim of his ingenuity was young Robert Elwell, who had 'put him on' to the Blue Star scheme.

Parvis, at Mary's first cry, had thrown her a sobering glance through his impartial glasses.

'Bob Elwell wasn't smart enough, that's all; if he had been, he might have turned round and served Boyne the same way. It's the kind of thing that happens every day in business. I guess it's what the scientists call the survival of the fittest – see?' said Mr Parvis, evidently pleased with the aptness of his analogy.

Mary felt a physical shrinking from the next question she tried to frame: it was as though the words on her lips had a taste that nauseated her.

'But then – you accuse my husband of doing something dishonourable?'

Mr Parvis surveyed the question dispassionately. 'Oh, no, I don't. I don't even say it wasn't straight.' He glanced up and down the long lines of books as if one of them might have supplied him with the definition he sought. 'I don't say it *wasn't* straight, and yet I don't say it *was* straight. It was business.' After all, no definition in his category could be more comprehensive than that.

Mary sat staring at him with a look of terror. He seemed to her like the indifferent emissary of some evil power.

'But Mr Elwell's lawyers apparently did not take your view, since I suppose the suit was withdrawn by their advice.'

'Oh yes; they knew he hadn't a leg to stand on, technically. It was when they advised him to withdraw the suit that he got desperate. You see, he'd borrowed most of the money he lost in the Blue Star, and he was up a tree. That's why he shot himself when they told him he had no show.'

The horror was sweeping over Mary in great deafening waves.

'He shot himself? He killed himself because of *that*?'

'Well, he didn't kill himself, exactly. He dragged on two months before he died.' Parvis emitted the statement as unemotionally as a gramophone grinding out its 'record'.

'You mean that he tried to kill himself, and failed? And tried again?'

'Oh, he didn't have to *try* again,' Parvis said grimly.

They sat opposite each other in silence, he swinging his eyeglasses thoughtfully about his finger, she motionless, her arms stretched along her knees in an attitude of rigid tension.

'But if you knew all this,' she began at length, hardly able to force her voice above a whisper, 'how is it that when I wrote you at the time of my husband's disappearance you said you didn't understand his letter?'

Parvis received this without perceptible embarrassment: 'Why, I didn't understand it – strictly speaking. And it wasn't the time to talk about it, if I had. The Elwell business was settled when the suit was withdrawn. Nothing I could have told you would have helped you to find your husband.'

Mary continued to scrutinize him. 'Then why are you telling me now?'

Still Parvis did not hesitate. 'Well, to begin with, I supposed you knew more than you appear to – I mean about the circumstances of Elwell's death. And then people are talking of it now; the whole matter's been raked up again. And I thought if you didn't know you ought to.'

She remained silent, and he continued: 'You see it's only come out lately what a bad state Elwell's affairs were in. His wife's a proud woman, and she fought on as long as she could, going out to work, and taking sewing at home when she got too sick – something with the heart, I believe. But she had his mother to look after, and the children, and she broke down under it, and finally had to ask for help. That called attention to the case, and the papers took it up, and a subscription was started. Everybody liked Bob Elwell, and most of the prominent names in the place are down on the list, and people began to wonder why—'

Parvis broke off to fumble in an inner pocket. 'Here,' he continued, 'here's an account of the whole thing from the *Sentinel* – a little sensational, of course. But I guess you'd better look it over.'

He held out a newspaper to Mary, who unfolded it slowly, remembering as she did so, the evening when, in that same room, the perusal of a clipping from the *Sentinel* had first shaken the depths of her security.

As she opened the paper, her eyes, shrinking from the glaring headlines,

'Widow of Boyne's Victim forced to Appeal for Aid', ran down the column of text to two portraits inserted in it. The first was her husband's, taken from a photograph made the year they had come to England. It was the picture of him that she liked best, the one that stood on the writing-table upstairs in her bedroom. As the eyes in the photograph met hers, she felt it would be impossible to read what was said of him, and closed her lids with the sharpness of the pain.

'I thought if you felt disposed to put your name down—' she heard Parvis continue.

She opened her eyes with an effort, and they fell on the other portrait. It was that of a youngish man, slightly built, with features somewhat blurred by the shadow of a projecting hatbrim. Where had she seen that outline before? She stared at it confusedly, her heart hammering in her ears. Then she gave a cry.

'This is the man – the man who came for my husband!'

She heard Parvis start to his feet, and was dimly aware that she had slipped backwards into the corner of the sofa, and that he was bending above her in alarm. She straightened herself, and reached out for the paper which she had dropped.

'It's the man! I should know him anywhere!' she persisted in a voice that sounded to her own ears like a scream.

Parvis's answer seemed to come to her from far off, down endless fog-muffled windings.

'Mrs Boyne, you're not very well. Shall I call somebody? Shall I get a glass of water?'

'No, no, no!' She threw herself towards him, her hand frantically clutching the newspaper. 'I tell you, it's the man! I *know* him. He spoke to me in the garden!'

Parvis took the journal from her, directing his glasses to the portrait. 'It can't be, Mrs Boyne. It's Robert Elwell.'

'Robert Elwell?' Her white stare seemed to travel into space. 'Then it was Robert Elwell who came for him.'

'Came for Boyne? The day he went away from here?' Parvis's voice dropped as hers rose. He bent over, laying a fraternal hand on her, as if to coax her gently back into her seat. 'Why, Elwell was dead! Don't you remember?'

Mary sat with her eyes fixed on the picture, unconscious of what he was saying.

'Don't you remember Boyne's unfinished letter to me – the one you found on his desk that day? It was written just after he'd heard of Elwell's death.' She noticed an odd shake in Parvis's unemotional voice. 'Surely you remember!' he urged her.

Yes, she remembered: that was the profoundest horror of it. Elwell had died the day before her husband's disappearance; and this was Elwell's portrait; and it was the portrait of the man who had spoken to her in the garden. She lifted her head and looked slowly about the library. The library could have borne witness that it was also the portrait of the man who had come in that day to call Boyne from his unfinished letter. Through the misty surgings of her brain she heard the faint boom of half-forgotten words – words spoken by Alida Stair on the lawn at Pangbourne before Boyne and his wife had ever seen the house at Lyng, or had imagined that they might one day live there.

'This was the man who spoke to me,' she repeated.

She looked again at Parvis. He was trying to conceal his disturbance under what he probably imagined to be an expression of indulgent commiseration; but the edges of his lips were blue. 'He thinks me mad; but I'm not mad,' she reflected; and suddenly there flashed upon her a way of justifying her strange affirmation.

She sat quiet, controlling the quiver of her lips, and waiting till she could trust her voice; then she said, looking straight at Parvis: 'Will you answer me one question, please? When was it that Robert Elwell tried to kill himself?'

'When – when?' Parvis stammered.

'Yes; the date. Please try to remember.'

She saw that he was growing still more afraid of her. 'I have a reason,' she insisted.

'Yes, yes. Only I can't remember. About two' months before, I should say.'

'I want the date,' she repeated.

Parvis picked up the newspaper. 'We might see here,' he said, still humouring her. He ran his eyes down the page. 'Here it is. Last October – the—'

She caught the words from him. 'The 20th, wasn't it?' With a sharp look at her, he verified. 'Yes, the 20th. Then you *did* know?'

'I know now.' Her gaze continued to travel past him. 'Sunday, the 20th – that was the day he came first.'

Parvis's voice was almost inaudible. 'Came *here* first?'

'Yes.'

'You saw him twice, then?'

'Yes, twice.' She just breathed it at him. 'He came first on the 20th of October. I remember the date because it was the day we went up to Meldon Steep for the first time.' She felt a faint gasp of inward laughter at the thought that but for that she might have forgotten.

Parvis continued to scrutinize her, as if trying to intercept her gaze.

'We saw him from the roof,' she went on. 'He came down the lime-avenue towards the house. He was dressed just as he is in that picture. My husband saw him first. He was frightened, and ran down ahead of me; but there was no one there. He had vanished.'

'Elwell had vanished?' Parvis faltered.

'Yes.' Their two whispers seemed to grope for each other. 'I couldn't think what had happened. I see now. He *tried* to come then; but he wasn't dead enough – he couldn't reach us. He had to wait for two months to die; and then he came back again – and Ned went with him.'

She nodded at Parvis with the look of triumph of a child who has worked out a difficult puzzle. But suddenly she lifted her hands with a desperate gesture, pressing them to her temples.

'Oh, my God! I sent him to Ned – I told him where to go! I sent him to this room!' she screamed.

She felt the walls of books rush towards her, like inward-falling ruins; and she heard Parvis, a long way off, through the ruins, crying to her, and struggling to get at her. But she was numb to his touch, she did not know what he was saying. Through the tumult she heard but one clear note, the voice of Alida Stair speaking on the lawn at Pangbourne.

'You won't know till afterward,' it said. 'You won't know till long, long afterward.'

Mary Williams

THE THINGUMMYJIG

SHE'D always been afraid, even as a child. Of the stiff-backed aunt who'd brought her up, her governess, the austere housekeeper with keys dangling on a chain from her waist, the dour cook, and the two elderly great-uncles who paid occasional visits to the large square house.

The house, Froggetts, stood close to a squelchy dark marsh. She was frightened of that too, with its sombre rooms, long dark corridors, and creakings of doors and floorboards. But most of all she feared Great-Grandfather.

He lived mostly in two rooms upstairs, and had become in her imagination the symbol of all evil that befell her . . . an awesome ancient judge responsible for scoldings and whippings, . . . though she seldom saw him . . . looming always in the background, with the power at any moment of calling doom upon her.

The sound of his stick thumping on the sitting-room ceiling struck terror into her heart and when her aunt said, 'If you dare do "this or that", I'll tell your grandfather,' her knees shook so much they nearly crumpled under her.

His appearance was grotesque; long white beard and whiskers covering a face so gnarled and old only the eyes seemed alive . . . fierce beady eyes darting here and there under bristling brows, quicker than a snake's about to strike. At the rare times he came downstairs to greet his brothers when they called, he was propelled down by the man Joseph in a curious kind of chair, step by step, until he reached the hall, where he swivelled the thing round himself with annoying speed, head thrust forward from humped shoulders.

On such occasions Clarissa crept away quietly to avoid him as long as possible, until the inevitable tea-time when she was forced to sit at the immense mahogany white-spread table, with her fearsome elders around her. It was on one of these days that she first saw the Thingummyjig. That is . . . *properly*. She'd half glimpsed him many times, once poking his head round a chimney-pot; at another watching her from a dark corner of her vast ugly bedroom where she'd been sent in disgrace, at others just slipping along the landing or behind the ponderous grandfather clock in the hall. He was small and round with large feet and hardly any legs at all, having no hair on his head, but wearing a peculiar kind of hat like a clown's.

He was generally smiling, and his smile reached from ear to ear, or *would* have if he had any. Actually there were none to be seen, so the effect was rather like a thin red line drawn in a curve across the surface of a huge turnip. Many children would have been scared. But Clarissa wasn't. Smiles were so rare in her life. So when she met him face to face by the arbour on an afternoon of her great-uncle's visit, she was relaxed suddenly, and smiled back.

After that they became friends, and gradually as the days passed, the little girl realized that the Thingummyjig was not only funny, but clever. When something nasty was going to happen he generally managed to appear and warn her. And if it was *very* bad, he could stretch himself from a ball into a long snake with such a frown on his face she was almost frightened herself.

It became an understanding between them that she never divulged his presence to the adults. Several times, when she was irately questioned by her aunt or governess concerning who she thought she was talking to, she was on the point of answering 'the Thingummyjig': but managed to restrain herself in time. So the secret liaison between them continued unchecked until the day of her eleventh birthday, when her great-grandfather disappeared.

Most of the morning Clarissa had roamed about the garden, partly because a family party was being held for her in the afternoon which meant the old man would be down to meet his relations, and partly because she wanted support, moral or otherwise, from the Thingummyjig.

She hated and was terrified of the approaching party which meant she'd have to be on such good behaviour, she'd inevitably drop something or say the wrong thing when one of the old men addressed her. If she'd had a pretty dress to wear things might have been easier. But Clarissa, despite her name, was a plain child, and her aunt considered spending money on such useless vanity as an immoral waste, a fact Clarissa well knew and understood, thanks to the Thingummyjig. Oh yes; the Thingummyjig was very wise. Though he hadn't much voice to speak of . . . just a thin high kind of squeak in her ear, he taught her a great deal.

That being the case Clarissa wasn't unduly surprised when the old man disappeared in his wheelchair during the early hours of the afternoon. The Thingummyjig had whispered something was going to happen, so it didn't really shock her at all.

The rest of the household, naturally, was in a panic.

'He was *there* . . . sitting in his chair under the elm with his pipe and paper before him, only ten minutes ago . . .' the aunt said with undisguised hysteria in her voice. 'What could have got into him? He seemed better than usual, more contented, and was *so* looking forward to the party . . .' her words trailed off into a nervous gasp, before she added, 'There's only one way he could have taken . . . down the drive and out of the gates towards the marsh. Someone would have seen him the other side, at the front of the house . . . we were all there preparing the tables and seeing the places were properly laid. *You* . . .' turning to Clarissa, 'did *you* see him move, Clarissa?'

Clarissa shook her head dumbly, eyes and mouth solemn in her pale face. She had a sly conviction the Thingummyjig knew something about it, but as none but her believed in him there was no point in saying so.

Naturally a search party was organized immediately, but it was not until early evening that the old man's body was found, still seated in his invalid chair that had sunk several feet into the dark mud of the marsh, head tipped back just above the oozing water, glassy eyes staring from greenish-grey face, mouth open and filled with slime, beard and hair bedraggled with weed.

A great tragedy, everyone said, resulting from an ancient man's sudden desire to see again the wide expanse of marsh where he'd wandered as a child. The brakes of the chair were intact, there was nothing at all wrong with the mechanics. The kindest verdict therefore was death by misadventure, which was duly recorded.

Shortly afterwards it was decided Clarissa should go to boarding-school, which meant naturally a sundering of her childhood relationship with the Thingummyjig.

She told him so the day before she left, and he didn't like it at all. From being a tubby ball of a creature he became suddenly a looming black snake-like thing with vicious red eyes and a fiery tongue darting from his down-drawn elongated mouth.

Clarissa drew back. 'Go away,' she shouted. 'Go away, do you hear? I don't want you . . . ?'

She turned and ran into the house, almost knocking her aunt over in the hall.

'*Clarissa*. What's the matter child?' Her thin hand closed in a claw-like grip on the girl's arm. 'Tell me, do you hear . . . ?'

'The Thingummyjig,' Clarissa blurted out. 'It was . . . it was . . . well, nothing,' she amended lamely. 'Not anything really. Just . . .'

'I know. Imagination. You're tired and overwrought, because of going to school.' For the first time Clarissa sensed real concern in her guardian's voice. 'Well, my dear, we've probably kept you too long at home. But with grandfather alive it was difficult . . . try and understand. I hadn't the power or money to do as I wished for you. Now it will be more fun. At school you'll make friends in time. *Real* friends of your own age. You'll see.'

Her words proved to be prophetic, although it took a whole term for

Clarissa to become adjusted to the new life. And during all that time she did not see the Thingummyjig once. Not even when she returned to the house for holidays, though she knew if she let herself she might easily see him lurking in the shadows or poking from a door. But she didn't. As far as she was concerned the Thingummyjig had disappeared from her life for ever.

Or so she thought.

Following her last term at school she went to university to take her degree in English, with a view to obtaining a teaching post in the future. She was not attractive and considered marriage highly unlikely. Students and tutors accepted her with a certain respect simply because she had undoubted imagination and a capacity to study. Otherwise she went through the usual routine of college life rather like some shy brown bird, unnoticed by more colourful companions. Then, shortly before graduation, she heard that her aunt had died, and as she was the sole heir to the estate, she had to leave immediately for Froggetts.

The late autumn sky was lowering over the marsh when the taxi drew up at the house, spreading an eerie glitter of greenish-black over the desolate flat lands. A solitary wildfowl, wings outspread, rose squawking into the air from the terrain beyond the garden. There was a seeping chill wind blowing; and the few trees waved black and leafless bordering the front drive.

As she went up the path to the door, there was a drawing of bolts and a shivering glow of light from the hall. The housekeeper stood waiting to receive her, a little more bent, her face thinner and more austere from age, her voice more disapproving as she said, 'So it's yours now, Miss. Sad . . . very; that the mistress had to go so sudden, I mean.'

'Yes.' Clarissa remarked, putting her case down at the foot of the stairs.

'We've no boy or man now to cart things about,' the woman resumed pointedly, 'and I'm not young any more.'

'Of course not. I can quite well carry it myself,' Clarissa told her.

'Your room's all ready,' the housekeeper continued, still in dull cold tones. 'Your old room. And the mistress is laid out beautifully in the front sitting-room. I knew you'd wish it that way . . . to see her once before the lid was closed.'

Clarissa shuddered.

'Oh I don't know. I . . .'

During the bleak pause she could feel the ancient retainer's eyes boring as though into her very soul.

'Yes, Miss?'

Clarissa, intimidated, pulled herself together quickly. 'Naturally. Yes. You're quite right of course.'

But the idea was more than distasteful to her; actually quite horrible. She hated dead things, and ever since her great-grandfather's funeral so many years ago, had been depressed by the very mention of the word. If there had been a way of getting out of her aunt's, she'd have taken it; and it was then she began to think of the Thingummyjig, recalling from the past the lumpy squat shape with the round head, large feet and no legs . . . the familiar crony of her childhood who'd possessed such power to help and warn her of approaching crisis. Why had she dismissed him so cruelly on that far-off day before being packed off to school? She recalled with shock the writhing violent thing he'd become . . . the stretched neck and burning eyes emanating such hatred. Well, no wonder after all he'd done for her.

Poor Thingummyjig.

Later, when she'd gone to bed, following the enforced ordeal of looking down on her aunt's swathed form in its oblong coffin, she tried to pull her mind to normality once more, telling herself over and over again there was *no* Thingummyjig; there never had been, really, it was just . . . but *what* was it? At that point her brain boggled, because she knew she was fooling with the truth. In the past only the Thingummyjig had made life for her possible. If *he* hadn't pushed the chair into the marsh on her eleventh birthday she'd never have escaped from Froggetts or gone to school or university, her great-grandfather would have lived on and on, with his awful bangings and threats of punishment . . . of . . . 'Thrash her, woman. It's discipline she needs, thrash her.'

And she'd had more than she could bear . . . until she'd found the Thingummyjig. Now she was back again in the beastly house, with the ugly memories rearing and torturing her almost to madness.

'Oh Thingummyjig,' she whispered without realizing it, 'come back, please; forgive me; help me, Thingummyjig.'

Outside a lean black branch of tree tapped at her window, claw-like, resembling the dark silhouette of a skeleton hand. There was the moaning of fitful wind from the marsh; a sighing and creaking through the undergrowth and huddled bent bushes of the garden as clouds raced over the face of the moon.

Then she saw it . . . pale round visage above a squat body, with fat fleshy fingers fumbling at the woodwork where the air blew between glass and frame, wide mouth extended in an exultant malicious grin.

She sat up with a lurch of her heart, crying 'Thingummyjig, Thingummyjig,' eyes wide and staring, arms raised towards him. The window opened soundlessly, and he was on her counterpane seated like some midget troll eyeing her with a strange unholy knowledge. The giant mahogany wardrobe, old-fashioned dressing-table with its archaic ewer and jug, and looming chest of drawers, which a few moments before had so oppressed her, were suddenly diminished to no consequence. 'What shall I do, Thingummyjig?' she whispered.

He slithered off the bed and padded on flat soundless feet to her door, with a curious rolling gait like that of some large ball. When he turned his moon face towards her his small sloe eyes held a reptilian glitter that told her he'd worked things out. He was hers again to do what she wished at her bidding, so long as *he* wished it too.

He had forgiven her for rejecting him those many years ago.

So she slipped on a pair of light shoes with a dark coat over her nightdress, and followed his slithering form along the landing, down the sombre staircase and through the flagged hall that was in complete darkness, to the front door. She lifted a hand mechanically to the bolts and lock. They gave at her touch with the merest whisper of a grating sound; then she was outside on the drive, running softly after the Thingummyjig, who lolloped and sprang, laughing gleefully but soundlessly through the cold air, turning every few seconds to beckon her on, a childlike, absurd, but incredibly evil-looking creature, with a lusting vengeful gleam in his fleshy lascivious face. There was nothing remotely comical about him any more; but in her gratitude at having him there, and faith in his capacity to free her from the haunting dark horror of Froggetts, she didn't notice it.

Not even when they reached the churchyard where her grandfather lay buried.

Then, with a sudden squeal, the loathsome little creature bounced up into the air, landing like a balloon on the black slab of marble, sitting with legless large feet akimbo, grinning impishly in the moonlight close against the upright memorial stone.

As the eerie light fell in a bluish beam across its face, fear slowly spread in a welling wave of terror through Clarissa's numbed mind. Her teeth were chattering as she whispered pleadingly, 'What is it, Thingummyjig, what's the matter?'

The stretched mouth widened further for a moment, before it flickered and died into a grimacing distorted sneer that lengthened and became one with the snaking black neck reaching and quivering above her, eyes mere dots of angry fire, darting tongue spitting and snarling, as a voice . . . no longer the Thingummyjig's, but her great-grandfather's voice muttered maliciously, 'Why did you push me into the marsh, Clarissa? That was a very wicked thing to do . . . ?'

Too terrified to move, she watched all that was left of the Thingummyjig merge into the frightful spectral shape of the old man. He was smiling, a ghastly threatening smile, one tooth-fang jutting from the decayed jaws. Green slime dripped from his straggling white hair, he had a skeleton hand outstretched to claim her, as the mournful wind carried the echo of his voice . . . 'Naughty girls must be punished, Clarissa . . . you know that, don't you . . . and it was a *very* wicked thing to kill me . . .'

She screamed once. The sound rose more shrill and high than any wild bird's into the damp night air. Then, suddenly, there was a thud as she fell face down on the slab of the old man's tomb.

In the morning she was found by the gardener lying quite dead wearing a dark coat and night attire fallen over her grandfather's grave. There was no indication of why she'd gone there, although the general opinion was that the poor lady had become unhinged by her aunt's death, which must have revived memories of the old man's tragic demise those many years before, inducing a heart attack.

Only one thing puzzled the authorities . . . a small scrap of paper in her pocket on which she'd scribbled . . . 'Thingummyjig, please help me, I need you . . .'

Thingummyjig! What an idea. Obviously grief had shocked the unfortunate creature back into the realms of childhood. The human mind was a queer thing and no mistake. And after all they *had* been a united family at Froggetts.

The housekeeper said nothing. It was not her place. But her opinion was entirely satisfactory to herself. Most people got what they asked for in the end, and Miss Clarissa had certainly deserved her fate.

An unruly wilful child, and a feelingless creature into the bargain.

Nemesis.

That was it.

Mary Elizabeth Counselman

THE HOUSE OF SHADOWS

T HE train pulled up with a noisy jerk ~~~~ ~~~~ d I peered out into
the semi-gloo~ ~~~~ at ~~~~ the place? – 'Oak
Grove'. I could rea~~~~ I sighed wearily.
Three days on the tr~~~~ roll, the cinders,
the scenery flying past ~~~~ ision and hurried
down the aisle to where t~~~~ dy off.

'How long do we stop h~~~~

'About ten minutes, ma~~~~ ~~~~ I stepped from the train to the
smooth sand in front of the station. So pleasant to walk on firm ground
again! I breathed deeply of the spicy winter air, and strolled to the far side of
the station. A brisk little wind was whipping my skirts about my legs and
blowing wisps of hair into my eyes. I looked idly about at what I could see of
Oak Grove. It was a typical small town – a little sleepier than some, a little
prettier than most. I wandered a block or two toward the business district,
glancing nervously at my watch from time to time. My ten minutes
threatened to be up, when I came upon two dogs trying to tear a small kitten
to pieces.

I dived into the fray and rescued the kitten, not without a few bites and
scratches in the way of service wounds, and put the little animal inside a
store doorway. At that moment a long-drawn, it seemed to me derisive,
whistle from my train rent the quiet, and as I tore back toward the station I
heard it chugging away. I reached the tracks just in time to see the caboose
rattling away into the night.

What should I do? Oh, why had I jumped off at this accursed little station?
My luggage, everything I possessed except my purse, was on that vanished
train, and here I was, marooned in a village I had never heard of before!

Or had I? 'Oak Grove' . . . the name had a familiar ring. Oak Grove . . .
ah! I had it! My roommate at college two years before had lived in a town
called Oak Grove. I darted into the depot.

'Does a Miss Mary Allison live here?' I inquired of the station-master.
'Mary Deane Allison?'

I wondered at the peculiar unfathomable look the old man gave me, and at his long silence before he answered my question. 'Yes'm,' he said slowly, with an odd hesitancy that was very noticeable. 'You her kin?'

'No,' I smiled. 'I went to college with her. I . . . I thought perhaps she might put me up for the night. I've . . . well, I was idiot enough to let my train go off and leave me. Do you . . . is she fixed to put up an unexpected guest, do you know?'

'Well' – again that odd hesitancy – 'we've a fair to middlin' hotel here,' he evaded. 'Maybe you'd rather stay there.'

I frowned. Perhaps my old friend had incurred the disapproval of Oak Grove by indiscreet behaviour – it seems a very easy thing to do in rural towns. I looked at him coldly.

'Perhaps you can direct me to her house,' I said stiffly.

He did so, still with that strange reluctance.

I made my way to the big white house at the far end of town, where I was told Mary Allison lived. Vague memories flitted through my mind of my chum as I had seen her last, a vivacious cheerful girl whose home and family life meant more to her than college. I recalled hazy pictures she had given me of her house, of her parents and a brother whose picture had been on our dresser at school. I found myself hurrying forwards with eagerness to see her again and meet that doting family of hers.

I found my way at last to the place, a beautiful old Colonial mansion with tall pillars. The grounds were overgrown with shrubbery and weeds, and the enormous white oaks completely screened the great house from the street, giving it an appearance of hiding from the world. The place was sadly in need of repairs and a gardener's care, but it must have been magnificent at one time.

I mounted the steps and rapped with the heavy brass knocker. At my third knock the massive door swung open a little way, and my college friend stood in the aperture, staring at me without a word. I held out my hand, smiling delightedly, and she took it in a slow incredulous grasp. She was unchanged, I noticed – except, perhaps, that her dancing bright-blue eyes had taken on a vague dreamy look. There was an unnatural quiet about her manner, too, which was not noticeable until she spoke. She stood in the doorway, staring at me with those misty blue eyes for a long moment without speech; then she said slowly, with more amazement than I thought natural, 'Liz! Liz!' Her fingers tightened about my hand as though she were afraid I might suddenly vanish. 'It's . . . it's good to see you! Gosh! How . . . why did you come here?' with a queer embarrassment.

'Well, to tell the truth, my train ran off and left me when I got off for a breath of air,' I confessed sheepishly. 'But I'm glad now that it did . . . remembered you lived here, so here I am!' She merely stared at me strangely, still clutching my hand. 'There's no train to Atlanta till ten in the morning.' I hesitated, then laughed. 'Well, aren't you going to ask me in?'

'Why . . . why, of course,' Mary said oddly, as if the idea was strange and had not occurred to her. 'Come in!'

I stepped into the great hall, wondering at her queer manner. She had been one of my best friends at college, so why this odd constraint? Not quite as if she did not want me around – more as if it were queer that I should wish to enter her house, as if I were a total stranger, a creature from another planet! I tried to attribute it to the unexpectedness of my visit; yet inwardly I felt this explanation was not sufficient.

'What a beautiful old place!' I exclaimed, with an effort to put her at ease again. Then, as the complete silence of the place struck me, unthinkingly I added, 'You don't live here alone, do you?'

She gave me the oddest look, one I could not fathom, and replied so softly that I could hardly catch the words, 'Oh, no.'

I laughed. 'Of course! I'm crazy . . . but where is everybody?'

I took off my hat, looking about me at the Colonial furniture and the large candelabra on the walls with the clusters of lighted candles which gave the only light in the place – for there were no modern lighting fixtures of any kind, I noted. The dim candlelight threw deep shadows about the hall – shadows that flickered and moved, that seemed alive. It should have given me a sense of nervous fear; yet somehow there was peace, contentment, warmth about the old mansion. Yet, too, there was an incongruous air of mystery, of unseen things in the shadowy corners, of being watched by unseen eyes.

'Where is everybody? Gone to bed?' I repeated, as she seemed not to have heard my question.

'Here they are,' Mary answered in that strange hushed voice I had noticed, as if someone were asleep whom she might waken.

I looked in the direction she indicated, and started slightly. I had not seen that little group when I entered! They were standing scarcely ten feet from me just beyond the aura of light from the candles, and they stared at me silently, huddled together and motionless.

I smiled and glanced at Mary, who said in a soft voice like the murmur of a light wind, 'My mother . . .'

I stepped forward and held out my hand to the tall kind-faced woman who advanced a few steps from the half-seen group in the shadows. She seemed, without offence, not to see my hand, but merely gave me a beautiful smile and said, in that same hushed voice Mary used, 'If you are my daughter's friend, you are welcome!'

I happened to glance at Mary from the corner of my eye as she spoke, and I saw my friend's unnatural constraint vanish, give place to a look, I thought wonderingly, that was unmistakably one of relief.

'My father,' Mary's voice had a peculiar tone of happiness. A tall distinguished-looking man of about forty stepped toward me, smiling gently. He too seemed not to see my outthrust hand, but said in a quiet friendly voice, 'I am glad to know you, my dear. Mary has spoken of you often.'

I made some friendly answer to the old couple; then Mary said, 'This is Lonny . . . remember his picture?'

The handsome young man whose photograph I remembered stepped forward, grinning engagingly.

'So this is Liz!' he said. 'Always wanted to meet one girl who isn't afraid of a mouse . . . remember? Mary told us about the time you put one in the prof's desk.' He too spoke in that near-whisper that went oddly with his cheery words, and I found myself unconsciously lowering my voice to match theirs. They were unusually quiet for such a merry friendly group, and I was especially puzzled at Mary's hushed voice and manner – she had always been a boisterous tomboy sort of person.

'This is Betty,' Mary spoke again, a strange glow lighting her face.

A small girl of about twelve stepped solemnly from the shadows and gave me a grave old-fashioned curtsey.

'And Bill,' said Mary, as a chubby child peeped out at me from behind his sister's dress and broke into a soft gurgling laugh.

'What darling kids!' I burst out.

The baby toddled out from behind Betty and stood looking at me with big blue eyes, head on one side. I stepped forward to pat the curly head, but as I put out a hand to touch him, he seemed to draw away easily just out of reach. I could not feel rebuffed, however, with his bright eyes telling me plainly that I was liked. It was just a baby's natural shyness with strangers, I told myself, and made no other attempt to catch him.

After a moment's conversation, during which my liking for this charming family grew, Mary asked if I should like to go to my room and freshen up a bit before dinner. As I followed her up the stairs, it struck me forcibly – as it had before only vaguely – that this family, with the exception of Mary, were in very bad health. From father to baby, they were most pasty-white of complexion – not sallow, I mused, but a sort of translucent white like the glazed-glass doors of private offices. I attributed it to the uncertain light of the candles that they looked rather smoky, like figures in a movie when the film has become old and faded.

'Dinner at six,' Mary told me, smiling, and left me to remove the travel-stains.

I came downstairs a little before the dinner hour, to find the hall deserted – and, woman-like, I stopped to parade before a large cheval-glass in the wall. It was a huge mirror, reflecting the whole hall behind me, mellowly illumined in the glow of the candles. Turning about for a back-view of myself, I saw the little baby, Bill, standing just beside me, big eyes twinkling merrily.

'Hallo there, old fellow,' I smiled at him. 'Do I look all right?' I glanced back at the mirror . . . and what it reflected gave me a shock.

I could see myself clearly in the big glass, and most of the hall far behind me, stretching back into the shadows. But the baby was not reflected in the glass at all! I moved, with a little chill, just behind him . . . and I could see my own reflection clearly, but it was as if he was simply not there.

At that moment Mary called us to dinner, and I promptly forgot the disturbing optical illusion with the parting resolve to have my eyes examined. I held out my hand to lead little Bill into the dining-room, but he dodged by me with a mischievous gurgle of laughter, and toddled into the room ahead of me.

That was the pleasantest meal I can remember. The food was excellent and the conversation cheery and light, though I had to strain to catch words spoken at the far end of the table, as they still spoke in that queer hushed tone. My voice, breaking into the murmur of theirs, sounded loud and discordant, though I have a real Southern voice.

Mary served the dinner, hopping up and running back into the kitchen from time to time to fetch things. By this I gathered that they were in rather straitened circumstances and could not afford a servant. I chattered gaily to Lonny and Mary, while the baby and Betty listened with obvious delight and Mary's parents put in a word occasionally when they could break into our chatter.

It was a merry informal dinner, not unusual except that the conversation was carried on in that near-whisper. I noticed vaguely that Mary and I were the only ones who ate anything at all. The others merely toyed with their food, cutting it up ready for eating but not tasting a bite, though several times they would raise a fork to their lips and put it down again, as though pretending to eat. Even the baby only splashed with his little fork in his rice and kept his eyes fixed on me, now and then breaking into that merry gurgling laugh.

We wandered into the library after the meal, where Mary and I chatted of old times. Mr Allison and his wife read or gave ear to our prattling from time to time, smiling and winking at each other. Lonny, with the baby on his lap and Betty perched on the arm of his chair, laughed with us at some foolish tale of our freshman days.

At about eleven Mary caught me yawning covertly, and hustled me off to bed. I obediently retired, thankful for a bed that did not roll me from side to side all night, and crawled in bed in borrowed pyjamas with a book, to read myself to sleep by the flickering candle on my bedside table.

I must have dropped off to sleep suddenly, for I awoke to find my candle still burning. I was about to blow it out and go back to sleep when a slight sound startled the last trace of drowsiness from me.

It was the gentle rattle of my doorknob being turned very quietly.

An impulse made me feign sleep, though my eyes were not quite closed and I watched the door through my eyelashes. It swung open slowly, and Mrs Allison came into the room. She walked with absolute noiselessness up to my bed, and stood looking down at me intently. I shut my eyes tightly so my eyelids would not flutter, and when I opened them slightly in a moment, she was moving toward the door, apparently satisfied that I was fast asleep. I thought she was going out again, but she paused at the door and beckoned to someone outside in the hall.

Slowly and with incredible lack of sound, there tiptoed into my room Mr Allison, Lonny, Betty, and the baby. They stood beside the bed looking down at me with such tender expressions that I was touched.

I conquered an impulse to open my eyes and ask them what they meant by this late visit, deciding to wait and watch. It did not occur to me to be frightened at this midnight intrusion. There swept over me instead a sense of unutterable peace and safety, a feeling of being watched over and guarded by some benevolent angel.

They stood for a long moment without speaking, and then the little girl, bending close to me, gently caressed my hand, which was lying on the coverlet. I controlled a start with great effort.

Her little hand was icy cold – not with the coldness of hands, but with a peculiar *windy* coldness. It was as if someone had merely blown a breath of icy air on me, for though her hand rested a moment on mine, it had no weight!

Then, still without speaking but with gentle affectionate smiles on all their faces, they tiptoed out in single file. Wondering at their actions, I dropped off at last into a serene sleep.

* * *

Mary brought my breakfast to my bed next morning, and sat chattering with me while I ate. I dressed leisurely and made ready to catch my ten o'clock train. When the time drew near, I asked Mary where her family was – they were nowhere in the house and I had seen none of them since the night before. I reiterated how charming they were, and how happy my visit had been. That little glow of happiness lighted my friend's face again, but at my next words it vanished into one that was certainly frightened pleading. I had merely asked to tell them goodbye.

That odd unfathomable expression flitted across her face once more. 'They . . . they're gone,' she said in a strained whisper. And as I stared at her perplexedly, she added in confusion, 'I . . . I mean, they're away. They won't be back until . . . nightfall,' the last word was so low it was almost unintelligible.

So I told her to give them my thanks and farewells. She did not seem to want to accompany me to the train, so I went alone. My train was late, and I wandered to the ticket window and chatted with the station-master.

'Miss Allison has a charming family, hasn't she?' I began conversationally. 'They seem so devoted to each other.'

Then I saw the station-master was staring at me as if I had suddenly gone mad. His wrinkled face had gone very pale.

'You stayed there last night?' His voice was almost a croak.

'Why, yes!' I replied, wondering at his behaviour. 'I did. Why not?'

'And . . . you saw . . . *them*?' his voice sank to a whisper.

'You mean Mary's family?' I asked, becoming a little annoyed at his foolish perturbation. 'Certainly I saw them! What's so strange about that? What's wrong with them?'

My approaching train wailed in the distance, but I lingered to hear his reply. It came with that same reluctance, that same hesitancy, after a long moment.

'They died last year,' he whispered, leaning forward towards me and fixing me with wide intent eyes. 'Wiped out – every one of 'em exceptin' Mary – by smallpox.'

Richmal Crompton

🦂

ROSALIND

I had known Rosalind long before Heath saw her. I don't know where she came from originally. I think she was serving in a shop before she became old Follett's model. If you remember old Follett's paintings, you'll remember what she was like – a girl about seventeen, with creamy skin, dewy grey-blue eyes, wonderful jet-black lashes, and a mop of short red-gold curls. I remember noticing that the upper outline of her lips was the perfect arc of a circle. Her nose was delicious – a hint of the *retroussé* about it and something childishly immature. She was small and graceful – not so much fairy-like as elfin-like . . . Of course, people talked when she went to Follett, but I happened to know that there was nothing in it. She was a perfect child, and old Follett treated her as though she were his daughter. He was a terrible old man, with a reputation like a piece of tissue paper, but Rosalind appealed to some hidden streak of fatherliness in him. I used to call at his studio a good deal and Rosalind was almost always there. When she was not posing for him, she was cooking his meals or mending his clothes or cleaning the studio. She made him change his underclothing. Periodically she cleaned his greasy old velvet jacket. Left to himself he was the most filthy old ruffian I have ever met. He had a villainous brown beard that reached almost to his waist, and that no amount of persuasion would induce him to have cut.

I think it was Follett who first made her dress in brown and gold. I never saw her wearing any other colours – apart from her models' costumes . . . always warm brown with a touch of golden yellow.

It was I who first took Heath at his own request to Follett's studio. And, curiously enough, it wasn't any of the Rosalind pictures that had attracted Heath. It was some sketches of Canterbury that he had seen in an exhibition that had attracted him and, hearing that I knew the artist, he had come round to ask me to introduce him. That was like Heath . . . He wasn't an artist and he wasn't particularly interested in art, but he was always darting off down side tracks – becoming suddenly interested in something, pursuing it madly for a time, then tiring of it as suddenly and wandering on aimlessly till some fresh interest attracted him. He was having an art phase just then . . .

I had known Heath from childhood. He seemed to have all the gifts that

Fortune could bestow – good looks, money, charm, ability, position – yet he just missed being what he might have been. He wasn't quite reliable. You could never be quite sure of him. He could do things so easily that he generally seemed to put off doing them altogether. He could have been a successful poet or novelist but he had no patience for effort or disappointment. Even in athletics, in which he excelled, his 'off-days' were more numerous and erratic than other people's. When he promised to do anything for you, it was safer to assume that he'd forget. You must know the type. There are thousands of men like that, but Heath's good looks and charm seemed, somehow, to place him apart.

He fell in love with Rosalind at once. We sat in the studio and talked art, or rather old Follett held forth and we listened. Old Follett could always hold forth by the hour. Rosalind brought in sandwiches, and made coffee at a little machine on the table among the tubes of paint and palettes. I noticed that night for the first time how beautiful her hands were. She wore rather an absurd dress that Follett had designed for her – heavy brown silk made in a medieval style with a great Medici collar of gold lace. It didn't suit her a bit, but it made her look delicious and childish and – heartrending, somehow.

Anyway, I saw Heath watching her and knew that he'd fallen in love with her. I knew the signs of Heath's falling in love. I wasn't sure about Rosalind herself. She hardly looked at him, but with some women that's a bad sign.

Heath didn't mention her when we went home. I knew that he had had countless love-affairs but I had an idea even then that this had gone deeper than most.

I wasn't surprised when I heard that he was having lessons from Follett. He went there every evening. They must have been queer lessons. Follett had no more aptitude for teaching than Heath had for learning. But Follett could talk. Follett loved to talk . . . Follett, with his enormous expanse of brown beard and his greasy velvet jacket, a palette in one hand, a brush in the other, striding about the studio, talking, talking, talking. Heath sitting on the paint-stained table, his eyes fixed on Rosalind . . . and Rosalind moving about softly with her young graceful movements, her adorable mop of curls, her delicious nose and mouth, not looking at either of them. Follett never sketched Rosalind when Heath was there, and never allowed Heath to sketch her, so he may not have been as obtuse as he seemed. Of course, he could not resist the ridiculously high fee that Heath offered for his 'lessons'. I think Heath was tortured by the suspicion that Follett was her lover.

Then Follett died. I was out of England at the time, but I saw the news in the papers. I wondered what would become of the ramshackle studio with its broken-down chairs and tables – and Rosalind.

I went there the day after I returned to London. Heath opened the door.

He was very voluble and excited. He'd bought the studio and all its motley furniture. He was an artist. He was working hard. He didn't mention Rosalind, but when she came into the studio with coffee and sandwiches it seemed quite natural. She had altered – glowed into radiant beauty without losing that rather poignant look of childishness. Her happiness was patent to anyone who looked at her. She was gloriously, recklessly happy. I think it was partly her ecstasy of happiness that gave her that curious look of pathos. Heath was the same. They were desperately in love with each other. And he was working hard. The strange thing was that he had a distinct talent for art (just as he seemed to have a distinct talent for anything he put his hand to), and was turning out stuff that was extraordinarily good in its way – bizarre, striking, and really original.

I went there every evening. Heath had, for the time being, quite dropped out of his old circle. He spent all his time in the shabby little studio tucked away in a corner of Chelsea, playing at being an artist and adoring Rosalind. I used to watch Rosalind curiously. I have never seen a woman so happy, so deeply in love, so regardless of past and future. Her eyes hardly ever left Heath. They worked together, laughed together, talked together, cooked together, washed up together. It was all a glorious game. They often forgot my presence; and Heath would take her in his arms and kiss her passionately on her lips as though I had not been there. I seem to see her now, leaning back in his arms in an anguish of ecstasy, her eyes closed, her face pale . . .

I sometimes wondered what went on in Rosalind's mind. Did she really think it could last, or had she decided that their present happiness was worth all the sorrow that was to come? Certainly she showed no apprehension, no foreboding. Yet no one could have seen them then, so young, so passionately in love, so handsome, without knowing that tragedy must be close on their heels. That sort of thing is too perfect to last in this life . . .

It had no more occurred to Heath to marry Rosalind than it had occurred to Rosalind that he should marry her. Heath would be Viscount Evesham when his father died, and there was a strong streak of racial pride in him. I had always known that when Heath married he would marry a woman of family and breeding and culture, a woman who could take her place in the world as Lady Evesham. He would not necessarily love her, but he would deliberately choose such a woman.

The present Viscount Evesham was very old and feeble, and I thought that the end of the Rosalind idyll would come when he died and Heath became Viscount Evesham. But it came sooner than that. It came when Heath knew that Rosalind was going to have a baby. That pulled him up sharp – sobered him, took the carefree joy and happiness from the situation. Rosalind was so pleased herself that it was some time before she realized his attitude. At first, when she saw how he had changed towards her (he could no more hide his feelings than a child), she thought that he was ill. It was some time before she realized that her wonderful secret brought him only disgust, embarrassment, and anxiety. The knowledge killed something in her, something that had been childishly joyous and trusting. It brought something very old and rather bitter into the lovely little face. I am not sure that she did not suffer more, then, than at anything that happened later. I remember a visit I paid them about this time. They were still in the studio. Heath was morose and silent. He avoided looking at her as though he found the sight of her distasteful (she had had about four months of her time and her boyish slenderness was gone). She was a white, unhappy ghost.

Of course, it wasn't like Heath to let any bonds hold him but those of his own inclination. He began to be seen again at his clubs and at his friends' houses. He visited Rosalind less and less frequently. Then one day he told me that he had sent her down to the country 'till afterwards'. 'She'll be better away from London,' he said. But I knew that the real reason was that he wanted her out of sight and, as far as possible, out of memory . . .

I'd met him several times at Frene Court before I realized what was in the wind. At first I hoped that it was Hope Cross, who was always staying there, but I soon discovered that it was Helen. He'd deliberately picked her out as the future Lady Evesham. She was everything he wanted his wife to be – of irreproachable birth and breeding, intelligent, cultured, dignified. In appearance she was the opposite of Rosalind. I've met people who called her colourless. She was ivory pale with soft waves of pale *cendré* hair, light-blue eyes, and calm sculptured lips. She looked like a princess lost in an enchanted forest. I'd been in love with her all my life, but I'd been waiting till I'd got a decent position to offer her. Now I knew I'd no earthly chance against Heath. To do Heath justice, he never knew that I loved Helen.

He came in one evening to tell me that Helen had accepted him. He was exuberant, excited, happy, almost the Heath of the Rosalind days. I could have hated him if it had been possible to hate him. But somehow you couldn't hate Heath. He was so infernally attractive . . .

'And Rosalind?' I said rather brutally.

His face darkened.

'I'll go down and tell her,' he said shortly.

'You'll provide for her and the child, of course?' I said.

He glared at me like a bad-tempered schoolboy.

'Of course,' he said.

I went down to see Rosalind the week after he'd told her. She was lying on a sofa very near her time. She still wore one of her brown and gold dresses. She was a ghost of her old self. Her face was sharpened and drained of its colour, her little mouth was set in lines of piteous suffering and bravery, her eyes were dull as though their brightness had been washed away by floods of salt tears . . . All her radiance was gone – and yet there still remained that poignant look of childishness that made her so pitiful.

'He told you?' I said.

She nodded, biting her pretty twisted lips.

'Rosalind,' I said, 'don't – don't take it so hard. You're young. You've all your life before you. You'll have the child.'

'I don't want the child,' she said in a dull little voice, 'now that he won't share it with me. I never thought it would be like this. I thought he'd be pleased.'

'Now look here, Rosalind,' I said with that abominable cheerfulness with which one tries to rally depressed invalids, 'you mustn't take it like this. You'll forget in time.'

'I shan't. I don't want to forget.' Then the colour crept into her pale cheeks and she clenched her fists. 'I can't *bear* to think of . . . her. I won't let her have him . . . Oh, she shan't . . . they shan't . . .'

I was surprised. And I was frightened.

'Rosalind,' I said gently, 'don't do anything foolish.'

She was suddenly still and very quiet.

'What sort of thing do you mean?' she said.

'I mean . . . don't tell Helen . . . or anything like that.'

'Oh, no,' she said in that strange little voice. 'I didn't mean anything that would make him angry with me . . . I don't think I shall live long, anyhow,' she ended.

I returned to my idiotic self-imposed task of 'cheering her up'. She watched me with a little smile as though she were amused.

The next week the baby was born dead and Rosalind died a day or two later.

I was with Heath when the news came. I guessed what it was from the sudden look of relief on his weak handsome face. He had been frightened. Helen was a deeply religious woman and an idealist, and he had been terrified of her finding out about Rosalind and the child. If it did not actually put an end to the engagement, it would bring him down with a pretty heavy bump from the pedestal on which she had set him. And now by an extraordinary stroke of luck both Rosalind and the child were dead . . .

'That's that,' he said as he handed me the telegram.

It was as if he said: 'A satisfactory end to an unsatisfactory business.'

At that moment I think I actually hated him.

I went abroad for two months after that and on my return I noticed that Heath was not looking well. He seemed to be developing 'nerves'. He started at every sound.

I stayed the weekend with him at his father's house in the country. It was something of a strain. We kept so carefully to impersonal subjects, avoiding both Helen and Rosalind and his approaching marriage. We rode in the woods on the Saturday afternoon. It was autumn, and the trees were turning to vivid reds and golds. As we were returning he reined his horse in suddenly with a quick jerky movement.

'Did you see her?' he whispered sharply.

I had seen before he spoke. We were passing an open grassy path at right angles to the one where we were riding. At the end was an enormous beech tree, a riot of browns and golds. As we passed and looked down the avenue, a gust of wind tossed a low branch that almost swept the ground, and just for a second in the shadowy distance it took the likeness of a girl dressed in brown and gold.

'It was the branch in the wind,' I said, 'a trick of the shadows.'

He bit his lip.

'It wasn't,' he said between his teeth, 'I'm always seeing her.'

Characteristically he had not entered the studio since he tired of Rosalind, neither had he taken any steps towards selling or letting it. I've forgotten how Helen came to know about it. I suppose that he or I mentioned it in some casual reference to old days. When he saw Helen's interest in it he quickly changed the subject, but Helen began eagerly to ask questions. Where was it? How big was it? Why hadn't she seen it before? He answered sulkily, but we were all used to his sulkiness. There was something rather attractive and boyish about it. Helen persisted. He must have a house-warming there. She must see it. Heath and I and she must have a picnic tea there the next day. She'd bring provisions and make tea for us . . . Heath objected. It would be damp. The place would be inches deep in dust. It was a barn of a place. He'd run her down to the coast instead and they'd have a decent picnic there . . . better than a mouldy old studio. But Helen persisted.

'Darling, I'd no idea you were an artist. I'm too thrilled for words. I must see it.'

She laughed as she spoke, her blue eyes alight, the sunshine turning the waves of her fair hair to silvery gold . . . I can see her now. Heath gave in with a bad grace, then allowed himself to be teased back into good humour.

The picnic was foredoomed to failure from the start. The air of the studio struck strangely chill though there was bright sunshine outside. It seemed like a haunted place. I saw Helen shiver and draw her furs around her as she entered. Heath's face looked grey in the sudden gloom. The windows were filthy. The cord that drew back the blind from the skylight was broken and we could not reach it. The corners were full of cobwebs. Everything was covered with dust. The table was a medley of dirty paint tubes, paper, brushes, and palettes. A clay figure seemed to grin horribly from a dark corner. On a plate on the windowsill was a mouldy peach. There was a damp *dead* sort of smell over everything. And suddenly I had a vision of the place as it had been – bright and cosy and clean, full of love and light and laughter; Rosalind going to and fro with the inevitable coffee and sandwiches, Rosalind sitting on the hearthrug bobbing cherries, Rosalind laughing her hauntingly sweet little laugh, Rosalind in Heath's arms on the very spot where Helen now stood. No wonder the place was cold and grey and – heart-broken.

Helen gave a sudden little cry and we both turned to her.

'What's the matter?' I said quickly.

'Nothing,' said Helen. She looked startled, half-amused, half-ashamed. 'I'm so sorry. It was nothing. I – it must have been the sunshine on the dark oak. Just for a second it looked as if the door were open and a girl stood there dressed in brown and gold, then when I looked properly I saw that the door was closed and it was just the sunlight on the dark oak. I'm sorry I startled you.'

Of course, the thing was hopeless after that. Heath went white to the lips. He kept looking behind him into the dark corners of the room. When the door creaked as we were having tea he dropped his cup and saucer with a clatter. I could see perspiration on his brow. He kept moving his dry lips as he gazed fixedly at the closed door. Helen was splendid. She carried off the situation – made tea, laughed and chattered, and refused to notice the tenseness of the atmosphere.

After tea she opened a portfolio that lay on the table and began to look at his sketches. Of course, the first one she took up was one of Rosalind – Rosalind dressed as a page boy, her lips curved into a deliciously impudent smile, her mop of red-gold curls aflame in the sunshine. Rosalind – instinct with life and laughter and roguery . . . Poor little dead, unhappy Rosalind . . .

'What an adorable child!' said Helen. 'Who is she?'

Heath had got himself in hand by this time.

'Oh, just a model,' he said almost casually.

Later, when Helen and I were looking at the view from the window, I saw him take out that sketch and slip it into his pocket.

There was another portfolio full of sketches of Rosalind which Helen never found. I saw Heath's eyes wander to it constantly as if afraid lest she should discover it, and once he carelessly pushed it still farther out of sight beneath some papers.

But Helen was genuinely surprised and impressed by the quality of Heath's paintings, and that gradually soothed him. He was always childishly susceptible to praise.

I didn't see Heath for some time after that. Our next meeting was a curious one. It occurred to me suddenly to go down to see Rosalind's grave. I hated to think of it untended and uncared for. I thought I might make some arrangements to have it looked after regularly. I took a train from Town to the village station and went to the little churchyard. When I found the grave I stood motionless with astonishment. It was February, but the grave was literally covered with roses and orchids freshly laid upon it – the most expensive roses and orchids it was possible to buy. Then I saw Heath coming round from behind the church to it. He'd brought armfuls of roses and orchids down from Bond Street and laid them on the grave with no means of keeping them fresh – no water or tins or anything like that, simply laid them in heaps on the grave of Rosalind and his child. He showed no embarrassment at being found there, no surprise at finding me there. He said, as casually as if we had met at the races: 'There's a train down in about fifteen minutes. Are you coming?'

We walked back to the station in silence. I looked at him curiously. He was thinner. His face was lined and – jerky, somehow. He looked on wires . . . and there was suffering in his face. When the station was in sight, he said suddenly:

'Did you see the baby?'

'No.'

'I didn't, either. I couldn't get down.' (That was Heath all over. He'd managed to persuade himself that he'd wanted to get down to Rosalind and the child and hadn't been able to.) 'But I'm glad it was a boy. She'd wanted a boy.'

Then I knew what had happened. His love for Rosalind was creeping back into his heart . . . the old, passionate, now torturing, love. I'd always known that Rosalind had gone deeper than any of his previous love-affairs. I'd suspected that it was Helen's suitability to fill the position of his wife that had attracted him rather than love for her. And now love for Rosalind, an aching, torturing, longing for Rosalind, stronger than any other passion he had ever known, was haunting him. Poor little unhappy ghost. She was amply avenged now.

We parted at the London terminus.

'You coming my way?' I said.

'No, I'm going to the studio.'

'Taking up painting again?'

'No.'

No, he wasn't taking up painting again. He was sitting alone in the haunted studio, longing for her, feeding his cheated love on memories of her every word and gesture, listening for the echoes of her silvery laughter, looking through the portfolio he had hidden from Helen . . .

His marriage day drew near. You will understand that, apart from my own feeling for Helen, I wasn't happy about the marriage. Yet I thought that once married to Helen he would forget Rosalind and learn to love Helen. No one could help it. And Helen would be an ideal wife for him. She was so wise. She would manage him so well. I wanted him to be happy. With all his faults and weaknesses he was a likeable fellow . . . And Helen – he could give her the sort of position she seemed born to fill.

I was to be best man, of course. Heath and I went down to stay at the inn at Craigford where Helen lived with her aunt Lady Frene. Lady Frene was deaf and very rheumaticky and doesn't come into the story. We arrived the day before the wedding and Helen insisted on our going to lunch with them. She said that she knew it was unconventional but it seemed so silly not to. We were all a bit on edge. Together we would be able to 'laugh it off'.

That lunch was a strange meal. The sunny panelled dining-room was very different from the dusty cobwebby studio, but that lunch with Helen reminded me of the never-to-be-forgotten 'picnic' in old Follett's studio. There was the same electric atmosphere, the same sensation of standing on the crust of a volcano. Heath was unlike himself – feverishly gay at one minute and morosely glum the next. I thought again how white and drawn his handsome face looked. Helen was her usual self – charming, interesting, the perfect hostess.

After lunch Helen suggested that we should go for a walk. I believe she hoped that it would clear the air and restore Heath to his normal self. I think we all felt a heavy sense of apprehension, a dim foreboding of evil, all except Heath, who now seemed feverishly excited.

I want to tell what followed as accurately as I can, but it happened so quickly that it is difficult.

We were walking along the road. On the side on which we were walking was a hedge, on the other the high wall that surrounded the grounds of Frene Court. A motorcar was coming towards us at a moderately slow rate. We all saw it for some time before it was abreast of us. Just as it came abreast of us Heath stepped forward suddenly into its direct line. The driver had no chance to pull up. It simply knocked Heath down and went over him. Yet it was not as if Heath deliberately stepped in front of the car. He did not seem to see the car. It was as if he had started forward suddenly to cross to the other side of the road, car or no car. Nothing mattered except to reach the other side of the road. That was the impression I had as he stepped forward.

The driver was a good fellow. He took us all back to Frene Court and then drove like fury for a doctor. But Heath was dead when we picked him up from the road.

It was the day after the funeral. I felt that I'd got to have things out with Helen. It looked horribly as if Heath had deliberately committed suicide to avoid marrying her, but I was sure it wasn't that.

I found Helen in the garden. She looked very pale and very beautiful in her black dress.

'Helen,' I blurted out, 'he didn't do it on purpose.'

'I know,' she said, 'it was the girl on the other side of the road. She beckoned to him just as the car was passing.'

'What girl?'

'Didn't you see her? She wore a long brown dress with a gold Medici collar. She had a child in her arms and she held it out to him and beckoned.'

'I saw nothing.'

'He did. Didn't you hear?'

'Hear what?'

'He gave a little cry when he saw her, and then he ran to her . . .'

'There was no one there,' I said, 'the road was quite empty.'

'Who was she?' she said, as if she had not heard me.

'I saw nothing,' I repeated doggedly.

'Whose baby was it?'

I shrugged my shoulders. I felt horribly shaken.

'Hers, presumably, as she was holding it,' I said, trying to speak in the half-bantering tone in which one humours a romancing child.

She replied in a voice that was barely audible:

'And was it – his, too?'

'I can tell you nothing,' I said, 'I saw nothing.'

Helen had a bad breakdown after that and was ordered abroad for a year. We were married two years later and have been perfectly happy ever since. But we have never mentioned either Rosalind or Heath's death to each other. I think we feel that we owed him that much loyalty at least.

Dorothy K. Haynes

❧

REDUNDANT

H E had always taken jobs that nobody else wanted.
'Taken' was perhaps the wrong word. It implied choice, and
Hamish never chose anything. He simply accepted what was left.

He had always been a shy and lonely man, a man who didn't make friends
easily. Girls never looked at him, dumb and awkward as he was, and he had
nothing to offer in conversation with men. Mostly, people treated him with a
kind of ribald affection, a humorous shake of the head, an exasperated but
delighted, 'And what's Hamish been up to now?'

Hamish had usually been up to something laughable. He was a willing
worker, first to clock on and last to leave, but he had a reputation for doing
the wrong thing, little mistakes, small inefficiencies which mounted up, in
time, to minor catastrophes. Sooner or later, every job he took would end.
He was never fired, or angrily dismissed; he was too well-meaning for that.
Simply, he was made redundant, but not nobly redundant, with a handsome
settlement as a reward for years of service; merely unwanted after a period so
short that there was no time for benefits to accrue.

That was his life. As he grew older and less able, less confident, the jobs
he was offered became more and more humble; from a trial period in a pool
of janitors to a dustman, a temporary picker-up of rubbish in the park, and
once a kitchen porter, hefting bins full of fish guts and cabbage leaves and
wads of sodden paper. Always, redundancy came in the wake of his
well-meant enthusiasm. As a janitor he mistimed the heating cycle, and left
the school gates unlocked; as a dustman he spilled rubbish on the road; in
the park, boys upended his litter bag in a high wind, and in the kitchen he
was too weak to handle bins more than half full.

The job he liked best had been a watchman's; not a posh security officer,
with a uniform and a dog to guard him and keep him company, but an
ordinary watchman by a hole in the road, with a brazier by the door, and red
lamps round the hut. This job lasted longer than all the others. It was a
pleasure to him, because he was on his own, with no one to criticize or sap
his confidence; but the work came to an end, the holes in the road were

filled, the lamps and cones and his little hut carried away on a council lorry, and he was redundant all over again.

It was some time after this, after a spell of being out of work, that he wakened feeling feverish and ill. The days came and went, his head ached, his stomach heaved, and then one day there was a thumping and crashing at the door, and people all around him. The neighbours had missed him, the milkman had had no answer to his knock, and the police had broken in and carted him away to hospital.

It was comfortable there, everyone was kind, and the mates who had worked with him on the building site came in to visit him; but they would not let him lie in peace. They seemed to think that he was ready to give up and die. 'And you don't want that, lad, do you?' they coaxed. 'You know what that would mean? You'd be last in the churchyard. You'd be the *Watcher of the Dead*!'

It didn't sound so very bad, but his mates explained it very clearly, as everything had to be explained to Hamish. It would be a job he couldn't escape from. It would be his, a cold and lonely vigil, until he was released by the next one to die, the next reluctant candidate; and that might be a very long time.

It didn't matter. He was beyond choice and effort. Hamish, cold and giddy, whirled unresisting down a dark echoing tunnel; and at the end of it was his new job, his last job, the one which nobody else wanted.

As he drove in state to the graveyard, spruced and formal in the tight enclosing coffin, he felt he had never started work in such style. The men who had visited him stood around in dark suits and black ties as words of cheer and encouragement were read over him, but all the time there was a shaking of heads and a murmur of sympathy. 'Fancy this happening to Hamish!'

He didn't care. He had a new job, a job with responsibility and a title to go with it. *The Watcher of the Dead*. It was like having his name in gold on an office door.

Patiently, he got to his feet to begin his first perambulation of the night. The gates were locked, the walls were high, and there was no one to see him as he half hirpled, half glided on feet which left no mark on the damp grass.

It was a calm night. Whoever would have thought the sky could be so blue at midnight? Little gold clouds like puffs of smoke reflected late sunshine or early moonshine – he couldn't be sure which – and the whole cemetery was visible, dim and dark blue. Here, in a low iron railing, was the grave of Mrs Swan, who had run out burning and birling when her home went on fire. *She* wouldn't have been much use as a watcher, poor mutilated thing. And there was Isaac Prosser, who had served ham and cheese at the front of his shop, and taken betting lines at the back. He had fallen dead of a stroke, and been buried with great ceremony, but there had been no reprieve for him. He had had to do his stint at the cemetery; and here was little Billy Slater, who had been picked up in pieces after falling over the cliffs on holiday looking for gulls' eggs.

Billy had never served his time. His parents saw to that. Hamish remembered it now with a new understanding. His funeral had met up with the corpse of Torquil McLachlan, who ran the Stag Hotel, and died of drink, and from that minute it had been a neck-and-neck race. It was not decent, the two hearses roaring and edging each other off the road, but Billy's parents were damned sure their laddie was not going to be landed with such a gruesome job, and him not twelve years old. Torquil's driver had had a dram or two before setting out, and his Rover squashed its wing at the churchyard gates. So Billy Slater nursed his bandaged body in peace, and Torquil became Watcher of the Dead.

There had been many after him, and now Hamish had taken over. He was keen, but lonely, lonelier than he had ever been working on his own. It was what the men had warned him about, telling him the disadvantages of the job – long hours, no pay, and no one ever to talk to – but it was not as bad as they had made out. He was not quite sure to whom he was responsible, but he was determined to give full satisfaction.

Never were the graves guarded so well. Crosses and cherubs, urns and hourglasses, he knew them all, the weather-blasted sandstone, the gilt-lettered granite, the upended jam jars, and the marble books open at consolatory texts. He checked them all, in the hours between dark and dawn, and as a bonus to Those Over Him, he sometimes did voluntary overtime in the daytime.

He leaned against the headstone, his feet following the line of the grave, his shoulders level with the last inscription, HAMISH McDONALD McCLURE. He had watched the men carving it, fitting the name and date beneath the names and dates of the other McClures, but they had not seen him. No one could see him in sunlight. The bright day hid him as it hides flames, so that they could talk about him as if he did not exist, though they looked over their shoulders and lowered their voices as the marble chips flew and passed through him.

'I thought Hamish would have been at rest by now. Tommy Bain was gey far through with the pneumonia, but it seems he's got the turn. His mother was tellin' me this mornin'.'

'Just as well. How could a wee laddie like Tommy manage the watching?'

'How does *Hamish* manage?'

It raised a laugh, though an uneasy one. Hamish, standing diffidently aside, wanted to answer back, and say that he was managing fine. He had nothing to complain about; only, when the men packed up their tools and moved away, he felt for a moment as if the sun had gone in; that was all.

He had another task to perform: the task of summoning those to die.

To begin with, he worried about this. Without instruction or supervision, he had no idea how or where to go about it, or whom to call. In the past, there had always been someone to take him in hand, with a few dos or don'ts, a quick runthrough of rules he couldn't always take in, but on which he could always get advice if he asked. Now there was nothing but a sensing in the midst of his nothingness, a compulsion which told him it was time to set out on a journey; and there by the gate was a black cab, an old black cab with a tired horse with hair as grey as cobwebs; and he knew to go into the driving seat and take up the reins and let the old horse go on its way.

They went through the gate like dissolving steam, and ambled on slowly along the empty road. Such an old cab it was, creaking and trundling, but the man inside was elated. It was the first time he had ever had a job with transport laid on for him. He let the horse go where it willed, and it plodded on past cottages and farms, where people pulled back the curtains furtively and peeped out at the noise. They could see nothing. They shook their heads and let the curtains drop, but Hamish knew that their faces were white and their hearts sinking to their stomachs. The death coach had passed; but if it was not for them, this time, who knew how long it would be before it stopped at their gate?

And then the coach did halt at a big house, a prosperous stone house with carriage lamps at the door and music behind lighted windows. The grey gravel crunched and ground under the wheels, and suddenly the music stopped and the lights went down. Inside, people were wailing. They had heard the sound, and knew what it meant. The horse stood for a while, patient in the grey moonlight, and then clopped away over the churning stones; and they went on and on, dreamlike, to a broken-down steading where the animals set up a terrified clamour, though there was nothing to see; and Jimmie Gow's wife choked over a scream, because though her husband was now past hearing, he heaved in the bed as if he wanted to be away.

They stopped at many places after that: a closed shop in the town, a new bungalow, and a hospital with dim lights burning. People out late, or up early before dawn, paused and covered their ears and prayed; and Hamish was neither sad nor sorry. He was only doing his job, and he had put in a good night's work.

He repeated his errand many times – he did not know how many; the nights were long, and colder now, and time was no longer a matter of day or night. He knew that if he had done his task properly, it would bear a harvest of souls, but he did not connect the harvest with himself. So far, nothing had happened. The strong took a long time to sicken, and the sick to die.

He was confident now, on top of his job, and no longer lonely. The mourners who came to lay flowers and stand in silence or merely sit and think in the quietness were company for him. He learned, considerately, to keep out of their way, because they had enough to bear without the grue that gripped them when he passed. Anyone meeting him would have screamed. He would have screamed himself at his own reflection, his face all hollowed and wasted away, hair in long wisps on a yellow skull, and his loose robe hiding a transparency of skin over skeleton; but what he wore he thought of as his uniform, clothes for the job, a suitable outfit for what he had to do; and he did it willingly, prowling the paths, inspecting the lairs and memorials, and making way, all the time, for those he still thought of as his betters.

Thus, when the gravediggers arrived with their planks and spades, he did not resent their talk, and the disturbance they made in his territory. They began to delve, deep and narrow, and worms crawled fatly out of the mounded soil. Hamish had an uneasy familiarity with worms; he imagined them . . . somewhere . . . wriggling and . . . he turned away, and the diggers paled as he passed.

The next people who arrived came in more seemly manner, carrying a new box of elm, bright with brasses, and gift-wrapped with ribbons and coloured wreaths. Hamish relaxed into gratification. For once, he had done everything properly. One of those he had bidden had come, according to plan, and this time no one could fault him. He had always known that, given time, he could work as well as the next man.

The last of many words were spoken, the coffin lowered, the last earth pattered down. The mourners left, with wet hankies, looking back with grief and regret. Hamish settled himself against a yew tree, almost inflated with job satisfaction. Tonight he would make another foray, transport laid on, and the job progressing at his own pace and discretion.

The shade beside him shouldered him away, snivelling soundlessly. Misery and dejection, resentment and terror surrounded him like a smell. As he was edged farther and farther away, Hamish realized now where his zeal had led him. Of all the corpses, one had to be last; and the last one would supplant him.

It was all wrong. This thing beside him dreaded his task, and he, Hamish, did not want to relinquish it. Surely they could come to some arrangement?

Surely . . . ? But there was no appeal. Slowly, he felt himself seep and settle into his grave like water into a sponge, the trust, the routine, the responsibility of time unmeasured gone as if it had never been.

Once again, he was redundant.

A.L. Barker

THE DREAM OF FAIR WOMEN

'I S it really called that?'
'Why not?'
'Couldn't you have found somewhere else!'
'You asked me to suggest somewhere Janine wouldn't find you and you could rest up. This is it. The landlord owes me a favour. Are you going to quibble about a name?'
'I can't stand women. I've done with them.'
'You? You won't be done till you're in your wooden overcoat.'
'I mean it. So far as I'm concerned it's not a dream, it's a bloody nightmare.'
'It's a poem by Tennyson.'
'So it's a poem by Tennyson! But if Janine tracks me down—'
'Beach – he's the landlord – will see her off.'
'I tell you she's sworn to kill me. And she'll do it.'
'It beats me how you get into these situations.'
Selwyn grinned. 'That's because you don't know the power of love.'
He made Miller take his key and go to the flat and check that Janine was out. Then he went in and got his things together. She had locked the wardrobe but he had no qualms about breaking it open. He took the whisky and gin, he liked whisky and she liked gin and he reckoned she deserved to suffer for illegally impounding his clothes. He frisked the mattress, felt in the space under the Sleepeezie label. It was empty, as half expected, seeing that he had removed some cash from there only the day before. But it was worth a look, she was such a creature of habit. He could say that twice, he could say anything boring about Janine twice.
'She's mentally unbalanced,' he called to Miller, who was keeping watch from the front window. 'If she's crossed she goes bananas.'
'Find yourself a nice homely girl with money.'
'All women are crazy, I've definitely done with them. Come on, let's get out of here, I don't feel safe.'
In the car on the way to the pub Miller said, 'Beach isn't exactly

mild-tempered either. He's an ex-Commando, so don't start anything unless you want your neck squeezed.'

'Is he married?'

Miller nodded and grinned, showing his eye-teeth. 'I'd be surprised if you started anything there.'

It turned out to be a Victorian-style red-brick hostelry in a mini-minor road, not much more than a lay-by, off the motorway. Miller could be right, Janine wouldn't come looking for him here. Selwyn, observing the thick carpets, claret-shaded lamps and claw-footed chairs, guessed that it was pricey. He needn't mind, he had the money Janine had been putting by for a new cooker, it would see him through the week and he was entitled to a spell of comfort – morning tea and newspapers in bed, full English breakfasts, three-tiered lunches and brandy after dinner.

Beach, the mine host, looked out of character with the place. He was beetle-browed, no longer young, but big in hams and fists, with a hot hard eye and hairy nostrils. Miller introduced Selwyn as 'this friend who's having trouble with his life-style and needs peace and quiet to sort it out'. Beach finished what he was doing, wiping the bar counter with a piece of mutton cloth before he shook hands. It was like being saluted by something cold, damp and powerful: a boa constrictor. Miller said, 'If anyone comes asking for him, he's not here, you've never seen him, or anyone like him.'

Selwyn, who was wiping his shaken hand on the seat of his trousers, put in, 'Especially if it's a woman asking.'

'What sort of woman?'

Miller said, 'Tall, slender, thirtyish, foreign-looking.'

'Blonde or brunette?'

'Dark brunette.'

'That goes for a lot of women that come in here.'

'Home-dyed,' said Selwyn. 'And built like a race-horse, she's got the same twitchy skin.'

'Money?'

'Excuse me?'

'Do you owe her money?'

'Certainly not.' Selwyn had perfected the art of clearing his face and retracting his ears with a boyish openness which most people – women, anyway – found irresistible. Beach found it totally resistible and gave him a non-complicit stare. 'It's an emotional entanglement, you know what I mean. She'll get over it. But she's liable to say and do things she'll be sorry for later on.'

'I'll put you at the back,' said Beach. 'If you see her coming you can get away down the fire-escape.' He wasn't smiling and there was no twinkle in his eye.

Selwyn thought it politic to laugh, so did Miller. 'You'll be OK, Sel. Call me if there's anything else I can do.'

'You've done enough,' said Selwyn. Later he might need to borrow Miller's car, but as of now Miller was welcome to go. Selwyn clapped him across the shoulders. 'I won't forget it, sport.'

He was probably doing Miller a favour. The inn, tucked away as it was, couldn't be much patronized and whatever Miller owed the landlord would be covered by the introduction of a paying guest. At present, anyway, Selwyn was prepared to pay. If he became unprepared by force of circumstance there might have to be a reappraisal.

A little old man with legs like a jockey and wearing button gaiters carried his bag upstairs. He opened a door on the first landing.

'Here we are, sir, I hope you'll be comfortable.'

'If I'm not you'll soon hear about it.'

But he approved of the room. It was dignified, full of solid, well-polished furniture and good old Turkey carpet, not Janine's plastic wrought-iron chairs and skid-mats on bare parquet. The bed was double, well-sprung, noiseless, the pillows plump, the eiderdown billowy and pink satin.

He lay down, closed his eyes and summoned a few erotic memories. When, sighing, even soulful, he got up, the short winter dusk had set in and the room was full of substantial shadows.

He was not, and never had been, a fanciful type. His school reports complained 'lacks imagination', but in the one and only important respect that was not true. He had plenty of imagination when it came to the little old three-letter word that made the world go round. One of those shadows looked uncommonly like a woman. Wishful thinking, of course.

He switched on the light and the shadows vanished. There was a sort of tallboy with a vase on top which could have looked like a figure, a woman's if he was sufficiently wishful. Whistling, he unpacked his clothes and hung them in the closet; he was of a sanguine disposition and Fate, or Nature, or the law of averages would provide.

He filled the bath and tipped into it half a bottle of Janine's bath oil which he had taken more to annoy her than because he liked it. It made the gloomy old hotel bathroom smell like a sauna and streaked the bath bright green. Afterwards he put on his dressing-gown and drank Janine's gin. This was the life and he was grateful to her for putting him up to it.

While he shaved he took a good look at himself. He had not been born with money but he had the remote next best, a thoroughly prepossessing exterior. In fact women were too damn prepossessed and couldn't wait for the property to become vacant. Which was how the trouble with Janine had started, over some wretched girl who thought she owned him.

He stroked his nose. Roman, Janine called it. It wasn't, it was Greek. And his skin, olive and warm, with greenish shadows after his shave, had positively obsessed her. He watched his smile light up his face and he couldn't wonder, he honestly couldn't, at the damage he inflicted. He couldn't be blamed for it either.

He dressed and went down to dinner. The tables in the dining-room were all set, white cloths and sparkling glasses, cutlery for three courses, bread baskets and napkins folded into bishops' mitres.

But company, though expected, did not arrive. He ate with a thousand of his selves reflected to infinity in the mirrors that lined the walls. The food was above average, country pâté and toast, followed by veal cutlets, creamed potatoes and button sprouts, then a nice apple charlotte with clotted cream, cheese and biscuits.

The woman who waited at table was as black as the ace of spades. He asked her what her name was.

'Rosanna.'

'That's two names, Rose and Anna.'

'Just the one. Like glory.'

'Glory?'

She drew the cork from his bottle of wine with a report like a gun shot. 'Hosanna in the highest.'

He watched her take her big hips away between the tables. She was majestical, even stately. In her own country she would rate as a beauty. But looking at her was like looking at a newly black-leaded grate.

When she brought his veal chops he raised his glass to her. 'Bottoms up.'

She inclined her head and smiled, not the melon grin of her kind, no more than a quirk of her lips. 'I hope you enjoy your meal.'

He saw her afterwards serving behind the bar. He didn't stay long. There was nothing to interest him, executive types talking about 'demand-promotion', elderly housewives, and a man with a smelly dog.

Anyway, he had demands of his own to promote. He was thinking of getting away somewhere warm for the winter. It would need organization to stretch Janine's cooker money to pay for his bed and board here and buy him an air ticket to Cyprus or Benidorm or wherever. He needed to think – and take a look at the fire-escape.

On the way up to his room he met a woman. He was deep in thought and didn't see her until they came face to face, or rather, knee to knee. It gave them both a surprise – wholly pleasant for him. As she stood on the stair above he was close enough to follow the blush that ran swiftly and softly from her neck to her temples. He did not stand aside, his hand went out to the banister rail and his arm barred her way. He smiled deep into her eyes and that again was a wholly pleasant experience.

She was young, but not too young, mid-thirties perhaps, he could see tiny scarlet threads under her skin. He could also see that she was a natural pure blonde. But she had raven black brows and lashes which, contrasting with her corngold hair, stopped his heart as well as his eye. Over her blue silk dress she wore a frilly apron, decorative rather than menial.

'I do beg your pardon,' he said warmly.

She lowered her eyes and made a movement, not quite a curtsey, nor yet a bob, but it acknowledged his status as a paying guest – and a promising male. All without a trace of coquetry or coyness.

He would have handed her down the stair but she drew back and stood against the wall so that he could pass.

'Mrs Beach?' She lifted her chin, smiling. 'My name's Selwyn.'

She nodded and next minute was gone, slipping away down the stairs and along the passage to the bar. Whistling, he went up to his room.

But he couldn't settle to his own affairs. He kept thinking about the woman. It was the old story, he was about to start something. Only this time he had a feeling that a start had already been made. Who by? Mrs Beach? He had only seen her for a couple of minutes but he could see she wasn't bold like Janine, nor forward. She had class, something he tended to forget women could have. It was in the way she looked at him, sure of her quality and expecting his to be up to the same standard. Well, he wouldn't disappoint her, there was a best in him, let her bring it out and see how good it was.

'Mrs Beach, you're a peach.' He went to the window and looked at the fire-escape. His plans had changed, he might be staying longer than first budgeted for, and there were other emergencies besides fire that he might want to escape from.

He decided to go back to the bar and have another look at Mrs Beach. But she wasn't there. Beach and the black woman were getting ready to close. She was rinsing glasses, Beach was rearranging chairs. He stood, a chair in each hand, and stared at Selwyn, eyes as hard as bullets. Selwyn did not ask him where his wife was; he disliked the idea of talking to Beach about her.

Hopefully, he thought, he might find her upstairs. He hung about outside his room and when he went in, left the door ajar. The dress she wore made a whispering sound when she moved and he would certainly hear if she passed by.

All he heard was Beach's heavy tread going along the passage and up the next flight of stairs. Selwyn shut his door and went to bed.

Next morning he was wakened with tea and newspaper, brought not by

Mrs Beach, as he had confidently expected, but by the old fellow with elliptical legs.

'I hope you slept well, sir.'

'Where's Mrs Beach?'

'Gone shopping.' The old fellow drew back the heavy curtains and let in a blaze of light.

Selwyn flinched. 'Hey, I ordered the *Sun* newspaper, not the bloody solar system. Leave the curtains.'

'I beg your pardon, sir.'

'Another thing, Barney, I want a pot of tea in the morning, and biscuits, not one cup going cold.'

'My name's Harold, sir. I'll see about the tea.'

'Ridden many winners, Barney?'

'Harold, sir. Winners, sir?'

Selwyn pointed to his legs and the old fellow put his hands over his knee-caps with the gesture of a girl covering her modesty. 'That's the arthritis, sir.'

Selwyn burst out laughing. There was no point in getting up right away, so he ordered breakfast in bed.

He looked through his newspaper. News didn't interest him, girlie pictures did. He had once gone so far as to cut out the best ones and stick them on the wall in the bathroom at the flat, but Janine and the steam between them soon curtailed that little show.

It was after eleven when he strolled downstairs. He left the inn and walked along the road, thinking he might meet Mrs Beach coming back from shopping.

The sun had gone in, the clouds were building up for rain or snow. This was marginal country, the fields still spattered with clay from the excavations for the motorway, the hedges broken down and a dredger like a dead dinosaur rusting in the ditch. He could hear the roar of traffic on the M-road, but the only traffic in this lane was an orange Mini, driven by Rosanna. She lifted her hand to him as she passed. They had it made over here, he thought. A car to come to work in! In her own country she'd be walking barefoot with a bundle on her head.

Chilled to the bone – he hadn't put on a top coat – he turned back. The name of the inn still irked him. 'The Dream of Fair Women'. Whose dream? Not Beach's, that ape wouldn't have the delicacy to dream. Though he did have one of the fair women. Selwyn found that he actively objected to the notion that he and Beach had the same tastes.

He was the only one for lunch and again he was served by old Barney, creaking across the dining-room with his thumb in the soup. Selwyn sent it back. 'When I want a taste of horse in my Brown Windsor I'll say so.'

'Sir?'

'Is Mrs B back from shopping?'

Barney picked up the plate and his thumb went under the soup to the base of his nail. 'Mrs Beach is in the kitchen.'

Selwyn went to the lounge after lunch. He kicked the fire into a blaze and stretched himself on the Knole settee. It was sleeting outside, the room was twilit and warm and he fell asleep.

A sound wakened him, a sort of remote whispering. He knew what it was before he opened his eyes. It deeply and deliciously disturbed him. He sat up and saw her walking slowly to and fro in the firelight.

'Hallo there,' he said, sounding surprised, though he was not. He believed his luck, he was lucky in love, only when he was out of it did his troubles begin.

She stopped, turned to him, and now that the whisper of her dress had ceased he was left with the astonishing contrast between her black winged eyebrows and golden hair. It could have been a mistake, but Nature did not make that kind of mistake and it was an unqualified triumph. The skin of her lips was so fine and so full of warm blood that again there was a contrast, almost fierce, between the redness of her mouth and the pallor of her face.

'I waited for you,' he said, and another voice, not the one he used every day but one which he reserved for private and primary communications, said, 'I've been waiting all my life.'

And he knew that if he never spoke another, he had just spoken something which was a whole truth.

Standing before him, head bowed, her hands clasped in front of her, she too seemed to be waiting, for his wishes – his pleasure. He felt himself go hot, then cold, then hot again, and put up his hand to her. But his reach wasn't long enough, or his arm wasn't right, or his timing, and he did not quite touch her. 'I don't even know your name.'

She raised her head, and with that slight movement her dress whispered. He had not yet heard her speak. Perhaps she was dumb? Was that what Miller had been getting at when he said he would be surprised if Selwyn started anything?

Selwyn could have laughed out loud. Words he could very well dispense with when he started anything – words and clothes. Smiling broadly, he stood up to look deep into the neck of her dress to the beautiful shadow between her breasts.

'I'm called Alice.' She glanced up from under her lashes and as quickly lowered her eyes.

'In your Alice-blue-gown.' He made a move towards her, but she bent away from him like a flame in a draught. 'You're not scared of me, are you?'

'No. It's my husband I'm scared of – he is so terribly jealous.'

'I don't blame him.'

'So terribly jealous,' she said again. 'It is terrible to kill someone out of jealousy.'

'Kill?'

She drew herself together, clasped her arms about herself, suddenly cold perhaps, or fearful, or in pain. 'A young man, a student, he was just a boy. Years ago. He came here to work in his vacation and my husband murdered him.'

'For God's sake!' said Selwyn. 'Why?'

'He thought he was my lover.'

'Was he?'

'I never had a lover.' She raised her face to his, opened her eyes wide, violet eyes – the only colour he had ever seen to match it was in one of those old-fashioned carboys in a chemist's window. 'I only had my husband.'

Selwyn felt quite dizzy. 'How could he – I mean, how did he get away with murder?'

'He strangled him and hanged him from a beam in the cellar. He made it look as though the boy had killed himself, you see.'

Selwyn, who did not see, said, 'Why should he kill himself?'

'Because of unrequited love. That's what everyone thought. But my husband thought I requited it.'

'How can you go on living with someone like that?'

She smiled. Selwyn sensed an awful lot in that smile, but was unable then to appreciate just how much, and how awful. 'Next time I shall make sure there's a witness.'

'Next time?'

'Next time he kills someone.'

He flung out his hands with the impulsive gesture which had endeared him to so many women. 'There's no reason why it should happen again! Don't be scared on my account. I'm not a boy, I'm a man of the world, I can take care of myself.'

'Ah, you—' She uttered a sigh. It said plainer than words that she knew the difference – and all the other differences there would be between a man and a boy.

But instead of taking his hands, her own flew to her throat. She murmured, 'Tonight.' Any of the women he knew who still remembered how to colour up went blotting-paper pink and puffy. Alice Beach blushed the tenderest shade of rose.

'Where?' he said eagerly. 'What time?'

A sudden gust of wind hurled heavy rain, or hail, against the window. He had turned his head to look, and in that moment she slipped away. When he turned back the room was empty.

'Damn and blast!'

'I beg your pardon, sir?'

That was Barney, bringing in an armful of logs.

'Where did Mrs Beach go?'

'I came in the back way, ain't seen nobody.'

Selwyn was joined in the dining-room that evening by a gang of commercials. They were having a reunion and kept Rosanna busy fetching wines from the cellar and chasers from the bar. He wanted to ask where Mrs Beach was, but decided not to prejudice anything. For all he knew she had made arrangements which would not bear inquiring into at this stage.

He sat at his meal, scarcely aware of what he ate, going over in some detail his expectations for later on. He was able, because of many past encounters, to vary the opening gambits. He couldn't make up his mind which he would prefer. One thing was certain, Alice Beach was intended for him. And he for her. The mutuality was going to make it a memorable experience. His bones, as well as his flesh, melted at some of his expectations.

When the salesmen started singing a smutty song to the tune of 'Annie Laurie' – it wasn't even original, just the same old smut from his schooldays – he got up and went into the bar.

It was still sleeting outside, there weren't many drinkers in the 'Dream' that night – the man with the smelly dog which was wet-through and smellier than ever, and some girls and boys getting stoned on vodka and Cokes. They looked under age, Beach probably couldn't afford to turn them away. He was leaning on the counter reading a newspaper.

Selwyn got himself a double whisky. He sat quietly taking it between his teeth and his tongue and turning over in his mind the question of whether Beach could have done murder. He had been wondering – not all that often, having better things to think about – since Alice had told him. The man was certainly an ugly customer and had plenty of bad coming to him. But on the whole Selwyn was inclined to think she had exaggerated, kidded herself. A woman, any woman, loved the idea of murder being committed on her account.

The salesmen came in from the dining-room and at once the bar was in an uproar. They had had a skinful, they were all in the same hairy skin together, jolly old pals, auld acquaintance never to be forgot, buddies, all for one and one big headache for all. They were singing another worn-out classic, about the nun and the undertaker. Beach was kept busy as they ordered and counter-ordered and forgot to pay, and spilled their drinks.

Selwyn had to laugh, watching him run to and fro, wild-eyed and sweating, trying to cope. A beerpull jammed and he lost his nerve and started bellowing.

Barney appeared, none too readily. 'I told you to fix this bloody thing!' shouted Beach. ' Get Rosanna. Where is she?'

'Got a headache.'

Selwyn wasn't surprised to hear that. He strolled over to the bar and watched Beach wrestling with the beerpull. 'Give me another whisky.'

Beach looked up with hatred. 'You'll have to wait. Can't you see I'm single-handed?'

'So was Rosanna.' Selwyn winked. 'It's your turn now, sport.'

He went upstairs after his third whisky. He knew when to stop. Alcohol was good, was practically medicinal at such times. It was a guarantor. But only up to a point, beyond that point was no return, only rapid deterioration. He meant to acquit himself perfectly tonight, for her sake as well as his own. 'I never had a lover,' she had said. He was filled with the pure and uplifting spirit of selflessness.

It was also reasonable to suppose that the first place she would look for him would be in his room.

He undressed, put on his pyjamas and dressing gown, tucked a silk cravat over his pyjama-collar. She was a creature of refinement and delicacy. There would be no time to waste, but she would require a little dalliance and – he rinsed his glass and put it ready beside the remains of Janine's gin – a little of the guarantor.

An hour passed. He had left his door ajar and a dozen times went out into the passage to look for her. He heard the salesmen go, packing into their cars, engines roaring and tyres screeching as they belted along the lane. They'd be lucky if they ran into nothing worse than a squad-car and breathalyzers. Afterwards, all was quiet downstairs. He looked at his watch and saw that it wanted but half an hour to closing time.

She wasn't coming. Either she had been prevented or she had been teasing him. Even ladies could be teases. Especially ladies. He cursed her aloud.

'Damn and blast you, Alice Beach!'

'No – please!'

He swung round. She was there in her Alice-blue, holding out her arms to him, her golden hair ablaze, her cheeks shining with tears.

'My dear – I didn't mean it!'

He started towards her, but she put her finger to her lips. 'Shhhh—'

'I thought you weren't coming!'

'Oh, nothing could stop me now!'

'Why did you leave it so late?'

'Late? If you knew how long I have waited!'

It was more of a wail than an exclamation. He went cold, and did not immediately go hot again. 'What about Beach? Won't he be coming up soon?'

'Not yet, not just yet.'

It occurred to Selwyn that she didn't even know how long a love-making would take, how long it *could* take.

'We don't want to hurry anything,' he said, and went to close the door, 'but I've been waiting too.'

She flung up her hands in a quaint, old-fashioned gesture of protest. 'Not here – it cannot be in this room.'

'Why not? It's the safest place. I'll lock the door.'

'He has a pass-key, he'll come looking for me. We must go somewhere else.'

'Where?'

'Come—' She slipped out of the room and was gone. When he went into the passage she was standing at the point where the stairs went up to the second floor.

'Not up there,' said Selwyn. 'He sleeps up there.'

'You must trust me.'

He was close enough to see how her eyes shone and her parted lips. She was breathing fast, and so was he, but her breasts moved in perfect rhythm as if there was a soft little motor under them. And the Alice-blue dress whispered to him.

He said hoarsely, 'I don't care where we go so long as it's now!'

'It is now – I promise.' She ran up the stairs and opened a door. He followed, found they were in a room, in darkness. He could just make out the shape of a bed, the clothes tumbled, a mound of eiderdown. It looked promising.

The time for delicacy was past. He threw off his dressing-gown and cravat, stood in his pyjamas. There was a movement on the bed, she was waiting for him.

'Alice—' he groped among the bedclothes.

At once several things happened. A light was switched on. Selwyn blinked, dazzled and disbelieving. A black face was looking up at him from the pillow. At the same moment he heard Beach's voice in the passage below. There was no one else in the room, no Alice, just himself and Rosanna. She raised herself on her elbow, her eyes rolling white with alarm.

'What are you doing here?'

He might have asked her that, but Beach's footsteps were on the stairs. He cried, 'Where's Alice? Where is she?'

'Alice?'

'Alice Beach – Mrs Beach—'

It wasn't possible, yet Rosanna's skin seemed to darken. The shine went out of it. She said, 'That Mrs Beach has been dead a long time.'

'Dead?'

'Killed in a car accident four, maybe five, years ago.'

'Goddamit!' cried Selwyn, 'That's crazy, up the creek! She was here a minute ago. She's framing me, why I don't know, but it doesn't matter now—' It was a matter, now, of self-preservation. 'Beach is coming—'

'He is coming here.'

'You've got to help me – Rosanna, I'll make it worth your while – I'll have to brazen it out – he can't object – it won't look – I mean it's not as if you're his wife, is it?'

'I am his wife.'

'What?'

'His second wife.'

Selwyn's jaw dropped. His mouth fell open and dried. Then Beach came into the room, and there was a moment of crammed and unpeace silence. Beach took in the scene – Selwyn in his pyjamas, Rosanna in the tumbled bed. A moment was enough, even for Beach, a man of not especially quick intelligence. He was also a plain man, and in that moment became downright ugly.

He made for Selwyn, unstoppable as a tank making for an enemy trench. Selwyn ran round the bed, shouted with all the strength of his lungs. He found he was trapped, his back to the wall, but, desperate, kept shouting. For help, for understanding – for a little more time. Beach's hands gripping his throat stopped him at last.

He didn't see Barney come running as fast as his crooked legs would bring him. Barney arrived in the doorway, stood and gaped. It was really all he was required to do. Had Selwyn been the fanciful type, and had the opportunity – which, naturally, he had not – he might have recalled at least one promise Alice Beach had kept: 'Next time I'll make sure there's a witness.'

Rosemary Pardoe

THE CHAUFFEUR

COURTHAM House, in its present form, was mostly built during the reigns of Henry VII and his notorious, much-married son; although portions of earlier work are incorporated into its walls. The building is generally considered to be the best Tudor Manor in Cornwall, and since being taken over by the National Trust twenty years ago, it has become a popular spot with day-trippers. In summer the courtyards and lovely tiered gardens are thronged with holidaymakers; and their cars block the small country lane which runs past Courtham Quay on the River Tamar, and forms the only access to the House. In winter, however, and especially in the evenings, it is a beautifully lonely and isolated place, despite the fact that Plymouth is no more than fifteen miles away.

My friends Edwin and Marion Farrow live in a rambling contemporary cottage attached to the main building. It was converted several years ago from two diminutive dwellings, one formerly occupied by the chauffeur; and thus the ground-plan is very peculiar and confusing, making it all too easy to lose oneself when on a visit.

The Farrows are a pleasant, middle-aged couple with a quiet sense of humour and a good line in conversation. Edwin is a writer on antiquarian matters, which is how I came to know him. I have an open invitation to stay at Courtham at any time, but until one chilly March a year or so ago, I'd had no opportunity to take up the offer. Therefore when I managed to get down to Cornwall for a week's holiday, I was determined to spend part of it with Edwin and Marion. As it turned out, they were kind enough to ask me to stay for the whole week.

My days were devoted to leisurely drives in the surrounding countryside, stopping whenever I came to a church, and sometimes taking photographs for my collection of post-1600 wall paintings. I've been told on many occasions that I miss the most interesting examples by confining myself to those produced after 1600, but my retort is always that earlier work is well covered by other researchers, and anyway my area of study is just as fascinating, not only historically but artistically too. No one who has seen, for instance, the lovely twentieth-century paintings in Denton church,

Northamptonshire, could doubt that. However, this is not the subject of my story, and I am in danger of getting sidetracked.

Each evening during my holiday, the Farrows and I would sit snugly around their fragrant log fire – a necessity with the frosty weather we were having then – and enjoy a sherry while we chatted about the places I'd visited that day. One night, just before we started thinking about making a move to go to bed, the subject of ghosts came up.

'Courtham has a ghost, you know,' smiled Edwin, 'but I'm afraid it is a very traditional one: in the House there is supposed to be a blood-stain which magically appears and disappears on the anniversary of a particularly nasty murder. It's unfortunate for the veracity of this legend that, as far as anyone knows, there have been no murders or violent deaths at the Manor; and I for one have never seen the blood-stain! It should definitely be taken with a pinch of salt . . .'

'But, Jane,' interrupted Mrs Farrow, 'we must tell you about our very own phantom. It's much more interesting.'

'Yes, please,' I said eagerly, sleep forgotten for the moment.

'Well, sometimes when I'm in the house on my own,' Marion began in her delightfully musical voice, 'I hear a car drive up and go into our garage – it's the one just outside our gate, by the way; close to where you park your Mini. The first few times it happened, soon after we moved here, I naturally assumed that it was Edwin returning home unexpectedly, but when I went outside to look there was no one about and the garage was empty. Once, I remember, I thought I heard him come home, and I went to the gate, only to see him drive up, three or four minutes later. In those days I was too embarrassed to tell anyone about my experiences, and when Edwin asked why I was waiting for him I made up some silly story about a premonition. He must have wondered whether I'd gone mad!'

'But not long afterwards,' her husband added, 'I also heard the mysterious noise when I was alone in the cottage and Marion had the car. Since then it has recurred countless times.

'Our theory is that the ghost is Mr Watkins, the old chauffeur who lived here when Courtham was still in private hands. He loved his job so much, and was heartbroken when he had to retire at the age of sixty because of arthritis. He died a few years before we came down here in 1964, so we never knew him, but there are many accounts of his single-minded devotion to work. We think that his death gave him the opportunity to return to his duties in spirit form.

'Your bedroom, Jane, was once part of Mr Watkins's cottage, but nobody has ever seen anything odd or sensed any unnatural atmosphere, either there or in the garage. In fact one often gets a warm feeling of peace and contentment. If we have a ghost he is obviously very happy, and neither of us would dream of trying to get rid of him.

'Now I come to think of it, though, I haven't heard him for some months now – have you, Marion?'

'No, it's been nearly a year since the last time,' Mrs Farrow pondered, 'I'm starting to miss him. . . .'

The conversation moved on to other topics and shortly thereafter we all went to bed.

When I awoke next morning, light was pouring in through the little diamond-paned window in my room. Inexplicably I was still incredibly tired and an extra half-hour's lie-in seemed very inviting – I didn't even have the energy to check what the time was. It was when I tried to turn over that I became aware of something worse than normal, early-morning lethargy. My limbs felt as though lead weights had been placed on them, and I had an unpleasant feeling of dizziness. I was not even quite sure of my own identity . . . my one overpowering emotion was of frustration. Whoever I was, I knew that I should be getting up – I had a job of some sort to do, and people were relying on me. However, try as I might I could not move an inch. Then quite suddenly, the weight lifted and my confusion disappeared along with it.

Over a lone breakfast a little later (the Farrows having eaten an hour earlier, at eight o'clock), I tried to account for what had happened to me. I was positive that it had not been a dream, and as far as I knew I was not ill: certainly I felt fine now. The suspicion grew that the old chauffeur was involved. But *how*? Perhaps there was a slight chance that I might get a clue from his grave, although it seemed unlikely. Still, there could be no harm in paying it a visit, so when Marion came in to see me off on my day's expedition, I asked her where Mr Watkins was buried. As anticipated, it was in Lanstock churchyard, only ten minutes' drive away and the closest village to Courtham. I had already been to the church once, on the previous day, but it would be easy enough to drop in again on my way north to the area on my morning's itinerary.

Lanstock graveyard was larger than I had expected, and finding the tombstone took me some time. Eventually I spotted it – a small grey tablet inlaid with plain black letters. The inscription was unspectacular:

> Joseph Watkins
> 1885–1960
> Blessed are the meek

'That doesn't tell me much,' I sighed, disappointed in spite of myself: it had been foolish to hope for an explanation of my strange experience. There was little point in staying, but I remained for a few moments gazing at the well-kept plot, with its neatly cut grass and vase of fresh daffodils wilting slightly in the cold air. 'Someone still loves the old man,' I thought.

Towards the middle of the grave was a patch of some herb or decorative weed; self-seeded rather than deliberately placed there, by the look of it, but apparently tolerated by the person who tended the plot. I'm no botanist and I could not recognize the plant, but its scanty dark-green leaves were quite attractive and a little like those of a primrose in shape and texture. Of course, in March there were no flowers to aid identification.

Suddenly I felt an irresistible urge to bend down and pull out the entire patch by its roots. I was completely unable to control my actions and, almost before I realized what I was doing, there was not a single stem left in the earth. An ugly area of bare soil about ten inches in diameter, and a small pile of uprooted, aromatic herbs at my feet, bore witness to my misdeed. I stepped back, stunned – why had I done such a thing? Normally I would never dream of picking a wild flower, let alone killing it by removing it bodily from the ground. That, to me, is unwarrantable vandalism.

Only for a minute did I feel this self-doubt, and then a flood of happiness and satisfaction washed over me. I *had* done the right thing. Why, I did not know, but there was a good reason for the removal of the plants. I extracted one from the forlorn pile, wrapped it carefully in tissues and put it into my bag for later identification – if my memory served me right I had seen a small paperback book on herbs in Edwin Farrow's extensive library.

As the day wore on I had other things to think about, including an unseasonable snowstorm which trapped me in Callington church for an hour; and Joseph Watkins and his grave slipped my mind completely. So, at tea-time, as I drove through the slush into my usual parking position tucked around the side of Courtham House, I didn't think twice when I saw Marion Farrow leaning on the cottage gate, looking around with a curious expression on her face.

'You just missed our ghost,' she called out, as I waved and went to unload my camera equipment from the boot. Apparently five minutes earlier she had heard a car driving up and thought it was me, until she realized that the distinctive sound which tyres make as they splash through melting snow was absent.

'It's good to have the old fellow back,' she said happily. 'I wonder where he's been.'

I suspected that I knew why the chauffeur had not been about his usual duties, and more than ever I was convinced that I'd acted correctly in taking the herbs from his grave. Now all I needed to do was to name them and discover why they'd had such an effect.

After tea I borrowed Edwin's book on the subject: *British Herbs* by Florence Ranson; and after some initial difficulty caused by the fact that the book contained only line drawings, I managed to identify the plant with a fair degree of certainty. It was wood betony, and Miss Ranson's description included the following relevant information: ' ... it is ... often found around old churches and ruined abbeys. The reason for its cultivation in these places is that it was considered a sure charm against "evil spirits ... and the forces of darkness" ...'

I would add that as well as keeping evil revenants in their graves, betony is evidently also capable of restraining good and harmless spirits. After I explained my thoughts to the Farrows they agreed to convince whoever was looking after Mr Watkins's plot that all suspect weeds should be removed as soon as they appeared.

That night and for the rest of my holiday I slept better than I have ever done, and I awoke full of energy. I cannot truthfully say that I felt any sort of 'presence' in my bedroom, but there was an atmosphere of peace and joy which had not been there before. My one regret is that I personally did not hear the ghostly car. Perhaps I will be more fortunate next time I go down to Cornwall.

Joan Aiken

✦

THE TRAITOR

O H yes – I once lived in a house with a ghost (said the old lady, gazing steadfastly into the red fire) – in fact with several ghosts. And they took no notice of me. It taught me a most painful lesson, one that I am not likely to forget.

It happened in the year when a great many small local libraries closed through lack of funds, and a lot of librarians were suddenly looking for jobs. I was one of them. Middle-aged lady librarians were two a penny, and nobody seemed particularly anxious for my services. I have always been rather solitary, from childhood on, without friends or relatives – I will explain why in a minute; and in this difficulty I hardly knew where to turn. But fortunately, just at that point, I saw the advertisement in *The Lady*: 'Elderly gentlewoman seeks pleasant Companion with a predilection for reading aloud.'

Now reading aloud has always been one of my greatest pleasures; first, with my dear mother when we had very few other resources; and then in Birklethwaite Library, where I ran a regular Reading Circle in the children's section twice a week, for I don't know how many years, and enjoyed it fully as much as any of my listeners.

So I wrote to the Box Number of the elderly gentlewoman, was interviewed, and happily we both took a liking to one another. She was, indeed, a most delightful person, wholly alert, although in her eighties, intelligent and humorous, in appearance a mixture of owl and eagle, with piercing dark eyes, a small beaky nose, and wayward hair standing up on end like white plumes. What she thought of me, I do not know, except that it was sufficiently well to offer me the post, above a number of other applicants; what I thought of *her* was that I should immensely enjoy her company, and probably learn a great deal from her too. It was arranged that I should commence my duties in two months' time.

Mrs Crankshaw's surroundings were as pleasing as her personality: she lived in a Georgian mansion called Gramercy Place under the slopes of the South Downs, and I looked forward to unlimited walks in the surrounding countryside during my free hours; but to my disappointment, before it was time to take up residence with my new employer, I had a letter informing me of a change of plan.

The poor lady had suffered a slight stroke. 'Nothing of consequence, I am already better, apart from being confined, at present, to a wheelchair,' she wrote with characteristic firmness, 'but I have decided that it would be practical to move to a less solitary environment – better for you, too, my dear Miss Grey. My lawyers are hard at work on the purchase of another house in a small agreeable town – in fact, the purchase of *three* houses which will be converted into one, so that, if we have less outdoors, we shall have plenty of *in*doors, and shall not be on top of one another, which I think is most important. The builders are only waiting for completion to start tearing down partitions, and I trust that our original plans will be put back by no more than a month or two.'

She did not mention the name of the small agreeable town, and I waited with interest to learn where it was, confident that our tastes would coincide in this, as they had in other matters.

The purchase went through, but the building work dragged, as such work always does, and it was more like nine weeks before Mrs Crankshaw was able to transfer herself from the nursing-home, and her furniture from Gramercy Place, and write to me that she was ready for me to come and take up my duties in the new residence.

When she did so, the address gave me a shock – the first of several. For she wrote from The Welcome Stranger, Stillingley; and Stillingley was the town where I had spent my childhood, after my father had gone to prison.

And when I reached my destination I received the second shock. For The Welcome Stranger turned out to be the house where my mother and I had lived, now joined together with the houses on either side of it.

'They were all for sale, so I bought the whole little old Tudor row,' said Mrs Crankshaw comfortably. 'Luckily my brother's legacy gave me plenty of leeway. (I told you didn't I, that he had died, and left me some money?) And it is right that the houses should be joined together again, for apparently, back in the seventeenth century, the whole building was one large inn; only in those days it was called The Bull. But since there is already a Bull Inn in the town, I thought I would choose another old coaching-house name. Besides, it is prettier. The coach entrance was that archway that runs through to the yard at the back.'

I could have told her that. I could have told her a great deal more. I had spent thirteen years in that street, in the middle house, and knew every crooked step in it, every beam and cranny, as well as the palm of my own hand. It was wonderful how little the builders had changed; as Mrs Crankshaw said, the building had been one house two hundred years before; all they needed to do was to knock down a few partitions.

The third and worst shock came as we were having our first cup of tea in the white-panelled parlour – which had been my mother's study where, three days a week, she worked at translation, and read proofs for publishers (on the other three days she had an editorial job on the local paper).

I had asked Mrs Crankshaw why she picked this particular town – did she have any connections with it?

'Oh yes,' she said, tranquilly sipping her Lapsang Souchong. 'My brother lived here, in Pallant House, for a number of years. I used to visit him, and always thought it would be a pleasant place in which to settle if, for some unfortunate reason, one was debarred from living out in the real country. My brother was a judge, you may have heard of him: Sir Charles Sydney.'

And of course I had heard of him. He was the judge who had sentenced my father. That was why my mother had moved to the town, after Father had gone to prison. First we had to give up our own house, we could not afford it. Secondly, visiting would be easier – only an hour's bus ride to the jail where Father was serving his twenty-five-year sentence. But also, having learned, during the trial, that Stillingley was where Sir Charles lived, my mother, apparently at that time, nursed some obscure notion of meeting him in the street or in the Pallant Gardens, or after church on Sunday, and trying to make an appeal to him. 'For anyone can see that he is a *good* man,' she repeated over and over, with tears in her eyes, 'and your father is a good man too; nobody denies that. Somehow, somehow, there *must* be some way of getting his sentence annulled, or at least reduced – I am sure there must be.'

But this plan came to nothing, because, first, she never ran into Sir Charles or plucked up the courage to approach him. I think he was a very busy man, hardly ever to be seen in the streets of the town, mostly up in London. And, secondly, after serving only two years of his sentence, my father died; of a broken heart, Mother said. I sometimes think it is just as well that he did not live on into the times of glasnost and perestroika and the end of the Cold War; all that has happened since his conviction makes what he did – sending some not very important scientific information to a colleague in Moscow – seem so pitifully trifling. My father was a civil servant, and of course what he did was strictly forbidden, and counted as treason. But he was a man of tremendously high principles, a pacifist and a conscientious objector; and he felt strongly that all scientific information should be shared equally all over the world. So he was prepared to go to prison for his beliefs. He took himself and his principles to prison; and he left me and Mother out in the cold. Or rather, he left me in prison too . . . .

I often thought that he had behaved very unfairly to Mother and me. Either he should not have married and had a family, or he should have chosen some other job. I was only five when he was taken off, and I missed him dreadfully for a number of years. He had been a kind, affectionate father, and used to play lots of games with me. One was called Treasure Islands, a guessing game, trying to find out about each other's treasures; and we told long sagas, each taking up the story in turn; or we did cookery, inventing new dishes from a list of ingredients all beginning with the same letter: apples, anchovies, artichokes, arrowroot.... Heartburn holidays, father used to call those afternoons.

So it was an incurable grief when he vanished away to prison, and a worse one when he died. Mother never married again. She and I reverted to her maiden name of Grey when we moved to Stillingley, because she used to get a lot of hate letters from people who said that Father was a traitor. People seem to have unlimited time for acts of spite to other people who have never done them any personal harm. And about ten years after Father's death, Mother also died. And I took a course in Librarianship with the small amount of money she left me, and became a librarian, and worked in libraries for twenty-five years. After Mother's death I never went back to Stillingley. We had no close friends there, because of the quiet life she chose to lead, so it was not at all probable that anybody in the town would recognize me. (Nobody did; partly because the town had changed a great deal. All the little old corner shops had gone, and instead there were tourist boutiques. Walking about the familiar streets, I felt like a ghost myself.)

So, my dears, I expect you can understand why, when Mrs Crankshaw said, 'My brother was a judge: Sir Charles Sydney,' I did not at once and honestly exclaim: 'Why, he was the judge who sentenced my father to twenty-five years for sending treasonable communications to Soviet Russia,' but instead gulped, bit my tongue, knelt to lay another log on the fire, and kept quiet.

Oh, what a difference it would have made if I had not done so! If I had told her that this house was my childhood home. For, once having embarked on a policy of concealment, I was, of course, obliged to go on; there never came an opportunity to change my mind, toss discretion aside, and proclaim: 'Oh, by the way, Mrs Crankshaw, I forgot to mention, when we moved in, that your brother sent my father to prison.' That seemed out of the question. And, although I had never in any way blamed her brother – who was only doing his duty, acting on his principles, as Father had acted on his – there was no slightest hint of resentment or anything of that kind – yet, nevertheless, the fact that I was keeping this major secret from her had some kind of crimping or smothering effect on our relationship; happy and friendly although that became.

Well – it *must* have, mustn't it?

But the worst result of all was what I am now going to tell you.

When Mother and I first arrived to live at Middle House, we were busy carrying baskets and jugs and suitcases in through the back door, when I was a little dismayed to observe an eye carefully scanning us from the window of the house next door. And when I say an eye, I mean literally nothing *but* an eye: the bottom left-hand corner of the lace curtain was twitched aside, leaving just room for one muddy grey optic to peer sharply over the window-sash and study our possessions.

This gave a decidedly chilly, sinister impression; it could not have been more misleading.

After a day or two spent in getting settled, we began to receive the impression that there was a tremendous amount of back-and-forth, come-and-go, to-and-fro, between the two little houses on either side of us. Upper House, Middle House, and Lower House, the row was called. We occupied Middle House; Upper and Lower Houses appeared to be inhabited by two couples who could not have enough of each other's company. Mr and Mrs Brown, Mr and Mrs Taylor were their names, we learned from the postman; and we soon discovered why they all lived in one another's pockets – it was because Mrs Taylor and Mrs Brown were sisters. In no time at all they had invited us into their highly polished front rooms, resplendent with pot plants and cage birds, and they had given us their life histories. Mrs Taylor and Mrs Brown – Di and Ruby – were Cockneys, had originally been evacuated to Stillingley in World War One, had fallen in love with local boys, married them, and never returned to London. Their husbands, Fred Taylor and Jim Brown, were, respectively, a bus conductor and a builder's foreman. By the end of three weeks, they were playing a very important part in our lives. Fred, every two days, used to bring us fish from Portsbourne, which was at the end of his bus run, and was a monument of sense and experience when it came to practical matters. Jim could deal with any household emergency, could fix leaking taps or loose wiring, mend windows, replace fallen tiles. Ruby and Di supplied the light relief; especially Di. She was a stand-up comic, a harlequin of a woman. Not at all good-looking, she was lean and rangy, with vigorously permed pale-grey locks and skin like uncooked frozen pastry. It was her eye that had peered from under the curtain in Ruby's kitchen. The sisters were perpetually in and out of each other's houses, exchanging pots or clothes, borrowing salt or soap, telling jokes or gossip. 'Roo? Are you there, Roo? Got a minute? Come and take a look at this! Di! Di! Got a pinch of bicarb – a few mothballs – a forty-watt bulb – a spoonful of honey?'

Although the husbands had relatives in the town – plenty of them – the two couples formed such a compact group in themselves that they hardly required other company. But they were immensely, infinitely kind to Mother and me. They became our family – surrogate uncles, aunts, grandparents, cousins. 'You're so *different* from us!' Di sometimes said wonderingly to Mother. That was because Mother spoke several languages and could translate from German and Russian. Our neighbours themselves had the unassuming modesty, the simple unobtrusive diffidence, of completely happy people. They saw no need to assert themselves; they already had all they required.

It was not long before Mother had told them everything about Father's prison sentence. She had resolved never to mention this circumstance to a single soul in Stillingley; she disclosed it all to Ruby and Di, Jim and Fred, without the least hesitation. She did not even ask for their discretion; she knew by instinct that they would never mention the matter to anybody; and they never did.

They listened to her tale with wondering sympathy, wholly without passing judgement.

'Well; he had to do what he thought right, didn't he?' said Fred.

'And so did the judge; all the same, it does seem a proper shame,' said Jim.

'All that time away from you; it's like as if you were a widder,' sighed Ruby.

'And poor little Snowball here, so many years without her dad,' grieved Di.

From then on they were even kinder to us.

Trip-trap and clitter-clatter through my childhood run the feet of Ruby and Di back and forth outside our dining-room window. 'Di! Ruby! Listen to this! Can you let me have a lump of dripping? Come and look at the bird, Di! D'you think he's poorly?'

They insisted on our sharing in the products of all their activities: marmalade, chutney, pickled onions.

Soon it was: 'Missis Grey? Are you busy? Can you spare a minute?' And quickly the Mrs Grey gave way to 'Ianthe' (which they shortened to 'Ianth'). But, scrupulously, delicately, they never dropped in on my mother during the hours of daylight; Fred, the chieftain of the tribe, had decreed this. 'She's the breadwinner, see? You gotta respect that and not go bothering her, you two, mind, while she's workin'.'

Fred and Jim, Di and Ruby; they were like the biologist's ideal, a completely self-sufficient society without the need of any outside agency or supplies.

Only once a year, at Christmas, did they summon huge hosts of other relatives whose arrival was heralded, weeks before, by monumental piles of Christmas cards which, as soon as they arrived, were slung on zigzag strings across and across the front rooms, in among the cyclamens, the tinsel, poinsettias, mistletoe, and folding paper bells. Then they had a Christmas party. After the first occasion we carefully avoided those parties, which could last for six, seven, eight hours at a stretch; Mother explained that she really had to go on working over Christmas and could not afford all that time off.

'But what about the liddle 'un? *She* don't have to work.'

'She's shy,' said Mother firmly.

Those parties did indeed have a numbing, shattering effect, as one munched one's way through more and more sausage rolls and sandwiches, drank more and more lethal mixtures of alcohol and fruit juice, while trying to keep up a continuous fixed smile at the tireless crackle of repartee from cousins, nephews, uncles, and indestructible great-aunts. All these relatives adored and respected our quartet, and would have liked to be invited much more often than once a year. 'But we don't want 'em,' said Fred, Ruby, Di, or Jim. 'We're comfortable just on our loney-own, thank you *very* much – with Ianth and the young 'un.'

So time passed for us, peacefully enough; we were buttressed, comforted, and contained by the strong dependable structure on either side.

When I was seven my father died in jail and, during that time, Fred was of silent, sterling support to my mother. He rented a car and drove her to and fro during Father's illness; he drove her to the crematorium, sternly excluding his wife, brother-in-law, and sister-in-law. 'No, she don't want you lot; it's a family occasion, see?' And he himself would have stayed outside the chapel if she had not insisted on his coming in, and then he stayed firmly on his own at the back. A surprising number of other people turned up, Mother told me (I was in bed at the time with measles); there were quite a few journalists, and old friends from past days. Mother was glad to dodge them after the ceremony and take refuge with Fred in the rented Rover.

That night my mother and the four neighbours held a kind of wake for Father. I expect she felt she owed it to them; it was what they would have expected. Fruit cake, cold ham, sherry, and whisky; lying upstairs in bed, feverish, with painfully aching ears and throat, I heard the subdued hum and grumble of voices down below gradually grow more cheerful, an occasional laugh ring out.

'How can they?' I thought, thrashing and tossing in bed, wretched, sick, and furious. Fred came up with a jug of lemonade and found me so, tears hissing on my hot red cheeks like water on the surface of an iron.

I glared at him, kept by manners and convention from saying what I felt.

But he understood perfectly well.

'I know, I know,' he said, settling his stocky bulk down with caution on my cane-seated chair. 'You think we're all heartless down there, don't you, tellin' jokes to your mum and makin' her laugh? But she's done a deal of sorrowin' already, and she's got a deal more to do; she needs a bit of a break. It ain't unfair to your dad; I expect he'd do the same. I dare say he liked a bit of a laugh in his time, didn't he? I expect he told you a good few jokes?'

Reluctantly I nodded.

'Well then,' said Fred. 'Just you remember, dearie; death ain't all black plumes and caterwauling. You got to carry on as best as you can.'

Fred saw us through various other troubles. When our cat died, he helped bury her; when my first boyfriend dropped me, left me a stricken thirteen-year-old grass widow, he managed to make me believe there were as good fish in the sea, which helped at the time, though in fact he was wrong, for I never acquired another.

And then, when I was fifteen, Ruby died. She had been growing gradually thinner and more gaunt; there was less vivacity in her jokes. She underwent an operation; spent painful weeks in bed at home, tended by Mother and Di. Then Fred said to me one day: 'I've got to tell you this fast – we're going to lose her,' and bolted blindly out of our kitchen. He himself was losing weight at a rapid rate; after her death he became, suddenly, a shrunken thread of a man. Di and Jim took him into their house, as they said he shouldn't be on his own. By this time I was sixteen, about to go off on a residential course at the other end of England. Fred was in bed, ill, when I left, I kissed him goodbye and never saw him again. Jim soon followed; it was as if, once the structure and symmetry of the group had been damaged, its individual members were vulnerable, badly at risk. Jim died of bronchitis, coughing his lungs away. He had been a heavy smoker. Poor Di could not bear her life without the others around her.

'It just don't seem right,' she said to Mother. She developed heart trouble and died in the ambulance on the way to hospital. Now the houses on either side of us were up for sale; and one day, at my residential college, I received a telegram to say that my mother had died of pneumonia, very suddenly, in the local hospital. Like Di, she was unable to manage without the rest of the group to support her.

After letting Middle House for a couple of years, to support me through my training, I sold it, having no wish to return there. New neighbours were installed on either side. The thought of Upper House without Fred and Ruby, of Lower House without Jim and Di, of our own house without my mother, was not to be borne; I would have felt like a survivor from a holocaust. I found a plain job elsewhere, in a plain library in a plain provincial town, and entrenched myself in books, catalogues, indexes, and reading aloud.

Until the day, over twenty years later, when I found myself back there, installed in The Welcome Stranger, with Mrs Crankshaw.

She, in her wheelchair, professed herself wholly delighted with the three houses fashioned into one. The builders had made ramps for her, so that her domain was entirely on the ground floor – bedroom at one end, living space in the middle, kitchen at the other. So her living quarters were constructed from Mother's and my old kitchen-dining-room, where Ruby and Di had clattered continually past the window. Her bedroom was Ruby's front room, where the terrifying Christmas parties had taken place. I could sit reading *Dr Thorne* aloud to Mrs Crankshaw and think of all those spangled cards fluttering overhead, and Fred's nephew Peter rolling his eyes under the mistletoe. My bedroom was upstairs (my own old bedroom, as it fell out) and there I lay at night, listening to the house creak and rustle gently round me; Mrs Crankshaw had installed gas-fired central heating.

After a few weeks, Mrs Crankshaw said to me, 'Miss Grey – Lucy – I am quite delighted with this house, and with our arrangement; I hope that you are too? But would you say – entirely without prejudice – that the place is slightly haunted?'

'No one has said anything of the kind to me, Mrs Crankshaw,' I fenced.

'Oh, won't you call me Moira, my dear, don't you think we have reached that stage by now? No, of course I had no such intimation from the agents or the lawyers or the builders – but then, one never does, does one? Just the same, I do begin to wonder. During the last twenty years there seem to have been a great many occupants. Do you think it was because no one cared to stay very long?'

It was true that since the time of Ruby and Fred, Jim and Di and my mother, the three little houses had changed hands repeatedly. Nobody seemed to have stayed more than a year or so.

'But that need not mean a thing,' I argued, quite truly. 'The whole town is in a – a state of transition. House prices are rising so fast, people buy them as investments, do them up, and move on. Also, the place is becoming more of a tourist centre than it – than it probably was twenty years ago.'

It was becoming harder and harder to maintain my pretence of never having lived in the town before. I felt worse and worse about it. Because our relationship – Moira's and mine – was, in all other respects, so happy, open, and free; she was beginning to seem like a beloved aunt, or cherished older sister; one of those relatives I had never been blessed with. We were able to talk to one another about every possible topic – except one; and our reading-aloud sessions were periods of calm, undiluted pleasure.

'What is giving you the idea that the place might be haunted?' I asked with caution.

'Why, there are times – especially when you are reading to me, my dear – when I am almost convinced that I can hear *voices* – voices perhaps in the next room, or somewhere else about the house, or perhaps in the little lane at the back.'

'Perhaps they are real voices?' I suggested hopefully. 'Echoes, you know, from the lane.'

The little lane – along which Ruby and Di used to run to and fro all day – was a right of way and led to the public library, my long-ago haunt of comfort and instruction.

'Well, yes, sometimes they might be real,' agreed Mrs Crankshaw, 'but not always. Not late at night. And the voices inside the house *must* be ghosts – mustn't they? Unless I am going potty.'

'And that you certainly are not, dear Mrs Crankshaw,' I said fervently.

'Moira, my dear – Moira.' Her hawk-eyes gleamed.

'What *kind* of voices do you think you hear?'

'You are sure you don't hear them yourself?' she inquired wistfully.

'No, I'm afraid I don't. Not at present. Perhaps I shall, by and by.'

Oh, how I wished this! For she said, 'Well, there are several different voices. That's why I'm sure it can't be just my imagination – for I never was very imaginative, you know, even as a child, I was the most prosaic little creature, and never cared particularly for pretend games or fairy stories. How could I invent something like this? What I hear is most often women's voices – quite raucous and cheerful, with a Cockney twang to them. Not a bit like our good neighbours up and down the hill.'

The good neighbours up and down the hill were nearly all antique dealers, who went in for a good deal of packaged refinement and ersatz chumminess; the females wore tweeds, and the males neatly trimmed beards.

'And you hear the voices particularly when I am reading to you?'

'Yes, is that not curious? It is precisely like – you know when you tune into a radio station, and at first it comes through perfectly clear, and then, by degrees, some foreign station comes in and jams it; though that is not quite the case here, for I can always hear you, my dear Lucy, perfectly well – but then in the background the voices begin.'

'Always women's?'

'No; the women are the most frequent, but occasionally I get male voices farther back – two different ones, I am fairly sure, one quite deep-toned and gruff, the other higher and more nasal.'

'Can you hear what they *say*?' I asked with quivering interest.

'Not yet, my dear. But let us hope that in due course I shall! Really, nothing so interesting has happened to me for years – and I am sure that I owe it all to your company in this pleasant place, my dear Lucy; I am so very happy that we had the luck to find each other.'

Her words filled me with mingled guilt and relief. Relief that she appeared to be deriving so much pleasure and interest from the phenomenon – many old ladies might have felt very differently; guilt that it was too late for me to be more candid and forthcoming about my friends; I felt I was doing them serious injustice by not telling her all about them.

Oh, what a tangled web we weave! . . .

While Mrs Crankshaw kept exclaiming in her satisfaction at what a warm, welcoming atmosphere the place had – 'Just like its name! I christened better than I knew!' – I, perhaps because I found myself in such a curious moral dilemma, felt the house curiously cold and unresponsive. No echoes came back to me, not a sound, not a signal, from the happy childhood hours I had passed there. And some of them *had* been happy: moments of hope, before my father died, moments of peace and companionship when my mother and I read aloud *Villette* or *War and Peace* in late spring evenings with a pale moon looking solemnly in at my bedroom window; moments of triumph when I had done well at school; or moments of pure fun when Di and Ruby were clowning and Fred and Jim, with us, were laughing at them.

I could not escape the impression that the house was displeased with me. I should have come clean; and I had not.

Mrs Crankshaw began to have remarkable dreams.

'I see such faces! Such real characters! Can they be people whom I have met, at some point during my life, and completely forgotten? They seem so extremely real. There is one extraordinary woman – a tall, bony, angular creature, with false teeth, and such a laugh! I have dreamed about her several times. Her name is Vi or Di – something like that. I must say, she is very entertaining. I wonder if I can be developing mediumistic powers in my old age? I must talk to the Vicar about it.'

She talked to the Vicar, but he was new and young; had come to the town long since the days of Fred and Jim and Ruby and Di. He could make nothing of Mrs Crankshaw's dreams. He assured us that, so far as he knew, nobody had experienced anything of this kind in the house.

I thought, also, that Mrs Crankshaw might be developing mediumistic powers. Was what was happening a kind of telegraphic flash passing over from my memory to hers? Was she picking up scenes from my past – my carefully suppressed past – and, as it were, printing them off in the darkroom of her mind? Did she see these things because I was there?

Or was she receiving entirely new impressions? Were the ghosts of Jim and Fred, of Di and Ruby, still floating around, still present in the house –

disturbed, perhaps, by my arrival, by the builders' work – available to Mrs Crankshaw because she was so happily, generously ready to receive them – but not choosing to reveal themselves to me?

That was indeed a chilling thought.

I could imagine – all too easily – Fred's quarter-deck voice. (He had been a petty officer once, long ago, before he retired from the navy and took to bus-conducting.) I remembered how sternly he had said: 'She's the breadwinner, see? You gotta respect that and not go bothering her, you two.' I imagined him saying: 'You shoulda told the lady the whole story, Snowball, right from the start. Now you put yourself in what they call a false position. And you put *us* in one too.'

Oh how I longed to apologize, to confess, to have matters somehow set right!

One morning Mrs Crankshaw called to me, in a voice of pure astonishment:

'Lucy! Somebody pushed my wheelchair!'

Contrary to her hopes, she had never recovered the use of her legs; her upper body was active, but below her hips she was motionless. Because of the ramps, all the ground floor of the house was accessible to her; she had a self-propelled wheelchair with an inner and an outer wheel.

She could spin herself around, very easily, through her downstairs domain, and did so, all day long. It was only when we went out of doors that I pushed her. But the wheelchair had a self-activating brake, a locking device which automatically engaged when the chair came to rest, so that it could never accidentally roll.

'Somebody,' said Mrs Crankshaw, with absolute conviction, '*some*body disengaged the brake and pushed me over to the front window.'

'You are quite sure that you didn't, almost unconsciously, do it yourself?'

She thought about it. 'No, my dear. Because my tiresome old fingers are growing so arthritic and stiff these days that when I heard a horse's hoofs go clopping past outside, I did just wonder, would it be worth unlocking the brake and rolling myself over to take a look out of the window. But I decided not to bother – and then, you see, some kind agency did it for me!'

I felt – believe it or not – a prickle of jealousy.

I said, 'Dear Mrs Crankshaw. I am so very sorry about your hands. Let me give them a rub with embrocation. And you know that wherever I am about the house, if you give me a call, I'll always *gladly* come and move your chair –'

'Oh, my dear, I know you will! And my hands are nothing – a trifle. With so few disabilities, in this charming house and with your company, I am a very lucky old person. And now, it seems, I have a friendly ghost to push me about as well.'

She laughed with real pleasure.

But I felt nervous. Bitterly ashamed, of course – for how could I possibly mistrust my kind friends enough to suppose that they might do Mrs Crankshaw any harm? Just the same, from then on I kept a very sharp eye on the position of her chair, and would casually move stools or small tables into its possible path, so that it could never roll very far.

Several times during the next few weeks the chair was moved again, always to anticipate some vague wish that Mrs Crankshaw had hardly yet expressed, even to herself. 'They positively forestall my needs,' she said, laughing. 'It really is *most* interesting, my dear Lucy. I am so *sorry* that you can't see them.'

For now she was beginning to get a glimpse of them – in odd, short flashes.

'Rather like a flickering, faulty television screen,' was how she expressed it. 'And, yes, sometimes in colour, sometimes black and white. Colour comes most often at twilight – black and white during full daylight. At night they seem to fade completely – just the reverse of what one expects of ghosts.'

Bit by bit, she described them.

'There is the tall, rangy woman. These are all quite modern spectres, my dear. No ruffs, or crinolines, or nonsense of that kind. The tall woman wears high-heeled leather kneeboots and a long narrow tube of a skirt, with an apron over it, and layers and layers of cardigans. Very often she has her hair in curlers. She is always the strongest image. Then there is a shorter woman, who nearly always has a piece of knitting in her hand.'

Dear Ruby! The number of hideous fancy-stitch sweaters she had knitted me! Which I was obliged out of politeness (and need also) to wear until I had outgrown them.

'Then there is a stocky thickset man who wears a dark-blue uniform. Perhaps he is a postman? I get a feeling of great kindness and dignity. And a little gnomelike fellow who spends hours poring over a folded-up square inch of newspaper, and always has a cigarette dangling from his lip. He is the faintest of them – but still, he is growing clearer as the days go by.'

'Just those four? No others?'

No grey-haired, thin-faced woman with hornrimmed glasses, busy at her typewriter?

'No, you greedy creature,' said Mrs Crankshaw, laughing. 'Aren't four well-constructed honest-to-goodness spooks enough for you? *How* I wish my dear brother Charles were still alive; he used to be such a sceptical materialist, would never admit even the possibility of ghosts. What a good time I should have, telling him about mine! I really begin to feel as if they were my own family – my family of phantoms.'

To hear her say that gave me a terrible twinge. And then she began to speak of writing to *Psychic News*. 'This is such an interesting phenomenon, my dear. I feel it should be shared with experts.'

'But', I argued, 'then they would want to come down and inspect and investigate, and put in watchers and try to take pictures with infra-red light – or however people do photograph ghosts; do you really want all that going on in your peaceful house?'

She glanced round the pleasant white-panelled parlour.

'Well, no,' she conceded. 'Perhaps not.'

In fact, to me, the house was *not* peaceful any longer. It seemed to throb with reproof and reproach. I knew that the time had come when I must, I absolutely must confess all, and make a clean breast to Mrs Crankshaw.

And what a poor figure I was going to cut! Deceitful, dishonest, hypocritical, cowardly, dishonourable – but, above all, shabby and perfidious to my good friends. Was it so surprising that they seemed to have turned against me?

I decided to make my confession one evening, after our reading-aloud period, between tea and supper. That was our easiest, happiest time, when we were most completely in tune with one another; then, I thought, I would have the best chance of winning forgiveness and understanding from Mrs Crankshaw for my long course of deceit.

All day my heart rattled painfully inside my ribcage. Mrs Crankshaw occupied herself as usual, in reading newspapers and political journals, in writing letters to her bedbound friends, with sketching and solitaire and petit point; she was a most self-sufficient person. Occasionally she would raise her eyes from the card table or embroidery pillow to remark, 'There goes the tall lady past the window, carrying a birdcage with a canary in it. Do canaries have ghosts too, poor little things?' Or, 'Now I see the man in blue. He is carrying one of those rush baskets that fish used to be sold in; do you remember them? Do ghosts eat fish?'

Oh Fred, I thought. He would be bringing the fish for my mother and me. Oh dear, *dear* Fred, why can't I see you too? I'll tell her this very evening. The minute that we have finished our stint on *Wuthering Heights*. And then perhaps, perhaps they will show themselves to me.

We had our reading session, installed as usual: Mrs Crankshaw on the sofa, comfortably snugged in, with cushions behind her and a rug over her knees; myself in the rocker with the table lamp at my side. Twilight was falling fast.

I read aloud several chapters. We were very close to the end.

'Shall I stop here?' I said nervously, clearing my throat.

'Oh no, *do* go on, my dear – if you are not becoming hoarse? Do finish the book. I don't know *how* many times I have read *Wuthering Heights*,' said Mrs Crankshaw with satisfaction. 'And it gets better every time.'

'Are you – are you hearing the voices?' I asked.

'Just a little. They are chatting comfortably in the background. Not intrusively, you know – but like people in the next room who know that we shall stop our reading and talk to them by and by.'

So I read on; read the last two chapters, came to the last line: '*I wondered how anyone could ever imagine unquiet slumbers for the sleepers in that quiet earth.*'

Closing the book, I let a silence of a few moments elapse. The room was almost dark now, apart from the bright circle of my reading light. I glanced about – hoping for a glimpse of a long tube skirt, a head of curlers, a pair of leather kneeboots, a dark-blue uniform jacket. But there was nothing.

'Mrs Crankshaw: there is something I have to tell you. Something I should have told you long ago, at the very beginning of our friendship. *Listen* . . .'

But I had left it too late.

Mrs Crankshaw's head had fallen back peacefully on her cushion; her hands, relaxed, lay open on the rug. She had gone for good, and left me all alone in that silent, silent house.

Elinor Mordaunt

THE LANDLADY

THE word 'ghost' brings to the mind's eye – shrinking even in thought – an apparition of the dead, the dank smell of death. At least that is how I used to take it; though I am sure I do not know why, for after all I believed, as we are all taught to believe, that the spirit – that impalpable essence of a ghost – is stronger than the body; and that being so there is no reason why it should not shake itself free at any time, and fluttering its wings be off on its own business, or pleasure, untrammelled by time or space. Why should there not be ghosts of the living as well as of the dead? Why – come to that – should not the word stand, simply and solely, for the true ego of any one of us?

Still, as I have said, there was that dread of the very word 'ghost' until we took Number Eight, The Paragon, Denis and I.

The Paragon was built in an oval, with a garden and plane trees in the centre of it; an oval of tall, narrow houses; all the rooms apart from the attics and basement panelled in white-painted wood.

Some of the houses were detached or semi-detached. But Number Eight was not even this; though in some strange, spiritual way there was never any house more completely detached and aloof, so that I do not believe that it so much as acknowledged the others, unless by the support they gave it; any more than a proud woman of the exclusive Victorian day acknowledged the individuality of the servants who ministered to her wants.

Apart from a small writing-room, which fronted the staircase, the whole of the first floor was occupied by the drawing-room, running the entire depth of the house, with two tall, narrow windows at the front, overlooking the oval; an arch in the middle and a large rounded bay-window at the back.

From this window, above the hawthorns and laburnums, the one giant chestnut in the long narrow back garden, above the steep slope of the red-tiled roofs and chimneys of the lower part of the town, one caught a glimpse of the river, with its forest of masts and funnels, its haze of silvery smoke or mist; and far, far away, the blue hills of Highgate.

We took the house, furnished, through land agents and lawyers, without any real idea to whom it belonged. The drawing-room was done in silk rep of a palish green – neither emerald nor willow, but something between both – and a shiny chintz, white, powdered with tiny black specks and bunches of rosebuds. The writing-table was very small with a sloping top; the other tables, all of rosewood, and unnecessarily large, were like pools of reflected light dotted with islands of morocco-bound books. There were a good many mirrors and a good deal of valuable china, vases and Dresden figures and bowls filled with pot-pourri, the scent of which permeated the whole room and the landing outside.

It sounds like a silly sort of a room, but it had charm as everything which belongs to a past generation does have, at least for me; and during that exceptionally hot summer it was grateful as a woodland bathing pool, overhung with willows.

Denis and I laughed at it and laughed at ourselves for liking it, but like it we did; not only the drawing-room but the whole house; the elegant twirl of the staircase; our immense mahogany bed, the huge wardrobe, the washing-ware – big basin and jug and tiny basin and jug side by side, like mother and child; the scent in the upper rooms, not of pot-pourri but sandalwood: sandalwood everywhere, in the drawers and wardrobes – wardrobes like houses.

Still, it was the drawing-room which held me most. Young and newly married, one of a large, cheerful family, I had begun by being almost unendurably restless during the long hours when Denis was away attending to his duties at Woolwich; noisy too, banging doors and swishing about, singing, whistling, too busy to settle down to anything.

But the drawing-room at Number Eight quietened me; so that before a couple of months had passed, the rather boisterous spring merged into a tranquil summer, I moved more sedately. How Denis laughed when I replaced my high-heeled shoes, with their irritating tap over the polished floors, with a pair of child's flat dancing slippers; while for the first time in my life I sat down to sewing – hand sewing, none of that feverish rattle and whirr of a machine, with the good, the tender excuse that the tiniest of all garments call for the softest of seams.

Hour after hour I sat still in that pensive room with the wash of pale, green-tinted air passing through its entire length from window to window – I who had been forever on the jig, never for one moment alone – choosing by preference what must have been known as the back drawing-room; laying down my work for long intervals at a time, and gazing out of the window over that expanse of which I have already spoken.

At first my mind was curiously blank; then – for the first time in my life, as with the sewing – I began to think; to reflect, to speculate, with no chance of running myself out in words, upon life: suffering; the unreason, the waste:

generation after generation like seasons, waxing and waning: the hopes of spring: the fulfilment of summer; the ripening and decay of autumn; and then old age and death, like a shut mouth, grim and undeviatingly silent. Along with all this I pictured my mother's thoughts and feelings before my own birth: my own unborn child grown to maturity and I, myself, with all earthly desires dropping from me like leaves from a tree: Denis and I old, old people, having spent years in the difficult support of life which must inevitably end, for all our pains; a life which could, by no manner of means, prove uninterruptedly happy. Though, after all, what was happiness? For the first time in my life, twenty-two long years, I differentiated between happiness and pleasure, amusements.

The days, wonderful late-spring and early-summer days, flowed by me like the air. I grew curiously intimate with the portraits on the white wall, water-colours and pastels of young women in short-waisted dresses and side curls; young naval officers with immensely high collars; an admiral smiling and scowling: a group of children with a liver-and-white spaniel: a portly divine in a black gown with white bands. I knew them all, I even talked to them – to them, and to *that other*.

Denis caught me at it one day. I felt like a lunatic and said so: 'Everyone's a bit queer at these sort of times,' that was the excuse I made, though he had showed no special surprise; I remembered that later, puzzled over it; for after all, we were not the sort of people who, normally, talked to ourselves.

'You're far too much alone.' Even that was tentative, a half question. 'Why don't you have Stella here?' – Stella was my sister – 'or if you can't stand relations, one of your own friends to stay with you for a bit? Molly Seton, or that Morris girl you used to be such desperate pals with?'

Stella! – Molly Seton, the Morris girl! In that house with – well, with *that*!

'I don't feel as though I were alone,' I answered slowly, thinking not so much of my words as of the queer meaning they had for me.

'You don't seem very sure about it.' Denis eyed me curiously; if I had not been so wrapped up in myself, I might have known that he too was wondering, trying to find out, test something he himself guessed at, the something which I might have in my own mind.

'Dear thing, all I know is that I've never been so happy in all my life.'

'Oh, well, so long as you *are* happy – though it doesn't do to mope; nothing so bad as moping, my mater says; and she ought to know, with eight of us all told.' He was very abrupt and matter-of-fact; a little disappointed too, or so it seemed.

But what could I have said? Even if I had realized what it was he wanted to get at: for it was only just then that things really began to shape themselves, become definite; that I, myself, was able to separate realities from pleasant, half-dreaming fancies.

It fixed itself like this, with odd simplicity and clearness. There was a tall vase of clouded glass standing upon one of the many tables in the drawing-room, and when I arranged it with some tall sprays of delphinium I had known the risk I was taking; for it was ridiculously badly balanced, as all Victorian vases are, fashioned for short-stemmed, dumpy bouquets.

The parlour-maid came into the room with a letter; there was a whisk of air between the two windows and the door, and in a moment the vase was over, with a thin stream of water – luckily the thing held next to nothing – running over the table and in among the books.

I called to Ada, but she had noticed nothing, was already half out of the room – one of those tiresome bustling servants – going about their work in a sort of whirlwind, very starched and clean-looking, and nothing more to them.

I jumped to my feet, but someone else was before me. I heard an exclamation which was like a breath of dismay: I saw – yes, I *saw* it, as plainly as I can see my own hand, now, stretched out in front of me – a small white hand, a wisp of a handkerchief, stemming the stream. There was some effort to raise the vase – I *felt* rather than saw this; but the sigh at the sense of failure was plain enough, following upon that first exclamation of dismay:

'Oh dear, oh dear!'

It was all like that, the keeping in order I mean, the anxiety over the precious trifles in that tenderly cared-for house, a casket of reliquaries. Sometimes, indeed, it seemed almost beyond bounds. 'Fussing?' No, no – Heaven only knows what I would have called it if I had been subjected to it from any of my own people; but here and now, and coming in the fashion it did, I rather liked it. It gave me a sense of being looked after; for that somebody, whom we seemed to have taken over along with the house, was concerned about me too: sometimes of set purpose, or so it seemed; sometimes because it fitted in that way. For ten to one if the sun threatened the rep curtains or chair-covers, it was tiresomely in my eyes also, though I was too indolent to get up and draw the blinds; lazily watching for, *expecting*, the hand on the cord, the faint flash of turquoise and diamonds – and for a long time that was all I saw.

Running down the polished stairs too – did someone really exhort me to be careful, was it in the air, so to speak, or did I just imagine it? Anyhow, there was nothing of irritation in my quick – 'All right, all right!' While there was real pleasure in the thought that someone else was watchful over the new life already so dear to me.

All the same, there was one thing that did really irritate me, and such a little thing, too. A tall candlestick of turned mahogany stood at Denis's side of the bed. Now Denis never reads in bed and I do, so what more natural than that I should transfer it to my side? – or more exasperating than that it should, each night, be moved back to its old place?

I tried it again, and again and again and again, until my irritation melted into amusement, and the thing became a quite good-natured duel between myself and that other. One night I actually heard it being moved, the soft 'tut, tut' to which I had become accustomed, followed by a distinct banging down – something like temper there! – of the candlestick upon the little table at the further side.

Jumping up, I walked round the foot of the bed in the moonlight, recaptured it and put it back in the place I myself had chosen for it.

'If you go on like that we shall have to leave the house,' I said firmly, and there was a gasp of dismay, followed by a soft chuckle – proving a distinct sense of humour, for *It* – oh, but why should I pretend like that? – *She*, bless her heart, knew that I was joking; was as sure as I myself that I could not bear the thought of my child being born elsewhere.

To my surprise, Denis – who I had thought was asleep – broke in with:

'Easy, old girl. Though, by Jove, it really is getting a bit beyond a joke!'

'What?' I almost screamed at him in my surprise.

'Well, the way she goes on. One can't call the place one's own. As for dropping cigarette ashes on the carpet! You should just have seen her face – never again, as I value my life!'

'Seen!' I was amazed, and dreadfully jealous: Denis to steal such a march upon me! 'Seen! Oh no, it's impossible!'

'What! Do you mean to say you haven't seen her?'

'Well, no, not exactly,' I admitted grudgingly, 'her hand, the whisk of a flounce or handkerchief.'

'Well, I've seen her,' his voice was almost unctuous with pride. 'Look here, light that candle, I suppose it's still at your side.'

'I've got my hand on it – firmly.' I struck a light and we both sat up in bed, for this was the sort of thing that was not to be taken lying down. But for Denis – Denis who, for all that he was such a darling, I had taken as being, in the nicest sort of man-way, a trifle insensitive – to have seen her, actually seen her, was almost beyond bearing.

'But not really – a sort of shadow – not like a real person,' I protested stupidly.

'My dear, she wears a cameo brooch and frocks which touch the ground all the way round – buttoned up to her throat; rows of buttons; and sometimes a fold of lace round her neck, and a what do you call it? – a sort of chest protector of lace stuff.'

'A plastron?'

'I don't know what the devil the thing is, but I've seen old ladies wearing them in real life. Not that she's not real enough! Grey hair puffed out over her ears and a little pink-and-white face, all crumpled up like the petal of a poppy-bud; her mouth drawn together – a tight bud that, but awfully sweet. A good deal bothered with us, the liberties we take with the house, and yet amused, at times; liking us on the whole – sort of tender and wistful. That night when you refused to come up to bed because you were in some sort of a paddy with me – remember that, eh, silly kid! – and I picked you up and carried you upstairs, she drew aside on the landing with a rustle of silk – queer sort of silks she wears, colours running into each other all the time, so you can't tell t'other from which—'

'Shot silk?'

'– Maybe, I'm hanged if I know – anyhow, she drew back to let us pass, flattened out against the wall, and laughed – a charming laugh, so soft and really amused; sort of as though she liked us to be there and young and in love – eh, old thing? – though we do make hay of her house.'

'Her house – Den, does that mean that you think . . . ?'

We were slipping into that careless married fashion of not finishing our sentences, taking the understanding for granted.

'Well, that's what I do think, that it belongs to her.'

'Belonged, you mean, centuries, oh centuries ago!' I don't know why, but the thought of anyone not seen being near, really near – in point of time, more than anything else – gave me the creeps. 'Ghosts don't come – well, all at once.'

'Don't you believe it, my dear.'

'Well, I shall know when I've seen her. The cheek of it! to let you see her and not me, when I think of the liberties she takes; straightening the things on my dressing-table and all – and *they* do belong to me. Why, she won't even let me leave my rings about loose, hangs them all up on the little china tree thing.'

'She must have taken tremendous care of everything. Look at those polished tables; by Jove, there's not a stain on any single one of them – the Lord only knows what would have happened if I put down a lighted cigarette, or anything like that.'

'The wonder is that there weren't any, we're the first and only tenants – that's why she feels it so.'

'Oh, Den, but that's impossible.' I was obstinate upon that point.

'How do you mean?'

'Well, ghosts don't come like that – at once.'

'She's not a ghost, I tell you, at least not in the ordinary way. I ought to know, I've seen her.'

That piqued me: 'If she's a ghost, she's dead – dead as a doornail, all ghosts are, so don't be silly,' I said, and turning round on my side I loosed my hold on the candlestick and blew out the candle.

It was in the same place when I awoke next morning, and for some reason or other this made me feel ashamed, in disgrace, left to my own miserable, haphazard ways.

The whole of that day I heard and felt nothing of her, not so much as a breath. 'I've hurt her,' I thought, 'perhaps she'll go away and I will never see her after all.'

I made my confession the first thing when Denis appeared home that night, contrite and abashed; feeling very small, curled up on his knee in the half light before dinner.

'I knew she was really alive, knew it the whole time; only I was jealous – just frightfully jealous, Den – I didn't know it was in me.'

'Jealous! Of a ghost?'

'Idiot! Of you seeing her and not me. But what do you think – really think?'

'Well, they say that there are – it sounds utter bunkum, but still there you have it – and I won't believe for a single moment that she's really dead – emanations or manifestations, or something of that sort. Supposing anyone was everlastingly longing to be back in some place they loved most frightfully – longing and longing, thinking of nothing else; you know when you long for anything like that the way you feel as though something were emptied out of you – it does seem that they might sort of slough themselves clear of the restrictions of space; yearn their spirits out of their bodies – actual bodies – dragging the appearance of it with them. If she, the little lady, had never lived anywhere else, loved this house in the way we love each other, she might – it seems feasible enough – almost *must* come back to it.'

'*She* – you speak as though you know who she was.'

'Why, the owner, of course.' He looked surprised, and no wonder; though it seemed strange to realize that Denis, whom I had thought of as much less subtle than myself, should have jumped at once to what I now realized as the only possible conclusion.

'Our landlady – oh, Den, but it makes us feel awful outsiders, frightfully in the way! Are you sure, though – was it a woman we got the house from?'

'I can't be certain. Don't you remember we just took it through the agent? – but of course it must be. Anyhow, we'll go and see him and find out tomorrow.'

All that evening I went softly, shy and ill at ease, a little resentful; once in bed, however, that queer feeling of half-amused tenderness came back to me. I had planted the disputed candlestick down, almost aggressively, on my own side of the bed, but I now leant across Denis and put it back in its old place. After all, she had been used to have it there, sleeping all alone in that great bed: and where was the sense of letting her worry her soul further out of her poor little body, frail enough already in all conscience as Denis saw it?

We went and saw the house agent next day, finding him as florid and bland as most of his breed are: a forced geniality masking the most complete indifference to damp and drains, along with life and death in general; that same species of geniality as is achieved by the really competent trained nurse.

It seemed that he could not tell us anything more than we already knew of the owner of the house: a lady – that was all he was sure of, and everything arranged through the lawyers.

We left things as they were for close upon a month after this, and then I began to get really fussed, and so did Denis. By this time we both saw her equally clearly, and it could not but strike us that she was somehow or other failing, the heart going out of her. She no longer kept us in such order: that familiar 'tut, tut' gave place to a sigh. I believed that she lay upon the sofa, one of those inconveniently curved and ridiculously small contraptions of Victorian days, for at times I found the cushion dented: my cushions, too, the originals being worked in Berlin wool and beads – there was one of Rebecca at the well, all beads, and only imagine the impress of that against one's cheek! Anyhow, it comforts me now to feel that she did like my cushions, immense and downy; though the very fact of their not being shaken up after use was enough to show you how she was changing! Why, in the beginning – no, even towards the middle part of our acquaintance, she never missed tucking in the loose chintz covers after Denis or his friends had been lounging on the chairs or sofa: more *pretending* to be horrified than anything else, I think, because there is no doubt about it, she liked them, laughed at their jokes if they weren't too – oh, well, you know, too modern; the sort of things we do joke about in mixed company nowadays.

Oh yes, there was no doubt about it that she was failing, wearied and played out to indifference: failing and fading, her dear little face growing pinched and pale, her frock rubbed and worn; her plastron – why on earth couldn't they have called them plasters and have done with it? – flattened out and depressed looking.

Then one day she came and stood by the drawing-room fire – for by this time the days were getting chilly, the summer nearly at an end – with one hand on the mantelshelf staring down into the blaze, with just such an air of dwindled faintness as those pale water-colours; so wistful that my heart bled for her.

'Oh, do, do, *do* tell me what it is,' I cried; but she only shook her head, straightened a couple of little Dresden figures on the shelf and moved away with a sigh.

It was not until she was gone that I realized what was wrong with her hands – the rings, turquoise and diamond, all gone, nothing but a fine gold keeper left; while the low-heeled, slim slipper on the foot turned sideways upon the twirly steel fender was rubbed and worn at the side, almost in holes.

'Something's got to be done,' I said to Denis when he came home that evening. 'She's got so frightfully thin, and what do you think – her rings are gone; just slipping off, I suppose, poor dear!'

'There may be another reason.'

'What do you mean?'

'Well, hard up, and all that, you know.'

'Denis!'

For a moment or so we gazed at each other in dismay.

'I believe you're right,' I said at last. 'Always the same dress, and getting very shabby. Oh – but *very* shabby; her shoes too. Fretting her soul out of her body, if she's really alive . . .' I paused; even then I could not really grasp it. 'And poor as poor. Well, if she is alive – and she won't be for long if she goes on like this – she'll have to come back here. We'll go and see that lawyer man tomorrow, eh, Denny?'

'You can't move house at this juncture, young woman, let me tell you that.'

'Well, I don't see why we should move; the place is big enough in all conscience.'

'Peggy!' I can never forget his look of amazement. 'You! You who wouldn't have anyone, not even one of your own people, here!'

'Well, she *is* my own people! After all, one has spiritual countries of one's own, places which are native to one from the first moment one sees them. And why not spiritual relations, who are far more real relations than the brothers and sisters and children of the man your mother happened to marry; or the woman your father married, either? They only pleased themselves, never really thought of us, or the sort of people that we might like to belong to us. But I've lived in the same house with *her* for six months, and know her and her dear little soft pernickety ways; and I'm sure she'll be a good influence for Thing-um-y-jig – particularly if it's going to be a girl,' I added ungrammatically: 'Thing-um-y-jig' being the temporary name with which we had endowed the impending offspring; anything to make out, even to each other, that we did not care, that there was no sort of sentiment about either of us.

'Well, the Lord knows I'll be only too glad for you to have someone with you, and it will be some sort of a help to her, too, if it's really come to that – pawning her rings and that sort of thing, you know.'

'Oh, Denis, it's too piteous, and here we are making ourselves at home in her house all the time.'

'But look here, old thing, after all there is the rent!' It was the first time we had either of us so much as thought of it. 'She can't actually starve on five guineas a week, you know.'

'Perhaps there are debts. That perfectly horrid-looking man in the portrait over the mantelpiece in the dining-room, with the leer and the underlip, and the *too* fine eyes, for instance. – Her father? What do you think?'

'Brother more likely; she's old enough. Blown everything, the devil, and left her to clear up the mess. Anyhow, we'll hunt out the lawyers tomorrow; and it's time for bed now. Come along, old thing.'

We turned out the lamps and left the room; at the door I turned and tweaked Denis's sleeve. The dying fire had flared up in a spurt of flame, and there she was; her arm resting along the mantelshelf, her head drooping upon it – too dispirited even to draw back her skirt from the heat of the fire, and that alone would have shown you if you had known as much of her as I did.

She looked up and gazed around her. For the moment Denis and I were wiped completely out of the picture; I realized that, while the gaze of those pale, wonderfully candid blue eyes was so yearning, so intense and tender that there was no mistaking what it was – a sort of goodbye, a drawing to herself once more, and maybe for the last time, everything that she loved best.

We went up to London next day – for it is only the post-office people who count us as already in it. At first I thought that the lawyer – who looked, as they say of wine, as though he had been 'laid down' for a very long time, his shoulders showing a pure bottle-like slope, his face cobwebby with fine wrinkles – established, or rather binned into, a set of frowsty chambers in Bedford Row, would tell us nothing; but Denis, who can charm a bird off a bough when he likes, gained his point with some very mellifluous lying, something about feeling that we really weren't paying so much for the house as it was worth, and we got her name, Miss Julia Champneys – Julia! Could it have been anything else? Julia, the soft syllables of it! – and the address of a boarding-house in Bloomsbury – such a boarding-house too!

The maid who answered the door, with an apology for a cap at the back of her head, a general air of having been dragged backwards through a gorse-bush, and that insolence which always goes with a certain type of imbecility, said she did not know if Miss Champneys would see us.

'She's here in her room, sick; I ain't sure as she'll see anyone,' that's what she said, scratching the instep of one foot with the heel of the other; though after some time, helped by the passing of a coin, we prevailed upon her to show us up into the drawing-room and go and find out.

Drawing-room! – drawing-room! *This* after the exquisite order and restfulness of Number Eight! What could the bedrooms be like in a house with public reception-rooms such as this? – A mausoleum, with crumbs in the crack of every chair, the dust of ages over the tables, and more woollen-ball-fringed antimacassars than I had ever seen in all my life before; small wonder that our landlady's soul had, at times, longed itself clean out of her body.

After a while the unspeakable maid came to tell us that she would be there 'in a brace of shakes', and then after another considerable pause – I had an idea that she had to travel downwards from the very top storey, some horrible, chilly, sloping-roofed place, for she was blue with cold and trembling with exhaustion – Miss Champneys herself appeared; desperately anxious, her wide blue eyes scared, her mouth tight with small perpendicular lines, braced up against disaster; for it was clear enough that our presence had put the fear of God into her – Denis's expression, not mine – that she made sure we'd come with some complaint about the house, some idea of wriggling out of our agreement, for her very first words were:

'If there's anything I can do to meet you in any way, if there's anything not quite right—' She broke off, staring; timid and bewildered as she well might be. Denis and I had been holding hands like two children when she came into the room, I myself frankly clinging: for— Oh, well, after all, it is not the sort of thing that happens every day, meeting the reality of an appearance, I mean, and she was so *like*, so precisely and amazingly like – stupid of us to be more scared by that than by anything else; but there it was, though after all it was not only our gaucherie which took her aback. There was more to it than this – amazement on her side, too; a slow dawning, unwilling realization, a painful acknowledgement of something which, at first sight, seemed impossible, upsetting every sort of calculation.

'Oh! – but I didn't realize – I couldn't have believed that – the maid said Mr and Mrs Maudesley, and of course I knew that was the name of the tenants, but – but not you – oh, not you!' She wrung her hands together in despair, those thin little hands, as though confronted with some idea which she could not get round: 'I made a mistake, confused you with— Oh, I don't know – I don't *know* – it's beyond me, that's what it is – beyond me. Why, all this time—' She shook her head trembling from head to foot, her face white and piteous, the tears running down her cheeks. 'You – you who I thought—' Her gaze was all for Denis. – 'Oh, of course, of course, at Number Eight – but I didn't realize – that's it, I didn't realize—'

I was on my knees at one side of her, Denis in a low chair at the other; we both held a thin white hand, patting it – I had the one with the thin gold keeper. The whole affair was so completely incredible that it was impossible for anything to seem more out of the way – outrageous, than it was. I even took out my own handkerchief and dried her eyes, pressed one hand to my cheek and kissed it; murmuring over her:

'Don't worry, dear, it's all right – indeed it's all right!'

'I thought – I thought—' She turned from one to the other, her confusion far greater than ours; for, after all, she was true to – what do they call it? – oh, sample – too wonderfully, wonderfully true; every fold of her dress, the rubbed sides of her satin slippers, showing how she sat with her tiny feet crossed – the dear ghost of Number Eight. But she herself was only too evidently disappointed, taken aback and that hurt me; for we really are – oh, well, quite nice.

'What did you think – what could you think? Of course we knew you, you are part of the house – the house we love. But Denis and I? Why – oh, but you don't like us!' I was shocked to the soul.

'I do – I do! I always liked you, loved you. Only I didn't know – oh, I didn't know,' she cried desperately, glancing from one to the other. 'I went back to the house – you know I went back to the house?'

We nodded.

'I couldn't keep away. It seemed dreadful, poking and prying like that, with the place let and all, but believe me, I couldn't keep away. Then when I saw you there – I am getting old and stupid, things confuse me – I forgot about the tenants; it was shocking of me, but I forgot – I quite forgot – I thought you were—'

'Yes – yes?' we bent nearer; I had one arm round her, fragile as a fledgling bird. 'Only just met her,' you say? Why, hadn't I lived with her for weeks and weeks and weeks, at a time when I was thinking and feeling more than I had ever done in all my life before? And anyhow, what does the length of time since you have first actually met a person matter, one way or another?

'Yes, yes,' I prompted her, 'you thought . . . ?'

'I don't know – I don't really know what I thought.' She shook her head helplessly. 'But – my dear – I wasn't always old – people were kind enough to say I was a pretty girl once – and it seemed to me that you were myself, as I used to be, and that you, sir' – she turned and faced Denis bravely, her crumpled cheeks pink, her eyes like sapphires, 'you – you, who are young enough to have been my son – were the gentleman whom I was once going to marry, and who was killed just before our wedding day. It sounds very silly, as everything of that sort does sound silly from old people, though I'm sure I don't know why – and maybe you'll think I am queer in my head – perhaps I am – sometimes I am afraid of that, but there it is – I quite forgot – it was dreadful of me, but I quite forgot about the tenants. You did not seem like real people, you know, just tenants; and it seemed that, perhaps, having given up the house and gone away, which was a very great wrench to me – for I had never lived anywhere else – that – I don't know I'm sure, I don't know – but it seemed that I was to be given a sort of dream life as a compensation; one feels so dreadfully young inside, that's the worst of it all – so young and full of hope. Don't you see – oh, don't you see?' She spoke almost fiercely, beating her two small, ringless hands up and down upon her knee. 'I didn't know what was true – I didn't *want* to know.'

'But lately, dear Miss Champneys,' I said, 'lately you've not been so happy?'

She shook her head, gazing in front of her with so faraway an air that I believe, could I but have opened the door of the drawing-room at Number Eight, at that very moment, I would have found her there. 'It has seemed to be slipping away – everything, everything, but the house. And even that seems difficult to reach – a long way off. I'm not very strong, I sometimes think – my heart, you know, so stupid – that the time will come when I may never see it again. Last night, for instance . . .'

She hesitated for so long that Denis prompted her: 'Last night?' with a glance across at me.

'Last night I thought I was saying goodbye to it for ever, and then nothing mattered: nothing! Not even he – the gentleman I spoke of, and who I was stupid enough to take for you, Mr Maudesley – nothing and nobody, only – only the house and the things in it. It is part of me, you see,' she went on eagerly. 'It really is a peculiarly lovely house, and it's part of me, in the same sort of way' – she flushed, turning her head a little aside, her eyes strained and wistful and very bright – 'as I have always felt that married people must be part of each other. It seems as if I can never, never leave it, however much I want to, however much I know I ought to, so long as there is any life left in me.'

'But you mustn't leave it, you mustn't live away from it; that's really what we came about. You belong to each other,' said Denis; then, hesitating a moment, ventured on a joke which sent my heart up into my mouth; but she took it well:

'Why, it really isn't moral for two people like you and that house to live apart.'

'But there are reasons' – she drew herself a little more upright, smiling, yet a trifle chilled, on her guard, as that generation is when it is driven to speak of pecuniary affairs – 'private expenses and obligations which make it impossible. That is unless you don't care for it, you are tired of it,' a piteous blend of hope and anxiety chased themselves across the small, delicately featured face.

'It isn't that, but we want you to come and stay with us. There isn't any heart in the house without you.'

She flushed scarlet: 'It's sweet and dear of you; but I couldn't – I really couldn't! Why, I hardly—'

'If you're going to say you hardly know us, I can't stand it!' I broke in, rising to my feet and standing before her, with an odd sense of being half child and half judge, looking my very worst, I know, awkward and frightfully determined. 'Look here, I'm supposed to be going to have a baby, and I know something will go wrong if you're not there at Number Eight. Anyhow, I won't have it at all in that case – so there!' I added, perfectly ridiculously.

'She's too much alone, it would be awfully kind of you,' put in Denis.

'Oh, if it's that – if I can really be of any use—' The little old lady rose from her chair, clinging to both our hands, trembling from head to foot. 'Oh, my dears, if you only knew what it will mean – like going to Heaven – like other people's Heaven!'

She said it again when we parted from her on the landing, for she would not let us take her upstairs back to her own room: 'It will be like going to Heaven.'

I went downstairs with Denis, and then ran up again halfway – I dared not venture on more – and listening, heard her move very slowly up that intolerable flight of stairs; with a long pause between every two or three steps, a still longer one at each landing.

The tousled maid came brushing past me with a bucket, and I pressed a ten-shilling note into her hand:

'Don't let her come down again today; and see to her, help her pack – my husband's coming to fetch her away tomorrow.'

I believe that she did her best; anyhow, she took her tea up to her own room – and one knows what that means in such places, the utmost concession – it came out later, because:

'She was all right when I took her tea up to her,' that's what she said, crying – actually crying. 'A bit excited and trembly like, that's all!'

I could not settle to anything that evening, neither could Denis; though we were oddly scared of putting our fears into words even to each other.

She had never come into the dining-room – I fancy that she must have shirked that portrait – but anyhow, he left the door open for her, jumped on the parlour-maid when she shut it, naturally enough, for it was a chilly evening, colder in the house than out of doors, or so it seemed.

Upstairs in the drawing-room, we each took a book; but I doubt if we either of us read a word. It was late when we got up to go to bed, and Denis was, oddly enough, making up the fire afresh, when he blurted it out – what I knew to be in both our minds:

'I wish to goodness we'd brought her back with us!' – for there was no sign or sound of her; while it seemed as though every room in the house had drawn itself close together, holding its breath, waiting for something which might be the end of a race.

By some odd chance the housemaid must have put the twisted candlestick at my side of the bed when she did the room; though I did not discover it until about two o'clock in the morning, when I could lie still no longer and stretched out my hand for the matches.

I thought I might have found her in the drawing-room. No, that's wrong, I did not think, I hoped despairingly, for I *knew* – all the time I knew; I had heaped up the fire again, was crouched before it, determinedly waiting, when Denis came down and carried me up to bed in his arms, with no single word of rebuke, or – bless him for his understanding – false optimism.

For of course he knew, and I knew, and the house knew, that there was nothing really to wait for, that the life and soul – yes, yes, despite our own youth, and many friends, and the little Julia who came later – the real life and soul of the house had gone out of it.

Why did she say that, 'Like going to Heaven'? Oh, well, I'm sure she would not like Heaven, the real Heaven; I was bitterly, resentfully sure of that. To take her there, just then, when we were going to make her so happy. She would only peak and pine, I knew she would, was certain of it; so certain that for months and months I thought that God would set her free, that she would come back to us – and Number Eight.

NOTES ON THE AUTHORS

Joan Aiken (b. 1924), daughter of the distinguished American poet Conrad Aiken, has written nearly a hundred books, ranging from adult mystery novels to a wide range of titles for children. *The Whispering Mountain* won the 1969 Guardian Award, and *Night Fall* won the 1972 Mystery Writers of America Award. Her series of 'horror, suspense and fantasy' collections, which attract an overlapping readership of both adolescent and adult readers, include *A Bundle of Nerves* (1976), *A Touch of Chill* (1979), *A Whisper in the Night* (1982), *A Goose in your Grave* (1987) and *A Fit of Shivers* (1990). These nerve-tingling fables mix paranormal events with compassion and wisdom in exemplary fashion. Her latest work in the genre is *The Haunting of Lamb House* (1991), set in her birthplace, Rye, Sussex. 'The Traitor' is previously unpublished.

Audrey Lilian Barker (b. 1918) achieved early success with her first collection, *Innocents*, which won the Somerset Maugham Award in 1947. Her subsequent titles include *Apology for a Hero* (1950), *The Joy-Ride* (1963), *Lost Upon the Roundabouts* (1964) and *Femina Real* (1971). Her most recent short-story collection is *Any Excuse for a Party* (1991). She has written over a dozen memorable tales of the supernatural, notably 'Lost Journey', 'The Little People' and 'The Dream of Fair Women', which originally appeared in the anthology *Stories of Haunted Inns* (1983).

Ann Bridge (pseudonym of Mary Dolling Sanders, later Lady O'Malley, 1891–1974) spent a varied and colourful life with her diplomat husband, Owen O'Malley, in China, Turkey, Dalmatia and other locations, all used to great effect in her best novels: *Peking Picnic* (1932), *The Ginger Griffin* (1934), *Illyrian Spring* (1935) and *The Dark Moment* (1952). Her ghost stories, which include 'The Buick Saloon', 'The Accident' and 'The Station Road', were collected in *The Song in the House* (1936).

Dorothy Kathleen Broster (1877–1950) took full honours in History at St Hilda's, Oxford, before women were admitted for university degrees. When she returned after the First World War, she was among the first women to receive a BA and MA. She was, together with Marjorie Bowen and Margaret Irwin, one of the most successful historical novelists of her generation. Much admired for her painstaking accuracy as well as dramatic power, she is reputed to have consulted eighty original works before embarking on *The Flight of the Heron* (1925). Her best supernatural fiction appeared in the rare collection *Couching at the Door* (1942), from which 'The Pestering' is taken.

Mary Butts (1890–1937) was the great-granddaughter of Thomas Butts, patron and friend of William Blake, and she spent her childhood at Salterns (described in her book *The Crystal Cabinet*) surrounded by forty-two of Blake's original pictures. Encouraged in her writing by Ezra Pound and Ford Madox Ford, she quickly became an innovative poet and novelist, and a prominent figure in literary circles. Among her writings are *Ashe of Rings* (1926), *Armed with Madness* (1928), *Imaginary Letters* (1928), *Death of Felicity Taverner* (1932) and *Scenes from the Life of Cleopatra* (1935). She admired the stories of M.R. James and Charles Williams, and several of her own tales involve the supernatural. 'With and Without Buttons' is taken from her posthumous collection *Last Stories* (1938).

Antonia Susan Byatt (b. 1936) is noted both as novelist and as literary critic. She has written two books on Iris Murdoch, and a study of *Wordsworth and Coleridge in Their Time* (1970). Her novels include *Shadow of a Sun* (1964), *The Game* (1968), *The Virgin in the Garden* (1979), *Still Life* (1985) and the 1990 Booker Prizewinner, *Possession*. 'The July Ghost' was first published in 1982.

Mary Elizabeth Counselman (b. 1911) is one of America's leading practitioners of the ghost story, with many stories to her credit over the past fifty-seven years. Among her tales are 'The Three Marked Pennies' (1934), 'The Black Stone Statue' (1937), 'The Shot-Tower Ghost' (1949), 'Unwanted' (1950), 'A Handful of Silver' (1967), and many more. Two collections of her stories have been published in Britain, with slightly varying contents, but under the same title: *Half in Shadow*. 'The House of Shadows' (which originally appeared in the American *Weird Tales* magazine in April 1933) is one of her best ghost stories, but has not been published in Britain before.

Richmal Crompton (R.C Lamburn, 1890–1969) earned worldwide fame as the creator of the immortal schoolboy 'William'. This eclipsed her impressive *oeuvre* of adult fiction, which included several tales of horror and the supernatural (including 'Rosalind', 'Hands' and 'The Haunting of Greenways'), collected in the volume *Mist and other Stories* (1928).

Daphne du Maurier (1907–89) achieved enormous popularity with her bestselling novels *Jamaica Inn* (1936), *Rebecca* (1938), *Frenchman's Creek* (1941) and *My Cousin Rachel* (1951) and her horrific short stories 'The Birds' and 'Don't Look Now' – all filmed. She was always fascinated by 'the unexplained, the darker side of life', and retained a strong sense of 'the things that lie beyond our day-by-day perception and experience'. 'The Pool' is taken from her collection *The Breaking Point* (1959). She was created a DBE in 1969.

Elizabeth Fancett has been one of Britain's most talented and original writers of ghost stories during the past twenty years, and has contributed to many anthologies in addition to Capital Radio's *Moments of Terror* series. 'The Ghosts of Calagou' is published here for the first time.

Lady Antonia Fraser (b. 1932), daughter of Lord Longford and wife of the playwright Harold Pinter, has been equally successful as biographer and novelist. Her first historical biography, *Mary Queen of Scots* (1969), received instant acclaim and won the James Tait Black Memorial Prize. She has also written mystery stories including *Quiet as a Nun* (1977; adapted for the television series *Jemima Shore Investigates*), *The Wild Island* (1978) and *A Splash of Red* (1981). 'Who's been Sitting in my Car?', from Giles Gordon's anthology *Prevailing Spirits* (1976), was her first published short story.

Celia Fremlin (b.1914) is one of Britain's most gifted writers of suspense novels, noted for special psychological twists and her gift for seeing horror in the ordinary. Her first novel won an Edgar Award from the Mystery Writers of America. 'Celia Fremlin's excellent English mysteries always centre on some apparently average, "normal" family situation gone terribly wrong', commented *Publishers Weekly*. Besides her elegant thrillers she has also written several excellent ghost stories, including 'The Combined Operation', 'The Locked Room' and 'Don't Tell Cissie', from her collection *By Horror Haunted* (1974).

Clotilde Graves (1863–1932) was a highly successful Irish-born playwright and novelist. She wrote many books under both her own name and the *nom de guerre* 'Richard Dehan'. Her most popular success under the 'Dehan' alias was *The Dop Doctor* (1910), a novel set in South Africa. 'A Spirit Elopement' appeared in her collection *Off Sandy Hook* (1915).

Dorothy Kate Haynes (1918–87) first made her name with *Winter's Traces* (1947) and the collection *Thou Shalt Not Suffer a Witch* (1949), with illustrations by Mervyn Peake. A later collection, *Peacocks and Pagodas*, subtitled 'The Best of Dorothy K. Haynes', was published in 1981. Pamela Hansford Johnson wrote that her stories 'send fascinated readers back to the library in search of other books by the same cunning and delicate hand'. 'Redundant', one of several ghost stories by Haynes left unpublished at her death, now makes its debut here.

Margaret Irwin (1889–1967) won many admirers not only for her long series of historical novels but also for her supernatural classic *Still She Wished for Company* (1924). She claimed to have written her first ghost story at the age of five, and often returned to the genre with tales collected in *Madame Fears the Dark* (1935) and *Bloodstock* (1953). 'The Book' originally appeared in the *London Mercury* in 1930. The critic Joanna Russ described this story (in *How to Suppress Women's Writing*) as 'one of the most interesting stories of the supernatural I ever read'.

Margery Lawrence (1889–1969) specialized in Gothic and romantic melodramas: her 1931 novel *The Madonna of Seven Moons* became the most successful British film of 1944. She was also a strong believer in the occult and reincarnation, and many of her ghost stories were based on accounts she heard at *séances*. Among the writers in this anthology she was probably the most 'psychic', and accumulated much detailed information about life on 'the next rung of the ladder of experience'. She always claimed to keep in constant communication (via mediums) with her parents, husband and various close friends after they died. 'Storm', which describes the ultimate power and vengeance of the 'spirit of the sea', was originally published in *Cassell's Magazine* (December 1931) and retitled 'Mare Amore' in her collection of occult tales, *The Terraces of Night* (1932).

Penelope Lively (b. 1933) has been equally successful as a writer for both children and adults. Her brilliant evocations of the supernatural may be found in *The Whispering Knights* (1971), *The Wild Hunt of Hagworthy* (1971), *The Ghost of Thomas Kempe* (winner of the 1973 Carnegie Medal for an outstanding book for children), *A Stitch in Time* (winner of the 1976 Whitbread Award) and *The Revenge of Samuel Stokes* (1981). Outstanding among her adult novels is the 1987 Booker Prizewinner *Moon Tiger*. 'Black Dog' was first published in *Cosmopolitan* in 1986, and reprinted later that year in her collection *Pack of Cards 1978–86*.

Elinor Mordaunt (1872–1942) had a varied, eventful life, spending some years in Mauritius, which provided the settings of her early novels. Some important writers of the next generation – notably Rosamond Lehmann – were strongly influenced by Mordaunt's excellent novels on domestic themes, including *The Family* (1915) and *The Park Wall* (1916). 'The Landlady' originally appeared in her collection *People, Houses & Ships* (1924) and was later reprinted in the large omnibus *Tales of Elinor Mordaunt* (1934).

Edith Nesbit (1858–1924) is best remembered for her immortal children's classics, especially *The Story of the Treasure Seekers* (1899), *The Railway Children* (1906) and *Five Children and It* (1902), dramatized on BBC television. In the late-Victorian era she contributed some fine ghost stories, notably 'Man-Size in Marble' and 'John Charrington's Wedding', to *Argosy*, *Illustrated London News*, and other leading magazines of the period, and the bulk of these were collected in her aptly named volume *Fear* (1910). Among her later uncollected stories is 'No. 17', which first appeared in the *Strand* magazine in June 1910.

Rosemary Pardoe (b.1951) has helped to keep the ghost-story tradition alive and well through her annual series of *Ghosts & Scholars* (now in its thirteenth year) and related titles issued by her Haunted Library imprint. She has also written several fine supernatural tales (under the *nom de plume* 'Mary Ann Allen') narrated by the church restorer Jane Bradshawe. These stories were collected under the title *The Angry Dead* (1986), from which 'The Chauffeur' is taken. Her learned study of Joan, *The Female Pope* (co-written with Darroll Pardoe), was published by Aquarian in 1987.

Ruth Rendell (b. 1930) has explored the darker regions of the human psyche in a highly acclaimed run of books alternating her series detective Inspector Wexford (introduced in her first novel, *From Doon with Death*, 1964) with other suspense novels focusing on psychotic and obsessed minds. She has been awarded the Edgar for her collection *The Fallen Curtain* (1974) and the Gold Dagger for *A Demon in My View* (1976). 'The Haunting of Shawley Rectory' first appeared in *Ellery Queen's Mystery Magazine* on 13 December 1979.

Jean Rhys (*née* Ella Gwendolen Rees Williams, 1890–1979), daughter of a Dominican (Creole) mother and a Welshman, wrote some of the finest novels of the interwar years including *After Leaving Mr Mackenzie* (1930), *Voyage in the Dark* (1934) and *Good Morning, Midnight* (1939). After decades of neglect, her reputation was renewed with *Wide Sargasso Sea* (1966), inspired by *Jane Eyre* in re-creating the early life of Rochester's mad Creole wife. This was followed by two collections of short stories, *Tigers are Better Looking* (1968) and *Sleep it off Lady* (1976) from which 'I Used to Live Here Once' is taken.

Pamela Sewell (b. 1966) is one of the new generation of ghost-story writers, destined to keep this genre fresh and active well into the next century. She has contributed stories to various magazines. 'Prelude' is previously unpublished.

Lady Eleanor Smith (1902–45) was the daughter of the first Earl of Birkenhead, Conservative statesman, Lord Chancellor and Secretary for India. Stirring memories of his gypsy grandmother launched Eleanor on a successful literary career which reflected her strong interest in the theatre, pantomime, circus and gypsy life. Her novels include *Flamenco* (1925), *Ballerina* (1928), *Tzigane* (1935) and her most famous work, *The Man in Grey* (1941; filmed in 1943). 'Whittington's Cat' was published in the American edition of her collection *Satan's Circus* (1934), but did not appear in the earlier British edition.

Rebecca West (the adopted name of Cecily Isabel Fairfield, 1892–1983) was a perceptive and energetic writer both on political themes (*Black Lamb and Grey Falcon*, 1942; *The Meaning of Treason*, 1949) and as a novelist: *The Return of the Soldier* (1918), *The Judge* (1922), *Harriet Hume* (1929), *The Fountain Overflows* (1956), *The Birds Fall Down* (1966), *Cousin Rosamund* (1985) and *Sunflower* (1986). Her early reportage and journalism for *The Freewoman* and *The Clarion* was collected by Jane Marcus in *The Young Rebecca* (1982). She was created a DBE in 1959.

Edith Wharton (1862–1937) spent her early years in New York, but for most of her adult life she lived in Europe, mainly in France. She was one of the leading writers of her generation; her novels have been extensively reprinted by Virago, and include *The House of Mirth* (1905), *The Fruit of the Tree* (1907), *The Custom of the Country* (1913), *The Age of Innocence* (1920) and *The Children* (1928), which has recently been dramatized as a major film (starring Ben Kingsley, Kim Novak and Geraldine Chaplin). Her supernatural short stories are among the best to be found in American literature. 'Afterward' was originally published in *Tales of Men and Ghosts* (1910) and was reprinted in her definitive genre collection *Ghosts* (1937).

Mary Williams studied art at Leicester and London, and has been a columnist on various newspapers. After the war she wrote and illustrated several children's books (as Mary Harvey) and has also written novels under the pseudonym Marianne Harvey. In the last fifteen years she has achieved a greater output of ghost-story collections than any other woman writer. Among these are *The Dark Land* (1975), *Where Phantoms Stir* (1976), *They Walk at Twilight* (1977), *Unseen Footsteps* (1977), *Where No Birds Sing* (1978), *Whisper in the Night* (1979), *Ghostly Carnival* (1981), *Haunted Waters* (1987) and *Ravenscarne* (1991). 'The Thingummyjig' first appeared in her collection *The Haunted Valley* (1978).